MOTHER OF THE ACCUSED

LEANNE TREESE

Moxie Publishing

Leanne Treese/Moxie Publishing, LLC

P.O. Box 5323

Clinton, New Jersey 08809

www.leannetreese.com

Publisher's note: This is a work of fiction. Names, characters, places, and incidents are a product of the author's imagination. Locales and public names are sometimes used for atmospheric purposes. Any resemblance to people, living or dead, or to businesses, companies, events, institutions, or locales is completely coincidental.

Cover Design by JRC Designs/Jena R Collins www.jenarcollins.com

Fizkes/Shutterstock.com

Onzon/Shutterstock.com

Dod Pavlo/Shutterstock.com

Akasha/Shutterstock.com

Mother of the Accused/Leanne Treese – 1st edition

ISBN print: 978-1-7358961-2-0

ISBN ebook: 978-1-7358961-3-7

DEDICATION

To my beautiful mother, and moms everywhere.

"Making the decision to have a child is momentous. It is to decide forever to have your heart go walking around outside your body." — Elizabeth Stone, teacher and author

1

D*ay of the Trial*
Meredith

My heart beat so hard I thought its outline could be seen in my chest.

Zach sat next to Peter at the defense counsel table. Zach in the navy-blue suit we'd gotten two weeks ago. A stray tag stuck out the back. I wanted to tuck it in. A tiny, motherly gesture. One I would not have thought twice about months ago. But, now, Zach was on a trial for sexual assault and there was a literal barrier between me and my son. A security officer too.

Our conversation that morning, the final one, had not been the best. I'd tried to assure Zach - and myself - that the jury may believe his side of the story, that he might get acquitted. He'd shaken his head. "I know what I'm up against, Mom."

He'd looked at me strangely, then pet Barkley, the dog's giant tail thumping on the hard floor. Zach had stared straight ahead on the car ride over, swallowing then clearing his throat in a nervous rhythm. His hand trembled.

"You've got to believe in your own case," I'd admonished, desperate to instill a sense of confidence.

He'd given me a sideways look then reached out and squeezed my shoulder in a gesture of comfort.

It was worse than if he had argued.

Now, in the courtroom, I had to force my gaze away from him. I averted my eyes from his back, looked around. Judge Patricia Richardson's courtroom was stately, more so than the little district court we'd been in for the preliminary proceedings. A massive desk, the judge's bench, sat in the front, a space for a court reporter on one side, a law clerk on the other. Behind the desk, American and Pennsylvania flags buttressed a gold-embossed State seal affixed to the wall. Brown panels lined the walls which, combined with the absence of windows, made me feel trapped. Anxiety intensified my sense of smell, and I fought off nausea from the competing odors of perfume and sweat inside the crowded space.

A woman filled water pitchers at counsel table. She approached the court reporter after, their heads together. The court reporter laughed.

A regular day in their life.

The worst day of mine.

A man with a giant sketchpad made his way down the aisle, dragging an easel behind him. He set up in the front, near where the jury would sit. I could see his pad from my front-row vantage point, a white canvas to be filled with hand-drawn scenes of the trial. I stared at the empty juror seats which would soon be filled by the twelve strangers who would decide the course of Zach's life.

And my own.

I glanced around, saw a few familiar faces. Julie was the only representative of the soccer moms. Donna would have been there, she'd said, but there had a been a last-minute change in the work schedule. I spied Reed in the back, his plain brown shirt blending into the wall panels. He put his hand up in a half-wave. I touched the empty space where my engagement ring had been. Had my life not been completely derailed, Reed and I would have been on our honeymoon right now.

Most of the crowd, I realized, was on the prosecution side, behind the Dixons. Kelly and Scott, the victim's parents, sat in the front row as I did, a macabre version of the sides in a wedding ceremony.

"All rise."

The courtroom silenced immediately.

Vomit formed in my throat; I steadied myself on the banister.

Judge Richardson followed her law clerk, a thick file under her arm. She had a round, wrinkled face and rosy cheeks. She'd pulled her grayish hair away from her face in a way that accentuated clear, blue eyes. She looked like a sweet grandma. Normally, her appearance would have given me comfort, but I knew from Peter that her looks were a ruse. Judge Richardson was tough and rigid; she was no doting grandma.

"Please be seated." The judge sat down, adjusted her robe, pulled the court microphone closer to her mouth. "We are here on the matter of Commonwealth vs. Zachary Noah Morgan, docket number CP-25-CR-4288091-2020."

I wanted to stop her, to slow down time. *Stop. Stop. I'm not ready. I can't handle what comes next.*

The judge spoke over my internal concerns. "Counsel? Your appearances for the record."

The prosecutor, Yvonne Williams, and Peter both stood. Yvonne, in two-inch black pumps, had three inches on Peter. She reminded me of a gazelle, elegant and graceful. Her red-nailed fingertips pressed against counsel table, her dark hair fell forward. "Yvonne Williams for the Commonwealth of Pennsylvania."

"Thank you, Ms. Williams." Judge Richardson looked to Peter.

"Peter Flynn, Your Honor." He transferred his weight from one foot to the other.

Judge Richardson raised an eyebrow. "Can you state for the record who it is you represent, Mr. Flynn?"

Modest laughter filled the courtroom; Peter corrected the error. "Of course, Your Honor. I represent the Defendant. Zach, Zachary Morgan."

I hung my head. The botched appearance would rattle Peter. His foot jiggled under counsel table. Twice, I'd seen him wipe his palms on his suit pants. I'd barely spoken to him since Friday night, our paths crossing only twice. Both times, Peter seemed almost unable to look at me, our conversations rushed and shallow. I would have asked him what was wrong, but I knew already. The pressure of this day – representing the son of your childhood best friend – had taken its toll.

Judge Richardson directed her attention to Yvonne. "I understand that the Commonwealth has a preliminary matter."

"Yes. Your Honor." Yvonne stood. "I know this is unusual on the day of trial, but the Commonwealth and the defense have reached –"

Bang.

I twisted in the direction of the noise. The back door had been swung open. Bo Brooker, the detective who'd assisted Peter with the case, stepped through. My eyes widened. Bo hurried down the aisle without explanation or apology, her blonde ponytail streaking behind. She stopped at Peter, slid him a note.

He scanned it, looked at Bo.

She nodded.

Peter stood. "I request a recess, Your Honor."

2

One year earlier

Meredith

I stood alone in Reed's sun-drenched kitchen, a bowl of muffin mix on the counter in front of me. It was the kind of kitchen I'd always wanted: stainless steel appliances, granite countertops, and a double-oven built into the wall. The drawers closed on their own if you so much as tapped them. The first time I'd been over, Reed had made a point of showing me this feature. He'd opened one to demonstrate. "See, you just bump it and it goes in." He'd opened a second drawer, then a third, until, finally, I tried. "Handy," I'd said as I watched it slide into place.

It was a dream kitchen with everything I would have chosen if I had designed it myself, right down to the light blue paint on the wall. But, despite our engagement, the kitchen didn't feel like my own. Neither did the rest of the house.

It felt like Reed's home.

Worse, it felt like Lara's home, which, technically, it had been before her divorce from Reed.

In fairness, it had only been two weeks since Zach and I

moved in. The wedding was still in the planning stage, but my lease had run out and it made little sense for me to renew. To his credit, Reed had made a massive effort to make Zach and me feel comfortable. "Move anything anywhere," he'd said. "Mi casa es su casa."

Notwithstanding Reed's offer, I'd left our belongings in neat, labeled stacks on the edges of the garage. Reed pointed the boxes out a few times; I unpacked one. I set throw pillows from the box on his couch, folded an afghan and placed it on a side chair. My belongings looked strange next to Reed's, a mismatch. Like fancy shoes with sweatpants, my things, unfortunately, in the latter category. Still, Reed made a big deal that I'd put some items out. He even moved the afghan to a more prominent position.

Barkley padded over and sat by my feet, expectant. I pet his square head. "Hey sweetie." The colossal chocolate lab looked up at me; I bent down to his level. "You won't like muffin batter, Bark."

I remembered Barkley's adoption as clearly as if it had happened ten days ago, not ten years. I'd gotten him on impulse, four months after Noah died. It had been the first day where the weight of being a widow hadn't felt as if ten thousand pounds bore down on my chest. I'd rolled down the car window on the way home and forgotten, temporarily, the words of the police officer months before, the ones which had severed my world into two distinct spheres: before Noah had been hit by the drunk driver and after. Barkley had settled easily, a brown lump on the bed where my husband had once slept.

I looked now at Barkley, his eyes steady on mine. I reached into a cabinet, pulled out a treat, and placed it by his feet. He gobbled it in a single bite. I gave him a second then swiped my phone from the counter and texted Donna. *Can you bring Zach back by 11?*

Zach had slept over at Donna's the night before; he and her

boys were inseparable. Donna and I were, too. She'd been assigned to train me at Sunshine Therapies, an organization which specialized in physical and occupational therapy. It was the first job I'd gotten after Noah died. But, instead of the training me, Donna filled me in on office gossip, and invited me to pizza at her house.

I'd come to Donna's with Zach and a Tupperware container of store-brought cookies I'd tried to pass off as my own. Donna peeked inside and said: "Shoprite special two for one?" We'd both laughed. Our boys hit it off and our own relationship morphed into one where you didn't need to call first, you just came over. I'd spent countless nights drinking chardonnay on the Sullivan deck, countless afternoons next to Donna on the sidelines of soccer fields, our fold-out chairs side by side.

I pressed the send button and the sound of the text swooshed through the otherwise silent space. My phone lit up a moment later: a Facetime call from Donna. I punched at the phone with my thumbs and Donna's face filled the screen, her wild black curls at its edge.

"So?" Her familiar, raspy voice sounded. "Are you ready?"

"I'm ready."

Donna rolled her eyes. "Really, Mer? You're ready for all three of Reed's kids. Aren't the twins' babies?"

"They're seven. Hardly babies." I sat at the kitchen table and exhaled. "Okay. If you must know, I'm freaking out a little. I don't know how the girls will feel about me living here full-time. And I don't really know what Zach thinks." I paused. "Did he say anything?"

Donna snorted. "You think the boys talk to me? I've barely seen them. They might not even be alive." The screen bobbed as she walked to her basement door; its telltale squeak sounded through the phone speaker. She disappeared from view, returned a moment later. "Yup. They are."

I could visualize the scene. Zach and Donna's boys, Owen

and Carter, sprawled out on her plaid basement couches, out-cold bodies covered by a hodgepodge of afghans and quilts. Empty pizza boxes would compete for space with video game controllers and soda cans. The room would smell like teenage boy.

Donna's voice interrupted my thoughts. "Hey. Try to look a little nice, alright?"

I looked down. I had on athletic shorts and an old t-shirt. My hair, limp and straight unless I blew it dry, was swept into a ponytail. "It's a weekend."

Donna scrunched her eyes. "You're in a t-shirt. Is that really how you want to greet Lara?"

The few times I'd seen Lara, she been in stylish clothes. She reminded me of the type of woman who'd accessorize for a pop of color, or knew how to tie a sarong. She would definitely not wear shorts and a t-shirt. Even if it was a Saturday. I blew out a breath. "Okay. Fine."

"Thank you," Donna said, as if I'd done her a favor by agreeing. "And I'll get Zach there by 11."

I switched the phone to off and looked for the electric mixer. Again. It irritated me, probably too much, that it was not in the appliance garage. Two drawers later, I gave up and mixed the muffin batter with a spatula, spooned dollops of it into a pre-lined pan.

I pushed the muffins into the oven, then went to change, the image of a perfect Lara fresh in my mind. I pulled on a blue sundress and, without time for the whole shower-blow-drying experience, wove a French braid through my hair. I applied blush and mascara; then, at the last moment, pulled two bangle bracelets from a wooden box Zach had made me in eighth-grade shop class. The oven timer dinged; I started down the stairs.

Reed was on his way up, thick with sweat from his run.

"Wow. You look nice," he said. He leaned down and kissed the top of my head, his six-foot frame dwarfing my five-four one.

"Don't sound so surprised." I crossed my arms in mock frustration.

"Sorry."

I placed an index finger on his chest. "And, you stink, Dr. Edwards."

He held up a hand. "Showering now."

He started up the stairs; I continued down, bracelets clinking. *Why did anyone wear jewelry?*

I pulled the muffins from the oven. Pumpkin butterscotch. Zach's favorite. I arranged them on a tray, first in one level, then two, then like a little pyramid. I stood back to admire my handiwork, then stopped. What was I doing? I was wearing a dress. And *jewelry*. Now I was obsessing over muffins?

I needed to get a hold of myself.

The doorbell rang. I listened at the stair, the shower still running. Crap. I'd have to do this on my own.

I stepped toward the door, inhaled a breath, and opened. "Lara!" The word came out insanely enthusiastic, as if seeing Lara was the highlight of my day.

"Meredith." She stood in the doorway in gray capris and a coordinating sleeveless top. Her make-up was perfect, black hair in a ponytail so tight it pulled at the edges of her face.

I pushed the door open wider, but Lara didn't move. Instead, she turned to her daughters. "Girls, you remember Meredith?"

She'd said the words like a question. It was ridiculous; I'd been dating Reed for almost two years. Still, the idea that I might be a stranger seemed to affect the twins, Emma and Abby. They stared at me over matching pastel duffels.

Fortunately, Jamie, Reed's sixteen-year-old, had no tolerance. "Yeah. We remember Meredith, Mom. We've only met her, like, a hundred times." She slid into the foyer just as Barkley arrived, pink tongue out in greeting.

"Hey puppy." Jamie pet his head. "Barkley, right?"

"Right."

I looked at the dog, then at Lara. Her eyes were wide. The twins had abandoned their spot on the step and now stood further back on the walkway.

"Reed told you about Barkley, right?"

"Yes. I just didn't realize how big he was."

I glanced back at Barkley. He sat erect, eyes on Lara, tail wagging slowly. I felt a sudden need to advocate on his behalf. "Barkley's big, but he's a total sweetheart." I squatted down. "And he loves belly rubs. Don't you, boy?" I rubbed Barkley's belly. He promptly fell to his back and sneezed. "See?" I looked toward the twins. "Do you want to pet him?"

Emma and Abby stepped forward, small hands tentatively reaching out to Barkley, still on his back.

Lara pursed her lips, then inclined her head toward the walkway. "Can we speak?" Her tone was oddly formal, like she was summoning me to a principal's office. I didn't answer, followed Lara down the walkway. She stopped part-way, seemingly out of earshot of the girls. "I'd like to talk to you about the arrangements."

I turned the word in my mind. Arrangements? What was she was talking about? I said nothing and, instead, stood stupidly staring at her.

"With Zach." Lara interjected. "I have a sixteen-year-old girl. Zach is, what, eighteen?"

"He's seventeen. He'll be eighteen October 1st."

Lara pursed her lips.

"Zach's met the girls before," I added. "A bunch of times."

Lara opened and closed her hand like she had a cramp. "Two teenagers sleeping under the same roof should have some boundaries, don't you think? And will Zach have boys over? While my girls are here?"

"I —" I started then clamped my mouth shut. It was the first weekend we were having the girls since Zach and I moved in. I didn't want to start it by having an argument with Lara over her clear insinuation that Zach was not to be trusted around Jamie. "Reed converted the office as a bedroom for Zach."

"And friends? Other boys?"

The trace of anger I'd felt at the initial question expanded. What friends Zach had over was not Lara's business. And Reed and I could place and enforce any boundaries, if needed. First weekend be dammed, this was insulting. I was about to say as much when I saw Barkley's body hurtling, full speed, through the front yard. "Barkley!"

A wiry tan dog sprinted from across the street. Barkley chased the newcomer. The tan dog, faster and more limber, barely missed knocking into Lara. He caught up to Barkley and the two began to wrestle, biting and snarling in play.

"Barkley," I yelled. He ignored me. I looked to Lara. "He never does this." I took a step toward the still-wrestling dogs. A thin woman, impeccably dressed, materialized on the lawn. "Katina. Stop." The woman's tone so was commanding, both dogs sat. She wagged a finger. "Unacceptable, Katina." The dog followed the woman back home, tail between her legs.

I bent down, whispered in Barkley's ear. "See that, Bark. Unacceptable." When I turned back toward the front door, Lara and the twins had disappeared inside the house.

3

I found Lara in the family room.

"Just thought I'd make sure the girls were settled." She spoke as though this wasn't the house her daughters had grown up in, as if she and Reed hadn't divorced three years ago. Seeming to sense the ludicrousness of the statement, she added, "you know, now with the dog and all."

I glanced at Barkley who, having spent his daily allotment of energy on the wrestling match, lay panting on his side. I looked back at Lara. I realized then that, just as it was strange for me to be in another woman's house, it must be equally strange for her. I would water her garden, cook on her stove, interact with her children. And, though I'd dated Reed for a long time, permanently living in the house was different. We both felt it.

Reed appeared then, pink-skinned and wet. "Hey Lara. Want a drink?"

"No. Thank you." Her eyes fell to my throw pillows and the now-prominent afghan. "I should go. I'll just say goodbye to –"

The front door slammed. Zach walked in a moment later wearing a faded Phillies t-shirt and gray sweats. His hair, thick and black, stood up all over. There was a five o'clock shadow on his jaw. He suddenly looked much older than seventeen.

"Zach. This is Lara Edwards. The girls' mother."

Zach extended his hand. "Ms. Edwards. Nice to meet you."

I smiled internally. Zach was a master of polite interaction; he'd gotten that from Noah.

Lara took Zach's hand in both of her own. "Nice to meet you, too."

He extricated his hands from Lara's, gestured to his clothes. "I should probably get changed." He headed to the stairs, turned back when he reached the bottom. "Nice meeting you, Ms. Edwards."

Lara nodded and watched Zach for a moment, seemingly satisfied. My heart swelled with momentary pride before I scolded myself. What did I care what Lara thought about my son?

She took forever to find and say good-bye to the girls. Finally at the door, she handed Reed a bottle of skin cream for Emma's poison ivy, folded his fingers over it as if she'd given him a lost scroll. "Twice a day," she said with a lift of her eyebrows.

"Twice a day," Reed repeated, then shut the door behind Lara's retreating back.

I let out a breath. This was it. The first weekend. I'd spent time with the girls, obviously. We'd had meals together. But not breakfast at their house. It felt different somehow.

I followed Reed into the kitchen, set a bowl of fruit on the table. I blew out a breath. It would be fine.

"Breakfast," Reed boomed. Almost instantaneously, all three girls assembled at the table, Barkley collapsed by their feet underneath. Reed poured batter into a waffle iron. I found my muffin pyramid and placed it on the table next to the fruit. I slid into the seat at the end, next to one twin. Emma. I was pretty sure.

"That's Daddy's seat."

"Oh." I stood.

"We don't have certain seats, Em," Reed called from behind the counter. "Meredith can sit anywhere." He held out his hands in an expansive gesture, as if to encompass the entire room.

Emma scrunched her face up.

"Come to think of it," I said, "I'd like a seat by the window." I stood, moved around the table, and sat at its end.

Reed placed the waffles in the center, steam rose from the stack. "Should we wait for Zach?"

I waved my hand. "No. He's showering. Don't wait. He'll be down soon."

I pulled a waffle on to my plate; the girls did the same. No one spoke. The scraping of silverware and subtle chewing sounds amplified the silence. Was this normal? I glanced at Reed. He either didn't notice the silence or didn't care about it. I waited a minute, then another. Finally, unable to stand the quiet anymore, I threw out the obligatory "how's school?"

Thankfully, Jamie looked up from her food. She swallowed. "Good."

I stabbed a piece of melon, looked outside. "The weather's supposed to be warm today...."

It was awful. Awkward. Not at all what I'd pictured. I scanned my mind for another, better question just as Zach walked in, hair still damp. He took the seat next to mine, eyed the muffins. "Are those pumpkin butterscotch?"

I smiled and pushed the plate toward him. "They are."

Zach picked one up. "These muffins," he said seriously, "are the best muffins in the world." He pulled off the baking cup, then held the muffin, naked, in the air. "All hail the world-renowned pumpkin butterscotch muffin." He opened his mouth wide and chomped down. "Mm."

Jamie twisted her hair into a lopsided bun then leaned

forward. "Alright. I'm game." She took a muffin, pulled off a chunk and popped it in her mouth. She swallowed. "It's good."

Zach widened his eyes. "Good? That's it?"

Jamie took another bite. "Okay. Very good."

The twins each took one; Reed joined them at the table.

Zach gestured toward the large picture window that centered the kitchen. "You should put our bird feeder there, Mom. The one that sticks to the window."

I looked in the direction of his gaze. The window was an ideal place for the bird feeder. My Aunt Sonia had given it to us after Noah died. Sonia had insisted the ongoing flow of birds would have a soothing effect. I'd been doubtful; I put it up anyway. Two days later, the first bird appeared, then a second. Their presence provided an ongoing dialogue during a time when Zach and I had no words. We'd talk about the piggiest birds, the prettiest birds, the favorites. Later, commenting on the birds became less of a crutch and more a part of our everyday life. There's that fat blue jay again ...

"I think I know just where that is," I said, standing. "Is that alright with you?" I looked to Reed. "If we hang the feeder there?" I pointed to the window.

"Mi casa es su casa," Reed responded, sitting back. Jamie rolled her eyes.

Once in the garage, I scanned the boxes, grateful for Donna's insistence on labeling. "You don't want to get there and be like where the fuck are my oven mitts," she'd said.

Typical Donna.

I found the feeder and a bag of seed and returned to the kitchen. "Victorious."

"Great." Reed took the feeder, inspecting it as he walked to the deck. He secured it to the window, filled it with feed. He pretended to be a bird after, flapping his arms, running about the deck. The twins laughed, Abby so hard that she spit out a muffin piece.

Jamie shook her head. "Ladies and gentlemen, my Dad." The affection in her voice belied the quip.

Reed returned to the kitchen and gestured to the feeder. "Okay birds. Go!"

We collectively stared at the vacant plexiglass structure. A bird swooped through the yard, a good twenty feet away. "There's one," Emma yelled. It disappeared into a nearby tree.

"It takes a while for them to find a new food source," I offered. "Remember, Zach?"

Zach nodded. "It does. But once they do, they'll never forget." He turned to me. "Remember the round, gray one? Newman?"

"Hello Newman." I said the words like Jerry on *Seinfeld*, felt the blank stares of Reed and the girls. "You've never seen *Seinfeld*?"

Reed shook his head. "Never watched it."

I was about to protest the insanity of never having watched *Seinfeld*, about to insist that we start a binge-watch right then, when Jamie spoke. "Remember the first time we saw orange cat?" Her sisters and Reed affirmed; Jamie began the story. "So this stray orange cat kept coming in our yard. Mom hated him, but Dad kept feeding him. He kept coming back. It was getting cold so Dad decided –"

"He gave orange cat to Mom for Christmas." Abby blurted out the punchline.

Jamie shot her a look. "Mom loves orange cat. She still has him."

I tried and failed to picture Lara with a cat. Reed had never once mentioned him. It occurred to me then that there were no memories for this group. No fat bird, no orange cat. Should we be trying to create some? I stood abruptly. "So. What's on tap for today?"

Reed shot me a surprised look. We'd already discussed this

first weekend. We would not go overboard with activities, wouldn't set an unrealistic bar.

Jamie spoke before Reed could answer. "I was going to play tennis." She looked at Zach. "Wanna play? The courts are a few blocks from here."

Zach shrugged. "Sure." He looked at me. "Okay?"

I paused, remembering Lara's words. Would she want Zach and Lara spending time together alone? Was this the type of circumstance she'd been alluding to when talking about arrangements?

"Mom?" Zach stood with his plate and moved to the sink.

I shook my head. They would be fine. Lara was ridiculous. "Of course. Have fun."

"We have Jenna's birthday party," Abby stated.

Reed looked at me. "I was planning to drop off the girls at the party, then get some supplies for the Koi pond." When I said nothing, he added, "do you want to come?"

"No." I shook my head. "I'll get food for the barb-e-que. Burgers and hot dogs, right?"

The rest of the day unfolded organically. Zach and Jamie returned from tennis, hot and sweating. Reed labored on the koi pond. I picked up the twins from the party. When we arrived home, Reed called out. "Hey, pond's done. Come check it out."

The six of us assembled outside. The pond sat, six feet long, four in diameter, its edges covered by large slate stones. Reed had stacked a group of stones on one end to make a waterfall; a thin band of water trickled down. A frog statue spit from the pond's center, bits of spray landing on nearby water lilies.

I kissed Reed on the cheek. "It's beautiful."

"And now, for the best part." Reed rubbed his hands together, then pointed to a big, orange bucket. "Check it out."

The twins ran; Jamie and Zach sauntered behind.

"Fish!" Abby pointed to the bucket. Interest piqued, I

stepped toward the bucket and looked down. A half dozen koi swam in a circle, all some combination of orange, white, and black.

“Let’s release these puppies,” Reed said. He stepped toward the bucket and poured the contents in the pool. The twins squealed with delight. Jamie dubbed a solid orange one Sunkist.

I look at the fish, the family, not wanting the moment to end. It felt, already, like a memory. *Remember the koi pond?*

“Hey look.” Zach pointed to the feeder on the window, a cardinal on its edge. There was a collective cheer from the group. I breathed in a contented sigh.

Reed’s house finally felt like home.

4

I sat at a round table in the stark break room of Sunshine Therapies, a stack of green and brown papers in front of me. I picked up the only scissors I could find - little child ones - and began cutting around the dinosaur template. Most of the therapists at Sunshine worked with older patients; I was a pediatric occupational therapist.

Donna's unmistakable voice thundered in the hall. "God help me." She entered the room a moment later, ran a hand through her hair.

I looked up. "Was that Rose Rose I heard?"

"None other."

Rose Rose was an eighty-five-year-old self-proclaimed psychic. At every physical therapy session, she shared a new prediction about Donna's future. Most were harmless. In fact, two weeks prior, she'd told Donna to expect a big gift. When Donna got a free mug at the bank, she'd called me: "I think Rose Rose is on to something," she'd said.

Donna picked up a paper, took the tiny scissors from my hand, and began to cut. "How about I cut out dinosaurs and you deal with the crazy old people?"

I shook my head. "I can only do kids."

Donna fake-glared at me. "Rose Rose told me I would lose something very important." She placed a dinosaur on the pile.

"You are not seriously believing Rose Rose. She's crazy."

She made a face, and suddenly I realized the issue. Donna was in the midst of a contentious divorce, her days peppered with obnoxious attorney letters and veiled threats from her husband, Max. The boys were in the middle, fights about custody and parenting time ongoing. Max was adamant that the boys belonged with him; Donna was steadfast in the opposite. Add litigious attorneys, an affair, and a house they both wanted. It was a mess.

I tapped her hand. "Rose Rose is crazy. Plus, its Friday and there's the party tomorrow. You're still coming, right?"

"The Uncanny Hootenanny? Wouldn't miss it." She rolled her eyes. The Uncanny Hootenanny was Reed's annual Western-themed end-of-summer bash.

I swatted the air in her direction. "Stop it. Reed loves that party. Plus, Lara will be there. I'll need your support."

"Why does she come again? Aren't they divorced?"

I shrugged. "Reed says it's for the kids. They always threw the party together. He thinks it would be weird if he didn't invite her."

She lifted her eyebrows. "And you're okay with that?"

"It's fine, but I need you there."

Donna smiled. "Yeah, you do. I'll be there and I'll bring the boys." She placed an additional dinosaur on the pile, one with a big shlong.

I held it up. "Really?"

"Cut it off then. I'd like to do the same to Max." She smiled, a smudge of red lipstick on her front tooth. She picked up the dinosaur and gave an emphatic snip to the protruding bit of paper. She raised her eyebrows. "See how easy that was?"

"You're crazy. And you have lipstick on your tooth."

Donna wiped her tooth off with a napkin. "Better?"

"Better."

Donna pointed to her watch. "I've got to get going. I'll see you at that hot party tomorrow." She winked and disappeared behind the door.

I was glad Donna would be there tomorrow. It was the first joint party with Reed; it felt significant. The event was a glimpse into the future, a peek at how my life and my friends would coordinate with Reed's.

There was no reason to think it wouldn't go well.

5

The Uncanny Hootenanny was in full swing. Country music reverberated through an outdoor speaker. At least half the guests wore cowboy hats; a few had on boots. Everyone wore a bandanna. Reed gave those out at the door.

It was a perfect night for a party, still warm with a gentle breeze. Stars dotted a dark sky surrounding an almost full moon. Reed had set tiki torches throughout the yard and their gentle light provided a festive ambiance. I'd covered round rental tables with plaid cloths, scattered hay bales around for extra seating.

I leaned on the deck railing, spied Zach in the back of the yard with Donna's boys and Jamie. A few girls sat with them, Jamie's friends. Zach said something; the others laughed. I smiled, relieved that he seemed happy. I'd worried that accepting Reed's marriage proposal and forcing three instant siblings had been selfish but, to date, the transition had been seamless. Zach and Jamie clearly had a bond and, though he wasn't particularly close with the twins, Emma and Abby seemed to look up to him in a way he seemed to find flattering.

I took a sip of wine and observed Zach give the girl next to him a light punch on the shoulder. She laughed and put her hand on his knee.

"Meredith."

I averted my eyes from Zach and the girl. I turned just as Lara approached, a water bottle in her hand. She gestured toward the kids. "So. They seem like they're having fun."

"Seems like."

Lara had calmed down since the initial boundary conversation and, though I wouldn't call her a friend, our conversations had become less transactional. We'd even shared a joke about Reed's habit of singing country songs in the shower. "I swear he thinks that, if he's in the shower, no one can hear him," Lara had said with a head shake.

I observed the girl next to Zach put her head on his shoulder, her massive brown curls spilling down his back.

I leaned into Lara. "Hey. Do you know who that is? The girl next to Zach?"

Lara squinted in the darkness. "Oh." Lara said the word as though she'd just tasted something sour. "That's Paige Dixon."

I waited for an elaboration. None came. "What do you know about her?" I asked finally. Paige had oriented herself behind Zach and appeared to be drawing something on his back with her finger.

Lara turned to me with a surprised expression. "You don't know the Dixons? Scott and Kelly?"

"No."

Lara spoke low, like I was on the receiving end of a big secret. "Scott is the managing partner at a big Philadelphia law firm. Kelly's gorgeous, a former beauty queen. Miss Alabama, I think. Anyway, Paige is the youngest of three kids. She plays tennis with Jamie. The sister is a freshman at Columbia, the boy, Ethan, plays soccer. They live on the corner of Woodland Road, the one with the big converted barn."

I knew the home. A massive stone farmhouse with dormers set back from the road by an acre or more of lush grass. Black wrought iron gates, cursive Ds in their centers, circled the edge of the property.

"Should I be worried?" I joked.

"I would be."

I looked at Lara to see if she was kidding but I couldn't make out her expression in the dim light. "Why?"

"I don't know. Scott Dixon just doesn't seem like a guy you'd want to cross. Or have your son cross. And that's his baby girl."

Zach and Paige switched positions. He drew something on her back with his finger. It seemed harmless enough.

Lara leaned toward me. "Truthfully," she started, "I hate the whole teen date scene. Way too complicated, especially these days. Don't you just want to keep your kids in a vault sometimes? Just save them from everything."

I clinked her water bottle with my wineglass. "Cheers to that."

It may have been the wine, but I felt a kinship with Lara in that moment: two moms discussing the pitfalls of teens and romance.

The moment was interrupted by an arm on my shoulder. Donna. Crap. She'd been drinking for at least an hour, maybe more. A sober Donna was unpredictable. A drunk one? Who knew what she might say? "Hey you." I punched her lightly on the shoulder.

Donna kicked up her foot. "Check them out." She wiggled a red cowboy boot, then stumbled backward.

"Whoa." I grabbed her forearm, helped her upright.

Lara extended her hand. "I'm Lara."

Donna bugged her eyes out. "Reed's ex." She ignored Lara's extended hand and slapped her on the shoulder. Lara looked at the spot where she'd been hit, brushed it with her fingers.

I tried, and failed, to catch Donna's eye. Rednex *Cotton Eye*

Joe sounded through the speakers. Donna nodded her head then belted out the refrain. "Come on guys," she urged. "It's *Cotton Eye Joe*! Everyone dances to *Cotton Eye Joe*." She danced a few steps in place.

Lara's eyes swept over Donna's dancing form. "I think that's my cue to leave. I'm not much of a dancer." She turned on a navy espadrille, and disappeared into the house.

I looked at Donna. For a split second, I saw her as Lara would have: a drunk, middle-aged Mom with too tight clothes and too bright lipstick dancing unabashedly on the deck in her cowboy gear. In contrast, Lara would stand in the kitchen, perfectly poised, with that same judgmental expression she'd used when talking about "arrangements." Screw her. I downed the rest of my wine, grabbed Donna's hand, and danced.

The party ended after midnight. I saw Zach through the front window with Paige and looked away. I wouldn't stoop to spying. As much as I wanted to know what was going on in Zach's life, I wouldn't allow myself to be *that Mom*. If he liked Paige, if there was something there, I'd find out soon enough.

I busied myself by collecting stray Solo cups. I carried the cups toward the kitchen and spied Donna on the chair in the family room, her head on the armrest, body stretched out in front of her. I set the cups down and adjusted her head, covered her body with an afghan. She'd have to stay the night.

Carter approached, shook his mother's foot. "Mom."

Donna roused slightly then pulled the afghan up to her chin.

I picked up the cups. "Listen. No sense waking your Mom. Go find Zach. You and Owen can stay over. There are extra blankets in his closet." Owen looked at me, then his mother. "Thanks Mrs. Morgan." He disappeared up the stairs.

I finished basic cleaning. I found Reed passed out diagonally on the bed, his cowboy hat askew. He'd removed just one boot. First Donna, now Reed. Was it the punch? I unzipped

Reed's other boot, pulled it off, then pushed him toward his side of the bed.

After an abbreviated night routine, I climbed in beside him, tucking my body into his like a curl.

After what felt like no time, a tiny hand gripped my forearm. *What?* I squinted and opened my eyes. It was Emma, the red numbers of the alarm clock illuminated behind her. *7:01 a.m. What the heck.*

Abby shook Reed. "Dad," she said urgently, "it's balloon day. Remember? Balloon day."

I peeked at Reed, his eyes still shut. No way was he getting up for balloon day. Or anything else. I forced myself upright. "What's balloon day?"

Emma jumped from one foot to the other. "It's a big party. With tons of hot air balloons."

"Hundreds," Abby added.

"I forgot girls. I'm sorry." Reed spoke with his eyes still closed.

"It's early, Dad. We can still go." Emma attempted to pull Reed from the bed.

I looked from Reed to the twins. I could do this. I could take the twins to balloon day. It would be fun.

What could possibly happen?

6

Peter Flynn

I leaned back on the tree in the clearing, stared at the door to the ladies' room at the New Jersey Hot Air Balloon Festival, waiting for my mother to emerge. She was probably chatting with someone at the sink. Or worse, over the stall. She loved to talk; I wouldn't put it past her.

The morning ascent over, dozens of balloons lay dormant on the vacant field adjacent to the festival. Our balloon, white with multi-colored panels, lay between one shaped like a panda and one with the colors of the American flag. To the right of the balloons sat an asphalt runway lined with white-capped tents crammed with food and crafts. Rising above the tents stood two large moon bounces, a modest balloon-themed Ferris wheel, and an inflatable rock-climbing wall. Chipper music piped through speakers interrupted, periodically, with announcements for a show or a band. The air was thick with competing smells: hot dogs, French fries, funnel cakes. One man walked by with fried Oreos.

Come on, Mom. I glanced toward the bathroom entrance.

My heart stuttered.

Meredith Morgan. Walking out the ladies' room buttressed by two dark-haired girls carrying pinwheels and stuffed dolphins.

Shit.

I'd had a wild crush on Meredith in high school; she was never interested in me that way. Still, we'd become close friends, Meredith practically a staple in my household growing up.

I'd messed things up after her husband died and our relationship morphed from real friends to Facebook ones. I hadn't told her I'd moved back home, hadn't told her about my divorce.

I looked down with the immature hope that Meredith wouldn't see me. Then I could text her and let her know I'd moved back. I could make it seem as if I'd been here for a few weeks instead of nearly a year. That would be better that acknowledging the truth. I'd been too ashamed to reach out.

I glanced up. Meredith and the two girls stood still near the bathroom. It seemed like they were waiting for someone.

Oh no.

The thought came to me at the same time I saw my mother, her finger pointed in my direction. "There he is." She threw me a frantic, big-armed wave that would have made an air traffic controller proud. "Peter," she called out, "look who I found."

I lifted my hand up, watched Meredith approach. She was an older but still stunning version of the new girl who'd been my lab partner in seventh grade. She wore little make-up, no jewelry. Denim shorts showed off long, thin legs. A blue sleeveless t-shirt revealed firm, muscled arms.

"Peter." She enveloped me in a hug, then stepped back. "You look fantastic."

I shrugged, hoping the effort would convey an indifferent casualness about my changed appearance. But I was proud of my twenty-pound weight loss, of the muscle I'd gained. I looked better. At least that was good.

"Seriously, Peter," Meredith gushed. "I'm not sure I'd have recognized you." She paused. "I mean, not that you looked bad before, but -" She let the statement trail off.

I forced my face to look serious. "I'm highly offended. I spent years perfecting my bespectacled, pudgy-guy look. And to think all that effort went unappreciated."

She laughed. I'd always loved the sound of Meredith's laugh. I'd forgotten that.

"Well, the new look suits you," she said conclusively.

Before either of us could say anything else, Mom interjected. "I told Meredith that she and the twins could go up on the balloon with us this afternoon." She turned to the twins. "This is Abby." She put her hand on Abby's head, then did the same to Emma. "And this is Emma. They're both seven. They're the daughters of Meredith's friend."

I crouched down to their eye level. "Well, it's nice to meet you both. How's your day been so far?"

The girls immediately launched into a fragmented description of the days' activities. From what I could gather, the highlight was choosing the dolphins at a tent crammed with stuffed animals.

"There were hundreds of animals to choose from," Meredith said, lifting an eyebrow. "It took quite some time."

"Listen." Mom clapped her hands like the former schoolteacher she was. "I'll sign these three up to go. Peter, why don't you show them the balloon?" She disappeared in the crowd of patrons. Meredith typed into her phone then looked up and smiled at me, her teeth a bright white against tanned skin. "Just texting the girls' Dad to make sure he's cool with it."

Dad. Right. In the surprise of seeing her, I'd forgotten that Meredith was engaged. It came back to me now, the pictures on Facebook. I glanced at her hand, just to make sure. The ring was still there, big and sparkly and obvious. Did she really want to spend the afternoon with me and Mom?

"Hey. My Mom didn't talk you into this, did she? She means well but she can be pushy. Don't feel like you have to come."

Meredith stuffed her phone in her purse. "Seriously, Peter. Do you think you would need to push me into going on a hot-air balloon? I live for this stuff. Kingda Ka? Remember?"

I smiled. "How could I forget?"

In eighth grade, we went on a class trip to Great Adventure. Meredith couldn't find anyone to go with her on the Kingda Ka, a steel roller coaster with a four-hundred-foot vertical drop. I hate roller coasters so, of course, I volunteered. Had I been with anyone else, I would have bailed, but I wasn't going to seem like a wimp in front of Meredith. As if it had been yesterday, I recalled the irrational feeling that I would fall to my death, the churning of my insides as the cart twisted on the track. She'd insisted we check out our "ride photo" afterward. In it, she'd looked elated, hands up, big smile. I looked terrified in contrast, my lips pursed in a fear-drawn line. Meredith had teased me about that picture endlessly.

I held up my hand like a boy scout. "I promise I am much braver now. Plus, a hot air balloon doesn't move quite as fast as the Kingda Ka." I gestured toward the field. "Come on. I'll show you."

Meredith followed me, swung a hand of a twin in each of her own.

"So the whole balloon ride takes about four hours," I told her. "The ride lasts about an hour. I try to land on a field near my uncle's house. Mom usually likes to visit with them." I glanced at Meredith. "You know how she is."

She smiled. "Your Mom? I'd expect nothing less."

"Is that okay? Do you have time for the ride and a visit?"

"I literally have nothing to do today." She blew out a breath. "Does that make me sound boring?"

"Um. I'm hot air ballooning with my mother."

Meredith laughed. "How's your Dad? Is he here?" She looked around the immediate space.

"He wasn't feeling well." I wouldn't get into a long explanation about Dad's dementia right then. It had gotten steadily worse since I'd moved back; it was one of the main reasons I'd stayed. We'd planned to take him today, hoped the event would have eased him out of what had been a bad spell. But he'd refused to come. Mom had been crestfallen, her expression one of wearied disappointment. I'd called a caregiver and surprised her with the trip.

Meredith gave me a sideways glance. "That's too bad. Be sure to give him my best."

"I will. How are your parents?"

"Living in London now." She said it with an eye-roll. I didn't ask for details. Meredith had always believed her conception was an accident, her parents biding their time until she was grown and they could live the life they'd planned. True to her theory, her folks went on a six-month European vacation the week after she'd moved into her college dorm.

We reached the balloon. "Here she is." I gestured to the dormant mass on the field.

"Wow." Meredith took a step toward the gondola, fingered the thick cables that attached it to the balloon. "How much does this thing weigh?"

"It's about eight hundred pounds like this and two tons when it's inflated."

"Two tons? That's insane." She directed her attention to the twins. "What do you think, girls?"

Both girls looked understandably underwhelmed. On the ground, the balloon was nothing more than colored nylon and a basket. I crouched down. "The balloon looks a bit boring down here but, when it blows up with air, it will be giant. A hundred and twenty feet tall." I extended my arm. "That's about thirty of you. And, once you're in the air, you'll feel like you're floating."

The girls remained wide-eyed, but said nothing. It was probably me. As badly as I wanted my own, I'd always been inept around children.

"Okay then," I said, standing, "time to blow up this baby." I moved a giant fan to the opening of the balloon and turned it on. We stood, silently watching the balloon morph from a pile of nylon into a giant framework of white and colored panels.

Mom returned awhile later. She scanned the now seven-story balloon. "Good. Perfect. Well," she said, climbing into the woven wicker basket, "now's as good a time as any."

Meredith and the girls were strangely silent. I couldn't tell if they felt awe or regret at the prospect of the ride. "Last chance to back out," I joked.

Meredith looked at the twins. "Girls? Good? Do you want to go?"

The girls nodded, though one did so with her eyes sky-high.

I picked each girl up in turn, placed them into the basket. I turned to Meredith, held my hand out in a fake-gallant gesture. "After you."

She laughed and took my hand. "Why thank you, Mr. Flynn."

Once in the balloon, I lit the burner. Mom gave her standard safety instructions: don't touch the equipment, don't lean too far over the side.

I opened the blast valve. Slowly, the balloon left the ground, above the people and the fair. Though I had done it half a dozen times, there was something ceremonious about the initial ascent, that first moment of weightlessness, the feeling that you'd left your ordinary life behind.

"This is amazing," Meredith said after a few moments. "Wait. People are waving." The twins waved back with wild hand gestures. "Hey," Emma called. "Look at the Ferris wheel. And all the balloons on the field."

"Hey. Cows." Abby pointed to a grouping of black and white cows.

"The hills and the farmland," Meredith said, looking down. "This is so beautiful."

I watched Meredith take in the scene — farms with tall stalks of corn, winding roads with fast-moving cars, lush green hills. In recent trips, I had failed to appreciate the view; the entire venture seeming more a chore to help Mom and Dad than a cool one-of-a-kind activity. But, with Meredith there, the experience seemed new. The gentle breeze, the feeling of weightlessness, the inhalation of warm, clean air.

We floated in congenial silence with the occasional reference to something of interest spotted below: a cool restaurant, a playground with twisty slides, a blond boy chasing after a small, brown dog. The landing field loomed ahead; I didn't want the ride to end.

7

I glanced at Meredith in the balloon, her long, tanned legs stretched out in front of her. Her eyes were impossibly blue, the same color as the surrounding sky. She looked almost ethereal.

Mom's words interrupted my thoughts. "We need to descend." With a final glance at Meredith, I let air out. The balloon began to descend as we reached the clearing. About a hundred feet from our landing spot stood a picturesque white farmhouse with a large stone patio off the back. Outdoor chairs surrounded a firepit; colorful potted plants adorned the edges of the space. A big willow tree sat off to the side, tire swing gently moving in the breeze. Near the willow, sat a second, large tree, red Adirondack chairs underneath.

A couple emerged from the home and walked toward the balloon. The Harrisons, my Aunt Leigh, Mom's sister, and Uncle Mason, stepped toward us.

Mom called out to them. "Mason. Leigh." She waved both arms wildly as if, without that effort, they might have completely missed the giant balloon in their yard.

Mason and Leigh reached the basket.

"Evelyn." Leigh tapped Mom on the shoulder, then looked to the rest of us. "Hey guys."

Mom hopped out, hugged them both before gesturing back to the balloon. "Leigh and Mason, this is Peter's old friend, Meredith Morgan, and her friends, Abby and Emma."

"It's nice to meet you." Aunt Leigh took a moment to shake hands with each Abby and Emma; she smiled at Meredith.

"We've got some grub at the house," Mason added. "Stay a while?"

Mom didn't hesitate. "Of course."

Mason turned to me. "Do you need help deflating?" He gestured to the balloon.

I waved my hand at the balloon. "Nah. I got it. Thanks."

Mom fell in step with my aunt and uncle as they walked toward the house. I turned to the twins. "So girls, did you like the balloon ride?"

Emma nodded vigorously. "I can't believe we got to go up in a real hot air balloon." She held out her stuffed dolphin. "My dolphin loved it."

"So did mine," Abby held her dolphin next to her sister's.

I looked at the dolphins, bent down to be at their level. "Glad you enjoyed it, dolphins." Both twins laughed. I lifted each out of the basket. As soon as their feet reached the ground, they scrambled ahead toward the tire swing. I leaned toward Meredith. "Phew. I was seriously concerned those dolphins were not having fun. The way they were held over the side —"

Meredith gripped my arm. "I know. I thought one of them was going to drop. Could you imagine if it fell?"

"Think about the poor person below. You're walking along and, wham, a stuffed, pink dolphin hits you on the head." I held my hand out to Meredith.

Meredith took it and stepped out. "Someone might think it's divine intervention."

"Or an alien." I moved my hands as though underscoring a headline. "Pastel dolphins invade New Jersey town."

Meredith laughed. "Oh, Peter. I have missed you."

I stood still. Meredith missed me? Really? Or was she just being nice? I must have taken too long to respond because she spoke again. "This is where you say, 'I missed you too, Meredith.'"

I shook my head. "Sorry. Of course, I've missed you."

We stood back and watched as the balloon began to deflate, now a massive half lump on scorched grass.

"I was just talking about our seventh-grade bio class the other day," Meredith said. "Remember when the mice got out?"

I laughed. "Rest assured that the image of Mr. Turner running after those mice with an upturned bucket is seared forever in my mind. As is his mantra."

"And that's science, kids!" We said it in unison.

I inclined my head to the still deflating balloon. "We can leave it and get it packed up later." We walked in step toward the tire swing where one twin pushed the other. It felt natural, like it had when we were younger. We reached the willow tree with the swing. "Should we sit?" I pointed to the Adirondack chairs under the nearby tree.

Meredith eyed the house. "Will your Mom mind?"

"My mother," I said, sitting down, "will talk for hours with the Harrisons. Believe me, she probably won't even notice we're gone." I plucked a blade of grass from the ground and twisted it in my fingers. I watched Meredith sit. She gave me a sideways glance. I needed to tell her. "Sadie and I got divorced last year."

Her body straightened. "Peter. I'm sorry."

I pulled at the blade of grass. "It's for the best. We were never all that great of a match. You knew that."

Suddenly, the air felt thick with things unsaid.

After Noah died, I'd handled his estate for Meredith. The matter was simple, but the extra contact with Meredith gave me a glimpse into her widowed life. She had to be there for Zach, find a full-time job, and do everything Noah had always taken care of – bills, grass, trash. I filled the void. I mowed the grass. I fixed the sink. I repaired Meredith's tiny deck after work one Friday. We'd sat on it after, sipping cold beers from the bottle and watching Zach wheel around the yard on an old dirt bike. Meredith ordered pizza; Zach fell asleep on the couch. I kissed her then; she pulled away: "Peter, you're married."

Mortification and shame had coursed through my body. I'd misread Meredith; I nearly cheated on my wife. I came around less after that; Meredith barely called. Sadie and I ended up moving to New York and my relationship with Meredith became almost nonexistent. We'd never discussed the kiss.

Her voice pulled me to the present. "What happened?" She twisted her hair. "Or don't you want to talk about it?"

"We just grew apart."

I didn't want to discuss the real reason. Sadie couldn't get pregnant. It was me, it turned out. Our marriage couldn't sustain the news.

"That's too bad. I'm sorry."

"Yeah, well." I sat up, regretting the melancholic turn of the conversation. I made my voice purposely light. "How about you? How are the wedding plans?"

"Good. It's not until May." She shrugged. "It'll be small, family mostly."

Family. I breathed an internal sigh of relief that I would not make that cut. I attended her wedding to Noah, watched her declare forever love to another man. It was not an experience I wanted to repeat. I struggled for a neutral follow-up question when, gratefully, one twin hopped over on shoes with heels that lit up. "Can one of you push us?"

I could not stand fast enough. Anything to get out of a further conversation about Meredith's wedding. Both girls moved to the tire swing, gripped the chains with tiny hands. I pushed at their backs, they flew up and around, matching ponytails bobbing behind them. “Higher, higher.” I pushed as high as it would be safe, then let the tire circle and stop.

“We should probably go in,” Meredith said, standing. The twins, done with the tire, scrambled ahead. I fell into step beside Meredith. “How’s Zach?”

Her face lit up, more so, it seemed, then it had when she talked about the wedding. “He’s great. Applying to colleges.”

“Wow. College.” I knew superficial things about Zach from social media, but I hadn’t been a regular part of his life in years. College. I squelched a pang of regret for lost time.

Meredith stepped on to the patio. “I can’t believe he’ll be gone in less than a year.” She made a face, teeth crunched together, a pretend-scared look. “I’m not ready to let him go.”

“I can imagine. Does he have a first choice?”

“The University of Pittsburgh. We toured it in the spring and that was it. PITT’s his favorite. It’s five hours away but ...”

She let the thought trail off. I filled it in. “But awesome sports when you visit. Pirates. Steelers. Games at The Pete.”

Meredith laughed. “Leave it to you to bring things back to sports.”

We followed the twins inside the house. My mother and the Harrisons sat at a thick oak table lined with appetizers, Mason’s bacon cheddar dip in the center. “Yes.” I looked at Mason. “The bacon cheddar dip.” I swiped a chip and dipped. “So good.” I grabbed another.

We sat at the table, the twins with cookies and milk at one end, Meredith and me with wine and beer at the other. The conversation was easy. Meredith told a funny story about Barkley running away with some poor family’s picnic blanket at a park. “I had to chase him three blocks.”

I laughed; I could picture that. In fact, I was picturing it when I heard my Mom’s voice: “Peter’s single, you know.”

I spit out my beer. “Mom!”

"What? It's been a year. Maybe Meredith knows a nice girl."

I grabbed a napkin to clean up the spit-out beer. I glanced at Meredith, who looked as if she might bust out laughing. That, at least, made me feel less like a loser and more like she and I were cohorts. My mother was like this. Meredith knew that.

Meredith spoke then, her tone congenial. "Any woman would be lucky to have a guy like Peter. I'll keep my eye out, Mrs. Flynn."

"Thank you." Mom seemed gratified by the remark. She shot me a look and mouthed, "see?"

Things wrapped up not long after the 'Peter's single' comment. Meredith volunteered to help me put the balloon back in the truck. We worked together in silence and, once the balloon and basket were tight inside, I shut the door. Meredith leaned against it on one leg, her other bent. Long hair fell around her shoulders, her cheeks and lips pink from the sun. She looked sexy. I cast my eyes downward.

"Hey Peter."

I looked up, afraid she'd read my mind.

"Let's stay in touch."

I exhaled. "Of course."

She pushed herself from the truck. "I mean it. This isn't the obligatory 'let's do this again sometime.' I really want to be a part of your life again."

She seemed like she meant it. But could I do that? Knowing she was getting married again. Knowing I would again be the 'best friend not boyfriend.' I wasn't sure.

She took a step toward me. "Peter?"

I looked at her. As it had always been for me with Meredith, I couldn't say no. "Why not?"

8

Three weeks after the balloon festival, I sat across from Meredith and Reed at a Starbucks table. The store was crowded, the line snaking almost out the door. Frantic baristas in green aprons rushed behind the long counter. Patrons sipped lattes on benches outside, a gentle breeze blew the first fall leaves. I hadn't met Reed before, didn't really want to. But Meredith had been strangely persistent. Every time I voiced a made-up conflict for dinner or lunch, she came up with another date or activity. When she'd brought up attending a late season Phillies game, I offered meeting for coffee. No way was I sitting for hours with Reed and Meredith at a baseball game.

Reed sat across the table from me, his chair inches from Meredith's. She looked possibly more beautiful than she had at the balloon festival. Her hair was curled back from her face, revealing light make-up which accentuated her eyes. A tight-fitting black sweater revealed more of her figure than the loose-fitting t-shirt she'd had on at the festival. She wore jeans and moccasins, the kind with fuzz on the inside. I smiled when I saw them. Meredith had always loved things that were warm and fuzzy.

Reed was tall and lean with a goofy smile. He wore a cross-over bag on his chest. He leaned forward. "So," he said with a smile, "tell me about Meredith in high school. What was she like? What don't I know?" He sat back with a satisfied look.

I cupped my coffee. "Meredith? Nothing to tell. Outstanding student, superb athlete." I paused. "But you know that already."

I knew the response was lame. I glanced at Meredith. She twisted a lock of hair, her nervous tell. I felt the familiar twinge in my gut, the one I'd always gotten when Meredith looked uncomfortable.

"Okay," I said, looking at Reed. "Here are a few things you might not know. Meredith made varsity softball as a freshman. She was president of the French club. And she made dean's list every marking period." I picked up my coffee, comfortable with the surface details I'd given. Reed didn't know the real stuff. That Meredith ate peanut butter and jelly for lunch every day, that she wore lucky green socks for tests, or that, sophomore year, she'd hidden a stray cat in her bedroom for a month.

Reed punched Meredith lightly on the shoulder. "French club? You never told me that." He looked thoughtful a moment, then said, "Bonjour, Mademoiselle."

Meredith smiled. "Salut, Monsieur."

"Vous etes belle."

"Merci."

I looked at Meredith. I desperately wanted to tease her about the exchange but didn't know how Reed would take it. Instead, silence enveloped our table, the quiet amplified by the surrounding noise. Laughing people. Talking people. Shouting people. It felt as though everyone, save the three of us, had something to say.

After what felt like an endless silence, I cleared my throat. "So, Reed. Meredith says you're a pediatric dentist."

He nodded vigorously. “Yes. Yes. I’m the tooth doctor. My office is on Sycamore Street.”

I’d seen it. Reed had actually named his practice The Tooth Doctor. A sign with a personified molar wearing a surgical mask hung out front. Occasionally, a person dressed as the molar stood in the building’s front waving a giant cutout of a toothbrush. Had the molar actually been Reed? I opened my mouth to ask, then thought better of it. “Hey. What kind of prizes do kids get these days? I used to love those.”

“Prizes?”

“You know. Stickers, bubbles, key-chains.”

Recognition crossed Reed’s face. “Right. I don’t do prizes. I give out toothbrushes.”

Toothbrushes? “Cool.”

The dental conversation was followed by an equally painful discussion about my own job as an estate lawyer, a topic which bored even me. We followed the discussion about my job with one about an upcoming beer fest none of us planned to attend.

“It’s supposed to be sunny this weekend,” Reed said, looking outside.

The weather? God, no. Had it really come to a conversation about the weather? I tipped my head, then reached into my pocket and pulled out my phone as though it had just vibrated. “Shoot,” I said, looking at my home screen. “It’s my assistant. My 9:00 is early.”

“Bummer,” Meredith said. She looked genuinely disappointed. “Maybe another time?”

I stood but didn’t respond for fear Meredith would whip out her phone and schedule something. I kissed her on the cheek, shook Reed’s hand. “Nice to meet you.”

“You too, Peter.” He held my hand and gaze a bit too long. It felt kind of like a warning.

Were my feelings for Meredith, past and present, that obvious? Did Reed know about my failed kiss all those years ago?

He nodded, let go of my hand, then rapped my shoulder. "Better get to that appointment, mate."

The comment felt wrong, like I'd been dismissed. I stood awkwardly for a moment, then lifted my hand in a half wave to them both. Feelings of jealousy mixed with embarrassment simmered in my gut.

Never again.

9

I drove to my office, only a few blocks from the Starbucks. The space was one-half of a brick duplex in downtown Crasmere, not far off the trendy shops on the main road. The firm sign stood on a grassy plot in front, The Law Offices of Peter Flynn in bold.

I pushed open the door. My associate, Nate, stood at the front desk with Kim, our assistant. Nate wore jeans instead of his signature blue suit, a Phillies baseball cap on his head.

I set my briefcase on the floor. "What happened to you?"

"Lily happened. She was up since 3:00 a.m. and it was my turn for night duty. I couldn't fall back asleep." Nate bounced from foot to foot. "I'm going solely on caffeine right now." He held up a mug.

"Wow. That sucks." It was the obligatory thing to say; I didn't mean it. A loving wife? A baby? I'd give up sleep for either of those things.

Nate shrugged. "Babies, you know?"

I nodded. I didn't know, of course. But it wasn't as if Nate and I had long conversations about my infertility; it wasn't as if he knew I wanted children.

Nate set a stack of papers in front of Kim. "So you're good to get this Motion filed today?"

Kim pulled the papers toward her. "You got it."

Nate glanced at the clock. "I got to get home and change. Washington prelim." He left without a further word.

Nate and I had worked together at the law firm, Collin Decker. I left the firm to move with Sadie to New York.

When I moved back home and went out on my own, Nate sought me out. He hated the work he was doing at Collin Decker, wanted to start a litigation practice – criminal and civil trials. I didn't handle that type of case – I hate courtrooms – but the price of office real estate in downtown Crasmere was steep. Nate made a strong argument for the money he could bring in. Though unorthodox to combine my estate practice with a predominantly criminal one, I agreed.

Nate wasn't wrong about the money. His new client income almost outpaced my own. I'd have to make him a partner soon.

I exchanged niceties with Kim and disappeared into my office. I drafted a will, two powers of attorney, and answered a dozen emails about an upcoming real estate closing. Only the latter of these was remotely interesting. My client's shed was, apparently, on the border of the neighbor's property. The buyers wanted it moved.

At noon, Kim popped her head in the conference room. "Take out?"

"Of course. 31 South?"

"You know it." Kim held up the 31 South menu. "Belefer again?"

"Always the Belefer, Kim."

I heard Nate come in. Kim took his order and, within forty minutes, the three of us sat at the table in the conference room with sandwiches on paper wraps. I nodded my head toward an extra sandwich in the middle. "Who's that for?"

Kim smirked.

"Kim?"

"It's for Lucy. She asked if she could join us."

I shook my head. Lucy, our landlord who lived on the other side of the duplex, was a major source of amusement for Nate and Kim. They insisted she had a wild crush on me; I wasn't so sure.

Kim cocked her head and looked at me, her expression deadpan. "Do you think she'll bring you more banana bread?"

Nate smiled and tapped the table in front of me. "Or another fern?

I put my head in my hands. "The fern was for the *office*."

"Yet," Kim added, "she gave it specifically to you." She directed her gaze on Nate. "Nate, did Lucy give you a fern?"

"Nope. And I don't recall ever getting banana bread."

"And she didn't ask me to watch her pit bull. Poppy, right?" Kim was full out laughing now.

"Stop it."

Lucy's voice sounded at the front door. "Knock, knock."

I peeked out the window and saw her on the step, hand poised in a fake knock. She wore jeans and tall boots with a navy sweater, a sequined Minnie Mouse in its center. Sprayed brown hair framed a face with heavy make-up. A green gift bag swung in the crook of her elbow. Great.

"We're in here, Lucy," Kim called.

Lucy entered the conference room. Thick rose-scented perfume filled the space around her. She swung the gift bag in a dramatic gesture, then set it before me. "Thought you might like this for the office." She took the seat next to mine.

I pushed the package back to be opened later, when there couldn't be Nate-Kim comments, but Lucy tapped on it. "Come on. Open it now."

I glanced at her, then pulled a tissue-wrapped cylinder from the bag. I held up the gift. "Nice."

I had no idea what it was. No worry there, as Lucy was

excited to tell me. "It's a wax candle burner. You pick a scent and plug it in. I got you a few starter scents." She dumped the bag; circles of wax rolled on to the glass table. I saw Nate smirk in my peripheral vision.

I picked up a wax circle and held it. "Thank you. This is very thoughtful."

Nate switched on the television mounted in the corner. It flickered to life and Yvonne Williams, one of Crasmere Count's deputy attorneys, filled the screen. She stood behind a podium in a black suit jacket, hair sprayed in place, red lipstick so perfect it looked as if it had been painted on her face. She answered questions about a sexual harassment case she'd handled, her voice clear and commanding.

Lucy looked from the television to me. "Is she always this tough?"

I shrugged and nodded toward Nate. "Nate would know better. He's the criminal lawyer."

Nate gestured with his soda. "She's the best DA they have down there." He shook his head. "They move her around a lot, give her the big cases." Nate watched the television another moment, then whistled. "Man, she is a buster. I'd love to have a case against her."

"Really?" I looked at Nate. The last thing I would want is to have a case against a lawyer with a reputation like Yvonne Williams.

Nate picked up a triple decker club. "It'd be a challenge, right? She hardly ever loses." He took a bite of the sandwich and half-swallowed. "Winning a case against Yvonne Williams would be like taking down the queen bee."

Kim started at the television. "What's so intimidating about her?"

Nate put down his sandwich. "She's just lethal. I saw her try an assault case once. The accused was on the stand. She asked perfectly natural questions, one after the other. The accused totally relaxed on the stand, leaning back, thinking he has her. Then, boom, Yvonne asks the question that corners him. He knew it too. The guy looked like an animal in a trap. Ned Lenkins, the guy's attorney, he's objecting like crazy, but it's too late. She had him. He was done." Nate shook his head. "I think Lenkins almost pissed in his pants." He swallowed a big bite of his sandwich before continuing. "So, anyway, Yvonne Williams is king of the jungle down at the courthouse. She lives for the kill." He looked at his watch. "Ah. Client coming in. Gotta run." He grabbed the remainder of the giant club and breezed out of the conference room.

"Time for me to run too," Kim said, standing. "Got lots of time entries to input." She picked up her trash. When she reached the doorway, she winked at me.

I looked to Lucy, then stood. "Well, I ought --"

"Do you want me to show you how this works?" She pointed to the burner with a pink fingernail.

"This?" I picked up the burner. "Nah. Seems pretty self-explanatory."

Lucy picked up one of the wax scents and started to remove the plastic wrap. "Peter," she started.

Oh no.

She looked down at the table, continued to unwrap the scent. "If you aren't doing anything, I was hoping you might want to go with me to the Black Cat Ball on Halloween. The money goes to The Cat Depot. You know, the shelter for stray cats." She looked at me, her expression vulnerable. "I have tickets."

My first instinct was to say no. It would be easy enough to feign an excuse or say I wasn't ready. My divorce hadn't been that long ago.

Lucy shifted in her seat.

I opened my mouth to decline when an image of Meredith and Reed from the morning flashed in my mind.

Lucy put down the now unwrapped wax scent. "I understand if —"

"I'd love to go."

"Really?"

"Really. Count me in."

Lucy smiled. "Great. Wow. Thank you." She moved in a seeming attempt to hug me, then stepped back and bumped my shoulder. "Great," she said again.

I escorted Lucy to the front door, then went back to my office to avoid Kim and Nate. I sat in my office chair just as my cell phone rang. My mother's face filled the rectangular screen. I accepted the call; she started talking immediately and without pause.

"Peter. Can you get your father's medicine on the way home? Also, can you pick up Chinese food? I ordered takeout."

I pulled up my calendar though I knew I had nothing to do after work hours, nothing socially anyway. "I can do that."

I hung up the phone, feeling both childish and annoyed. A grown man should have his own place to live. But I couldn't, not with Dad's dementia worsening. Mom wouldn't be able to handle it.

I worked until five. When I pulled into my parents' driveway — medicine and Chinese take-out in tow — I saw a minivan parked at the top. One of Mom's bridge friends? I hoped not. They, like Mom, were always trying to set me up.

I walked toward the stone farmhouse Mom had inherited from my grandparents a decade earlier. The two-story home stood on an acre of farmland in front of dense woods. To the left of the main home stood a carriage house which had been converted into an apartment. To the right sat a red barn with horses, Mom's pride and joy. I made my way up the stone path. Freeloader, my favorite of the barn cats, stood on the path. I picked him up, scratched his chin. "Hey buddy." He purred.

I blew out a breath, prepared myself to meet and converse

with the owner of the minivan. Here goes nothing. I pushed open the door. “Food’s here!”

“Great,” Mom called out. “We have company.”

Of course we did.

I stepped into the kitchen.

Meredith was there.

10

"Meredith. Hey."

"Hey, Peter. Long time, no see." She chuckled.

I didn't respond, tried to work out why she was there. I must have taken too long because she stamped her foot. "Get it? Long time, no see because I saw you just this morning."

I smiled. "Yeah. Right. For coffee."

I set the food on the counter, and Mom gestured toward Meredith. "Hey hon, can you get down some glasses? Second cabinet to the right."

"Sure, Mrs. Flynn."

"Please, call me Evelyn."

I looked at them both. Neither seemed to think the scenario strange. I squinted at Meredith. She pulled down a glass. "What?" she asked.

I looked at Mom, then back at her. "Okay. I'm glad to see you, but what are you doing here?"

Surprise flashed across her face. "Oh, sorry. I thought your Mom told you."

Mom gestured toward her legs. "I called Meredith to get

some exercises for my knee. She was nice enough to come here and show me." She did a half squat. "See?"

I could not remember my mother ever complaining of knee pain. Had she really made up an injury as a ruse to get Meredith here? I shook my head.

"I'll get your father," Mom said finally, and breezed out of the room.

Meredith began to fill the glasses with ice. "Your parents' new house is beautiful." She moved to the large picture window which looked out on the yard. I glanced in the same direction. A bright sun beat down on an expanse of land lined by thick woods. The horses stood in a cluster at the far end of their enclosure, manes blowing in the gentle breeze.

"Oh, look." Meredith pointed at two of the horses. They ran next to one another, almost like a race.

"That's Fritter and Deo." I moved next to Meredith. "They act like siblings, always fighting and chasing each other." I pointed to a large, black horse in the back. "And that's Rebel. He's more of a loner."

"I can't believe there are horses in your yard." Meredith punched me gently on the shoulder. "Could you imagine if your parents had this house when we were in high school? I would have been here all the time." She paused. "Wait. I was at your house all the time anyway." She laughed. "Your Mom always had the best snacks. What were those oatmeal ones again?"

"Energy balls," we said in unison. Energy balls, a concoction of oatmeal, peanut butter, and chocolate chips, had been Mom's specialty.

I walked toward the refrigerator. "She still makes them." I opened the fridge door, took out a round cluster of oatmeal, and held it out.

Meredith's hands flew to her mouth. "Oh. I have to try."

I placed the ball in her out-stretched hand; she popped it in her mouth. "Oh my gosh. It tastes like childhood. I totally remember eating these after school and watching General Hospital."

"You and my mother watched General Hospital. I had nothing to do with that." I grabbed a stack of plates. Meredith set out silverware.

"Oh really? So you didn't care about Luke and Laura? And you didn't have a crush on Kristina Wagner?"

"Nope. Neither of those things. I just happened to be in the room while you and my mother watched. Total coincidence."

"Right. Of course. I'm sure you were doing something very important on that big recliner." She said it teasingly; it felt like old times. It was amazing how different this encounter was from the one just that morning. Fun and lighthearted instead of stilted and forced. I straightened the silverware. When I looked up, Meredith had a smirk on her face.

"What?"

She nodded toward the newly straightened forks. "Still a perfectionist, I see?"

I looked at the forks, moved a few out of line. "No. I'm much improved. Those forks being haphazard doesn't bother me a bit." I crossed my arms and glanced again at the table. "Not one bit."

Meredith grinned, then realigned the forks. "I know it's driving you crazy. I got you."

Before I could respond, Mom entered the kitchen, Dad on her elbow. I looked from my Dad to Meredith. I should have warned her about his dementia. She'd be expecting the jovial high school social studies teacher Dad had been, not who he was now. I tried to think of an excuse to get Meredith alone when Dad's face erupted into a smile. "Meredith." He looked legitimately thrilled.

I looked more closely at him, then realized the obvious: my Dad could clearly remember people and events from earlier times. It was his short-term memory that was problematic.

"Hi, Mr. Flynn," Meredith moved toward him.

"Psst." He waved a hand at her. "It's Karl."

Meredith gave him a hug; Mom looked at me over their heads. "Who knew?" she mouthed.

Dad gestured for her to sit. "Good to see you. What are you up to these days?"

Meredith told Dad about her job at Sunshine Therapies and about Zach. He asked numerous follow-up questions in a manner more engaged than he'd been in months. When we neared the natural end of the meal, I didn't want it to be over. Meredith's presence seemed to unlock a better version of my Dad.

Mom picked up a few empty plates just as Dad cleared his throat and asked, "should we play some horseshoes?"

I stared at him. *Had he just asked to play horseshoes?*

Over the summer, I had built a horseshoe pit in the backyard. Mom insisted the physical activity would be good for Dad's dementia. Plus, he'd always loved the game. I made the new pit a replica of the one from our old house but, when I showed it to him, he'd insisted I stole it. The rant had gone on, Dad insisting that he be taken back to the other house. It had been awful. A man I'd hero-worshipped my whole life had been reduced to a confused, angry mass on the lawn. After the incident, he completely ignored the pit; I put the horseshoes in the garage. He never mentioned it again.

Until now.

I looked at Meredith. She didn't know the backstory behind the horseshoes; she probably didn't want to play anyway. It was Friday night. Surely, she had something better to do.

"I'd love to."

"Really?" The word popped out of my mouth.

"Sure. Reed's out with his girls and Zach is at his friends' house. I'm totally free." She held her hands up as she said the last sentence.

Dad looked from Meredith to me. "Okay then. Me and my Evie against you two."

We followed him out to the pit. Meredith punched me lightly on the arm. "Don't worry," she whispered, "I'm a fabulous horseshoe player."

I rolled my eyes. "I have no doubt."

At the start of the game, Mom got a ringer on her first turn, then on the second. I was awful. Meredith was worse.

I leaned into her. "I thought you were a fabulous player," I whispered.

"Just warming up." Meredith picked up a horseshoe and held it toward me. "This is where we come back." She threw the shoe. It hit the metal stake with a clank then swung around.

"Ringer!" I held up both hands.

Meredith reached up and slapped my upturned hands for a double high-five. "See? And you doubted me."

I grinned, noticing, without wanting to, how blue her eyes looked. "Lucky break." I picked up a horseshoe and threw; it missed entirely.

"Hmm," Meredith said, her mouth a straight line. She bent down to get another shoe, her body lithe and athletic. I stared at her a moment, then forced my gaze away.

We finished the first game of horseshoes, then a second. I was a disaster in both. I tried to laugh my incompetence off as lack of practice but, the fact was, Meredith distracted me. The curve of her neck, the sound of her laugh. The look of concentration she got just as she was about to make a throw. I was grateful when Mom suggested we break for some wine on the covered porch.

We moved to the porch area and sunk into deep outdoor couch cushions just as the bright early evening slid into night. Mom brought out blankets and poured glasses of wine. I lit a fire. Flames from the pit burst in colored licks of red and orange, their brightness illuminating the space. Crickets sounded, twinkling stars lit up a dark sky. The conversation ebbed and flowed.

I closed my eyes a moment, pretended how it would be if this was it, my life. Meredith a staple in it again; Dad's brain not cursed with disease.

"Well."

I opened my eyes at the sound of Dad's voice.

"We're going to get to bed." He gestured to Mom who had dozed off, long fingers still clutched around her wineglass stem. Dad gently uncurled them, then set the glass on a side table. He helped Mom to her feet, put his arm around her shoulders, and guided her toward the house. "Thanks, Karl," she whispered.

I watched them a moment. I couldn't remember the last time I'd seen Dad care for Mom and not the reverse.

Meredith stood and poked the now-dying fire. Tiny orange ember bits flew out with the effort. She poured us each a bit more wine, finishing the bottle, then sat and held up her glass. "To old friends."

I clinked my glass to hers. "To old friends," I repeated.

Meredith leaned back and shut her eyes and I watched her, wishing, for a moment, that things could have been different between us. Back in high school. After Noah died. Now. I shook my head. It wasn't meant to be.

A buzz sounded from her purse. Her eyes flew open and, in what seemed like a single, fluid movement, she jolted up, unzipped the bag, and pulled out her phone. Scanning the message, she breathed out.

I tried, and failed, to decipher her expression. "All okay?"

"Yeah," she said, sliding the device back into her purse. "Just Reed letting me know the movie got out late." She exhaled. "It's crazy but every time my phone buzzes and I'm not with Zach, I always worry it's him, that there's been some emergency." She shook her head. "It's ridiculous. He's going to be eighteen next month. But it's a habit, you know? I don't know when I'll ever get over it."

I thought about my Mom. "Probably never."

She sat up and swatted my thigh. "Hey!"

I smiled. "What? It's true. That's just how mothers are."

"Dads too," Meredith said.

I didn't protest because I didn't know. A sliver of sadness slipped into my psyche; I forced it out. Meredith didn't know about my infertility and it had been too good of a night for self-pity. I held up my glass. "Here's to never getting an emergency call from Zach."

She held up her glass and clinked it to mine with a broad smile.

"Cheers to that."

11

Meredith

"So, this Peter. Is he hot?" Donna put her hand up to shield her eyes from the afternoon sun. "Wait." She stepped forward, cupped her hands around her mouth. "Come on, Carter," she yelled. "You can't let those get past you."

I watched Carter jog back to his place on the soccer field. He didn't acknowledge his mother.

Donna leaned closer to me. "Sorry about that. So. Peter?"

"Peter's an old friend."

Donna kept her eyes trained on the defense; the boy Carter was defending scored a goal. "Damn it," she said under her breath, then yelled, "you've got to do better than that, Cart."

The whistle blew for substitutions; the coach replaced Carter with a freshman. I braced myself. After eight years of standing with Donna on the sidelines of soccer fields, I knew this wouldn't go well. Donna was unabashedly vocal at her kids' sporting events, yelling at coaches, referees, other players. Once, after screaming at a high-school volunteer referee during a U12 tournament, an official asked her to leave.

But Donna didn't mention the substitution. Instead, she asked again about Peter. Her lack of focus on the soccer game was unusual. She must really want to get back to the dating scene. I glanced in her direction; she bumped my arm. "Okay, he's an old friend. But is he hot? Will he get the old juices going, again?" She threw a salacious smile in my direction.

"He looks different now than from the last time I saw him." I conjured up a vision of new Peter. "He's clearly been working out, and he has this new haircut. It's high at the top and –" I stopped myself. The truth was, I'd had trouble digesting Peter's new look. My Peter was squishy and comfortable, like an old teddy bear. New Peter had broad shoulders and biceps visible under his clothes. He had what seemed to be permanent five o'clock stubble that set off brownish-green eyes. I'd seen Peter twice since the night at his parents' house. Once for coffee, once for lunch. "He's not bad looking," I admitted.

"You've got to introduce me. I need to get me some." Donna moved her hips backward and forward suggestively. The gray-haired woman next to us threw a judgmental look. Donna oriented herself in the woman's direction and swung her hips again, this time more vigorously. The woman turned her back.

Donna leaned closer. "Seriously. This whole thing with Max and the divorce has been depressing. I could use a little fun. Can you set us up? Just one date?" She held up an index finger.

I didn't answer. Peter and Donna? Old best friend and new best friend? It was strange to think about. Peter was stable and comfortable. And Donna was Donna. Crazy and fun. Would Peter like that? Probably.

"Mer?" Donna prompted.

"Sure," I blurted. I pictured them together. Donna would overshadow him, her strong personality dominating his affable one. A surge of protectiveness coursed through me. "Peter's a nice guy," I said. "Be careful."

She threw me a look. "Jeez, Mer. I'm not going to hurt him."

I was about to respond when a player passed Zach the ball. Zach dribbled up the field, around one player from the opposing team, then another. My hands turned to fists. "Come on, Zach. Come on," I whispered. Zach passed the ball to Mikey, the center forward, who kicked it into the goal.

Donna held her hands up in victory. "Yes, boys! Get another, get another. You got this." She clapped with enthusiasm then turned to me. "Nice assist."

"It was a good one." I felt a swell of pride. I'd miss these games next year. I'd known the mothers for a decade, their sons on and off the same teams through the years. We soccer moms were moored together by shared memories: travel team tryouts, concession stands, the Beach Blast tournament in Wildwood. And, for me, the kindred group of other mothers made it easier to be a single parent.

The game continued; Zach's team dominated. When it was over, he waved to me. I waved back then watched as the blue number 9 on Zach's back disappeared among the mass of teammates heading into the locker room.

I turned around. A group of team mothers clustered in a circle near Donna. I stepped forward; the group moved to make room. The afternoon sun dipped behind puffed clouds; the sky darkened.

"So," Donna said, "dinner and wine? It's Friday. We know our boys won't be home." She rolled her eyes.

Julie and Terri, two of the moms, agreed to go and, a half hour later, we sat at the Crasmere Pub, a festive bar in the heart of town. Our table was directly in front of a wood burning fire; its subtle warmth enhanced my mood. The last few months had been good. Reed's girls had seemed unbothered by Zach's and my presence on their weekends, and pumpkin butterscotch muffins were now a staple along with the morning waffles.

Most Saturdays, Reed and I sat at the kitchen table after breakfast, bits of the morning paper spread between us. The twins would disappear into the basement for Disney-themed dance competitions on the Wii. Jamie and Zach would generally be in the family room. Every now and again, I'd hear one of them laugh or share something with the other. It felt good. Like a family.

A server appeared; Donna ordered two bottles of wine for the table.

"Two?" Julie questioned.

Donna shrugged. "There's four of us."

Julie looked as though she were about to retort, then seemed to think better of it. "Anyone done with college apps?"

There was a collective groan. "Zach just sent in PITT last week," I volunteered.

There was a smattering of updates on the other boys' applications before the conversation turned again to other senior year rites of passage: the prom, the May prank, the senior trip.

The server returned with our food and drinks; she poured each of us a glass of wine. Donna downed hers like a shot and looked at me. "Drive me home?" she mouthed.

"Of course." Thankfully, she moved from the wine to her oversized cheeseburger. As much as I loved her, Donna's behavior since Max left had been worrisome. She was angry more than usual and, anytime there was alcohol in proximity, she got drunk. I watched her down another swig of wine, made a mental note to talk to her. Maybe the drinking was just social, but maybe it was more. She might want help.

I pushed my concern about Donna's drinking to the back of my mind and leaned back. Whitney Houston's *I Wanna Dance with Somebody* blared on the speaker. Dancers moved on the floor between our table and the bar. Donna stood. "I wanna dance with somebody," she said, then pointed to a man at the bar.

"Oh no, Donna," I said.

"Oh yes." She approached the man, head bobbing, whispered in his ear. He looked at her then slid off the stool, took her hand, and began to dance. After a few moments, Donna called to the group. "Come on guys. Mike here doesn't want to dance with just me." The group, save Julie, met them on the floor. We danced until the next slow song. When it began, Donna gave Mike an exaggerated kiss on the cheek before returning to the table.

I drove Donna home. The boys' car was at her house when we arrived. Zach's too. I looked at her. She seemed about to pass out.

"You good, Don?" I asked.

"I'm good."

I took a deep breath. Maybe I could pass her off as tired? I helped her inside, set her up on the couch. After, I found all three boys in the kitchen, their faces caked with white, black, and red make-up. "Ah," I said, opening the cabinet where Donna kept the glasses, "haunted Halloween again?"

Zach, Carter, and Owen worked at Sleepy Hollow Haunted Halloween, a nature-farm turned Zombie Apocalypse every October weekend. Zach and Carter typically hid behind haystacks in a corn maze and jumped out at unsuspecting visitors; Owen was a guide. I hadn't been to Sleepy Hollow. I'd heard it was legitimately scary, but, looking at the boys in the bright light of Donna's kitchen, the idea of them frightening anyone seemed ludicrous.

I filled a glass with water for Donna. Zach tapped me on the shoulder. "Hey. We have to go." He paused a moment. "There's supposed to be a party after. If there is, can I go?"

I hesitated.

"No drinking," Zach volunteered.

I looked at him. He held up one hand like a boy scout. "I promise, Mom."

Underage drinking was a huge issue for me. If adults did stupid things when they were drunk, how could anyone expect teenagers – whose brains aren't fully developed – to manage. Excess drinking at any age was nothing more than a precursor to bad decisions. The man who'd hit Noah's car in a drunken stupor had been fifty-eight. Later, I'd learned that the man was a decent human being. Married, hardworking, a father of two grown girls. Didn't matter. His one stupid decision to drink and drive had changed all our lives.

"Mom?"

I exhaled. Zach was a senior. And a good kid. He'd given me no reason to distrust him. "Alright. No drinking and text me the address." I grabbed his phone off the counter to hand it to him. A text message from Paige Dixon flashed on his home screen: *C U 2nite.* There was a cartoonish image below the message, a figure obviously intended to look like Paige, popping out of a jack-o-lantern.

Oh.

I opened my mouth, then shut it. Universally, teenage boys would not want their mothers commenting on girls in front of their friends. Zach was no exception. I'd ask him about it tomorrow.

I handed Zach his phone and gestured for the boys to get together. "Let me get a picture." They collectively groaned but stood with their arms slung around each other, goofy smiles incongruent with their heavy, scary make-up. I snapped a shot then looked at it, a lump in my throat. Zach's senior year was flying by.

I wasn't ready.

The boys left. I found Donna in the family room, handed her the water. After a sip, she leaned back and closed her eyes. "Max filed for full custody."

It took me a moment to process the sentence. "What? Why?"

"Because he's an asshole." She got up, retrieved a stack of papers from a cabinet, and dropped them in my lap.

I scanned the documents, a motion for custody, Exhibits A to J affixed to the back. It seemed crazy; I looked to Donna. "But the boys are older. What's the point of switching things up?"

Donna laughed. "Who knows? According to Max, I'm a negligent mother. I drink too much. I don't supervise the boys. They don't do their homework. They don't get good grades." She leaned forward. "I mean, lots of kids don't get good grades, right? Lots of kids don't hand in homework." She paused. "Does Zach?"

"Not always." Surely Max couldn't be filing for custody over a few missed homework assignments.

"And do you know where Zach is every single night? According to Max, I should have constant tabs on these kids."

Donna didn't seem to want an answer. I was glad. I did know where Zach was every night. I put the documents on a table behind her, rubbed her shoulder. "I'm so sorry, honey. What does your lawyer think?"

Donna explained their legal strategy. The process sounded awful and expensive and reminded me of the conversations I'd had with Reed on the topic. His divorce from Lara had been horrific.

My phone pinged. A message from Zach: *104 West Riding Drive.* I didn't know the home. Did it matter? I had the address. *Fine.* I put my phone face down on the table and looked at Donna, still upright but with her eyes closed. She would not, I was certain, worry about Carter and Owen all night. She'd wake up in the morning and her sons would be home in their beds and she would not have wasted one second of her life on unrealistic and far-reaching 'what if' scenarios.

Unlike me.

I got up and shifted Donna's body on the couch, covered her with an afghan and set the water on the side table. I picked up my phone intending to give Zach a midnight curfew, then stopped myself. There would be no midnight curfews in college. Plus, I had to learn to stop worrying.

Zach would be fine.

12

Zach got home at 12:37 a.m. I know this because I was awake next to Reed's sleeping, snoring form, pretending, without success, that I was completely fine with Zach being out past midnight at a party at a stranger's house. He's almost eighteen, I'd told myself, like a mantra. Finally, I heard the click of the front door and my tense muscles softened. I fell asleep as quickly as if I had flicked an internal light switch to off.

Zach slept late the next day and, the next morning, ate two pieces of peanut butter and jelly toast, followed by scrambled eggs, followed by Fruit Loops. He drank the leftover pink milk from the bottom of the bowl, a habit I'd always hated.

"Zach."

"Sorry."

I dropped a new K-cup into the Keurig. "How was the party?"

"Fine."

I watched a thin band of coffee filled the waiting mug. "That's it? Fine."

Zach tossed Barkley a piece of crust. "The police came at the end. A neighbor complained about the noise."

"That's too bad." I waited, hoped Zach would follow up with more details, maybe mention Paige. "Anyone interesting there?"

Zach rinsed his plate, then stuffed it in the dishwasher. "Interesting how?"

"Just wondering who went that you knew. Besides Carter and Owen."

Zach blew out a breath. "I hardly knew anyone. It was a Crasmere School party."

"Oh." The Crasmere School was the town's private high school. State-of-the-art. Expensive. Jamie went there. So did Paige.

Before I could think of something else to ask, Zach disappeared. I heard his feet on the stairs, the sound of his bedroom door. Clearly, he didn't want to share about the party.

Maybe there was nothing to share.

I moved to the family room and switched on the television. It wasn't Reed's weekend with the girls and it felt excessively quiet. Boring, even. I sat on the couch, stared at a smiling woman on the screen carving a jack-o'-lantern. After what seemed like no time, she turned it around to reveal a perfect cutout of Elsa from Frozen. How? I struggled to even cut triangles.

I heard Reed come in, felt hands kneading my shoulders. I gestured to the television. "Check it out. Frozen pumpkins."

Reed glanced at the television. "Wow. Impressive. Should we try that with the twins?"

I looked up at him and raised an eyebrow.

He laughed. "Right, never mind. Anyway, speaking of Halloween --" He let the words trail off dramatically.

"Yes. Speaking of Halloween --"

"Rob has tickets to the Black Cat Ball that he can't use. It's tonight but it's supposed to be really fun. Tickets are impossible to get."

I sat up. I'd heard about the Black Cat Ball but had never gone. "Sure. What do you want to do for costumes?"

"I've got Rob's costumes. They're crazy. Wait." Reed hurried out of the room and came back a moment later with a giant, zippered garment bag. "Okay. Close your eyes."

"Close my eyes? Really?"

"Yes. It makes the reveal more exciting."

"Fine." I closed my eyes and heard a zipper, then the rustle of plastic, a strange anticipation in my chest. What would we be? Superheroes? Ghouls?

"Okay............ now!"

I opened my eyes. A smiling Reed held a Mickey Mouse costume in one hand and a Minnie one in the other. Not regular costumes. Super, over-the-top costumes. Dangling from the hanger of the Minnie costume were oversized yellow shoes, giant white gloves, and mouse ears centered by a red polka-dot bow. They were somewhat ridiculous.

"Fun. Right? And get it? We'll be MICE at the Black Cat Ball."

"Clever." I fingered the polka dot skirt, caught Reed's expression, unabashedly thrilled. "These are fantastic," I said, trying to improve my reaction.

Reed pulled on the oversized gloves and placed the mouse ears on his head. "Hot, right?"

"Most definitely." I put on my own gloves and ears. "We'll be the envy of the ball."

THE RENAISSANCE MARRIOTT staff had completely transformed their largest banquet room for the ball. Leafless trees adorned with fake spiderwebs and white lights sat in the center of the room. Several dozen tables dressed in royal purple linens circled the illuminated trees. On each sat three lit candles of varied heights, thick waxy drips on their sides. But for the flickering candles and tree lights, the room was dim. A band played *Monster Mash* on a stage in front of a wooden dance floor.

I picked a name card from the front table. It featured a photo of a cat for adoption, a description of the feline on the back. I inspected the card. The cat, Lemon, was a three-year-old female with white and gray fur who liked sunny spots and belly rubs. I held it out to Reed. "Are you in the market for a cat?"

He took the card. "No. But I heard it's almost impossible to leave here without one."

"Not me. I have Barkley. He'd hate a cat."

Reed put the Lemon card back on the table. He leaned forward. "Rob told me the MC gets people bidding actual money for these stray cats. It's insane. He said that, last year, some guy bid over five thousand dollars."

"Five thousand dollars? For a stray cat?" I couldn't imagine.

Reed flipped through the name cards. "Here we are." He flashed a card with Rob's name on it. "Table twelve. Let's find it."

I followed Reed past costumed pirates, cave dwellers, and a couple dressed like Fred and Wilma Flintstone. When we reached table twelve, I set my purse on the table. Something brushed against my leg. I looked down. A black cat stood by my foot.

I looked at Reed. "There's a cat." I pointed to it.

"I didn't tell you?" Reed picked up the cat.

"No." I looked at the animal, now cradled in Reed's arms. It blinked at me.

"Sorry. The cats for adoption walk around. It's like they're mingling with potential owners."

"Really?" I examined the room. Now that I knew they were there, I saw cats all over. Some on chairs, some roaming the floor. One yellow cat sat perched on a seat, licking its back leg. I turned to Reed. "Aren't people bothered by the cats everywhere?" I pointed to a cat on a seat. "Like that one?"

Reed shook his head. "Not as far as I know. People know what the event is. It's become trendy to attend. Like I said, it's hard to get tickets. Plus, the waiver they make you sign is like a mile long. And, if you want to bid on a cat, you have to fill out an even longer adoption form. It's quite the process." Reed looked at the name tag of the cat in his arms, then took its paw and made it wave. "Hi Meredith," Reed said in a New York accent. "I'm Banjo. Want to be friends?"

Banjo wiggled out of Reed's arms, unwilling, apparently, to be part of the ridiculousness.

"Do you think the cats ever scratch anyone?"

Reed shrugged. "I don't know. Probably, right? Hence the big waiver." He shrugged then pointed to a bar in the corner, the face of it covered with black spiderwebs. "Shall I get us drinks? Chardonnay?"

"Sure." Reed made his way to the bar, Mickey ears high above the crowd. The band played *Ghostbusters*. I tapped my foot; Banjo pounced on it. "Hey buddy." I picked him up; he started purring immediately. I could see what Reed meant now. It would be hard to leave without a cat.

"Meredith?"

I turned around. "Peter."

13

"Oh my gosh." I set Banjo down, hugged Peter, then stood back. He wore a Prince Charming costume, a red sash diagonal across his chest. He looked handsome, broad shoulders, hair slicked back with gel. I gave him a sideways glance. "I was wondering when my prince would come."

He shot me a look. "Ha. Ha. You look great."

"You think so? I thought I looked a bit mousy."

Peter slapped his forehead. "Oh my God, Meredith. Only you."

I smiled. "Reed and I just got tickets today. Have you been to this before?"

"No. I'd never heard of it, actually." Peter gestured around. "It's kind of cool though."

"It is. I heard it's a good moneymaker."

A woman came up behind Peter. She put her hands on his shoulders, whispered something in his ear. She matched him, a Snow White to his Prince Charming. "I'm Lucy," she said, extending her hand. "Peter's date."

Date? I don't know why it surprised me. Of course, Peter

would be here with a date. I shook Lucy's hand, smiled too broadly.

"Meredith's an old friend," Peter offered.

"Seventh grade lab partners," I added. My face flushed. "So, have you seen any of the cats?"

"Peter's in love with the toothless one. Nine." Lucy linked her arm through his as she said the words. The gesture seemed possessive.

Peter extricated his arm from Lucy's and made quotation marks with his fingers. "'In love' may be a bit strong but, if no one adopts her, I will. You know my parents' place. What's one more cat?"

"Or two or three." I wagged a finger at him. "I know how you are with animals, Peter Flynn." I looked at Lucy. "Peter has always loved animals."

Lucy shot me a quizzical look. I met her gaze, looked down. What was wrong with me? Why was I trying to one-up Peter's date?

Lucy turned to Peter. "We should find our table."

Peter held up their name card. "It's twelve."

"Who's at twelve?" Reed's voice boomed from behind me. He held out the Chardonnay.

"Reed," I said, taking the glass. "You remember Peter, right? This is his date, Lucy. They're also at twelve."

"Super." Reed shook each of their hands. "Great costumes. Love Disney."

The conversation moved from costumes to food. It turned out that both Reed and Lucy loved Thai food. A long discussion of Thai restaurants ensued. I turned to Peter and bumped his arm. "You clean up nice, Prince Charming."

Peter shrugged. "Costumes were Lucy's idea. Yours are good too."

"Reed's idea."

Peter looked down. "Hey girl," he said. He bent down and

stood with a white and orange cat. "This is Nine. I think she's stalking me."

I stroked Nine on the head. "Smart girl. Maybe she wants you to adopt her. Maybe she knows all about the big farm."

Peter looked Nine in her eyes. "Is that true, Nine? Do you want to live on the farm?"

Nine wriggled in his arms; Peter set her down. The lights blinked. "I guess it's time for the event," he whispered.

I sat between Reed and Peter at the table. The band stopped playing and a man in a tailed tuxedo appeared behind the microphone, the MC. "Hello Fuurrriends! Is everyone feline fine?" The audience groaned. "We'll I'm Steve Perkins and let me tell you, we have some PAWSitively CLAWsome kitties for adoption tonight." Steve pointed a remote at a large screen in the front of the room. "We have Lemon and LeBron and Mr. Whiskers." As he said each name, a photo of the corresponding cat appeared on the screen. "And we have Meadow and Reggie and Nine." At the mention of Nine, Lucy squeezed Peter's hand. Steve resumed until fifteen cat pictures filled the screen.

Steve paused a moment. "Now," he continued, "I'll let you enjoy your MEOWnificant meals and get to know these kitties. The auction will start when the MICE cream is served."

I laugh-snorted; Peter put his head close to mine. "You're loving these puns, aren't you?"

"They're PURRfect."

Peter shook his head in mock derision. "Only you."

Dinner continued with a slideshow of cat pictures on the big screen as a backdrop. Every time Nine's photo appeared, Lucy squealed and bumped Peter's arm. Irrationally, a spasm of jealousy surged inside me each time she did it. I reminded myself I was there with my fiancé. I shouldn't be concerned with Peter and his date.

Steve reappeared when the ice cream came out. He held a black and white kitty in his hands, the cat's picture on the screen behind him. He moved to the microphone. "This is Kazooie. Eight months old. Fiesty and cathletic." Steve paused. "Let's start the animal shelter donation at $200."

Still holding Kazooie, Steve started to speak in the voice of an auctioneer. "Do I see a two-hundred-dollar donation? I see a two-hundred-dollar donation from the lady in the back. Do I see three-hundred dollars? Is there three-hundred dollars?" He pointed to a man in an astronaut costume. "Three-hundred dollars to the astronaut man. Anyone for a four-hundred-dollar donation? Is there a four-hundred-dollar donation?"

Bidding for the right to adopt Kazooie reached $1,100. The astronaut man and a woman in a witch costume had engaged in a heated bidding war. The woman won, her ultimate donation $1,500.

Reed whispered in my ear. "See. It gets crazy."

Nine's picture flashed on the screen.

Lucy screamed. "Peter. It's Nine."

A woman wearing a tight-fitting cat costume handed Nine to Steve. "Okay," he started. "We have Nine here. Nine is our oldest cat. She's ten. But don't let that fool you, my friends. She's got a lot of Cattitude." He stopped for effect; there was a smattering of groans from the audience. "So let's get the bidding going for Nine." He resumed his auctioneer personna. "Okay. Is there a $100 donation for Nine? A one hundred-dollar donation?"

Lucy bumped Peter's arm; he held up his paddle.

"One hundred dollars from Prince Charming. Is there a two-hundred-dollar donation? A two-hundred-dollar donation to a good cause?"

A woman dressed as Dorothy from The Wizard of Oz raised her paddle. Steve pointed at her. "Two hundred dollars to Dorothy. Do I see a three-hundred-dollar donation? Is there a three-hundred-dollar donation? Peter raised his paddle. "Prince

Charming has bid three hundred dollars. Is there four hundred dollars?"

My phone buzzed on the table. I turned it over; Zach's name and picture flashed on the screen. My heart dropped, and my mind immediately flew toward worst case scenarios. An accident. A robbery. A horrid illness.

I exhaled. It was probably something mundane. He wanted to have a friend over or see if he could use the credit card for some Xbox purchase. I stood, whispered to Reed. "It's Zach." I pointed to the phone and hurried toward the entryway, picking up the call as I walked.

"Mom, it's me. The police were just here."

14

Peter

The MC, Steve, was speaking; I didn't register his words. I stared in the direction Meredith had gone.

"And Nine going to Dorothy for nine hundred –"

Lucy pulled my hand up.

"Wait," Steve said. "Prince Charming and Snow White are back in. We have nine hundred and fifty for Nine, do I see nine hundred and fifty..."

Steve chattered on. I raised the paddle twice more; it was the last one that did it. Steve leveled a gavel on the podium and announced,"Nine to Prince Charming for one thousand, one hundred and fifty dollars."

"You got him, Pete!" Lucy looked as if she might jump out of her seat.

The woman in the tight cat uniform took Nine from Steve's arms and made her way to our table. She handed me the cat. "Congratulations, sir."

I stared at Nine. She blinked at me, the act a seemingly triumphant gesture. She'd just fooled a lawyer into spending $1,150 to give her a nice home.

A photo of a new cat — Lemon — appeared and Steve took the mic again. "What a Caturday so far. Am I right?"

I laughed. Meredith would love that pun. Where was she? I looked back at the door just as it swung open, Meredith in its frame. She took hurried steps toward the table, her face cast downward.

Something was wrong.

I stood when she reached the table, still holding Nine. "What is it?"

"The police were just at the house," she whispered. "They were asking Zach a bunch of questions. They said he -- " She looked around, didn't finish the statement.

I digested her words. The police were questioning Zach? Before I could respond, Meredith tugged on Reed's sleeve, whispered in his ear.

Reed stood, his expression bewildered. "The police? Why?" His voice was loud.

The others at the table glanced in our direction. Lucy looked up at me. "Pete?" I didn't answer; she stood and joined the group. We moved to the edge of the room, a circle of four.

"I don't know why the police were there," Meredith said. She waved her hand in a casual gesture. "But I should probably go home."

"Alright. We can go." Reed reached into a pocket in his costume and pulled out keys.

I looked at Meredith. Her eyes were wild, her face flushed. There was definitely something wrong. "Do you want me to go?" I blurted. "I'm not a criminal lawyer, but maybe I could figure out if something more needs to be done."

Reed met my eyes. "Is that really necessary? It's probably some silly kid thing." He gripped the keys tighter.

Meredith put her hand on Reed's forearm. "I think it might be good for Peter to come. Zach's a bit spooked. I think having a lawyer talk to him would help."

Reed remained silent. Steve goaded on bidders for Lemon, his voice a backdrop: "Eight hundred from the Wicked Witch of the West? Do I have eight-fifty? Do I have eight-fifty for Lemon? Eight-fifty to the pirate in the back."

"And you're sure you don't know what this is about?" Reed asked. "Seems strange."

"It is strange," Meredith said, a sliver of frustration in her voice. "That's why I need to get home."

Reed blew out a breath. "Alright."

I looked at Meredith, completely forgot about Lucy. She touched my shoulder. "So you're leaving now?" Hurt flashed across her eyes.

Shit. I felt like a dick. I didn't like Lucy, not romantically, but she had tried to treat me to a nice night. My actions were unfair to her, but I couldn't shake the feeling that there was something serious going on with Zach. Meredith needed my help. "I'm really sorry, Lucy." Nine wriggled; Lucy pulled him from me.

"How will I get home?" She stroked Nine's head; the cat squinted, then closed its eyes.

Reed held his hand up. "I'll take you. If that's okay?"

She nodded toward him. "Sure. Thanks."

"I'm really sorry," I blathered. "I'll make it up to you. Dinner?"

Her expression softened. "Okay. Dinner it is." She lifted Nine up. "And I'll take care of this little lady."

Reed rapped my shoulder. "Call if you need anything."

I couldn't imagine calling Reed even if I did need something, but I nodded anyway. Meredith hurried out of the ballroom; I followed. We found my car in silence. I put the address she gave me into my GPS. Once on the main road, I glanced at her. She stared straight ahead, hair twisted tight around an index finger.

"The police told Zach a girl said he attacked her at a party."

"He hit a girl?"

She paused; I looked over. "No," she said, "sexually."

"Oh." I was glad for the darkness; I knew I looked shocked. I don't know what I'd expected. Underage drinking. Open container. Not this. Shit. "Like a rape?" I asked finally, my heart pounding.

She shook her head. "I don't know. I don't know all the details. Zach was speaking so quickly it was hard to understand. I figured I should just get home." She picked at one of the white polka-dots on her Minnie skirt. "I'm sorry I'm dragging you into this. It's just Zach sounded so upset and I figured with your legal background –" She let the sentiment trail off.

I touched her shoulder. "It's fine. I'm glad to help if I can, but I'm not a criminal lawyer. I'm not sure how much I'll know." I paused. "If we need to, I can call Nate, the other lawyer at my firm. He does criminal stuff."

"Thanks." Her voice was barely audible.

I glanced at her as we passed under a streetlamp. The light illuminated her face, stricken and worried.

"Come on, Mer," I said, my tone gentle. "It might just be some kind of misunderstanding. We don't know anything yet. Nothing's happened."

She nodded. "I know. But why would the girl say that about him?"

"I don't know. But let's not assume the worst." The GPS directed my next turn and I navigated the car on to a residential street with large cookie cutter houses, most adorned with pumpkins and ghosts and related Halloween décor. Music emanated from one house, a line of cars on the street in front of it.

Meredith pointed. "The house is up there on the left. Number 12."

I pulled into the driveway of a white two-story colonial home set back from the road by a square patch of grass. An array of pumpkins sat on the front steps, a fall wreath on the door. Pretend gravestones adorned otherwise barren gardens. In a different circumstance, the decorations would have seemed festive.

She squeezed her eyes shut. "Alright," she said, seemingly more to herself than to me, "let's figure this out." She emerged from the car and walked in stockinged feet toward the entrance, the oversized Minnie shoes in her hand.

I followed. An ominous feeling formed in my gut, like, once we walked through the door, reality would shift in a way that could not be undone. I pushed the feeling aside. I had no concrete information, no reason to believe the worst.

Meredith pushed open the door and stepped into a two-story foyer with a giant chandelier. I followed. Pictures in silver frames lined heavy dark table, the largest depicting Meredith and Reed at a restaurant. Big smiles for both, a lit candle on the table between them. A streak of jealousy surged through me; I forced my gaze away.

"Zach?" Meredith called. No answer.

I followed her down a hallway to an expansive kitchen, then toward the room that connected to it.

"There you are." Meredith entered a cozy space with plaid couches, a green armchair, and a large television. Pictures of Reed and his girls and a few of Meredith lined a shelf along with books and knick-knacks. There was one photo of Zach, a formal one. Probably his senior portrait.

Zach sat hunched on the couch in a gray sweatshirt, his phone on his lap. A large dog, curled by his side, looked at us, then thumped his tail on the cushions. Zach half stood. He looked nothing like the bony kid with scraped knees I'd remembered. He was muscular, manlike. His eyes were the same color as Meredith's.

"Are you alright?" Meredith asked.

Zach shrugged. "I guess. The police were here." He looked again in my direction; Meredith followed his eyes.

She waved at me. "Do you remember Peter Flynn, my high school friend?"

Zach gave a near imperceptible shake of the head.

"He's a lawyer. I thought he might help us untangle what's going on."

They both looked at me then, expectant. The same ominous feeling I'd had in the car returned. It felt like a bomb was about to explode in my hands.

Meredith took a seat next to Zach. She adjusted the Minnie skirt, pulled the headband from her hair. "It'll be alright," she whispered and squeezed Zach's shoulder.

I perched on the edge of a chair and asked the only question I could think of.

"What happened?"

15

Zach shut his eyes, then opened them and looked at me. "A police officer came. He said he had a few questions for me about a girl I know, Paige Dixon. I know Paige, so I let him in. I didn't think whatever it was had anything to do with me. I thought maybe Paige was hurt or missing or something." He looked down then back up. "The officer asked if I'd been to a Halloween party last night, if I'd seen Paige there."

I undid the top button to my costume. "And did you?"

Zach nodded. "Yeah. We were both at the same party. The officer kept asking questions about it. I answered them. Then he told me Paige said I forced myself on her, that I started to take off her clothes and –" he stopped. I waited. "He said that I was starting to –"

He stopped again, and I realized how awkward it must feel to be recounting the accusation to his mother and a stranger. I was about to intervene when he exhaled and told Paige's account in a single breath: "She told the officer I was touching her in a sexual way and that she didn't want me to."

I nodded and pushed myself further into the armchair.

"And your side of the story?"

"I didn't do it." He crossed his arms.

"But were you with her?" Meredith interjected. She angled her face so she could see Zach.

"We kissed. That's it." He held up his hands.

"Were you drinking?" Meredith asked.

Zach paused, picked a piece of lint from his jeans. "No," he said finally.

Meredith pulled at the bow of her Minnie head band, brows knitted together. After a moment, she looked at me, eyes questioning. "Is it normal that the officer came here and questioned Zach? Wouldn't he need a warrant or something?"

I reached down to the recesses of my criminal law knowledge, shook my head. "I think he would only need a warrant to arrest him," I said. "Not to talk."

Zach sat up straighter. "It seemed like he just wanted my side of the story."

Meredith looked at Zach. "And that's it? He just left after asking you the questions?"

"Yeah. He left his information." Zach nodded to a business card on the side table. "The officer said if I remembered anything else to call him." He glanced at the card. "He kind of seemed to be on my side."

I swiped the business card from the table and looked at the name. Officer Lyle Jenkins. I had no idea who that was. I looked from the card to Zach. "This Officer Jenkins might seem like he's on your side, but I don't think I would talk to him again. At least not until I talk to Nate. He's the lawyer at my office who does criminal law."

"I only told him I didn't do it."

He seemed upset; I forced my voice to be calm. "I know. I'm sure it's fine. But let's just wait and talk to Nate, okay?"

"Should we call him now?" Meredith looked from me to Zach. "I mean, just so we know what we're dealing with?"

"Um." I checked my phone. 10:10 p.m. Would Nate even be up? I glanced up, ready to put off the call until morning, but when I saw Meredith's pained face, I changed course. "I'll try him." I dialed Nate, listened to what felt like a dozen rings. I was about to hang up when I heard his voice.

"Well, if it isn't Prince Charming. You rocking that costume? How's the ball? How's Lucy?"

Lucy. The ball. It seemed so long ago. "Actually," I said. "I'm here at my friend's house. The police came to talk to her son, Zach. The officer said a girl alleged that Zach sexually assaulted her at a party last night." I pressed the speaker button.

"Oh, shit. That ain't good." Nate's voice boomed through the room. "How old's Zach? If he's under eighteen, the police shouldn't have questioned him without a parent present."

"He's eighteen," Meredith called out.

"You're on speaker, Nate," I explained. "Zach and his mother are here. Could you tell them what, if anything, they should do next?"

"Well don't fucking talk to the police." He paused. I could visualize him shaking his head. "Excuse my language. Just don't talk to the police. If they're talking to you, Zach, they're trying to get information. They're trying to build a case for arrest."

A look of horror flashed across Meredith's face. "Zach already spoke to the officer," she said quickly, her voice tinged in desperation.

"Who was the officer?" Nate asked.

I read from the business card. "Lyle Jenkins."

"Alright. If he's who I'm thinking of, he's pretty young, a new guy. What'd you tell him, Zach?"

Zach recounted his conversation with the police officer.

"All that's fine," Nate said. "Nothing incriminating. But don't talk to him again. Don't talk to anyone about last night, okay."

Zach nodded. "Okay."

"And your friends, anyone who was there, tell them not to talk either. Not without lawyers present, anyway."

Meredith put her head in her hands; Zach's expression had morphed into one of shock.

"Hey Pete," Nate continued, oblivious to the emotional havoc his words were creating. "Text me the number for that officer. I'll call him, let him know that, if he's going to arrest Zach, he should call me first. Then Zach can turn himself in."

Meredith's head shot up. "Turn himself in? We don't even know what he's been accused of."

"Yeah," Nate started. "He'd turn himself in only if they're going to arrest him anyway. Otherwise, they'll come to your house or his school in a squad car. Most people don't want that."

Meredith stared at the phone, her face shell-shocked. Zach looked equally appalled.

"Okay," I said, desperate to quell the emotional onslaught of Nate's words. "We'll cross that bridge if we get to it. Anything they should do now?"

"Just, like I said, keep quiet. Don't talk about last night." A baby's wail sounded in the background. "Jeez. Lily. That kid never sleeps."

I wrapped up the conversation, switched off the phone.

We sat in silence. I couldn't think of anything to say. In the span of five minutes, Zach's matter went from a possible mix-up to a possible arrest.

Meredith held up her phone and looked at Zach. "I'm going to call Mrs. Sullivan," she told him. "Tell her that Carter and Owen shouldn't talk to the police."

Meredith moved to the kitchen. Filtered words from her conversation filled the otherwise silent space: "Paige Dixon." "Police." "Arrest."

I looked at Zach. He started straight ahead, an almost catatonic expression on his face. I wondered if he'd told the whole story. Had he been drinking? Had they just kissed? I hadn't seen Zach in a decade, didn't know if he was the kind of boy who would assault a girl. He didn't present that way, but who knew? It wasn't like attackers had a specific prototype.

Meredith returned. "Mrs. Sullivan's going to tell the boys not to talk to the police." She looked to Zach. "Did you know anyone else at the party?"

Zach shifted on the couch; the dog jumped off. "Not well. It was a Crasmere Friends party." He paused. "Jamie was there."

"Right." Meredith nodded, looked to me. "Jamie is Reed's daughter," she explained.

A car door slammed outside. Meredith whipped her head toward the front of the house. "That must be Reed now."

A moment later, he appeared in the doorframe of the family room, Mickey ears still on his head. "All okay here?" He loosened the tie of his costume.

Meredith stiffened. I felt a surge of protectiveness, then stopped myself. She was probably just nervous to tell Reed, to tell anyone, what Zach had been accused of. It wasn't as if he'd been caught speeding.

"I'll fill you in in a minute," she said. "We should really let Peter go now. I've intruded on his evening enough."

Reed stepped forward, looked at me. "Thanks." He extended his hand.

I took it, gripping harder than normal. "No problem. Thanks for getting Lucy home."

"She's got Nine," he said. "She told me to tell you."

Nine. In the craziness of the evening, I'd forgotten about the cat. "Right." I let go of Reed's hand, tried to decipher his expression. He stepped toward the door. I wanted to stay, to make sure Meredith was alright. The thought, I knew, was ridiculous. Reed was her fiancé, not me. I was just an old friend, barely in her life anymore. Still, I met Reed's eyes, hoped he could read the warning in them. *You better handle this well.*

16

I drove home after leaving Meredith's. My sleep was less than restful, filled with half-conscious thoughts about Meredith and Zach and the potential arrest. Still tired in the morning, I made my way to the kitchen. Dad had the sports section of the paper spread in front of him; Mom pushed scrambled eggs in a pan. "How was the ball?" she asked, her voice unabashedly delighted that I'd done something social. It was the same tone of voice she'd used when I was a boy.

"Fine." I grabbed a mug and poured coffee.

Mom put down the spatula. "Come on. Give me something."

I rattled off a few details in a sleep-deprived haze, checked my phone for a text from Meredith. Nothing.

"Did you see anyone you knew?"

"No," I lied. I couldn't tell Mom I'd seen Meredith. The admission would open too many questions and I couldn't discuss the fact that the police had questioned Zach. Though the firm was not officially representing him, it seemed prudent to maintain the attorney-client privilege. Plus, keeping quiet was the right thing to do. Meredith wouldn't want people to know.

"No one?" Mom questioned. She set a plate of eggs down in front of my Dad.

"No one interesting." I swiped my phone off the table and stood. "I'll go check on the horses." I took a swig of coffee, grabbed a coat, and stepped outside. My breath made smoky puffs in the crisp air. I reached the barn, leaned against it, pulled out my phone and stared at the home screen. Should I text Meredith? Make sure she was okay? I punched a message - *How'd things go?* – and hesitated only a moment before pressing send, the electronic sound of the message filling an otherwise tranquil scene.

Dots signaling a return text appeared, disappeared, then reappeared. I watched them intently. What was happening? What did she want to say? Her response finally appeared: *Long story. Can you meet for a walk?*

Yes. Of course.

We made plans via text to meet at the Crasmere Gorge, a trail I knew to be one of Meredith's favorites. An hour later, we stood at the entrance of the gravel path that curved along the trajectory of a river. The river water flowed over groupings of large stones and fallen logs, tiny rapids on its surface. Fall trees in bursts of orange, red, and yellow stood on tall hills buttressing both sides of the path.

Meredith zipped up a puffy red jacket and shoved her hands in the pockets. Her cheeks were pink, her lips slightly chapped. But for the worried expression in her eyes, she looked normal – a pretty woman out for a walk on a beautiful day.

She began to walk, high ponytail swinging with swift steps. "Thanks for last night. I really appreciate you coming over."

"Of course."

We navigated around a boy and a jumpy brown dog, then a group of bikers. Meredith quickened her gait, eyes straight ahead, hands in her pockets. She didn't speak, seemed almost to forget I was there. But there had to be a reason she'd asked me to meet her. She must want to talk about something. We walked longer in silence until, finally, I couldn't stand not knowing anymore. "Did it go okay with Reed last night?" I prodded.

She took a few steps before answering. "I didn't tell him."

Didn't tell him? That didn't seem right. Reed would want to know why the police where there. Before I could ask the question, Meredith spoke again.

"I told him about Paige's accusations. I just didn't tell him she said the boy who attacked her was Zach."

"Oh." I walked a few paces, digesting her omission. "Makes sense," I said after too long a silence.

"It really doesn't," she admitted.

I opened my mouth to protest; she waved at me.

"I know it's weird I didn't tell him. He's my fiancé, I should be able to share anything." She paused. "But blended families are strange. You're still getting to know each other's kids and there's this weird dynamic of wanting to show yours off in the best light somehow." She stepped to the side to give a group of kids on bicycles room to pass. "At least that's how it is with me, anyway. I still feel like I want Zach to make a good impression."

I blew out a breath, again felt inadequate to speak on the subject of children. Still, from what I saw last night, Zach seemed like a nice kid. I couldn't imagine Reed thinking poorly of him. "I'm sure Zach's made a good impression. A police visit wouldn't change that. And he says he didn't do it. It's not like he's been convicted or something."

She nodded. "I know and, honestly, that's a big reason I didn't say anything. I figure if nothing comes of the accusation, why bring it up?"

I didn't answer. It seemed like, if Reed was the kind of man

Meredith deserved, it would be a comfort to share the burden with him; she'd want to tell him.

"Anyway," she continued, "you're probably wondering why I asked you here."

I was, but I didn't say so.

"I just –" she started. "You and Donna are the only people who know about the police questioning Zach. I trust you and –" She stopped walking and moved to a space off the path between two large stones. We stood siphoned off from the path, a private enclosure. "My roommate in college was raped," she whispered.

"What?" I was sure I misheard her.

"My roommate in college was raped," she repeated, her voice still low.

"Shannon?" I'd met Meredith's roommate at her wedding. She was adorable, a doppelganger for Tinkerbell.

Meredith shook her head. "No. My freshman roommate. Natasha. She transferred." She blew into her hands.

"God. That's awful." I shook my head. "Did they get the guy?"

"She didn't end up pressing charges. The school wasn't particularly supportive. And she thought her parents would be mad."

I didn't respond, my thoughts on how any man could do that to a woman, overpower her sexually, against her will. And to be mad at the woman? That never made sense to me. Be mad at the guy. I opened my mouth to voice the sentiment, then shut it. For all I knew, Zach was the guy.

"Look. I know it probably seems weird that I'm bringing this up but, whenever I see or hear anything about rape or sexual assault, I think of Natasha. I remember how awful it was, how changed she was. She became depressed and withdrawn. It was hard for her to talk about the attack, really hard. I went with her to the school administration when she made the report. She could barely get out the words. The Dean we talked to seemed to not believe her and all I could think of was why would she make this up? Why would she make herself vulnerable, recount all these painful details? Why would anyone?"

I stood speechless, followed Meredith's obvious train of thought: what benefit would it be for Paige Dixon to lie about what happened with Zach?

She leaned back on a large tree. "I mean, maybe Paige is an exception, maybe she's crazy or jealous or something, but it has always been my belief that, when a woman reports a rape or attack, it's because it happened."

"I agree," I said, "but we don't know much here. Maybe there's something more to it. Something that has nothing to do with Zach."

Sadness shaded her eyes. "Maybe. I believe Zach. He's my son and I can't picture him attacking a girl." She shook her head. "This whole thing is tearing me apart. I'm sorry. I just needed someone to talk to and I didn't want to tell Reed and –" She shut her mouth and leaned into me.

I encircled my arms around her compact frame. "It'll be alright, Mer," I said. I hoped the words were true.

Days passed after the walk in the gorge, one after another. No arrest. No calls. No news. It was strange, the waiting. Everything went on as normal; yet, I knew there was an investigation underway. The feeling of not knowing what or if something might happen was disconcerting. I felt like I was waiting for an anvil to randomly drop from the sky.

Initially, Meredith called every day to see if I'd heard anything. Sometimes twice a day. But as one day merged into the next, then more than a week passed, the calls had trickled to a near stop. Meredith seemed to assume that Zach was in the clear. It seemed likely. Wouldn't something have happened by now?

I found Nate in his office, head buried in a document. "Do you think we're clear on Morgan?" I asked. "It's been over a week."

Nate looked up, a confused expression on his face. "Morgan?"

"Zach. My friend Meredith's son?"

"Right," Nate answered, a look of recognition crossing his features. "Yeah. Sometimes the investigations take a while."

My heart dipped. I'd been looking for affirmation, not cause to worry. "A week?"

Nate shrugged. "Sometimes."

I stared at him, irritated by his lack of urgency or concern. Then again, Nate didn't grow up with Meredith; he'd never had a wild crush on her. And, unlike me, he was used to cases where freedom hung in the balance. Still, I felt a need for some kind of closure. "How long do you think?" I asked. "Before we would know if the arrest is going to happen?"

Nate exhaled and met my eyes, his frustration evident but unspoken. "I really couldn't say, but I'd stop worrying about it. There's nothing you can do. If there's evidence to charge him, they'll charge him. If not, they won't. There's no timetable here." He stood. "Look. I've got court." He shoved the document he'd been holding into his briefcase and grabbed his suit jacket.

I watched his form retreat down the hall, then made my way to my office, disheartened by the conversation. I'd wanted Nate to say the chances of arrest were slim to none, that, if the police didn't have the evidence by now, chances were, they'd never get it. He'd essentially said the opposite.

I collapsed my office chair and again thought of Meredith. How her face lit up when she talked about Zach. How she said she wasn't ready to let him go away to school. The information she'd shared about her college roommate.

The District Attorney could not charge Zach. It would kill her.

My office phone rang; I pushed Meredith from my mind. I couldn't keep obsessing about a potential arrest. I had an office to run, a life, albeit sad, to lead. And, like Nate said, there was nothing I could do anyway.

I took the call then buried myself in work, even the tasks I'd long put off like signing up for mandatory continuing legal education classes. I texted Lucy and planned the make-up dinner. I felt better, more in control. My cell phone rang; I swiped it on without checking the ID. It was Nate.

"Hey Pete," he said. "I just got off the phone with Officer Jenkins. They've got a warrant for Zach. He needs to turn himself in."

17

Meredith

I stood outside the occupational therapy gym at work, gripped the phone to my ear. "What?"

Peter repeated the statement. I was to bring Zach to the police station so he could turn himself in. "I'll meet you there," he said.

"Zach's in school. I'm at work." I paused. "He's got a soccer game." My first thoughts, ridiculous ones. It wasn't as if Zach turning himself in was a voluntary appointment, one where we got to choose the day and time most suitable for our schedules.

"You need to go get him," Peter said. "Nate says the police and DA's office will work with him if he turns himself in."

I peered through the gym window at my client, Michael, an eight-year-old boy with gross motor challenges. I'd left him in the ball pit. He waved at me; I lifted my hand in response. "What is he even turning himself in for?"

"The assault."

I clutched the phone tighter, fought rising panic. Arrest. There was enough evidence for arrest. What had they found? "But he said he didn't do it." My voice rose and caught at the end. A new physical therapist standing by the hall supply cabinet glanced in my direction; I forced a smile.

"He's not admitting to the crime," Peter said. "But, if he turns himself in, the police will work with him. That's what Nate told me."

Work with him? What did that even mean? I pulled the phone away and started at it as though the issue were encapsulated inside its rectangular structure. I had the juvenile impulse to hang up.

"Mer?" Peter's voice, distant. "I know this is rough."

I pulled the phone back to my ear, took my anger out on Peter. "Do you? You've had experience with your teenage child getting arrested?"

Silence.

Regret slid into my gut. Peter had been nothing but helpful since this had all happened. "I'm sorry. I'm just stressed." I watched Michael climb a rope and swing into the pit. My supervisor, Beth, emerged from her office and looked around, presumably for me. I had to go. "I'll get Zach and meet you at the station," I said quickly.

I hung up and, forcing myself to be calm, strode across the gym toward Beth. "Sorry," I said. "My son's sick. That was his school."

Beth tipped her head in Michael's direction. "You can't leave clients unsupervised."

I pointed to the window in the doorway. "I was watching him from the hall."

She nodded as if assessing, then met my eyes. "Next time, get someone before you leave." She scrunched up her face. "Do you need to go to the school?"

Beth agreed to finish up with Michael and I started toward the high school. Ridiculously, the fiction that Zach was sick made me feel better. Like I was an ordinary Mom – a good one – ready to pick up my sick child on a moment's notice, ingredients for homemade chicken soup in my trunk. My mind clung to the illness fabrication until I pulled up to the high school entrance. Then reality barreled through like a runaway train. I was signing Zach out so the police could arrest him. *Arrest.* I didn't know what would happen after that. Would he be jailed? Would there be a hearing? There were a million questions I wish I could have asked Peter.

I turned off the engine, then clenched the steering wheel, my head on its top. I could just turn around. Find out more before leading Zach down what I felt in my gut was the wrong path. Zach turning himself to gain police cooperation felt akin giving up, like forfeiting a sporting event so the referees would be nicer. But I wasn't an expert. Peter and Nate both said Zach should turn himself in. They both said he'd be arrested no matter what. Did I really want Zach to be taken away in a police car?

I startled at the sound of a rap on the car window. "Meredith?" Julie stood at there, her face at the glass, impossibly close. I held up a finger. God. If there was anyone that I wouldn't want to know about the arrest warrant, it was Julie. Her kids were always excelling in something – school, sports, community volunteers. I liked Julie but, most of the time, she made me feel inadequate. And that was before Zach's imminent arrest.

I grabbed my purse and exited the car.

"Did you forget the AP test money too?" She held up a check made out to the College Board, then started toward the school entrance, a Coach purse swinging on her elbow. She looked back at me. "Or does Zach not take AP?"

My defenses rose and, like my mind was on autopilot, it fell to its default concern: how Zach stacked up against his peers and how that reflected on me as his mother. I knew the worry was absurd – who cared if Zach took advanced placement classes or not – but it was difficult to turn off a brain pathway that had been in place for nearly two decades. "He is," I said, following Julie into the entry vestibule of the school. "For psychology. I paid for the test already."

She tipped her head, seemingly surprised I had remembered something she had not. "Oh. What brings you here then?"

Shit. My mind whirred with possibilities. "Zach has an orthodontist appointment," I blurted. It was the most benign excuse I could think of.

She squinted, her eyes a question. "Zach has braces?"

Zach's braces had been off for years. "A retainer issue," I said, the second lie easier. I pointed to my own teeth as though this would make the story more believable.

Apparently believing me, Julie launched into a story about how her poodle ate her son's retainer. I could barely comprehend her words, but I knew enough to laugh when she was done speaking.

She pointed her index finger at me. "So keep that thing out of reach from Barkley," she said. I forced a laugh for the second time and, at last, Julie dropped off her check for the AP test and left.

I pulled the sign-out clipboard toward me, picked up the pen attached to it's top by a frayed string. My hand shook as I wrote, and I started at the space for Zach's school ID. I couldn't remember and I stood, silent, the pen dormant in my hand.

The receptionist, a woman I vaguely recognized but did not know, scrutinized my face. "Are you alright?"

"Yes. Fine." I looked down at the paper and back up. "I can't remember my son's ID."

She glanced at his name, punched it into the computer, filled in the space for the nine number digit on the board. "I'll get him." She called his classroom teacher for this period. "Zach Morgan for dismissal."

A few minutes later, Zach navigated the hall outside the office, backpack slung over his shoulder, coat in his hand. He smiled when he saw me; the vision broke my heart. I had, on occasion, taken Zach out of school for a surprise day. Beach trips when he was little, sports games when he got older. From his expression, I gathered he thought he we were going to attend the afternoon 76ers game or take an impromptu trip to New York.

He pushed through the glass doors to the front office, took in my expression. His smile vanished. "Did it happen?" he asked, his voice low.

Words caught in my throat. I stood, frozen. Zach threw me a quizzical look. When I didn't move, he took my elbow and guided me toward the door until my own steps took over.

"Am I being arrested?" he asked once we were outside and near the car.

I wanted to say no. I wanted to say gotcha. I wanted to actually take Zach to an orthodontist appointment and get McDonalds milkshakes after. Instead I stood, unable to move or speak, my hand on the handle of the car door.

"Mom," Zach said, his voice more urgent. "Am I being arrested?"

"We need to go to the police station," I said, unable to definitively answer his question, unable to admit out loud to Zach, yes, your arrest for a serious and terrible crime is imminent.

I drove toward the police station, a building I'd passed hundreds of times. I'd only been inside the brick building once, when I chaperoned the second-grade field trip there. I visualized Zach as he was then, missing front teeth, freckles, and skinned knees. An officer had taken fingerprints of every child for a souvenir. I recalled putting Zach's on the refrigerator with a red magnet shaped like a crab.

"What happens now?" There was a scared edge to his voice.

"You're supposed to turn yourself in." I forced my voice to be calm. "The police will work with you if you turn yourself in."

I repeated the words Peter had said wishing, again, that I'd had time to ask him more questions.

"But what happens then? After I turn myself in?"

I pressed the directional, pulled into the lot of the station. A line of police cars sat in front spaces like vehicular guards. I pulled into a space next to Peter's car and switched off the engine. I puffed out a breath, then looked at my son and told him the truth.

"I don't know what happens next."

18

Nate and Peter stood in front of the station, ties peeking from the tops of buttoned coats. Nate had his phone on one ear, his hand over the other. He spoke and paced at the same time. Peter stood next to him, straight-faced and grim.

I reached the area where they stood, Zach behind me. Nate held up a finger. He finished his call, something about theft and camera evidence, and it struck me that Zach was just another client to Nate, that his life didn't revolve around what happened to him.

Nate switched off the phone and looked at us. "Okay," he said, seemingly switching gears. "I talked to the arresting officer on the phone earlier, Jenkins. Because Zach has no priors and isn't a flight risk, he's not going to push for a high bail amount at the arraignment. He said he'll recommend 50k, ten percent." He shook his head. "The DJ in this jurisdiction is Gallo. He's a former cop and I think he'll run with the rec. So, listen, I'll take Zach in the station and he'll get processed. Jenkins will bring him to district court for the arraignment. You'll need 5k for the ten percent. He," Nate nodded toward Zach, "may sit in custody a bit while you get the bail processed. And if you need time to get the money." He puffed out a breath, seemingly satisfied with his counsel.

I stood, open-mouthed, so many alarms going through my head I couldn't form a coherent question. DJ. Prelim. Processed. Words which may have well been in a foreign language for all I understood them. A piece of me was embarrassed that I didn't know some of this. Surely, I should have some remote knowledge of police procedure or arrest protocol. But I didn't. I'd never had as much as a speeding ticket. I didn't even watch crime shows on television. The piece of me that wasn't embarrassed was angry. No one, not the police, not Nate, not the DA, seemed to consider Zach's side of things.

Nate touched Zach's shoulder. "Let's go in." He nodded to the station door.

"No." I moved in front of Zach.

Nate's face flashed surprise. "But Jenkins said he would work with us. And 50k, 10 percent is a good deal." He said it as though the words weren't legal gobbledygook.

"No," I repeated, anger and upset snaking up my gut. I jabbed my index finger toward him. "This may be routine to you, but I have no idea what you're talking about." My voice vacillated between anger and tears. "I've never been involved with the police or the law and neither has Zach. I don't understand half the words you just said. What I do know is that Zach says he didn't attack Paige, and no one seems to care." I took a breath then spit out the rest. "Why is this all happening with no one getting his side? His side matters." I kicked at the ground in frustration, took a deep breath to stave off tears. "It matters," I said conclusively.

Peter moved toward me, put his hand on my shoulder. "Of course, it matters," he said, his voice soft. "It's just, right now, they have Paige's side and the police think they have enough from her to look into this further. It doesn't mean Zach did it or that no one is going to care about what he said happened. We're just at the beginning. It still may end up Zach wasn't involved."

"It feels wrong." I crossed my arms then, feeling like a petulant child, uncrossed them.

"It's okay, Mom." Zach put his hand on my arm. "I'll be okay."

A wave of guilt surged through me as I realized Zach, who was probably terrified, felt he had to comfort me. I needed to pull it together. I looked to Nate. "Could you explain again what's happening. Please?"

"Sure. Sorry I rushed." He shoved his hands in his pockets and set forth the process a second time, slower and calmer. Zach would be booked at the station, then we'd walk the two blocks to the district court for what was called the preliminary arraignment. A district justice there would read the charges against Zach, give him the complaint and warrant, and set bail. The cop Nate talked to was going to recommend a low bail amount for the crime, $50,000 of which I'd have to post 10%. This was big, according to Nate, because bail for a felony – *felony!* – was typically much, much higher. Nate stressed that the preliminary arraignments were routine and that there was nothing to worry about. Apparently, district attorneys didn't even go to these types of proceedings; most defendants didn't have lawyers.

Despite Nate's assurances, it seemed to me that the preliminary arraignment would be anything but routine. Cops, bail, judges. These were not the staples of my life and I wondered, briefly, how anyone could be so laissez faire about a proceeding which ended either with an exchange of a large cash amount or loss of liberty. Zach interrupted my thoughts.

"Nate says I can't have this." He extended his arm toward me, his cell phone in an open palm.

I stared at the device a moment, wanting Zach to keep it.

The phone had always been a crutch for my parental anxiety. As long as Zach had it, he could reach me if he needed to. And vice versa. I did not want to be without that line of communication, especially with everything so unsettled.

"Mom." He slapped the phone in my hand. "I got to go in."

I shook my head. It was fine. Zach would be with Nate.

He disappeared into the station. I wanted to follow, knew that I couldn't. It was strangely similar to how I felt when Zach had his tonsils out at age nine. I'd watched the nurse push his hospital bed down the hall, wanting more than anything to follow the little bed as its wheels squeaked along the hard, cold floor. Then, as now, I'm not sure what I thought my purpose would be. Tell the surgeon what to do? Explain to the police that Zach was a good kid? All I knew is that waiting was agony, my mind full of horrid imagined scenarios.

Peter tipped his head toward the station door. "Do you want to go in and get warm?"

I nodded, followed Peter inside. Compared to the cool outside air, the heat inside the station felt excessively warm. I unzipped my coat, felt my cheeks flush. "So, we go to the district court right after?" I confirmed. "And I can take Zach home after that?"

"Right." Peter paused. "But you have to post the bail before getting Zach out. Do you -" he started then stopped again before spitting out the question. "Do you have the money?"

I did. Barely.

"Because," Peter continued, "I can lend it to you if you need it."

I shook my head. "No. You've done enough and I haven't even paid you or Nate anything yet. I've got it." I held up my purse as if the bills were inside. "I keep a check in my wallet. I can use that to pay, right?"

Peter didn't know. Of course, he didn't. I reminded myself

that he was an estate lawyer. The person who knew about criminal law was Nate.

When Nate and Zach finally emerged, I let out a breath of relief. I'm not sure what I'd expected, that Zach would look disheveled or upset or changed somehow. But he looked the same. Maybe the process would be easier than I'd thought. Maybe it was just as Peter said – the police just needed to look into a few things – and it would all be fine.

A momentary feeling of peace washed over me; it vanished as soon as we entered the district court. I'd seen the district court from the outside hundreds of times and never once wondered about the inside. Had I done so, I'd assumed the courtroom would look like they did in the movies, elegant and stately. Instead, it was a small space with a pocked ceiling full of dim recessed lights and streaky windows on one side. Rows of hard wooden benches stood front of the judge's enormous desk, two small tables for lawyers in the front of them.

Court was in session when we arrived. Lawyers, police officers, and litigants sat smushed on the benches amongst coats and briefcases and files. Those who couldn't fit stood against bland, tan walls, belongings pooled at their feet. Other than the people I presumed to be lawyers, few wore nice clothes, jeans and sweatshirts the dominant fashion. The door to the courtroom remained open. People filed in and out at random intervals, adding to the general disorder. I stood against the wall, Nate on one side of me, Peter on the other. Zach sat on the bench in the front with the arresting officer. He looked excessively young, a puppy admist a group of weathered dogs. The whole atmosphere felt surreal, like I was on the set of a terrible movie.

The district judge, Miles Gallo, called cases and conducted hearings, seemingly oblivious to the surrounding chaos. He had a black-silver hair, wire-rim glasses, chiseled features. In a different circumstance, I'd have thought him handsome.

A flood of thoughts, rational and not, teemed through my brain. One moment, I'd panic that Zach would be held over in jail and, in the next, I would imagine the judge dismissing the matter and say something entirely unlikely like: "Paige Dixon changed her mind." The churning emotions, combined with the stomach bile that inched up my esophagus, were so bad that I barely registered Nate whispering. I had to ask him to repeat his words.

"This is a preliminary arraignment," he said again. "This is what Zach's hearing will look like."

Oh. I stifled my nausea and zeroed in on the proceeding in the same manner I might have had I been told there would be a test after. The defendant, a pudgy, middle-aged man with a bright bald spot, sat in jeans and a sweatshirt. He didn't have a lawyer. A police officer sat beside him.

Judge Gallo called the case then the read charges, the latter of which were letters and numbers followed by words "robbery of a motor vehicle" and "receiving stolen property." He explained the man's right to counsel, then asked the arresting officer if he had an opinion on bail.

Watching the matter unfold, I was grateful that Nate had discussed bail with the police in advance. I didn't think I'd be able to sustain my composure if the matter had been unsettled. I'd yell out or throw up or maybe just cry.

The case concluded. The man stood and a police officer placed handcuffs on his wrists, clicking them shut with a snap. I stared at the metal clasps, watched the man move his wrists in vain. I knew it was part of the process. Nate had warned me that Zach would be handcuffed and held in a holding cell until I posted the bail which, I assumed, wouldn't take long. But knowing what would happen and seeing it happen were two different things. I gawked at the cuffs, at the man, at the door he disappeared behind. Was it the holding area? My mouth went dry, I leaned into Nate to ask him, when the Judge Gallo called out: "Commonwealth v. Zachary Morgan."

I clamped my mouth shut, my question for Nate stuck inside it. I gripped my purse, then opened it and pulled out my wallet. The emergency check was there, behind a twenty-dollar bill and two ones. I pulled it out and held the thin, green paper in my hand. I'd be ready when the time came.

Zach glanced at me, seemingly for approval. I nodded reflexively, and he took his place beside Nate at counsel table. I slid into a vacant seat on a nearby bench, moved to make room for Peter. He put his hand on my knee a moment, met my eyes. "It'll be okay," he said. I exhaled.

As he did with in the other proceeding, Judge Gallo read the case name and docket. Then he read off the charges: Sexual assault under 18 P.A.C.S. 3124. Aggravated indecent assault under 18 P.A.C.S. 3125. Indecent assault under 18 P.A.C.A. 3126. Said aloud and in succession, the crimes sounded horrific. It was difficult for me to imagine that these were the charges against Zach, my son, a boy so kind he let bugs outside on napkins.

As in the first matter, Zach's case turned to a discussion of bail and, again, an appreciation for Nate's arrangement with the arresting officer surged through me. As Nate predicted, Judge Gallo asked the officer his opinion on bail and, as agreed, the officer recommended $50,000, ten percent.

I'd expected Judge Gallo to issue the bail amount, but he sat still instead, brow furrowed. He read from a paper that I presumed to be the complaint, his glasses perched on the edge of his nose. "These are serious allegations," he said, looking up. "There's a significant danger to the safety of the community." He pushed his glasses back up, made his fingers into a steeple. "Sexual assault, aggravated assault, indecent assault." He looked at Officer Jenkins. "Very serious allegations, Officer. I'm not sure how you thought this bail amount was appropriate."

There's was an agreement, I wanted to scream. *The police said they would work with us.* I stared at Nate's back, willing him to say the words. *Tell him, Nate. Tell him.*

Nate jumped to his feet. "There's no priors, Your Honor. And Defendant has strong ties to the community. He's lived here his whole life." His voice went up an octave; I felt my stomach clutch.

The judge furrowed his brows. I held my breath. It felt like an hour passed; it was probably less than a minute.

Judge Gallo picked up paper again, examined it, then looked back up. "Bail is set at $250,000."

19

"But Your Honor," Nate started.

The judge held up his hand. "Sexual assault is a felony, Mr. Fletcher," Judge Gallo said. "$50,000 bail is not reasonable, not for a case like this. $250,000, ten percent." My eyes dodged from the judge to Nate to Zach in quick succession. That couldn't be it, right? There would be more arguments; Nate would bring up the agreement we'd have with the officer. That had to mean something.

There were no more arguments. Nate didn't protest. Instead, a police officer approached Zach, gestured for him to stand. Zach looked at me, the fear in my eyes reflected in his. The officer asked Zach to stand and put his hands behind his back. He clasped handcuffs around his wrists, guided him toward the same door they had taken the other man. I knew it was probably just the holding cell but it felt like the officer was taking Zach through a portal to an unknown, dangerous world.

"Wait." I stood, any sense of propriety or common sense obscured by panic at my loss of control. "What happens now? Can I see my son?"

Judge Gallo met my gaze. His expression softened in a way I wouldn't have expected. "You're Mom?"

I nodded.

"Your son will be kept in custody either here or at the jail until you or someone posts bail or a bond."

"But –" I started, thoughts flying through my brain. Ten percent of $250,000 would be $25,000. I didn't have that; I barely had $5,000. How would I get Zach out? Surely, he wouldn't just sit in jail. No one had proven anything. "I don't have the money," I blurted.

"You'll have to discuss that with your son's attorney, ma'am." He nodded toward Nate, now standing by my side, Zach's slim file in his hand.

"If I can't pay, he just goes to jail? That's it?"

"You'll have to discuss that with your son's attorney," Judge Gallo repeated.

"My son's in high school, Your Honor. I need to be able to talk to him, get him things he needs. Like his glasses." I felt unhinged.

"Ma'am," the judge said. "You need to talk to your son's attorney."

"But –"

"Ma'am." The judge's expression had changed; his prior look of compassion had morphed into a frustrated scowl.

"But –" I said again.

Nate put his hand on my arm. "Shhh," he whispered and guided me toward the door.

Shhh? Zach was handcuffed behind a door with a bunch of criminals. I had nowhere near the $25,000 needed for bail. And all Nate could say was shhh?

I held back a tirade of harsh words, allowed him to guide me out, vaguely aware of Peter behind us, carrying my purse and coat. Those left in the courtroom stared at me with pity as a walked, the semi-hysterical mother of the accused.

We spilled into the hallway and, seeming to sense my impending outrage, Peter gestured to the front door. I stepped out, didn't feel the cold. "What the actual fuck," I yelled as soon as the door shut behind us. "I thought the judge would accept the officer's recommendation."

"Sometimes they don't," Nate said. "It depends."

"It depends?" I threw my hands up, looked at him, my expression fierce. "My kid," I said, pointing at the building, "is in high school. He's now in police custody with God knows who. And he just gets taken to jail? If I can't pay, if I don't have $25,000, he just sits there. What kind of justice is that?" My chest heaved from the effort of yelling. A gust of wind whipped; Peter handed me my coat. I put it on without acknowledgement, shoved my hands in the deep pockets.

Nate turned to face me. "Look," he started, "there are a few options if you don't have the $25,000 cash." He explained that I could pay ten percent of the $25,000 to a bail bondsman and they would guarantee the rest. As long as Zach showed up for his hearings, I'd never owe the full $25,000. Catch was, the ten percent, $2,500, was the bail bondsman's fee.

"So even if Zach is eventually found innocent or the charges are dropped, I never get that money back."

Nate shook his head.

There was no doubt I would pay it. I'd have paid much, much more to prevent Zach from sitting in a prison cell. But it still didn't seem fair. No one had proven that Zach had done anything wrong; yet I had to pay this large, non-refundable sum. It may not have been a lot of money to some people, but it was to me.

I pulled my bank check out of my wallet and wondered, briefly, about defendants who simply didn't have the funds for bail, even with the help of a bondsman. Would they just sit in jail for weeks or months when, if they had only been wealthier, they could have been at home? Such a two-tiered system didn't seem right but it wasn't, couldn't, be my problem. I had enough to worry about.

I held up the check. "Who do I make it out to?"

Nate shot me a quizzical look. "We've got to go to the bail bondsman first."

"Alright." I checked my watch. "It's four now. We've got to get moving so I can get Zach." I looked from Peter to Nate. Neither said anything. "What?"

"Posting bail doesn't happen in an instant," Nate said. His voice had an air of trepidation; he took a step back. "Zach will have to spend the night in jail."

20

"What?" I felt unhinged. "I have the money. I can pay the bail bond fee." I held up my check, it's edge fluttered in the wind.

A group of people pushed out of the district court in a cluster, their voices too loud, too happy. I wanted to scream at them; I stared instead. A woman in the group held her hand up in response; I turned back to Nate.

"Well?" I waved the check.

Nate looked at his watch, a circular gold monstrosity that probably weighed half a pound. "It's five after four. There won't be enough time to process the bail before the transport vehicle leaves."

Transport vehicle. I'd seen them on the road — gold busses with blue stripes, the Pennsylvania Department of Corrections lettered in all capitals on the side. Of all the times I'd seen those buses, I'd never once thought about who was inside. I'd certainly never dreamed it would be Zach. I fought off an image of him on the bus, handcuffed and scared. I directed my gaze to Nate.

"Can't you tell them to wait? They can just leave Zach in

that holding room while I go post this bail." I held up the check again, as if my ability to pay was the only barrier.

Nate shook his head for the second time. "The bail bondsman has to process the paperwork," he said, his voice an irritating calm. "It takes a least a few hours. Plus, they close soon." He glanced again at the giant watch. "But, if we hurry, we can get the paperwork done now so it will be processed first thing tomorrow."

My heart lurched. I looked at the district court building. I wanted to go inside, figure out how to let Zach know what was happening, but I needed to get the bond office before they closed.

Peter seemed to read my mind. "I'll see if they'll let me talk to Zach. I'll let him know what's happening." I watched him hurry back in the building, wind pushing at his back.

I blindly followed Nate to the bond office, grateful for his long strides and hurried steps. Inside the office, my bail was processed by a cherubic-faced bond agent named Eve. "My son is in jail," I whispered, as if it were a secret.

We met up with Peter outside district court after I'd paid the fee and filled out the forms. "How was he?"

"He's alright. He understands."

I searched Peter's face for a clue as to the truthfulness of his statements. His expression was indecipherable. "Really?"

"He's alright," Peter repeated. "He knows it's just one night."

I followed up with questions about the other prisoners; choked on the word as I said it. Prisoners. Of all of the wild, anxiety-driven scenarios I might have imagined for Zach through the years, being a prisoner was not one of them.

According to Peter, there were three others to be taken on the transport bus. "They looked harmless," he offered. "One was a little guy." He put his hand down as if to demonstrate his size.

The statement did not comfort me. I tried to calm a rising sense of panic.

Zach was fine. There were armed guards at a jail. And it was just one night. I was making too much of things. "Well, can I see him? What's the address of the jail?"

"It's past visiting hours." Nate said the words so fast, they were practically slurred.

I opened my mouth, shut it. I didn't have the energy for more outrage. My head hurt; my body was numb. I couldn't remember the last time I ate. "Okay," I said.

Peter put his hand on my shoulder. "Are you alright? Do you want me to drive you home?"

I shook my head. "I'm okay." The words were a lie. I was not okay. And I would not accept that I couldn't see Zach. Of course I could visit him. I was his *mother.*

Peter walked me to my car. He left after assuring, again, that I was okay. His tall form disappeared around a corner; I googled the address of the prison.

I drove there, my mind preoccupied by the singular task of seeing Zach.

The reception area was bright white, the floor laid with square tiles in shades of tan. A woman with stringy brown hair sat at a desk behind a plexiglass barrier, a circular cut out in it's center. A row of orange-cushioned chairs faced the desk, lined up in a row like soldiers. The space seemed more like a medical office waiting room than jail reception, but what did I know? This wasn't my world. At least not until now.

I stepped to the glass, moved my face to the circular cut out. "I'm here to see my son, Zachary Morgan. He was just brought here from the court."

She nodded, tapped on a computer. My heart lifted. Nate had been wrong.

The receptionist continued to tap. I angled my face so I could see her computer screen. I'd expected to see Zach's name;

a list of visitation rooms, something that had to do with my request. Instead, I saw the familiar home screen of Facebook, a picture of two labradors on the top of the scroll. The woman typed a comment. I couldn't make out the words.

"I'm here to see my son," I repeated more forcefully.

She didn't look up, spoke in a rote voice. "Visiting hours are over. Tomorrow at noon. Sign up online." She pushed a flimsy paper with instructions through a thin slit in the plexiglass.

I stared at the paper, openmouthed, ready to plead for an exception.

My son is in high school.

It would just be a minute.

Please. I'm his mother.

The woman continued to tap at the keyboard, strings of hair obscuring the sides of her face. She seemed oblivious to my presence.

I swiped the instruction paper from the ledge, shut my mouth. I was too tired to maintain the fury I'd felt since Zach turned himself in. Peter had talked to him; he knew he'd be out in the morning. It would be fine. I'd probably cry or refuse to leave if I saw him anyway.

With a final glance at the receptionist, I blew out a breath and returned to my car. In the driver's seat, I stared at the mud Zach had left on the passenger seat dash a few days before. He'd put his dirty sneakers on it; I'd made a big deal. The concern seemed trivial now.

My phone buzzed, Reed's face on its rectangular screen. He'd texted twice already; I'd ignored both. No doubt he was worried. We hadn't spoken since the morning.

I accepted the call. Reed's voice sounded through Bluetooth car speakers. "Oh, good, Meredith. I've been worried. Are you alright?"

No, I was most definitely not alright, but Reed wouldn't know that. I hadn't even told him that the police were investigating Zach. He didn't know about the arrest. The hearing. Jail.

I gripped the steering wheel harder. "Long story. I'll tell you when I get home."

~

LATER THAT NIGHT, Reed and I laid side by side in bed, our bodies illuminated by moonlight filtered through half-closed blinds. "And Paige said it was Zach?" Reed propped his head up on his hand, bare chest peeking from the plaid quilt.

I stared at the bedroom ceiling. "Yes," I said, the undercurrent frustration in my voice unhidden. "I told you this when I got home."

"And what did she say happened again?"

I blew out a breath, angry that I had to repeat the statements I'd already made and, frankly, never wanted to make again. "She says he tried to force himself on her. There's a police report, but we don't have it yet. Zach said he didn't do anything."

"But the charge is sexual assault."

"Yes." I fought to keep my voice level.

"Sorry. Just trying to make sure I understand what happened." He paused. "Lara will ask, you know."

I sat up, the beginnings of genuine anger in my gut. "How will Lara even know? Honestly." I rolled away from him, pulled the pillow tight against my chest and stared at the wall. I hated everything about the moment. The room. The situation. Reed's concern about *Lara*. I closed my eyes. An image of Zach in jail formed in my mind.

"Well what evidence did the police have to arrest him?"

My body shot up again. "I don't know what evidence they have, Reed. They don't have to tell us yet for some reason." I laid back down on the bed with force; my head sunk into the pillow. "This whole thing is exhausting and confusing and upsetting. The last thing I need is an interrogation."

"Sorry. Just trying to figure out what's going on."

I glanced over at him, his mouth a thin line. He didn't look sorry; he looked upset and concerned. It was the opposite of what I needed right now. I turned away from him again, cradled my knees.

I pictured Zach on a thin mattress in a dirty jail cell with unsavory people surrounding him. I tried to block out the image but, as if it had its own power, it expanded to include irrational, horrible details based on movies I had seen. A tear slipped down my cheek, then two. Within moments, my gentle crying morphed into ugly heaving sobs. My body shook, tears dampened the pillow.

Reed sat up. "Oh my God, Meredith." He put his hand on my back. "I've been an ass. I'm sorry."

He sounded genuinely remorseful. I sat up and faced him. "I don't know what's going on," I choked out. "I can't imagine Zach would do something like this. He's not that kind of kid, you know?" Tears continued to streak down my face.

Reed put his arms around me and squeezed. "Shh. I know. I know."

I sat up and hunched over the edge of the bed, body still heaving with sobs. Reed rubbed my back. "We'll get it figured out."

I stopped crying, my body drained and empty as if tears had carried my emotions down an invisible drain. I laid back, closed my eyes. 'What if 'questions swirled through my mind:

What if they don't let Zach out of jail?

What if he gets hurt?

What if he's guilty?

My sleep was so disjointed that I was grateful when bits of morning light shone through the slits of the blinds. I opened my eyes and peeked at Reed. He lay bare-chested and still with a look so peaceful it would rival that of a newborn baby. I'd always found Reed's habit of deep sleeping to be endearing but, today, it angered me. How could he sleep like that when Zach was in jail? When his fiancée was clearly a mess? I gave his placid form a final look then set my bare feet on the floor and checked the clock. 6:11 a.m. Less than three hours until the courthouse opened.

It was almost time to get Zach.

21

I arrived at the district court before it even opened. Rationally, I knew there was no valid reason for me to be there. Zach wasn't scheduled for a hearing, and it wasn't as if my presence was needed to process the bail bond. Still, it felt like I should be there, a motherly guard.

I sat on the bench outside the courtroom, jiggled my foot. I looked at my phone, turned it facedown, then back up again. At 9:01, I called the bond agent.

"Paperwork's getting sent over now," Eve assured me.

From my vantage point on the bench, I could see inside the courtroom. Judge Gallo presided over the same chaotic process as he had the day before, just with different actors. The repetitive sequence of events reminded me of the movie *Groundhog Day*.

I leaned back on the bench, shut my eyes. Exhaustion competed with stress; my brain both foggy and alarmed. I sat up after a moment. Did it really make sense for me to stay there? I should be at the jail. That way, when the judge signed off, I'd already be there. I could get Zach right away. Of course, there'd probably be some unknown nuance, some extra hoop I had to jump through to get Zach, but I couldn't worry about that now.

I drove to the jail, pulled into a parking space, and waited. Time ticked by, agonizingly slow. I tried to distract myself with social media, then the news. Neither helped. The media feed was too frivolous; the news depressing. I checked the time.

God. How long did it possibly take to process bail?

My finger hovered over the button to call Eve again; I called Peter instead.

"I don't know why it's taking so long," he admitted. "I'll call the court."

He called back within minutes. "Judge just signed off," he said, a trace of triumph in his voice.

I thanked him and walked to the reception area so quickly it was almost a jog. Instead of the unfriendly woman from the night before, a man sat behind the plexiglass wall. I told him why I was there. He smiled and said "no problem." I exhaled a sigh of relief so long it was as if I'd been holding it for days.

A guard brought Zach to the front. I'd fixed so many horrid images about the jail stay in my mind that I was surprised he looked unscathed. I hugged him, tight, until he finally pulled away.

Zach was silent in the car. I squelched every motherly instinct I had to interrogate him about jail. We were both exhausted; there'd be time later to unpack the 'jail experience' if there was anything noteworthy. There wouldn't be, I told myself. The whole encounter was likely akin to an overnight at a nightmarish hotel.

As soon as we got home, Zach shoveled food in as if he hadn't eaten in weeks. I counted it as a win that he hadn't lost his appetite. He took a shower, took a nap. I fell asleep too, checked on Zach when I woke up. I stared at his sleeping form from the doorframe.

When he was younger, I'd loved to watch Zach sleep -- as an

infant, when his tiny chest rose and fell in a reassuring rhythm; as a toddler when constant activity succumbed to quiet; and, as a boy at night, hair wet from his bath, tucked into bed after nighttime stories. Now, of course, Zach went to bed on his own time frame, woke up by an alarm. I'd rarely seen him asleep anymore. But I could see now that he still slept on his side, still with a pillow between his knees, and still with one bare foot peeking out of the edge of the blanket. He was bigger but I could still make out the boy he'd been, same cowlicks, same smile, same freckle in the center of his left hand.

I tiptoed out and sat in the family room, my mind swimming with images from the past seventy-two hours. Judge Gallo. The handcuffs. The prison.

I thought of Natasha, my college roommate, too. Like it was yesterday, I could picture the two of us in the straight-backed chairs of Dean Carolyn Armstrong's office. Natasha told the dean what happened. Her face had been red, her words choked. She'd stopped the story three times to gain her composure. She'd exhaled when finished.

Carolyn Armstrong had reached across the desk, patted Natasha's hand, then asked a series of questions, the focus on Natasha's actions: Had she been drinking? Had they been kissing? Had she said no?

Natasha answered the questions with respect, but I could see the change in her countenance, the narrative shifting in her mind: the rape was no longer the fault of her attacker. It was her own. She should have been more forceful. She shouldn't have drunk the alcohol. She never should have gone to the boy's room alone. When Dean Armstrong asked if she wanted to press charges, she'd said no. She begged me not to speak of it on the walk back to our dorm, dropped out of school two weeks later.

I'd lost touch with Natasha, but I often wondered what happened to her. Was she scarred by that experience? Had being a victim inexorably changed her? Or did she move on and leave a productive and happy life, able to blot the horrible incident from memory? I didn't know. What I did know is that there was no way she had been lying. Why would she? What benefit would it have been for her to do so?

Thoughts of Natasha did not help my mental state, and I held on to the possibility this whole thing between Zach and Paige Dixon was some crazy misunderstanding. Maybe things would be straightened out before anyone heard about the arrest.

I swiped my phone from the side table and pulled up Facebook. On a whim, I typed Scott Dixon into the search bar. His page filled my screen, the header a photo of their family on a beach. In the picture, Scott leaned against a large rock, crashing waves behind him. He wore a white polo and navy shorts, his wife, Kelly, beside him in a floral blue dress. Dark hair flew back from her face, its absence accentuating blue eyes and flawless skin. An older girl, a cookie-cutter of her mother, stood next to her. A boy around Zach's age stood in front of Kelly, Paige to his left in front of Scott. The entire group looked like they'd stepped off the pages of a Vineyard Vines catalog.

I typed Kelly's name next, her header a photo of eight gowned girls in tiaras, all about five. Each stood with one hand on a hip, the other holding a rose. Kelly, made up and beautiful, stood in the center. I scrolled down and read her bio. Kelly had won several pageant titles, including having been the runner-up for Miss Alabama. She was the owner and operator of "Pretty Pageant Birthday Parties." The twins had been to one. It had taken me forever to get the make-up off their faces.

Unlike Scott, Kelly was a prolific Facebook poster. Along with the standard 'look at my kid doing a thing' pictures, Kelly's posts revealed impossibly beautiful vacation locales, stunning gardens (hers), and gourmet meals (also hers, apparently). One photo depicted a gourmet meal *in* the garden, the food displayed on an exquisitely set wrought iron table complete with flickering votive candles, wicker placemats, and casual bouquets of wildflowers. If Kelly Dixon had set out to make her life look perfect, she'd succeeded. I scrolled further down then, unable to manage my growing envy, swiped my thumb upward to the top of the screen.

A new post.

I scanned it, words jumping out at me in a jumble.

The post was about Zach.

22

I took a deep breath and forced myself to read the text, word by word:

WARNING. For those of you who do not already know, there was an attempted rape of my daughter, Paige Dixon, at a party the week before Halloween. Notwithstanding that Paige and a witness reported the incident to the police, her attacker, Zachary Morgan, is now free on bail. Please warn your daughters. Please share!!!

I PUT the phone face down on my lap as if doing so would somehow obliterate the content. I sat for a moment, panic coursing through my body, then picked up the phone and read the post again. It was awful. And public. I scrolled to the bottom. There were two likes already.

It seemed crazy. Zach hadn't been convicted of anything, only accused. We hadn't even seen the evidence against him. I started furiously typing a comment to point this out, then stopped myself. I should really talk to Peter before doing anything.

I called his cell. No answer. I called the office. The receptionist said he was in a meeting.

"Can you get him?" I asked.

"Um -- " She hesitated; I hung up. My hands shook. My breath quickened. I had to talk to Peter or Nate or both. The longer Kelly's post remained live, the more it would be seen or shared. I checked it again. Five likes. A share too.

I sent a text to Zach, still sleeping, and drove like a maniac to Peter's office. I burst in and saw Nate and Peter in a conference room with glass walls. Phone in my hand, I charged through the door.

"Meredith." Peter half stood.

I didn't respond and instead waved the phone. "Can she do this?"

"Do what?" Nate leaned back in his chair in such a casual manner it made me want to knock him off of it.

I slid the phone across the table. It skimmed across the slick surface, skittered toward its edge. Peter caught it just before the impending free fall. I didn't even let them read the post before continuing. "It's slander, right? Or tampering with the case. Something. Kelly can't just declare Zach the attacker." I pulled at my sweater, felt my hair, unbrushed since my earlier nap.

I knew I looked manic. I took a breath and tried to calm down.

"The post could fit the definition of libel if Zach is innocent," Nate said, his voice calm.

Rather than soothe me, Nate's tranquil demeanor made me more angry. I stood, my mouth in an "o", my fingers pressed so hard against the conference table their tips were pale. "So that's it? This is allowed?"

Nate spoke while looking at my phone. "No. It shouldn't be

allowed. I'll call the District Attorney's office and ask them to have Kelly Dixon take it down. The post could be a problem if the case goes to trial, tampering with the witness pool and all." He looked in my direction. "We'll get it taken down."

I moved to a chair and sat, out of breath from my outburst. "But it's out there now. People are going to think Zach did this." My voice hinted at a whine.

"Maybe not that many people have seen it," Peter volunteered. "It's been up less than an hour."

Nate lifted his shoulders. "Some people are going to think Zach did it no matter what. It's the nature of these cases. It won't affect the defense."

I stared at Nate. "The nature of these cases? This is my son we're talking about."

Peter looked from me to Nate. He extricated my phone from Nate's hand and gently passed it across the table. "I think what Nate's trying to say is that sometimes people have preconceived notions about sexual assault cases. We can't worry about that."

Though the sentiment was the same, Peter's manner of speaking calmed me. I twisted a lock of my hair. "I just don't want this to hang over him, you know. Every time someone sees him, I don't want the thought to be – hey, there's the kid who assaulted Paige Dixon."

"They won't, Mer," Peter said again. "People forget about stuff like this all the time."

I nodded, but didn't believe the words. If the police accused some other kid of rape or assault or any awful crime, I'd remember. In fact, when Zach was ten, the police arrested his summer camp counselor for selling marijuana. The kid ultimately graduated from Cornell University, but I still thought of the arrest when I saw him.

I shoved my phone in my bag and recalled the part of the Common Application for college which asked about criminal records. "What about colleges? Will they find out about this?

Does he have to put this down?" My voice was an octave higher than normal.

Nate shook his head. "He hasn't been convicted of anything."

I stamped my foot. "That's what I've been saying." I felt like I was in some weird paradox. The lack of conviction didn't seem to matter when the court required Zach to stay overnight in jail. Or when Kelly Dixon all but declared him guilty on her public Facebook account. But now it mattered? I didn't want to alert colleges about the accusation against Zach. I just wanted to understand the process.

Nate stared at me as though I might be crazy. Maybe I was.

"I just don't understand the rules here." I perched myself on the edge of a chair, tried to look calm.

Peter glanced at Nate. "Maybe it would be helpful if you explained the next steps."

Nate sat up. "Alright. There's the formal arraignment, but that's easy." He waved his hand as if a formal arraignment was inconsequential. "Next big step in the case is the preliminary hearing. The prelim's all about the DA's case but the DA won't want us to know everything, not right off the bat. They'll only show enough of their case to make sure it gets held over for trial."

I glossed over some of Nate's words, my mind fixed on the word 'hearing'. "Any chance the judge will dismiss the case at the hearing?" I felt a surge of hope as I said the words.

Nate shook his head. "Not really. We won't even start on figuring out the defense until after it's over."

I leaned forward, sure I misheard. "We won't put on any evidence?"

"Nope." Nate sat back. "Even if we had any, we don't want to tip our hand."

My thoughts churned. We were going to attend a criminal hearing and not submit a defense? That made no sense. "I want a defense," I said in my most authoritative don't-mess-with-my-kid voice. "I want a defense at the preliminary hearing."

Nate shook his head. "You don't. It doesn't matter. The preliminary hearing is not about credibility of the defense, it's only about whether the DA has enough evidence to proceed." He sat back. "Think of it like a medical procedure. A doctor would most likely run tests before ordering surgery. The prelim's like a medical test for the DA's office. The judge is trying to figure out if there is enough evidence to warrant surgery which, in this case, would be a trial." He paused, then added. "It's a really low threshold. I've never seen a case *not* held over."

I digested his words, their meaning slowly unfurling in my mind. Not only wouldn't Zach be exonerated in a few days, the only evidence presented at the hearing would be that against him. No one would hear, or care, what he said. How was that fair? "Will Paige testify?"

Nate scrunched up his lips and shook his head. "Not likely. Again. The DA will put on a little evidence as possible to hold it over. Probably just the police officer who took down the report."

What? Anger and confusion swirled in my gut. I stiffened; my jaw clenched. Peter must have noticed because his hand shot out and touched my shoulder. The gesture did nothing to reign in my rising temper. I took a deep breath and tried to form coherent words. "So, what I understand is that Zach will appear at a hearing with no defense and where the prosecution tries to give us as little information as possible. Paige won't testify, and the inevitable conclusion is that my son will be held over for trial." I paused for a breath. "Is that right?"

Nate looked abashed. He glanced away a moment, then said, "I will ask questions of their witnesses on cross examination."

"Why?" I said. "If the end result is that the court will hold Zach over for trial, why do anything? Why even show up?"

Nate and Peter both stared at me. I stood. "I need some air." I swiped my bag from the floor and swung out of the conference room. I passed the receptionist without acknowledgment and pushed open the front door. A cool breeze hit me when I stepped outside; I barely registered the cold.

The reality of the situation made me feel as if I'd been smacked in the face. There was no chance my life, or Zach's, would go back to normal next week. We'd be stuck in a vortex of confusion and mayhem where the rules didn't make any sense, at least not to me. And I didn't know how we would get out of it. Or what we would do in the meantime. Did we just go on with our regular lives? Go to school, go to work, pretend nothing happened? I'd barely been able to do anything since the police officer came to talk to Zach. The waiting and uncertainty would kill me.

I reached my car, pulled my keys out of my bag in a jagged motion. I heard footsteps behind me. Peter.

"Are you okay?"

"No." I turned to look at him, crossed my arms for warmth. Peter took off his jacket and put it on my shoulders. "This process is insane." I leaned against my car and put my head back. "It really sucks."

Peter puffed out a breath. "You're right about that. I'm a lawyer and it barely makes sense to me." He paused. "Hey. Sorry about Nate. I know he doesn't have the best bedside manner. Don't feel like you have to stick with him. If you want to get a different lawyer, I understand."

I shook my head. "No. He's fine. And I like that you're here." I looked at Peter's familiar face. "Thank God you're here, actually. I might have punched Nate back there."

Peter gave a small smile. "I still might." He kicked at the

ground. "I just wish I knew more about criminal law. I can't help you as much as I want to."

I pulled his jacket tighter and stomped my feet for warmth. "It's alright. You're good at what you do. I remember. After Noah died." I blinked. "I'm still waiting for the bill from that, by the way."

He smiled. "In the mail."

I tapped him on the arm. "You're a good friend."

I slid Peter's jacket from my shoulders, he waved at me. "Keep it. Looks better on you anyway."

I put my hand on the car door handle, not wanting to leave the safety of Peter's steady presence. I didn't want to find out about the aftermath of Kelly's post, didn't want to march forward toward a hearing where the only evidence provided would be that against my son. I stood still at the car door.

Peter put his hand on my shoulder. "Can I do anything for you?"

We both knew he couldn't. The only way out was through.

23

Zach went to school the next morning. It seemed the prudent thing to do. If the legal action moved forward after the preliminary hearing, Nate said it would take months until there was a trial. Months. We couldn't keep our lives on hold for months; we'd both go crazy. And Zach had a soccer game after school. His soccer-playing days were almost over; it'd be a shame for him to miss another game. Besides, it would be good for Zach to be out, good for both of us. A bit of normalcy after the past few horrid days.

I pulled into the high school parking lot and looked around at the familiar scene of high school fall sports. This, I knew. Cross-country runners in clusters, bulky football players pushing at tackling dummies. Girls in skirts with hockey sticks; tennis players on green courts. It made me feel happy, or at least normal, just being there.

I parked near the soccer field, hopped out, grabbed my folding chair from the trunk. I started toward the field.

"What the shit, Meredith?"

I turned and saw Donna, her phone in her hand.

I knew the issue immediately. "You saw it."

Kelly took down her Facebook post the day before; I'd convinced myself it wouldn't have made its way to my circle of friends.

"Yes, I saw it. I tried to call you. Why didn't you tell me the police arrested Zach?"

Why didn't I tell her? Because I was embarrassed, confused, dismayed, and upset. Because I wanted to pretend the accusation never happened. Because I didn't want anyone to know. I stood long enough without talking that Donna filled in the gap.

"Is Zach alright?"

I shrugged. "He's here."

Donna leaned forward. "I heard he was in jail. Is that true?"

I took a step back, alarmed. How did she know that? Did everyone?

"I heard –" she started.

I waved at her. "I can't right now. This past–" I stopped. I didn't know how to succinctly describe what the last forty-eight hours had been like. "I can't talk about it right now. I just want to have a normal afternoon." Bright sun peeked from a cloud and warmed my skin. "I really, really need a normal afternoon."

Donna's face softened. She pulled me into a bear hug, my body tight against hers. "You got it, baby. You got it."

She picked up my folding chair, and I followed her toward the field. She turned back to me. "Are you worried at all that the game's against The Crasmere School? Doesn't the Dixon boy play for them?"

I stopped. "Wait. The game's against The Crasmere School?"

Donna pointed to the red and white bus, The Crasmere School in block letters on its side.

"Shit."

"It won't be a problem," she said quickly. "No one recognizes who anyone is when they're in their uniforms. They all look the same."

I looked at Zach's team, now warming up on the field. Donna wasn't wrong. Unless you knew a kid personally or knew their number, it was hard to tell the difference between them.

"Don't worry," Donna said. "No one will realize." She headed toward Terri and Julie and set my chair down with a flourish. She patted on it.

"Hey guys." I slipped into the chair, stretched my legs out in front.

"Hey," Terri said, her tone muted.

She knew.

Of course, she knew. It didn't matter that Kelly Dixon took the post down. The damage was done; I'd have to address it. I opened my mouth, then shut it. I couldn't gather appropriate words. Hell. I couldn't gather any words. Coming here was a mistake.

Julie angled her face toward me. "We saw Kelly Dixon's post. What's going on?"

I blew out a breath, thankful, for once, for Julie's blunt nature. "You know as much as I do. Paige Dixon accused Zach of attacking her. Zach doesn't know what she's talking about."

"So, Zach says he's innocent," Julie confirmed.

"Of course, Zach is innocent." It was Donna. "No one is questioning that, are they?" The question was more of a mandate: no one was to doubt Zach's innocence. I felt a surge of affection, gestured to the space beside me. "Sit."

Donna plopped down and pulled a black water bottle from her bag. "Got the good stuff in here," she whispered.

I looked at the bottle. Did she really have alcohol in a water bottle at a soccer game? Concern flashed through me; I suppressed it. I had bigger things to worry about today.

I scanned the sidelines for Kelly Dixon. I spotted her on the far end, easy to recognize from the Facebook photos. She wore a short, white coat cinched with a tie, her dark mane pulled into a low ponytail. A large bag hung from her elbow; high heeled boots on her feet. She looked like she might just as easily have been at a high-end tailgate than a high school soccer game.

Donna followed my gaze. "Is that –" she gestured toward Kelly.

"Don't, Donna."

"But don't you want to confront her? Tell her off for the lies about Zach."

"No."

"I'd want to –"

"No," I said more emphatically. "Normal afternoon, remember?"

She leaned back; her posture defeated. "Right. But, for the record, if it were me, I'd be all over these sidelines setting the record straight."

"Well, you're not me and I want to be on the down low." I whipped sunglasses out of my purse, put them on, then looked at Donna. "See? Incognito."

The teams finished warming up, and the players took the field, Zach on offense in the number 9 position, center forward. I scanned the field for Ethan Dixon, but I only knew what he looked like from Facebook. I couldn't distinguish between the dozens of dark-haired boys on his team. He could be any of them.

The first quarter started. It may have been my imagination, but it looked like the boys from The Crasmere School were whispering to Zach between plays.

"That's outrageous," Donna said, slapping me on the knee. "They're trying to stoke Zach."

"We don't know that."

She crossed her arms. "You're too nice."

I watched, my attention zeroed in on what happened between plays. The sequence of boys from The Crasmere

School talking to Zach between plays repeated itself over and over, the conclusion obvious: they were trash talking. But Zach seemed to handle it fine, and I couldn't intervene anyway. It was something Zach would have to figure out on his own.

The half ended: Crasmere High School North, 4, and The Crasmere School, 2. Zach jogged with his teammates back to the locker room.

I wanted to stay still in my chair, shielded by my sunglasses, but my bladder, frustratingly and exceptionally small, felt uncomfortably full. "I gotta pee," I whispered to Donna and stood, scanning the area for Kelly. She was still with her group, arms gesticulating, booted heels dug into the grass. I'd run to the bathroom and back; I'd never see her.

I jogged to the port-o-potty row and stepped into one. When I stepped back out, Kelly Dixon was there.

Thank God for my sunglasses; they hid at least half my expression. But my mouth must have twisted in shock because Kelly stepped forward and said, "goodness gracious, that bad, eh?"

I stood still, unable to move.

Kelly continued, her voice a perfect Southern drawl. "I swear, they should allow parents to use the bathroom inside the school. These port-o-pottys are just plum gross."

I realized then that she didn't know who I was. Why would she?

She looked at me intently. "Should I just hold it? It's not worth it to go in there, right?"

I opened my mouth to answer when I heard Donna. "Hey!"

Oh no. I turned to her, waved my arms to try to stop the onslaught I knew was coming.

Too late.

"You have some nerve." She pointed at Kelly.

Kelly took a step back and assessed Donna like she was a wild animal. "Excuse me."

"Spreading rumors on Facebook. You have no right. Zach Morgan hasn't been convicted of anything. And the Crasmere School boys. Stoking him like that."

"What are you talking about?" Kelly's face morphed from confusion to anger. "Wait a minute," she said. "Zach Morgan is HERE? Playing in this game?" She looked from Donna to the field and back.

I put my arm on Donna's shoulder. She brushed it off. "Zach Morgan has as much a right to be here as your son."

Kelly inched closer to Donna, spoke in a low voice. "My son's not a criminal." She spun on her heel and walked away.

Donna started after her; I grabbed at her arms. I felt like a mother who'd lost control of her child. "Let it go. Come on."

She turned back at me, her face a grimace. "How are you not more pissed off by this? That woman," she gestured the direction Kelly had gone, "is saying horrible things about your son. She's calling him a rapist."

She emphasized the word rapist; I cringed. I *was* angry, horrified even, but it felt like, if I engaged with Kelly, Zach and I would get more entrenched in this awful nightmare. I didn't want to be entrenched; I wanted my life back.

"You're too nice," Donna concluded, her voice tinged with disappointment. She pulled peanut M&Ms from her bag. "Got these from the concession stand." She thrust them in my direction. "You're welcome."

I looked at the M&Ms and smiled. As frustrating as Donna could be, she was always thinking of her friends.

We returned to our seats just as the second half started. I couldn't say I really watched. I looked at the field, my mind on Kelly's words, and Donna's. I couldn't wait for the game to be over. I'd gather up Zach and we'd just hole up inside forever.

Zach played little in the third quarter; coach put him in at the start of the fourth. A few minutes in, a player shoved him, he fell to the ground. Rough play? Maybe. I couldn't tell. I kept my eyes trained on Zach even as the ball was at the opposite end of the field. His defender followed him, his mouth moving and moving and moving. Zach said nothing. The boy kept talking. He finally spoke back. The boy smirked, paused, then said something else. I saw the change in Zach's facial expression and watched in horror as my son landed a right hook.

24

The referee blew the whistle, held the red card over Zach's head like a matador. Play stopped. A team of coaches from The Crasmere School ran to help the boy; his teammates gathered around him like a human shield. Two helped him to his feet. He loped to the sideline, greeted by back-clapping and hair rumples.

Zach stood alone.

He stared at the place on the field where the boy had lain moments before. It was as if he couldn't quite work out what had happened. Finally, Carter jogged over, then the coach.

I sat, frozen. The coach whispered in Zach's ear. He nodded, gathered his things. He walked off the field alone, disappeared inside the thick brown door to the locker room.

Donna jumped up, pulled at my arm. "That's bullshit."

I didn't respond. It felt like every person was looking at me, every set of eyes waiting for my reaction. I didn't move until the play resumed, then stood and folded my chair, said a vague goodbye.

Donna followed me to edge of the parking lot. I stared at the cars. Where had I parked? I glanced around, half registering the cars, half thinking about what had just happened. What was Zach thinking? Was the boy okay? Would there be discipline from the school? I didn't know. To the best of my knowledge, Zach hadn't been in a fight outside a video game.

Then again, maybe I didn't know Zach as well as I thought I did.

Donna put her hands on my shoulders and oriented me thirty degrees to the left. "Your car's there, honey." Sure enough, my silver Odyssey stood where I parked it, ten feet away.

"Thanks." I opened the trunk and placed the chair inside. "I've got to get Zach." I inclined my head toward the locker room, then took out my phone to text him.

Donna touched my arm. "Wait. Are you okay?"

"Would you be?" The question came out more tersely than I'd intended. "I'm sorry. I thought this, being here --" I paused and looked around the familiar space. "I thought the soccer game would make things seem more normal. Instead, it's worse. I mean --." Tears started, a trickle. I pushed at them with my hand.

"Ah, Mer." Donna enfolded me in the second bear hug of the day.

The tears streamed down my cheeks in silent strips of wet. I fell into her. "It's awful," I whispered. Donna drew me closer, then waved at a waiting car. The driver went around us. She repeated the gesture a second time for a second car. When the third car pulled up, I let go, wiped my face. My phone dinged with a text. I glanced at it. "I've got to get Zach."

"Call me if you need anything." She held up her hand in a half wave.

I drove to the entrance of the locker room. Zach slunk out immediately, slid into the car. He leaned back on the headrest and shut his eyes.

I navigated the car to the edge of the parking lot, the soccer field on my left. The game was over, and stray players and parents peppered the field. Kelly Dixon stood with a group of women, her arms flying about as she spoke. Talking about the incident, no doubt.

I glanced at Zach. He held his right hand in his left; his eyes were closed. "What happened?" Zach didn't respond. I turned on to the main road in a jolt, squeezing in before a truck when there was barely enough room. The driver beeped. "I know you wouldn't punch someone for no reason. Did that boy stay something to you?"

Zach opened his eyes. "Stuff about me going to jail. Things that would happen to me there."

I stiffened. Of course, I'd thought about the horrors that might befall an eighteen-year-old convicted sex offender in jail. It was the dominant of what felt like endless, multiplying worries. But I'd hoped Zach's mind hadn't gone there. Too late now. Those boys probably put a dozen graphic pictures in his head. "Did you tell Coach Bryant?"

"No. I thought I could handle it."

I pursed my lips. Why did Zach have to 'handle' anything yet? There hadn't even been an investigation.

I searched my mind for a plan, my go-to elixir for anxiety. Worried? Make a plan. In the months after Noah died, I'd planned my days down to the hour. Time moved forward in tiny increments and, with each, my grief eased and the need for scheduling lessened until, one Saturday, I woke up with nothing to do. Zach and I ended up having a breakfast picnic at a nearby park with Barkley, then a puppy. We'd set up near the water and watched Barkley sniff, then wade, then swim, his small, brown head skimming above the surface like a seal. Zach had been elated, throwing sticks in the water for the puppy to retrieve. Finally, wet and exhausted, Barkley curled up on the picnic blanket and slept, Zach beside him. I smiled at the memory.

That was a good day.

This was an awful one.

I passed a McDonald's and pulled in on a whim.

"I'm not hungry, Mom."

"You have to eat." I took my place in the drive-thru line. "Come on. Cheeseburger? Big Mac?" My words, even to my own ear, sounded desperate. But he had to eat. Zach not eating meant something was wrong, and I desperately needed to pretend nothing was wrong. The car line snaked forward toward the order kiosk. "Come on. You have to be a little hungry."

"Mom –"

"Please."

He sighed. "Alright. Just get me the number 2 combo and water."

I pulled up to the window and ordered the food, supersizing the fries. "And two large milkshakes," I added. "Two large, chocolate milkshakes."

I pulled to the pay window and passed the food and one milkshake to Zach. I took a long sip of mine. "Mm. Good. Really chocolatey." He said nothing, his untouched milkshake dormant in the cupholder. I inclined my head toward it. "It's good."

He set the food bag on the floor. "I'm not five, Mom. You can't make things better with milkshakes and fast food."

I swallowed. The words stung in their truth. It was ridiculous to think that a soccer game or junky food would make things better. It wasn't as if we were dealing with something trivial like not getting invited to Timmy Kaiser's kindergarten birthday party. Zach faced serious criminal charges.

It was not the type of situation a mother could fix.

25

That night, Zach stayed in the office-bedroom under the guise of doing homework. Reed and I sat alone at the kitchen table, plates of lukewarm meatloaf and Birds-Eye green peas on plates before us. Normally, we talked easily but, since the arrest, there were too many landmine topics for our conversations to be natural. We avoided all discussions of the allegations but, at least for me, the allegations were all I could think about. And, now, I avoided any mention of Zach's fight on the soccer field, though I was fairly certain Reed must have heard about it by now.

Reed slammed the bottom of a ketchup jar. "How was the soccer game?" The ketchup shot out, bits of it dotting the table.

I reached out and wiped the spray, scrutinized Reed's expression. Did he know? "Zach's team won," I said after a moment.

"Close game?"

I stabbed a piece of the loaf, held my fork mid-air. "Pretty close."

I popped the meatloaf bite in my mouth, contemplated

whether Reed knew about the fight and was fishing for me to tell him. Probably not. Reed was transparent and direct; he wasn't one for games. If he knew about the fight, he'd say so.

Reed told a story about a five-year-old with six cavities. "And her mother gave her gummies on the way out the door," he concluded.

"Crazy," I said half-heartedly. I opened my mouth, intending to detail the altercation, then shut it.

No.

Maybe Reed would find out but, if he didn't, I'd avoid another strike against Zach.

It wasn't as if I knew every detail of Jamie's life or that of the twins. In fact, if Jamie got into a fight or the twins were in trouble, Reed probably wouldn't tell me either. He'd talk about it with Lara.

The night continued as normal, the next day too. I checked Kelly Dixon's Facebook page. In lieu of the caustic remarks about Zach's violent tendencies I'd expected, Kelly had posted a picture of exquisitely carved pumpkins on her front step. The caption: 'DIY fun!'.

I checked my email. Still nothing from Zach's coach. Nothing from the school either. It seemed almost like the entire incident had been a figment of my imagination, the lack of fallout a gift. The court had scheduled the criminal preliminary hearing the following week and, emotionally, I couldn't handle much more.

At work the second day after the punch, I sat in the break room planning an activity for my next client, a six-year-old boy with sensory integration issues. I could do something with sand. Maybe hide toys? I checked the file to see what the boy liked. Jungle animals. Perfect. I'd hide jungle animals in the sand for the first activity. I wrote it down just as Donna stepped into the room.

"Hey, Mer."

Her voice was different, passive. I looked up. She stood in place in the door, an oversized bag on her shoulder. "Hey. What's up?"

She cocked her head but didn't move.

"What?"

"Have you seen today's Crasmere Times?"

My heartbeat sped up. "No." I pushed aside my notes about jungle-themed activities.

Donna took the seat across from me. She pulled a newspaper from her bag and set in on the table. I scanned front headlines. Another political gaffe. A wildfire in California. Nothing about Zach. I exhaled.

She looked at me, then pulled out the local section, the headline in bold: "Zach Morgan at Center of Soccer Brawl." There was an oversized color picture of Zach standing on the field next to the fallen boy, hands on his hips. He looked imposing in the photograph, like a bully. My hand flew to my mouth. "Oh my God."

Donna talked, but I blocked out her words, my eyes on the article. The reporter summarized the criminal charges, noted that Zach had been arraigned the previous week. There was a quote from the boy Zach had struck and one from a Crasmere Friends coach. "It was hardly a brawl," I said finally.

"I know. It's bullshit." Donna smacked at the paper. "What are you going to do about it?"

"What can I do?" I leaned back and puffed out a breath. "I mean, it's no worse than Kelly's Facebook post, right? And Zach did this." I tapped on the article. "The story's not wrong."

"Even so." Donna picked up the part of the paper with the article and tore it in half, then again, then a third time. "The reporter of this story can go fuck herself." She opened her hand, and the fragments of the article fluttered haphazardly on the table.

I shook my head. "You're crazy."

She smiled, swept the article pieces off the table into a trash can. I watched them scatter into the basket for a moment before I remembered. "Shit."

Donna's head shot up. "What?"

"I never told Reed."

She bugged her eyes out. "About the fight? Why not?"

I said nothing; I should have told him. My omission seemed to signal something wrong with our relationship, a missing piece of trust. "I didn't want him to think badly of Zach," I said finally. "More than he already does."

Donna shook her head. "Zach's a great kid. Reed knows that."

"I'm not sure." I filled her in on the tension in my relationship with Reed since the charges, on his fixation with Lara's potential reaction.

She scrunched up her face. "Did Lara get his balls in the divorce or something?"

I laughed, but the lift in mood was short-lived. I stared at the article fragments. "How do I explain to Reed why I didn't tell him?"

"Tell him the truth. He's more worried about Lara than he is about you, and you're sick of it." She bent down, picked up a stray article piece, and put in in the trash. "And tell him to ask Lara for his balls back." She reached in her bag and pulled out a box of chocolate covered pretzels. "Your faves." She pushed the box toward me.

I picked up the box. "What's with all the food? First the M&Ms at the game. Now these?" I slid my fingernail under the tape.

"Food makes everything better. How is it you have gone so long without realizing this?" She plucked a pretzel from the now open box and took a bite.

I grabbed one; my phone rang. I pulled it out, flipped it around so Donna could see the caller.

Crasmere High School North.

I met Donna's eyes.

"I think things are about to get ugly."

26

"Suspended?" Reed paced in the kitchen.

"Just for a week." I said it as though it were routine, like Zach had received a slap on the wrist. "Principal Myers said she didn't want to do it. She thinks Zach's a good kid." This seemed important to point out. And it was true. When Zach left to get his belongings, the principal had told me how sorry she was. She'd said she'd received intense pressure to punish Zach. She'd even produced a folder of emails from parents complaining. I'd stared at the file in disbelief.

Reed stopped pacing and faced me. "Were you just not going to tell me this?"

"I –" I didn't feel like getting into with him about Lara. "It seemed like it was going to blow over."

"Still, you should have told me." He took a seat across from me at the table, pushed back a box of pizza. "And now he's suspended? Jesus." He threw his hands up.

I leaned forward, anger overtaking guilt. "That's your reaction? Really? Not, I'm sorry, Meredith, or how can I help, Meredith? It's not like if I had told you any of this, you would have taken Zach's side. You've been against him since the arrest." I sat back and crossed my arms.

"That's not fair."

"Isn't it?'

Reed got up and walked out. I stared after him. He was leaving? Now? I jumped to my feet and took a step, practically bumping into him when he came back through the kitchen door.

"This came yesterday. I didn't tell you because you had a lot on your plate." He thrust a folded paper in my direction.

I took the paper, unfolded it. A letter. On legal stationary.

Dear Dr. Edwards,

As you will recall, I represented your ex-wife, Lara Edwards, in your prior divorce matter. Ms. Edwards again retained this law firm to address a disturbing change in your living environment. She has informed me that you are currently living with a woman and her adult son, the latter of whom has been charged with serious sex crimes against a minor. It goes without saying that this fact constitutes a change of circumstance, warranting a judicial review of the current custody and parenting time arrangement. This office has commenced paperwork for the appropriate Motion. In the meantime, Ms. Edwards strongly feels it is in the best interest of your daughters to cease visitation at your residence so long as the criminally charged adult lives in your home.

Please contact this office to make alternate parenting time arrangements. I will wait to hear from you.

Very truly yours, Tookie Taylor

I read the letter twice. "Can she do this?"

Reed shrugged. "She's not supposed to. I have a custody order that lays out my time with the girls."

"Well, can't you enforce the order? You fought hard enough for it." Over the past years, Reed had shared details of his custody battle, a matter which cost him over ten grand.

Reed tore a piece of cardboard off the pizza box. "It's not that easy. Technically, I have a right to see them. But, if Lara doesn't bring them, there's not much I can do. I don't want to call the police. They'd just say call your lawyer." Reed ripped the piece of cardboard, set the jagged pieces on the table. He spoke again, not meeting my eyes. "It would be a little strange too, to have the girls here with Zach after all this."

My mouth went dry. "You're not suggesting you think that Zach would attack your girls?"

His head flew up. "No. But I can't say I don't see Lara's concern. She barely knows Zach." He looked down at the bits of cardboard scraps, now in tiny pieces on the table. "Anyway, I called her. I told her we were always here, she had nothing to worry about. I thought I had her convinced, but now there's this. A fight and a suspension."

My head dropped.

"No way Lara will let them come now."

I shut my eyes. Reed loved time with his girls. He was a hands-on Dad, the kind who genuinely enjoyed his kids. I pictured him dancing in front of the Wii, hips shaking, trying (not trying) to beat the twins in You Can Dance. I visualized his head bent forward next to Jamie's, patiently explaining a math problem. He had every weekend, every dinner with his girls blocked out on his calendar months in advance. He protected those days like cherished gems.

As for us, our time as a blended family had gone exceptionally well. I thought back to the first weekend the girls came over. Jamie and Zach teasing each other, all of us feeding the koi. We'd played cards on the deck until the sky turned dark, the twins taking breaks to catch fireflies in the yard.

Now, even if the girls came, it couldn't possibly be the same. Lara would tell them to avoid Zach, to be on guard. Awkward silences would take the place of spontaneous conversations.

"Reed, I'm sorry. This situation is such a mess."

"There is a possible solution," Reed said after a moment.

"Sure. What?" I leaned forward.

"Maybe Zach could stay at Donna's while the girls are here?"

"Oh." I sat back, contemplated the suggestion. Kick Zach out? Even for a few days a month, it didn't seem right. It wouldn't look right either. It would seem like he was too dangerous to even spend a weekend with his soon-to-be step-sisters. And, really, I didn't want him at Donna's. She'd been acting so erratically. Plus, she was dealing with the whole custody issue.

"Just until it blows over," Reed said quickly.

Barkley's collar jingled; the front door opened and shut. Zach. Taking Barkley for his nightly walk. I wondered, briefly, if he'd heard our conversation. Probably not. He usually had his Airpods in.

I picked at a crumb, still processing the request. Reed tapped on the table in front of me. "What do you think?"

What did I think? I hated the idea. But I understood where Reed was coming from. He just wanted to see his girls.

"I see why it might make sense," I said carefully. "But I don't think I can just cast Zach off. I mean, this has been hard for him, awful really. I don't think I can kick him out and then spend every other weekend like nothing's happening." I pictured the scenario a moment. Zach relegated to Donna's and me, having barbeques and movie nights like everything was fine. "Would you do that?" I said after a moment. "If it was one of your girls?"

Reed looked at table. "No," he admitted, "I wouldn't. I'm just not sure what the solution is."

"Me neither."

Reed got up and kissed me on the head, his lips lingering. "Maybe we should sleep on it. Bed?"

I nodded. "I'll just wait for Zach to get back with the dog."

Reed retreated to the bedroom. I leaned back against the kitchen chair, its hard surface unforgiving. I sat in stillness, an image of Zach in the principal's office earlier that day formed in my mind. He'd sat upright in the chair, sneakered feet solid on the floor, face devoid of emotion. He'd looked exactly like I'd felt.

I checked the clock. It was late. How long had Zach been gone? I didn't know. I pulled out my phone to text him, then put it away. It would do me good to get out in the fresh air, to talk to Zach privately.

I pulled on my coat and stepped outside. Cold air blasted my skin, a wake-up call. I walked at a brisk pace toward the park where Zach and Barkley usually stopped. I approached the small space; the outline of the small playground came into view.

I squinted in the dim light and saw Zach's form on a swing, Barkley at his feet like a loyal guard. I took the swing next to his. "Hey hon."

"Hey."

I swayed gently and looked at my son, his features illuminated by a streetlamp. I couldn't be sure, but it looked as if he'd been crying.

We swayed on our swings. Two women in leggings and running shoes power walked on the sidewalk near the park, both complaining about elementary school drop off. A car drove down the street, turned into a driveway. A woman with a high-pitched voice called for her dog.

"I heard you and Dr. Edwards," Zach said finally. "I can stay with Mrs. Sullivan."

I sat straighter, the swing jerked with my sudden movement. I'd been wrong about the Airpods. Zach had heard. "You staying at the Sullivans is the last thing I would want."

"Really, it's alright. It would make me feel better." A car drove by; Barkley stood at attention. "It's okay, boy," Zach whispered, then stopped his swing's momentum with his foot. "I've made such a mess of things."

I looked at him, recalled our conversation after the police had visited on the night of the Black Cat Ball. "You said it was just a kiss. That's hardly a mess."

He met my eyes. "And the fight?"

I shrugged. "Kid deserved it." It was the type of statement I thought would get at least a hint of a smile, but Zach sat stared straight ahead, his profile stoic. I tapped his knee. "We'll figure things out, honey. It'll be alright." It was the motherly thing to say and, the words out there, I felt more in control. I stood. "Come on. Let's get back now."

Zach remained on the swing, eyes downcast.

I looked at him and knew it. In my gut, I knew it. Something was wrong.

"Zach?" I sat back down on the swing.

He looked up, didn't respond.

"Zach," I said more forcefully

"I don't remember."

I took an intake of breath, looked up at the near-full moon, at the night sky peppered with stars. I did not want to ask, did not want to know. Zach continued.

"I don't remember. I was drinking and I don't remember."

I set my foot down. The swing stopped. "What don't you remember, Zach?" I held my breath, knowing the answer, wanting to be wrong.

The silence stretched out; Zach finally spoke. "I don't remember what happened with Paige."

27

Peter

"Zach doesn't remember what happened," Meredith whispered.

I gripped the phone tighter, squinted in the darkness. What time was it? I moved my head toward the clock on the nightstand. 12:15 a.m.

"He was drinking," she added.

I forced myself to sit up. If Meredith felt something was important enough to call me in the middle of the night, it must be big. "Sorry. I was asleep. What's this again? What about Zach?"

"He was drinking the night of the assault. He doesn't remember what happened with Paige."

The panic in her voice forced me awake. "Okay," I said, sitting up fully now. "Does he remember anything?"

"Just kissing her in a bedroom, apparently. They were drunk and passed out."

Shit.

"He said he felt sick and found a bathroom," Meredith

continued. "And he only remembers kissing Paige." She paused. "But he doesn't really know."

I blew out a breath.

"Is it bad?" She sounded desperate.

"No," I said automatically though it might be. But honesty was not what Meredith needed right now. I moved to the edge of the bed. "If Zach can remember leaving for the bathroom, I would think he'd remember attacking a girl, right?"

She exhaled. "Right."

"Look," I said in my most calming voice. "Why don't you get some rest? We can run this by Nate in the morning."

Silence.

"Mer?"

Crying. I pressed the phone closer to my ear. "Ah, Mer, shit. Are you alright?"

Her sobs got louder. It occurred to me that she was most likely in the house with Reed. *Her fiancé.* And, yet, here she was on the phone in the middle of the night with me. Anger shot through me at the thought of Reed sleeping through her pain. Or not caring about it. What was wrong with that son of a bitch? If it had been me .....

I stopped the thought. It wasn't me. That was the whole point of the conversation Meredith and I had all those years back, after Noah died. It wasn't me. I wasn't the one. But I was her friend and I was the one she was talking to. "Do you need me to come and get you?"

"No." She inhaled a breath, then a second. "No," she said again, more in control. Then she explained about the suspension and Reed's ex-wife's attorney letter. "I won't leave Zach with Donna and hotels don't take dogs." She paused. "We don't have a place to stay."

I didn't hesitate. "Yeah, you do."

~

Two days after I'd extended the invitation, Meredith stood in the family room of my parents' carriage house. She and Zach had arrived in the afternoon. Reed had insisted on following them in his own car. He'd parked behind Meredith's van, carried their duffels and pillows inside.

He checked out the space like a parent inspecting the site of an overnight camp. When his ridiculous house survey came to a natural end, he gave me a look, it's intent clear: he wanted privacy.

I met his eyes, then sat at the kitchen table and pulled out my phone. If Reed wanted privacy, he should have let his fiancée stay in her own home.

He stared at me a moment, then apparently realizing I wasn't going to leave, bumped me on the shoulder. "Thanks, Peter. This shouldn't be too long." He nodded toward Meredith and Zach like they were pets.

His plan, I knew, was for Meredith and Zach to move back and forth. But Meredith didn't like that idea; she'd already told me she thought the constant upheaval would add stress. They were planning to stay at the carriage house until they got their bearings. Apparently, she hadn't yet shared this plan with Reed. I glanced at him. "Meredith and Zach can stay here as long as they want."

He nodded and remained standing, awkward, as though he wanted to say something more. Too much time elapsed and he finally left with a little half wave. Meredith followed him out. I glanced at them out the front window, both standing by Reed's car. His mouth was moving. Saying what I couldn't imagine. "Sorry for leaving when you probably need me the most." Meredith said something back. I hoped it was "fuck you" but I knew it wouldn't be. Meredith was too level-headed to lose her temper like that.

She gave Reed a platonic kiss, then turned back toward the house. I averted my eyes, looked back at my phone.

She pushed through the door, her cheeks pink from the cool air. "It's homey in here." She gestured around the area. She wasn't wrong. The space was small with a wood stove that served as a fireplace, oversized plaid couches, and tables with stacks of books, magazines, and old family photographs. The family room adjoined a bright white kitchen with a round table next to a large picture window that looked out on the horse barn. There was a bedroom and a bathroom in the back; two twins on a roomy loft which served as a second space for sleeping. I'd lived in the carriage house when I first moved back home. I would have stayed but my Dad's health deteriorated and it made more sense for me to be at the main house.

"All my Mom." I stood and pointed to a stack of fluffy blue towels she'd left on the counter. "She even left you fresh towels."

Meredith eyed them. "Fresh towels, wow. I feel like I'm at a hotel." Her lips curled into a smile that vanished almost immediately. "I'm so sorry about this. Are you sure it's not too much of an inconvenience?"

I shook my head. "An inconvenience? Are you kidding? My mother is thrilled. When I told her you and Zach were coming, it was like I'd said the Queen of England and Prince Charles were on their way." I took a step back. "Seriously. It's fine."

She moved forward, picked up a towel, and held it to her nose. "These smell good."

"Well, those are the 'guest' towels." I made quotations with my hands. "My mother stores them in a closet with little packets of stuff."

"Pot-pourri?"

"Not sure. I just know I'm not allowed to use those good-smelling towels." I nodded toward them.

"Poor baby."

"That's right. I mean, what guy wouldn't want to use towels

that smell like --" I bent down and sniffed at a towel. "Some kind of flower."

She held one up. "Want to sneak one?"

"And risk getting caught by my mother? No way." I stepped back. "Oh. And she's invited you and Zach for dinner. She's making lasagna." I held up my hand. "Don't feel like you have to."

Meredith tipped her head as if considering. She had dark circles under her eyes, her posture bent. She looked exhausted. "Never mind," I waved my hand. "My Mom will drive you crazy with small talk. I'll fix you and Zach some plates and bring them down."

"Are you sure, Peter? We can get takeout."

I bugged my eyes out. "You're not seriously going to put me in a position to tell my mother you'd rather have takeout than her homemade lasagna? She makes the dough by hand, you know. And the sauce. Canned sauce is for people – "

"With no palate." She finished my sentence. "I remember. I would love some of your mother's lasagna. I'm sure Zach would too." She gestured to the loft. "Thank you."

"Alright." I stepped backward. "Lasagna on the way."

I returned an hour later with massive amounts of lasagna, salad, and crusty Italian bread. I arranged the food on the small table. Meredith called Zach down from the loft. Feet pounded on the stairs. Zach materialized in the kitchen a moment later, Barkley by his side.

"Hey Zach." The dog circled me. "Hey buddy." I pet the dog's massive square head. "Hey boy." Barkley's tail whomped on the floor.

I picked my head up, looked more carefully at Zach. He looked different than when I'd seen him at the night the police had first come to the house. Like Meredith, there were dark circles under his eyes, his cheeks sunken as though he'd lost some weight. It was almost as if he'd aged overnight.

I looked from Zach to Meredith. Both seemed in need of a good meal and a rest. I took a step toward the door. "Well, enjoy. And don't hold back. My mother has a whole other tray at the house."

Meredith reached out, put her hand on my shoulder. "Wait. Do you want to join us?"

I examined her expression. She looked sincere but, also, wearied in a way I'd never seen her. It was as though the light she normally cast off had been dimmed. The last thing she and Zach needed was me in their space. I waved my hand toward the food. "Nah. Hot, homemade lasagna is overrated. You two eat. I'll see you tomorrow."

Meredith pulled out a chair, her expression almost pleading. "Please, Peter."

28

I considered. I'd eaten with my parents, but I could eat more. More important, it felt like Meredith really wanted, almost needed, for me to stay. "Alright," I said, keeping my voice light. "Far be it from me to pass up a food offer." I moved toward the table, slid into a seat.

We ate in silence before Meredith gestured around the space. "So, I've been enjoying all the Peter photos around." She pointed at a photograph on the curio behind me. It was a picture of me around age three, tanned and chubby, holding up a sand crab at the beach. My expression in the photograph was so elated, it looked as if I'd just found a pot of gold.

I plucked the photo from its spot. "This," I said emphatically, "was my best day. It's all been downhill since."

Meredith smiled, a temporary uplift to her sad countenance. I felt encouraged, held up the picture again. "No. It's true. I mean, look at this face." I pointed to my face in the photograph. "Is this not the face of someone having their very best day?"

Meredith took the photo from me and inspected it with a

contemplative expression. "You do look pretty happy. And nothing this good has happened since? You're sure?"

"I'm sure," I said seriously. "This was my best day." I looked at her. "So. How about you? What was your best day?"

"My best day?" She tapped her finger to her lip. "My best day? Hm." She picked up a piece of bread and popped it in her mouth before continuing. "I think my best day was when I got the Fisher Price castle for Christmas."

"Really?" I feigned a disappointed expression. "So materialistic."

"Well, wait. You have to know the back story. I tested the castle in a department store before it came out. I kept asking for it and my Mom kept telling me it wasn't available, that the one I played with was just a test toy. But it was a really good castle with a working dungeon and a pink and green dragon." Meredith spooned salad on to her plate. "I kept begging until finally my Mom said the castle might never be available. It was just a test, maybe the company decided not to make it."

I lifted my eyebrows. "The plot thickens."

"Right. So when I got it for Christmas, the castle, the same one I'd played with, I was so excited. It was like getting something that you thought might never exist."

"Like seeing a unicorn."

She smiled. "Exactly."

"Hm." I buttered a piece of bread. "Okay. I'll accept that for now, but I think you have to dig deeper. I mean, look at this face." I pointed again to the sand crab picture then directed my attention to Zach. "How about you, Zach? What was your best day?"

He looked up from his plate. "Me. I –" He paused. "I'm actually not feeling that well. Would you mind if I just went up?" He looked to Meredith.

I looked at Zach's plate. His food was largely uneaten, his face drawn and pale. What had I been thinking? Talking about best days. Acting as if the visit was some voluntary social call. What wrong with me?

"Of course, hon." Meredith said. "I'll save the plate for you."

I stared wordlessly as Meredith hunted for aluminum foil. "Top drawer to the –" I started, but she'd already found it.

Zach looked to me. "Nice to see you again, Mr. Flynn."

"You too, Zach."

He disappeared up the stairs, Barkley behind him.

I caught Meredith's eye. "Sorry," I mouthed.

"It's okay," she mouthed back. "He's been having a rough time."

Of course, he was. Which is exactly why he didn't need practical strangers prattling on about sand crabs and best days. "I should go."

"No. Please stay." She met my eyes, sat, and tapped the table. "Please." She took the seat next to me. Fritter and Deo, two of the horses, entered the frame of the picture window. Meredith stared in silence. "I love them," she said after a moment.

"The horses?"

"Yeah. They're so majestic. I never thought of myself as a horse person, but there's something therapeutic about watching them." She scooted her chair closer to the window.

I looked at the scene. All three horses were now out, Rebel running along the back field. The two-story barn was set off to the right, white with brown trim. Three open windows, one for each horse, filled the back of the structure. At night, the horses often looked out in unison, a picture-worthy scene.

"Hey," I said suddenly. "Do you want to feed them? Get them set for the night?"

Her response was immediate. "Sure. Let me just check on Zach." She went up to the loft and returned a moment later. "All good."

"It's a bit of a chore," I warned.

"Well, I'll just watch you then," Meredith teased. She grabbed her coat and we set out.

"I've got to get them in first." We reached the field and I corralled the horses, walking each in with thick, black leads. Meredith watched from the split rail fence. I passed by her with Rebel and she smiled, a slight breeze blew at her hair.

So beautiful.

Still so beautiful.

I forced my gaze away. I could not allow myself to develop feelings for Meredith. Not again. Not under these circumstances.

I gathered myself, put Rebel in the stall, popped my head out the window. "Come on in. They're ready to eat."

Meredith appeared at the barn door a moment later. A cat skittered and jumped on the top of one of the barn stalls, a second cat meowed from the loft above. Meredith jumped. "Whoa. Cats. I forgot about that."

I picked up the cat on the stall. "This is Freeloader." I pointed upward. "And that's Visitor cat."

"Freeloader and Visitor?"

"Dad named them. He pretends he hates the cats but, on good days, he's always down here talking to them, bringing them milk." I set Freeloader down. "Okay. Let's get to work."

I showed Meredith how to shuck the stalls. I brought her to the loft above; we pushed fresh hay down. We filled silver buckets of water from the outdoor spigot, hung them on thick hooks. We prepared the food as the horses drank, a mixture of grain and oats. Once they were fed, I pulled plaid blankets from a trunk. "These keep them warm." Meredith helped me drape each horse in a blanket. She spoke to them much the way I did. "Why, aren't you a good horse? This will keep you nice and warm."

I locked the stalls, then pulled treats from a container on a shelf. "Now for the fun part." I showed Meredith how to feed horses from her hand, palm up, no movement. I watched as she fed Fritter, tentative at first, more confident with the second treat. Rebel licked her palm. She laughed and looked at me.

We stepped outside the barn after; Meredith washed her hands at the outdoor sink. "That was fun. You do that every night?"

"Most of them. My Mom does it sometimes, but it's getting hard for her."

The sun dipped below the horizon, bits of red and pink from its final rays colored the clouds. Meredith leaned against the barn. "It's good you're here for them, Peter. I know it can't be easy."

I shrugged. "I don't mind the chores or the errands or any of that. What's hard is my Dad. I hate to see him forget things, but it's even worse to watch him try to remember. He looks so hopeless then, like he knows he's slipping."

Meredith shut her eyes as if visualizing Dad struggling. She opened them, looked at me. "I'm sorry. I know how close you were to your Dad."

"Yeah. It's tough." I leaned against the barn next to her, looked out at the outline of an almost full moon in the darkening sky. "How are you doing with everything?"

"It's fine." She paused, her head swung downward. "Actually, it's been awful."

"I'm sorry."

"I'm so worried all the time now. About Zach, about the case, about how everything will go at the hearing next week. The only time I feel any peace is when I first wake up. I have about thirty seconds before I remember what's going on and the day spirals from there." She pulled her coat tighter around herself, blew a smoky breath into the air. "At least we have that meeting with Nate's investigator on Monday, Bo Brooker. I'm hoping that will somehow make me feel better."

"Nate says Bo's good."

"So, I've heard. Right when he told me her retainer amount." She rolled her eyes.

I opened my mouth, ready to offer to defray the cost, then shut it. Meredith was proud; she wouldn't want that. Plus, I'd already convinced Nate that he should do the criminal case for less than half of what he normally charged. In exchange, I'd agreed to draft free wills for an uncountable number of his friends and family. "It'll be worth it when Bo finds something," I said finally. I hoped to God the statement was true. We walked toward the carriage house.

Meredith stopped at the front step, her body illuminated by the porch light. For the second time that evening, I was caught off guard by her beauty. Flawless skin. Clear blue eyes. Perfect lips. I looked down, fought my natural inclination to turn red and stammer. It felt like I was in high school all over again.

She reached out and touched my arm. "Thanks for letting us stay."

"Of course. I wouldn't have it any other way."

"Well, I'm grateful for it, for you." She kissed my cheek. "Good night."

"Good night."

She disappeared into the house; I stared at the closed door. I was happy to have been able to offer she and Zach a place to stay, but I knew now it would be trouble. Because after just one evening alone with Meredith, one thing was clear.

I was still in love with her.

29

In the two days since standing with Meredith on the front porch of the carriage house, I convinced myself that any romantic feelings I'd sensed were merely a result of seeing her in person again. My attraction would disappear once I got used to her presence. And if it didn't? I was principled enough to keep my feelings in check. I would not be the man pining away for Meredith while she faced a crisis. My role was to provide stability and a place to stay and help with the case as much as I was able. That was it.

Nate had given me the task of talking to Meredith about the meeting with Bo Brooker. He didn't want her there, thought Zach would speak more freely if she wasn't in the room. And, though I felt a bit like a bit of a traitor, I agreed. No teenage boy wanted to talk about sex in front of his mother.

I made my way to the carriage house, a bit of unease in my gut. Meredith didn't come across as controlling as a helicopter parent, but she did give off a protective vibe. I was certain she would want to be present at the meeting with Bo.

She swung open the door before I knocked, held out a

hand. "You're not bringing more cookies from your Mom, are you?"

I shook my head. "No such luck." She stepped out and closed the door behind her. I tried not to notice her form-fitting jeans or the loose, gray sweater which looked sexy despite all odds. "I'm actually here to talk about the meeting with Bo tomorrow."

She tipped her head. "Yeah, I can't wait to meet her."

I took a second. "That's just it. Nate thinks it would be better if you didn't come." I said the words quickly, feeling like a school child delivering bad news to a parent as fast as possible.

"Oh." Her face was unreadable.

"It's just, we need Zach to tell Bo everything and he might not want to share everything with his mother in the room."

"Oh," she said again. She looked like she was processing; I kicked a pebble with my foot. "Will you be there?" she asked finally.

"I will."

"Can you tell me about it?"

Technically, I couldn't. Zach was the client and there was the matter of attorney-client privilege. "I'll tell you as much as I can," I agreed. "I'm sure Zach will tell you the rest."

She looked down, then up again. "Will he? He didn't tell me about the drinking. And all he'll say is that he kissed Paige. There has be more to the story, I would think. I've pressed him; he won't say."

I opened my mouth to respond but she waved at me with her hand. "It's okay. I'll stay back."

I agreed to drive Zach to the meeting the next morning. He emerged from the carriage house in khakis, a light blue button down, and what appeared to be new shoes. His hair was wet and brushed back, his face clean-shaven. He looked like he could be on the cover of a prep-school brochure.

The ride over was easy. We talked 76ers basketball the

whole way. I liked Ben Simmons; Zach was a Joel Embiid fan. We made our respective cases for why each was the better basketball player. The office loomed into view shortly after.

Once inside, I spied Bo Brooker through the glass door of the conference room. One hand fingered a blond ponytail; the other cupped a steaming paper cup.

I'd seen Bo at the office before but, outside the normal niceties, I'd not had a reason to speak to her. She always looked the same: ponytail, jeans, and t-shirts with funny sayings. The last one I'd remembered depicted a black cat holding a large bone with the caption, "I found this humerus." I'd snorted when I'd seen it, pointed at the shirt. "Ha!" Bo had looked at me as though she hadn't the slightest idea why I was laughing.

Nate waved us in.

I pulled open the heavy glass door and Zach stepped through. Water bottles and a Dunkin Donuts coffee box sat in the center of the table along with a box of munchkins, small plates, and napkins with ghosts that I assumed Kim had picked out before Halloween. Both Nate and Bo stood as we entered, Bo in a t-shirt which read "It's Jake, From State Farm." I opened my mouth to comment then, remembering the humerus shirt, shut it.

Nate made the introductions and Bo gave a brief description of her background. She'd spent five years in the investigation unit of the Crasmere Police Department before going out on her own. She'd been operating her investigative practice for seven years. She gave names of a few apparently high-profile cases she'd worked on. None were familiar to me, but Nate nodded in appreciation. "Questions?" Bo asked, her focus on Zach.

Zach gave a nearly imperceptible shake of his head. He looked sad and scared. I wanted to tap him on the back, tell him in would be okay. But, given I didn't know that, I said nothing.

"I read the police complaint, I've spoken to Nate but, really, I'd like to hear from you," Bo said.

Zach nodded.

"First, do you have a picture of the accuser?" she asked.

"Of Paige?" Zach clarified.

"Yes. I like to picture accuser and accused in my mind," she explained. "It gives me a better sense of things."

Zach scrolled through his phone, stopped, and slid it across to Bo. "This is Paige on the night of the party."

Bo inspected the photo a moment, then set the phone down in the center of the table.

I glanced at it. The photo on Zach's phone depicted an image of a girl in a tight-fitting police officer costume. The costume was short, barely covering the tops of her thighs. Full breasts spilled out its top, buttons undone to reveal cleavage. The girl wore high heeled tall boots and a massive amount of make-up. A pair of handcuffs hung from a red-nailed index finger.

Nate picked up the phone, bugged out his eyes. "This is how she was dressed?"

Zach shrugged. "Yeah. All the girls wear stuff like that."

"We can use this," Nate said. "The way she's dressed."

The implication was clear. Part of the defense could be Paige's provocative clothing. A girl dressed in such a way might be looking for sex. The idea seemed outdated; it felt wrong. I thought of Meredith and our conversation about her freshman roommate. She would hate the idea of a defense based in part on Paige's clothing.

"Let's not hinge the defense of how the girl's dressed," Bo said.

Nate held up his hands. "Sorry. Initial reaction."

Bo looked to Zach. "So, start at the beginning," she said. "Where were you before the party?"

"Right before?"

"Yes. Right before."

"I was at the Sleepy Hollow Haunted Halloween. I work there. There was a party afterward, a girl from Crasmere Friends. I didn't know her. We heard about the party from my step- sister, soon to be step-sister, Jamie."

Zach sounded mature and well-spoken. I couldn't help but think that Meredith would be proud.

"Wait, wait," Bo said. "Back up. Who's Jamie?"

Zach explained that he and Meredith had been living with Reed and, sometimes, his girls. He explained about Lara and about having to move out. When he was finished, Bo sat for a moment. "I'll want more on that," she said. "For now, let's stick to the party." She led Zach through a series of questions. A detailed picture formed in my mind.

The party had taken place in a two-story colonial tucked back in the woods on several acres of property. There were no adults in the home. Loud music blared through Bluetooth speakers and vaping inside the house produced pockets of liquid smoke. Outside, it smelled like weed. Beer cans peppered the kitchen table along with a giant bowl of vodka-laced punch. Zach didn't know how many kids were there, but estimated about thirty. Most wore Halloween costumes. Zach knew almost no one by name and could identify them only by costume: "I talked to The Joker" or "Paige was hanging out with two girls dressed as cats."

Bo moved to Zach's relationship with Paige. They'd dated over the summer and he had broken up with her a week or so before the party.

The fact that Zach and Paige dated was news to me. Zach had never mentioned it, and I was pretty sure Meredith didn't know. I wondered the reason for the break up when Bo asked the question.

"Why did you break up with her?"

Zach shrugged. "She was more into it than me. It was too

much, you know. I'm going to college next year. I didn't want a serious girlfriend."

"Was she mad?" Bo leaned closer.

Zach shook his head. "She didn't seem to be."

"Did you and Paige have sex while you were dating?"

Zach bristled at the question, then answered, "no."

"After you broke up?"

"No."

"Did you talk about it?"

"Yes, but it never happened."

Zach grabbed a water bottle from the center of the table and twisted off the lid. He took a sip and set it down. I felt a surge of empathy. It had to be difficult to talk about your sex life to a room full of strangers.

Bo walked him through painstaking details of his encounter with Paige on the night of the alleged incident. The general gist was that Paige had found Zach at the party. They'd both been drinking and hung out by the punch. Later in the night, Zach guessed 11ish, they went upstairs and entered a bedroom with pink walls, white furniture, and a framed photo of ballet shoes on the wall. Zach closed the door; they started kissing on the bed in the dark.

"And?" Bo tipped head.

"And we passed out. That's what I remember. When I woke up, I felt like my head was spinning and I left to find a bathroom."

"Do you remember having any sexual contact with Paige other than kissing?"

"No."

"Okay." Bo exhaled. She took a long sip of her coffee. For a moment, I thought the interview was over. I gave Zach a mental pat on the back for his composure and reached out to gather the used paper plates. Then Bo asked another question.

"What do you remember about being in the bathroom?"

Zach exhaled, almost as if he, too, thought the meeting had concluded. He described what he could remember about the bathroom. He'd sat against a wall facing the door. There were two sinks and a shower curtain with frogs on it. There was a rug, too, in the shape of a frog. He didn't know how long he was in there.

Bo tapped on the desk and leaned back. "Did anyone come in while you were in the bathroom?"

"One girl. Yeah."

I sat up. A girl? A witness? This could be good.

Bo lifted an eyebrow. "And did you talk to this girl?"

"Not really. She might have asked my name but I don't remember. I don't know her name," he said, as if anticipating Bo's next question.

"Well what do you remember about her?" Bo asked.

Zach paused. "She shot something into her arm with a needle. I don't know what it was."

My body deflated. The witness was shooting something in her arm. Drugs? That couldn't be good. The girl, if we ever found her, might have been high. She might not even remember seeing Zach. To her credit, Bo didn't miss a beat and asked the next question as easily as if Zach had said the girl was brushing her hair or reapplying lipstick.

"Do you know what time it was when the girl saw you in the bathroom?"

"No."

"Could you identify her?"

"She had on a short, black robe and a hat with a purple wig. I don't know what color her hair was." Zach paused. "I think she had brown eyes."

"Okay." Bo paused and reached for her coffee.

Zach sat up. "Wait. She had a tattoo on her calf. A four-leaf clover."

Bo placed the coffee down and leaned forward. "OK. Right calf or left?"

Zach looked thoughtful. "Left," he said after a moment.

"Ok, good. This is good." It was unclear if Bo was talking to Zach or herself, but she seemed energized by the snippet of information. I wasn't sure why. All we had was a girl, possibly a drug addict, dressed as a witch with a tattoo. It seemed little to go on. I dreaded Meredith asking me about it.

Bo asked a few more questions, then pushed back her chair. She nodded. "Lots to get started with here." She looked to Zach. "Is there anything else you think I should know or that your lawyers should know? Anything at all?"

Zach bit his lip. The silence stretched on.

I held my breath. Oh no. It was clear Zach wanted to say something and I sensed that, whatever it was, it wouldn't be good.

"Zach?" Bo prompted. "I work best if I know everything."

"I –" he started. He exhaled and took a moment before spitting out the sentence. "I told Carter I slept with Paige."

30

Zach and I spoke little on the way home.

He'd acknowledged to Bo what he'd told Carter wasn't true. It didn't matter. I'd read the criminal complaint. It included not only Paige's statement but one of her friend, Olivia Wade. Olivia had seen Zach on top of Paige in the bedroom. And, later, Zach bragged to his friend that he slept with her. Zach's unrelated, but still disturbing, fight on the soccer field didn't help matters.

Bo and Nate had both assured Zach that the investigation was just beginning, but he looked scared. We pulled into the driveway, tiny gravel rocks flying from the weight of my truck tires. I cut the engine. Zach glanced in my direction, eyes wide. "Can you not tell my Mom?"

Given the severity of the situation, it seemed telling Meredith should not be Zach's biggest concern. Still, he was kid. I'd probably have been worried about the same thing when I was his age. In fact, I knew I would. "I can't tell her," I said truthfully. "Attorney-client privilege." I paused, glanced at Zach's anguished face. I touched his shoulder, spoke again.

"Don't worry about your Mom. Your mother loves you. I mean, I've known her a long time. I've seen her love a lot of things. Like, when she was in high school, she had these two pet hamsters. God, she loved those hamsters like people love their dogs. You've seen it. You know. Just think about how she is with Barkley."

His lips turned up slightly. "Yeah. She loves that dog."

"And she loved your Dad." I oriented myself to see his full face. "But, in all the years I've known your Mom, I've never seen her love anything the way she loves you. The look on her face when she talks about you?" I shook my head. "I can only hope my mother loves me half that much." I paused. "Whatever happened that night, whatever you did or didn't do, your mother loves you and she's on your side."

Zach exhaled. "I know." He hung his head in a way that made my heart break. "That's why I feel so bad. This whole thing is killing her."

"Your Mom is stronger than you think. She can handle this." Even as I said the words, I wasn't sure I believed them. Meredith was tough, but Zach was her baby. If a jury convicted Zach of sexual assault?

The verdict would break her.

THE DATE of preliminary hearing inched up. I sensed Meredith's increased agitation as it neared. It wasn't what she said, it was how she looked. Tight-lipped with a stiff posture, a near constant look of unease in her eyes. I was not one who generally believed in auras, but I could feel the tension in hers. She knew the court would bind Zach over for trial; Nate had drilled into her that such a result was all but inevitable. Still, hearing the evidence against him, having an official trial date – these were the things she dreaded. I was almost relieved when the date for the hearing arrived. At least the anticipation would be over.

I didn't need to go to the hearing; Nate was handling the matter. Still, I felt like I ought to be there. For moral support, if nothing else. I dressed in my nicest suit, tied a maroon tie, heard the rattle of a car in the drive.

Reed.

I moved to the window and peeked out. Reed had insisted on taking Meredith and Zach to the hearing which, of course, I had wanted to do. I thought Meredith would have preferred me to take them too but, if she did, she didn't say so. And now Reed was here, taller than I'd remembered, standing on Meredith's step, his hand raised in a half knock. Before he could complete it, Meredith pushed open the door.

She and Zach stepped out, her hair in spiral curls, Zach's combed to the side. They both wore long, warm coats, Sunday best shoes. Reed half hugged Meredith, rapped Zach on the arm. It may have been my imagination, but I thought I saw Zach flinch.

They assembled into the car with solemn faces; Reed shuttled up the drive. If I hadn't known the context, I'd have guessed they were on their way to a funeral.

I grabbed a quick bowl of cereal and left, lest I be caught by my mother and peppered with well-meaning but nonetheless irritating questions about the case.

I slipped into my car. It was a gorgeous, crisp, fall day with a full sun and few clouds. The kind of day reserved for football or apple picking or playing frisbee in the park.

Not for this.

Not for a hearing which we all but knew would end up in the scheduling of a trial for Zach Morgan.

I snaked toward the district court, irritated by the slow traffic. I craned my neck, saw a crowd in front of the building. For Zach? No. It was just a preliminary hearing. "A routine matter," Nate had repeatedly called it.

I mentally skimmed my recollection of the newspaper for a big case that would draw this kind of crowd. I couldn't think of one. I inched forward in the traffic and saw people, kids really, holding signs which said, "One Step."

Fuck.

I'd seen that tagline in relation to Zach's case. It was meant to depict that Paige was one step away from being raped. I shifted my eyes from the high school kids to a group of reporters, microphones in hand.

I hoped Meredith and Zach had been here early enough to miss the chaotic scene. Or that Reed had enough sense to go through the back entrance Nate had told me about. Which he wouldn't because he wouldn't know about it. I blew out a breath. I should have insisted on taking them.

I moved forward in the traffic line far enough so that I was now directly in front of the building. I gazed in its direction then saw the long coats, the new shoes. Shit. Meredith stood on the outskirts, Zach by her side. Their heads were down.

One of the teen protestors looked at Zach.

No. No. No.

"That's him!" she pointed her sign in his direction.

The reporters turned, then surged, microphones out, cameras flashing. Meredith and Zach moved toward the door, pushed together, reporters around them. The protestors waved their signs with new vigor. Where the hell was Reed?

I pulled my car to the side and cut the engine. I ran across the street, narrowly missing a silver coupe. The driver blared his horn; I ignored him, adrenaline pumping through my body. I ran with giant strides until I reached the cluster of reporters.

"I'm Peter Flynn. My law office represents Zach Morgan."

The reporters turned from Meredith and Zach, questions firing at me now:

"Is your client guilty?"

"Is it true Zach Morgan was suspended?"

"Was Zach asked to leave his family home?"

I moved toward a microphone and opened my mouth, stalling. I made eye contact with Meredith, inclined my head toward the door. "My client--," I started. I watched Meredith and Zach disappear inside.

"Never mind. No comment."

The reporters collectively looked back to where Meredith and Zach had been standing, then continued their barrage of questions for me:

"Do you think your client will be bound over for trial."

"Does Zach Morgan have a history of violence?"

I didn't answer. The reporters followed, still talking, cameras flashing. I crossed the street and slid into my car. What the hell? Where had Reed been? And why didn't Nate warn us about the possibility of reporters?

I circled the district court for a parking space without luck, ended up having to park five blocks away. I jogged to the court, pushed open the door, reached inside my pocket. No attorney badge. Damn it. I'd have to wait in the security line. I took my place behind what seemed to be endless stream of unhappy people.

The sheriff's officers in charge of entry seemed to relish being slow and, when I finally got to the front, I set off the beeper. An officer pointed to me with an electronic wand. "Step to the side, sir."

"I have court."

"Step to the side, sir." She motioned again with the wand, then waved it over my body.

"Empty your pockets."

"I –" It was no use. I emptied my pockets, spilled the

contents into a little basket. The culprit ended up being paperclips. She waved me in.

I dashed through the crowd, toward Judge Gallo's court. 9:16 a.m.

The preliminary hearing surely would have started by now.

31

When I stepped into Judge Gallo's courtroom, the preliminary hearing was underway. I spied Meredith in the front row behind Zach, Reed, suddenly present, by her side.

Yvonne Williams, the district attorney handling the case, stood at counsel table in a fitted navy suit and two-inch heels, hair pulled back in a tight bun. She was in the midst of a direct examination of a police officer. I understood quickly that this man, Officer Jenkins, had taken the complaint from Paige Dixon. Jenkins was a kid, skinny with white-blonde hair. He looked so young that, but for the setting, I'd have guessed he was in high school.

At each question, Jenkins rubbed his blonde goatee, answered in formal terms which seemed in contrast with his youthful appearance: "The victim came to the police station at 1600 escorted by her parents" or "victim described the accused as a 6'1" Caucasian male." The academic nature of his speech lulled me into complacency. It didn't feel like Officer Jenkins was reporting on Zach; it felt like a television show.

Yvonne moved from behind the counsel table and stood in

front of him. She was at ease in the manner of someone who'd carried out preliminary hearings hundreds of times. "And what did the victim tell you when she arrived at the police station?"

Nate jumped to his feet. "Hearsay."

Judge Gallo swiveled his chair toward Nate. "Overruled. Hearsay testimony is allowed at a preliminary hearing, counselor. Commonwealth versus Ricker."

Really? I assumed Nate knew about the exception, that he was objecting on the outside chance of success, but I didn't. I knew from law school that hearsay testimony – when a witness states something someone else told him or her – was generally not allowed. That there was an exception for criminal preliminary hearings struck as palatably unfair.

Judge Gallo nodded toward Yvonne. "You may proceed with direct."

Yvonne repeated the question. The officer rubbed his goatee. "Said victim reported that she met Defendant at 104 West Riding Drive, Crasmere, Pennsylvania at approximately 021 hours."

Yvonne nodded. She asked further questions, laying the scene. Paige's report to the police, as told through Officer Jenkins, was strikingly similar to Zach's. They met at the party, kissed in an upstairs bedroom, and passed out. It was after this point where the stories diverged.

Yvonne took another step toward Officer Jenkins. "And did the victim say whether she woke up or not."

"Victim indicated she woke up at 023:39 at which time the Defendant was on top of her person?"

Yvonne paused. "Did the victim report any further contact with the Defendant."

I closed my eyes. This was it. The incident. Officer Jenkins explained in her terse formal language what Paige had reported. She'd been passed out and woke up to find Zach on top of her. He had one hand on her breast and one in her underpants. He'd unzipped his pants. She'd said "no" and "stop" and tried to push him off. According to Paige, Zach pressed his lips against hers, gripped her breast harder, pushed his hand further into her underpants, fingered her vaginal cavity. When a witness entered the room, he removed his hands, got up, and exited through a Jack and Jill bathroom.

Officer Jenkins went on; I felt sick. It was hard not to picture the scene as described, hard not to visualize Zach in the act, overpowering Paige. Zach was the size of a full-grown man; Paige petite. It would have been easy for him to force himself on her.

I shook my head. God. If I was picturing the scene, if I felt sick, how was Meredith doing? I craned my neck, glimpsed the back of her head. I couldn't tell anything from her back but I knew Meredith well enough to know she'd be gutted. My eyes moved to Reed. He sat a good foot away from her, arms dormant at his side. What an ass. Comfort the woman already. She's your fiancé, after all.

"I have nothing further, Your Honor," Yvonne announced.

Nate stood for cross-examination. As he had previously shared, his purpose was to ask questions which would make it seem as if the District Attorney did not have sufficient evidence, try to fit the facts into the sliver of cases which didn't make it through giant openings in the sieve of judicial procedure. He wouldn't succeed, of course. The threshold to bind the case over for trial was just too low.

Nate stood, put one hand in his pocket. He looked to Officer Jenkins. "Isn't it true, officer, that your testimony is based entirely on statements made by the victim and a second witness, Olivia Wade?"

The officer shifted on the stand. "Yes."

"You have no personal knowledge of what happened between Paige Dixon and the Defendant, isn't that right?"

"That is correct."

"You don't know, for instance, how dark the room was?"

"No."

"Where the witness was standing when she allegedly identified the Defendant?"

"No."

"If Ms. Dixon ingested anything that might have impaired her judgement?"

"No."

Nate continued his questions, effectively showed that, when it came down to it, Officer Jenkins didn't actually know all that much. Nate finished and sat; Judge Gallo angled his face toward Yvonne.

"Anything else, Ms. Williams?"

Yvonne stood. "No further witnesses, Your Honor."

I widened my eyes. No further witnesses? That was it?

Judge Gallo looked to Nate. "Any witnesses?"

Nate half stood. "No, Your Honor."

"Final arguments." Judge Gallo motioned to Yvonne.

She stood and in perfect, succinct sentences outlined the evidence as presented by Officer Jenkins. Repeated, again, the allegations as if they were truths. Nate argued that the entire prosecution case was based on hearsay.

My heart lifted. Maybe we had a chance. Maybe Nate had done enough. I held my breath, fixed my eyes on Judge Gallo. My recent memory could not recall anything I wanted more fervently than to hear the word 'dismissed' in the next thirty seconds. I tried and failed to read the judge's expression.

He moved his mouth closer to a small microphone. "In the case of Commonwealth vs. Zachary N. Morgan," he started. He cleared his throat before speaking again. "The court finds the Commonwealth has met their burden. All charges will be bound over for trial." He went over the conditions for bail, his pensive eyes on Zach. "No contact with the victim. Not in person. Not on social media. Not through third parties. Do you understand?"

Zach gave a barely audible "yes".

Judge Gallo continued with further conditions before turning to his clerk and asking what other cases were ready. Nate and Yvonne gathered their things. Zach sat still, back hunched, head down.

That was it?

I saw Meredith's head dip forward in the same manner as Zach's at counsel table. We'd known the outcome before the hearing even started, but actually hearing the judge hold the case over for trial made things real. The cogs of judicial process would start churning, Zach at the center of the wheel.

Nate touched Zach's back; he stood. I moved into the aisle, made my way toward Meredith. Her head was still down, spiral curls hanging, shielding her face. I'd almost reached her when Reed saw me. My presence seemed to uncork some recess of chivalry in his brain. He slid toward Meredith, put his arm around her shoulder.

I stepped back, unclear now, of my purpose. Nate was the trial lawyer. Reed was the emotional support, even if he sucked at the role. I was the third wheel friend-lawyer with no criminal law experience.

What was I doing here?

Meredith's soccer Mom friends weren't here. Donna wasn't here. Clearly, those friends had enough sense to know that Meredith would fill them in in her own time. I felt suddenly out-of-place, like a voyeur or stalker or worse.

I should leave.

I turned and stepped toward the door when I heard Meredith's voice, clear and loud.

"Peter, wait."

32

Meredith

Peter turned in the courtroom's aisle. I gestured for him to come forward, shifted away from Reed.

After barely acknowledging me all morning, Reed had been momentarily attentive, whispering that things would be alright. His words irritated me. He hadn't exactly been a beacon of support since Zach's arrest. But, now, suddenly, he knew things would "be alright." The words stung with insincerity. I'd opened my mouth to say as much but emotions – anger, anxiety, shame – crammed in my throat and I couldn't speak. Then I'd looked up and saw Peter's retreating back. I called out.

He now stood at the edge of the row, Reed between us. He looked past him and met my eyes. "Are you alright?"

"I –"

Before I could finish the thought, Zach turned to look, his expression a combination of shock and shame. Nate, next to him, picked up his briefcase. "Let's regroup in one of the conference rooms." He inclined his head to the door of the courtroom.

Zach stood. I reached out and squeezed his hand, looked directly in his eyes. I wanted to instill the message that I loved him, that the awful things stated by Officer Jenkins would never move that dial. I wanted to grab him, hug him, verbalize the sentiment, but Zach turned away from me, followed Nate toward the courtroom door. Reed stepped after them, hands deep in his coat pockets.

Peter waited for me. He leaned his head toward mine. "I'm sorry. That sucked."

"It did." It was all I could say. Notwithstanding everything that should have made this situation seem real – Kelly's Facebook post, the jail overnight, the preliminary arraignment – it wasn't until now that I really felt the weight of the charges against Zach.

I stepped into the aisle in front of Peter, my head in a fog. I took a few steps toward the door, then looked back. Peter was bent over where I'd been sitting. He stood with my coat and bag, held them up. "You might need these."

I looked at the items. "Oh. Thanks." I moved to grab them, but Peter shook his head.

"I got 'em."

We stepped outside the courtroom into the crowded hallway. Nate, Zach, and Reed were waiting for us. Reed met my eyes; his hard expression seemed to soften. "Sorry I rushed ahead," he whispered.

We followed Nate around a corner. One woman passed in front of me, her grip on the hand of a boy, twoish. The boy wore snow boots with light-up heels and stomped, heavy, on the floor. In a sudden movement, he extricated his hand from the woman's and ran ahead a few steps before losing his balance and tumbling on the hard floor. He wailed in pain, held his knee. The woman, presumably his mother, bent down, rubbed it, kissed his head. The crying stopped. I stared at the two of them. The magic of mothers when kids are small.

I watched the boy and woman a moment, wishing Zach's problems were small enough that they could be solved by a mother's kiss. When did motherly power to fix things stop? First grade? Puberty? I didn't know. I felt a hand on my shoulder and averted my gaze.

"Mer?" Peter gestured to a room. Nate stood, the door held open by his body. I followed Peter through the door to a dimly lit room. Despite a circular table and chairs, no one sat. Nate closed the door and the five of us stood against walls.

At the sound of the door slam, Reed spoke. "Well, that was a clusterfuck."

My head whipped in his direction. Reed rarely cursed.

"I mean, we put on no evidence. None." He threw his hands up.

I realized then that I hadn't explained the legal process to Reed as Nate had explained it to me. I'd been so busy avoiding the topic, I'd never given him the details. "Reed –" I started, but he waved me off and took a step toward Nate.

"Why didn't we present any evidence?"

"The preliminary hearing is about the District Attorney's case," Nate said. He gave Reed an explanation of the legal process. It did little to calm him down.

"Well, why didn't they put on any actual evidence?" Reed bellowed. "Where was the victim? Where was Paige?"

Nate again explained the process. Reed stood with balled fists and red skin and angry breaths that came out like pants. Had I thought his visceral reaction was borne out of concern for me or Zach, the strong emotion would have flattered me. But I suspected his fury was rooted in concern over Lara and his girls and his parenting time. I almost knew it was.

Reed looked from Nate to Peter, then directly at me. "We should get new lawyers. Let's get out of here."

I looked at him, face red, hair askew. Where was the affable man I'd agreed to marry? The one who had tea parties with his twins or surprised me with breakfast in bed. He seemed a stranger now.

"Come on, Meredith." He pulled his keys out of his coat pocket and gripped them, tight, in his hand.

I stared at him. I was not a huge fan of Nate, but it didn't seem that Reed should make this call. He hadn't attended a single attorney meeting or court proceeding until now. I opened my mouth to say as much when Zach spoke.

"I like Mr. Fletcher." He slid into a chair and looked up at me. "And I'm the client, right?"

"Right," I said.

"Then, if it's all the same, I'd like Mr. Fletcher be my attorney."

I nodded. Reed dropped his keys back in his pocket. He exhaled in a way that made it seem as his reserves of patience had been inexorably taxed. "Well," he said, placing his hands on the table, "what's the plan then?"

Nate tapped the table with the edge of Zach's file, the words Morgan, Zachary in scrawled writing on its edge. "We're still hunting down witnesses." He met Reed's gaze. "Our investigation just started. It's rough, because the kids were in costume and they didn't go to Zach's school. He doesn't know them."

Reed looked unmoved. "So how are you going to find them then?"

"Actually, our investigator wants to talk to your daughter, Jamie. We're thinking she can give us some names of the kids that were there."

Reed looked like someone had punched him. "Your investigator wants to talk to *Jamie*?"

"To find out the names of the kids," Nate clarified.

Reed shook his head. "Yeah. Great. My ex-wife will love that. Jamie being involved in a criminal investigation."

I looked at Reed, shocked that he would be so cavalier about the investigation that may exonerate Zach. The anger that had been brewing since the moment he'd picked us up, when he'd barely acknowledged Zach, reached a tipping point. "Exactly what would be the problem, Reed?"

He gave me a hard look. "You know how Lara is."

"Yeah, I do. We already moved out because of Lara's concerns. This is different. It has nothing to do with Jamie being in the house with Zach or whatever other bullshit she's worried about. This is about Zach getting exonerated. This is important."

Reed looked down with an expression that made it seem as if he were weighing his options. I couldn't believe it. What options? Was he really going to try to prohibit Jamie's involvement? I stared at him; he met my eyes. "I can talk to Lara," he said finally.

The room was silent, tense. Zach looked up from the table. "What's next?"

Nate launched into another abbreviation driven, hypertechnical explanation of the criminal process. From what I gathered, now that the preliminary hearing was over, Zach's case would graduate from district court to the Court of Common Pleas. We wouldn't get any evidence from the District Attorney's office until the case "hit the trial list." The next event was the formal arraignment.

My head spun. "I thought we already had the arraignment."

"That was the preliminary arraignment," Nate said. "This is the formal arraignment. But we don't appear. We'll waive."

I took in the words. The process felt foreign, almost made up, like Nate was a little kid creating rules to a board game as he went along. But I didn't have the energy to argue, made a mental note to ask about waiving the hearing later.

Reed pulled out his keys again, his features framed with disgust. "Chaos," he whispered but the room was small enough that we all heard. He held up the keys with a jagged movement and looked at me. "This is crazy. Let's go." He pushed open the door, expectant, it seemed, that Zach and I would follow.

His actions seemed pushy and unfamiliar. My nerves were frayed enough that I couldn't handle being confined in a car with him, even if it was only a fifteen-minute ride. I shook my head. "We don't live with you anymore, remember?"

He stepped back inside the room, the door latched behind him. His posture slumped. "Look, I'm sorry. This is stressful. I'm not at my best." He took a deep breath, then spoke again. "I'd really like to drive you and Zach back. Can I do that for you?"

I paused. Moments with Reed, better ones, flashed in my mind. Learning to windsurf together in Stone Harbor. Our attempt to make thai food and the joint decision, after two bites, to order pizza. Binge-watching *Breaking Bad* in bed, naked. I visualized Reed at the beach on one knee, holding out the diamond ring, asking me to marry him. Reed loved me.

He loved his kids more.

I couldn't blame him for that. Given a choice between Zach and Reed? Zach. Hands down.

I met his eyes. "Peter can give us a ride."

Reed dropped my gaze, his eyes slid toward Peter. He gave me a perfunctory kiss. "See you later."

"Sure."

The door shut behind him.

33

In the carriage house the evening after the preliminary hearing, I sat still, phone on my lap. My mother had left a message about Thanksgiving. They would not be 'Stateside' as she liked to call it. She'd prattled on a long apology, extended an invitation for Zach and I join them in England. "Of course, they don't really celebrate Thanksgiving here," she'd said.

Zach could not travel out of Pennsylvania let alone the country; it was a condition of his bail. But, of course, my parents didn't know Zach was out on bail. They didn't even know about the arrest. I gripped my phone. I didn't want to tell them. How would that even go? *Thanks for the invite, but the District Attorney has charged Zach with sexual assault.* No way. I would tell my parents at the last possible minute. If ever.

My phone buzzed. A two-word message from Reed: *I'm sorry.*

For what? I thought. Asking me to leave? Putting Lara's interests above mine? The initial refusal to let Jamie speak to the investigator?

I put the phone face down on the table, kneaded the knots

in my shoulder. I'd deal with Reed and my mother later. Right now, I needed a good, long soak in the tub.

Though I loved baths, it had always seemed a luxury to take one. If the idea ever crossed my mind, I'd come up with a dozen chores to do instead. Cooking, cleaning, helping Zach. But, today was different. I felt a visceral need for the comfort of the hot water, for the smell of clean soap, for the trickling sound of the faucet as the tub filled. It would be a way of washing the day, the testimony, and the hearing, away.

I entered the small bathroom and turned the faucet on the tub. It sputtered to life, a trickle, then a steady stream. I put my hand underneath, made the water hotter. Steam filled the small space, fogged up the round mirror. I got undressed and stepped in the water as the tub filled, lit the scented candles Evelyn had set on the sides. The candles sat between lush green plants, a wicker basket of bath products on one end. I scanned the products, picked up bubble bath, and poured it into the water stream.

I sat on the edge of the tub and watched the bubbly water rise before entering. I stretched out my legs and torso, directed my shoulders to drop, kneaded the still hard knots inside them.

I tried to banish the images of the day. But, as soon as I got my mind on something else, visions of the hearing crept into the edges of my thought and, suddenly, Judge Gallo or Officer Jenkins or Yvonne Williams were front and center. I honestly couldn't even recall what I thought about all day before this happened. Soccer? The college search? Dinner ideas? The subjects seemed foolish now.

I submerged all but my head under the water, bubbles up to my chin. The persistent thoughts of court persisted. The only beacon in my recollection was Peter. I visualized his face as he charged toward the reporters. He'd looked uncharacteristically fierce. I was positive that, had a fight broken out, Peter would have swung a punch on my behalf. He had gone to the hearing, he didn't have to, and he'd waited for me, clearly concerned. Peter had driven us home. When we'd pulled up to the house, he'd turned to Zach and said, "you're just in the first quarter of this, you know. There's a lot of game left to play." Zach had nodded and, though it didn't make things objectively better, his continued efforts to connect with Zach moved me.

It was more that Reed had done.

I heard a knock at the door. "Zach," I called from the tub. "Can you get that?"

Nothing.

Another knock, louder.

"Zach!"

Barkley let out a woof.

Still no response from Zach. Damn Airpods.

A third knock. I sighed and stood. Bubble-laden water slid down my skin. I dried off, quickly dressed, put a towel around my head like a turban. I made my way to the door and opened it, expecting to see the usual suspects: Peter. Evelyn. Donna. Instead, police officer Jenkins, the goatee-faced kid who'd testified at the trial, stood at the door.

34

"Officer?"

I stared at him, the police officer who'd said those awful things about Zach just this morning.

"Ma'am."

I pulled the towel off my head. My hair hung in a tangled mess of wet strands, bits of water dripped on the floor. Barkley raced down the stairs and sprinted around the officer with enthusiastic tail wags. "Barkley, stop." I grabbed his collar.

"Sorry to disturb you, Ma'am. Officer Chad Jenkins. Crasmere Police Department." He flashed a badge in a plastic holder. He seemed not to recognize me.

I looked past him to his patrol car, Crasmere Police in blocky letters on its side. "Is there something wrong?"

"I'm here about a missing person."

"A missing person?" Barkley pulled against my restraint; I gripped his collar tighter.

"Karl Flynn."

Peter's father. I let out a breath, afraid it had somehow been Zach, then felt bad for the thought. "Karl's missing?" I clarified.

"So, you know him?" Officer Jenkins pulled out a pad with

one hand, touched his goatee with the other. He looked even younger than he had at the preliminary hearing.

"Yes, I know Karl. I live here." I paused. "How long has he been missing?"

"His wife estimates he's been missing since 15:30 p.m." Chad paused, then added, "that's 3:30 regular time."

"Oh." I glanced at the clock. Karl had been missing for three hours.

"It's a problem," Chad Jenkins explained, "because Mr. Flynn has dementia. Did you know that?"

"Yes, I know that."

Chad's questions were irritating. What did he want? Barkley strained. I moved my hand to re-grasp but he broke free and circled Chad then jumped up, giant brown paws on the man's chest. "Sorry about that." I pulled Barkley off the officer and again held his collar. "Zach. Can you come get the dog?"

Zach's voice sounded from the loft. "Coming." I heard his feet thump on the stairs, realizing my mistake when he stopped short on the bottom one. His eyes locked on Officer Jenkins.

"Karl's missing," I said quickly. "The officer's here –" I let the sentence trail off. Why was the officer here?

"Can I look around?" Chad asked. He swirled his pen around at the interior of the carriage house.

Almost everything in the space could be seen from where we stood. "Is that necessary? Karl's not here."

"It's for the report, ma'am." He tapped his pad. "I've been charged with checking the premises and surrounding area for Mr. Flynn."

Apprehension formed in my gut. The police, once a beacon of justice in my mind, felt scary now. A piece of me believed Chad's backstory a ruse, that he was actually there to spy on us. He'd stomp through the house, find some errant piece of evidence, and cart Zach back to jail. I knew the thought was irrational. There was no evidence. Plus, Karl was missing. It was that last piece that brought me to my senses. "Of course."

Zach grabbed Barkley. Chad stepped into the house toward the kitchen, thick, black boots clomping heavy on the floor. He glanced at the kitchen, then turned left down the only hall, toward my bedroom and the bathroom before returning to the main area. I watched as he ascended the stairs to the loft and stood there. Too long. Why? What did he see?

"Officer?"

Chad turned and descended the stairs. He walked toward us, a serious expression on his face. He reached toward his waist, near silver handcuffs that hung dangerously from his belt. I held my breath. Chad pulled out a business card.

"Please call if you see or hear from Mr. Flynn."

I slid the card from his hand.

Chad tipped his hat. "Have a good night." He shut the door behind him.

Zach let go of Barkley, who raced in a circle several times before plopping on the rug.

"That was strange," I said. "I wonder why Peter didn't call?"

"He was here," Zach said. "You were getting the pizza. He'd asked if his Dad was here. I didn't think to tell you." He paused. "Sorry."

I shook my head and swiped my phone from the kitchen counter. "It's fine. You didn't know. I'll call him." I pulled up Peter's contact and pressed.

He answered on the first ring.

"Peter. I just heard about your Dad. I–"

"The police found him in town. They're bringing him back."

I exhaled. "Oh, good."

"Could you wait for him at the house? Would you mind? The police will get there before we do, I think."

"Of course. I'll go right now." I clicked off the phone, happy to do something for Peter. He'd helped me so much these past weeks; it felt good to be on the giving end instead of the receiving one. I found Zach. "I'm going to wait for Karl at the house."

Zach nodded toward the window. Chad was still outside playing cop, his flashlight now on a squirrel. "He was the one at the hearing today."

A vision of Chad Jenkins on the witness stand materialized in my mind. I pushed it away. Chad was here for Karl, not Zach.

"It's fine, Zach. He's just here to help find Karl."

We watched Chad pull out his phone and press it to his ear. He dropped it after a moment, made his way to the police car. Someone must have told him Karl had been found.

"See," I said to Zach. The police car ambled up the drive. I kissed him on the head. "I'll be back in a bit. Text if you need me."

I put on my coat and stepped outside. Just as I reached the main house, a squad car pulled up. Karl exited and entered the home. I met the eyes of one of the police officers and gestured to where Karl had gone. "The family asked me to stay with him until they get back."

The officer nodded. "They told us. Thank you."

I found Karl at the kitchen table, a bowl of red apples in front of him. I slumped in the chair next by his side. "You okay?" I angled my head to look at him.

"Good, fine. You?"

"It hasn't been my best day, Karl, if I'm telling the truth."

"Me either." He looked down. "I got lost." He met my eyes; his face held a distinct look of shame.

"It happens," I said though the words were untrue. People didn't typically get lost in towns where they'd lived for decades. A surge of empathy for Karl and for Peter and his Mom coursed through my body. Dementia wasn't easy.

My feelings of empathy were followed by feelings of guilt.

I'd brought more stress on Peter by moving in, by involving his firm in the case against Zach. He didn't need that. He and his mother had enough to handle with Karl.

Karl interrupted my guilt-laden thoughts. "You know," he said, picking up an apple, "I used to be able to get a whole apple skin with one peel. Stupid, but it used to help me relax." He rolled an apple toward me and chuckled. "Evie used to know if I had a bad day. She'd find me with a whole pile of naked apples."

I stopped the apple's momentum with my hand, recalled an image of Karl on the front porch of the Flynn's former home, a basket of apples by his side. I always thought he'd done it as a hobby; it hadn't occurred to me it was for relaxation.

"I remember. Mrs. Flynn used to make apple pie with them."

"That's right." Karl smiled widely.

"There was nothing like coming here and getting a big ole slice of Mrs. Flynn's apple pie." I paused. "I liked it best warm and with ice cream."

At the thought of the pies, my mind transported me to the Flynn household in the Fall. It smelled, always, of baked goods. Sometimes the apple pies, but sometimes pumpkin bread or peach cobbler. Evelyn would usually be in the kitchen, traces of flour on her clothes. Karl could be found either on the front porch or sprawled out on the family room couch, the Philadelphia Eagles on in the background. Friends of Peter were always welcome and, unlike my own home, there was always some group of kids at the Flynns. Playing cards, watching movies. Or dumb things like racing pumpkins down the driveway.

"Do you want to learn?" Karl's voice interrupted my recollection. He got up and retrieved two knives from a drawer. "I can teach you how to peel an apple in one shot."

I hesitated. Part of me wanted to go to back the carriage

house and crawl under a blanket. But part of me wanted to stay in the Flynns' warm home, insulated from all the bad things beyond it. "Sure," I said, meaning it. "I'd love that."

Karl handed me a knife and sat down. "Start at the top," he told me, demonstrating, "Hold the knife down tight and move the apple around it."

I placed my knife at the top and dug into the apple skin, then moved it.

"Move the apple, not the knife," Karl instructed.

I pressed down harder with the knife and moved the apple to the left. A bit of red skin peeled off. I smiled.

"That's good," Karl said. "Just keep turning it." He watched me a moment then said, "See? Apple peeling is good for the nerves."

I nodded. He wasn't wrong. The act of peeling took just enough concentration that I could forget my present circumstances, but not so much that the task itself became stressful. I pressed down at the bottom of the apple, the last bit of the long peel spiraled away. I held it up. "Ta da!"

"First try," Karl cheered. He rolled a second one across the table. "Might be beginner's luck. Try again." He winked.

I laughed and picked up the second apple just as Peter and Evelyn walked in. Evelyn strode toward Karl, a look of worry on her face. She touched his shoulder. "Are you alright?"

"I'm alright." He didn't elaborate on where he had gone. Evelyn didn't press him; her worried gaze remained.

"Karl's teaching me to peel apples," I volunteered. I pointed to two naked apples in front of me.

"Kid's a natural," Karl said.

Evelyn stared at the apples a moment then took a seat next to Karl. "You've always loved doing that."

I felt Peter's hands press down on my shoulders. He bent down, his mouth near my ear. "Thank you." He smelled woodsy. I hadn't noticed that before. New cologne?

I looked up at him, his face inches from mine. I kissed his cheek. My lips felt warm where they met his rough stubble, my face felt hot. "I should probably get going."

Evelyn waved in my direction. "I'll bring by some apple pie tomorrow." She inclined her head toward Peter. "Walk Meredith home now, will you?"

I shook my head. "It's okay, really. It's just right there." I pointed at the carriage house, in clear view of the window.

But Peter was already grabbing his coat. "Who am I to refute my mother?" He pushed open the front door and held it for me.

We walked the five hundred feet in silence, then stopped in front of an oak tree. I could see Zach inside, a professional basketball game on in the background.

Peter leaned on the tree. "How are you?"

"I might ask you the same thing. What a stressful night."

"Yeah. Not the best. My Dad got lost in town."

I nodded. "I know. He told me."

"Yeah." He shook his head. "It's rough seeing him like this. Like he's there and he isn't, you know?"

I nodded, reached out and squeezed his hand. "I'm sorry."

He shook his head as if to remove the image of his Dad. "Anyway. Thanks for waiting with him. I'm sure that's the last thing you needed today."

I shrugged. "It was a good distraction. And I do like apple peeling."

"A new hobby is born." He smiled then gave a half wave. "Try to get some rest." He turned toward the main house.

I stared at his back. I don't know if it was the stress of the hearing, the tension with Reed, or Peter's comforting presence, but something shifted inside me.

I didn't want him to go.

"Wait."

35

Peter turned, his face rough with stubble, features etched with concern.

Emotion coursed through me. I wanted to wrap my arms around his broad shoulders. I wanted to keep him with me all night, a barrier of comfort against the rising storm that had become my life. I looked into Peter's eyes, warm and empathetic. I felt an emotion shift inside me, one that no longer saw Peter as a just a friend. I moved toward him, stopped myself.

What was I doing?

I was engaged. I fingered my ring. Reed had been acting like a jerk, but we'd never called anything off.

I stepped back. It was late. I was tired. I couldn't trust these new feelings. And, even if I could, there was no indication Peter felt the same way. He had at one time but, back then, he'd been at a crossroads with his marriage.

"Mer?"

I shook my head. "Sorry. Just wanted to say thanks. For the help, the support," I gestured to the carriage house. "For the place to stay."

He held out his hands. "It's nothing."

I met his eyes. "It's not nothing. You've got so much going on with your Dad and trying to run a firm and here I pop into your life out of the blue with a major problem and all you do is help me." Emotion overwhelmed me as I spoke. "Your help is most definitely not nothing." My eyes started to fill, and I swallowed hard. The last thing I needed was for Peter to give me a sympathetic embrace. I'd start something physical if he did that. My emotions were too jumbled, too raw, for me to control my instincts. I forced a breath. "Anyway. Thanks." I turned toward the carriage house and strode toward the door.

~

A WEEK LATER, I sat on the Flynns' sun-drenched porch with Karl.

"Gin." I placed my cards down in a fan pattern on the table then sunk into the deep floral couch, arms behind my head in a teasing gesture.

Karl held up his cards and counted. "Ten, twenty, twenty-eight." He paused a moment then said, "fifty-three." He picked up the small spiral notebook and noted the score inside.

The gin rummy games started the day after Karl had gone missing. The caregiver called out and Evelyn asked if I could stay with Karl while she went to the dentist.

I'd found him on the porch, reclining on a couch but still awake. A hand-knitted blanket, one I recognized from the Flynns' old house, was strewn haphazardly over his legs. "Hey Karl." I glanced around the room and, in a cupboard over-stuffed with thrillers, picture frames, and ceramic bowls, spied a deck of cards. "Gin rummy?" I pulled down the deck.

We'd played twice since the initial game, five rounds at a time. The loser added up the face value of their cards; Karl recorded them in a tiny notebook with a pencil he tucked inside the spiral afterward. The first to get to 500 lost. Karl, so far in the day's round, was at 411.

"Just a few more games 'til I got you," I teased.

"Don't count your chickens." Karl shuffled the deck.

The games, Evelyn's meals — dropped off at the carriage house a few times a week — and the nightly routine of helping Peter with the horses had given me momentary bits of normalcy. Zach was scheduled for trial, but people, the Flynns, still ate, still cared for their pets, and still passed the time with silly card games. Normal people. Normal lives.

In truth, to an outsider, my own life might appear normal. Zach's suspension was over. He went to school; I went to work. We showered, dressed, ate three meals a day. But, in between these tenants of daily routine, lay the difference that had divided our lives into two distinct spheres: before the arrest and after it.

The sideboard in the carriage house kitchen had previously served as a hodgepodge for stuff, mainly things for the high school, the soccer banquet or senior class trip. The space was now a legal depository for court notices. Yesterday, Zach had received the "official" trial notice. It was a computer-generated form on paper so thin I could see through it. A printer had inserted Zach's name in the defendant space like thousands before him, as if he were just another person and not the kid who laughed at bad jokes, inhaled pumpkin butterscotch muffins, or slept with one foot outside the blanket.

My routine was different too. I grocery shopped at odd hours to avoid people. I no longer frequented HomeGoods or Target, instead shopping online. Twice, I'd turned Donna down for dinner. I never answered Julie's calls but responded with texts that said things like "hanging in there." I'd barely talked to a single person at the few remaining soccer games.

Zach was similarly isolated. He used to be out after school and on weekends. Since the hearing, he'd gone out just twice, both times to get school-related items from Carter. His personality was different too; it was as if my charismatic son had been muted.

Karl dealt the cards for the fifth and final round. Each of the cards depicted a different US. President and, at least once a round, Karl would provide a random fact. Last time, the detail had been about John Adams: "Did you know John Adams wrote over 1,100 letters to his wife?" I didn't.

Karl played the first card; I followed suit. We played in companionable silence; Peter came in halfway through. "Who's winning?"

I glanced up. "This game or overall?"

"Both."

"This game, me. Overall, your Dad."

"I'll catch up," Karl said, playing a card. He picked a replacement and held it up. "Jimmy Carter. He received the Nobel prize, you know. 2002."

Peter laughed. "The benefits of having a history teacher as a Dad."

The game concluded and Karl again marked scores in the tiny notebook. He stood and touched my shoulder. "Thank you, darling. I'm going to catch up next round." He ambled out of the room.

Peter took the seat Karl had vacated. He wore jeans and a navy pullover, his hair gelled slightly at the tips. His feet were bare.

He looked at me. "Hey. Thanks for playing cards with Dad. It's good for him. He's seems more like himself."

I scooped up the cards in a pile. "It's no problem. I enjoy playing. It keeps my mind off things." I paused. I hoped Peter would say something about Zach's case, some big break that would serve as a turning point: we found the girl from the bathroom or a kid saw Zach outside during the attack.

Something.

Anything.

Instead he said, "I have something for you." He stood and pulled his wallet out from his jeans. He sat as he opened it, removed two tickets. "A client gave me these. They're for the Chinese Lantern Festival in couple weeks. You and Zach should go." He extended the tickets in my direction. "It's in Philly."

I glanced at the tickets. "Don't you want to go?"

"Nah. You and Zach should use them."

I'd seen pictures of the festival from prior years, a spectacular display of lights featuring dragons, pagodas, sea creatures, and mythological beings. The event also featured Chinese food booths and artisans. Zach and I would have something to talk about that wasn't the trial, something to put on our calendar beside the dreaded court dates.

I took the tickets and held them a moment. It was a nice gesture, but it made me feel bad, too. Peter had already helped me so much and, here he was again, gifting tickets to a cool one-of-a-kind experience. He should go to the festival, take a date or his mother or someone. I extended the tickets toward him on an outstretched palm. "You should go."

Peter put his hand under mine and moved my fingers, so they curled around the tickets. "I've been to the festival before. Go and take Zach." He met my eyes. "Please." He let go of my hand and sat back.

I shut my eyes. Just when I thought the strong affection I'd felt for Peter the night Karl went missing was the result of stress and fatigue, he'd put the feelings right back in my heart, front and center. I opened my eyes and shifted away from him as if physical distance might lessen my emotion. "Thanks. You're the best."

Peter smiled. "Said no one ever, but you're welcome."

I said goodbye and made my way to the carriage house. Barkley greeted me when I entered, his fat brown paws pressed on my chest. "Hey Bark. Hey, boy." I took my coat off and spied

Zach on the couch, phone in hand. He looked up with the same distant expression he'd had since the preliminary hearing. "Hey."

"Hey hon." I crossed the small space, kissed the top of his head. It was a long shot but maybe having tickets to the festival would cheer him up. It was something different to do. I pulled the tickets out and flashed them. "Mr. Flynn gave us tickets to the Chinese Lantern Festival in Philadelphia."

"Cool." He did not look up. I persevered.

"You've seen pictures, right? Dragons and pagodas all lit up. Tons of Chinese lanterns. Thousands, I heard. It's cool." I paused to let the image take hold. When Zach said nothing, I added, "they have food too."

Zach glanced at me then back at his phone. "Nice."

"I think it will be really fun," I said, willing some measure of emotion into my son.

He looked at me a second time. "I'm sure it will be."

His tone was muted; his expression the opposite of excited. I tried to think of something else to say then stopped myself. I was being ridiculous. Zach was an eighteen year-old boy. He probably wouldn't have cared about the Chinese Lantern Festival even under the best of circumstances and certainly not now. I needed to stop trying to make things seem normal. They weren't normal.

I crossed the room, slid the tickets under a magnet on the fridge. When I turned around, I noticed a cardboard box on the sideboard. "What's this?"

"Dunno. It was on the front step when I got home."

I picked up the box, immediately recognized Julie's handwriting, a sealed note on the top. A present. My mind immediately conjured up fun items that could be in the box. Candy? Bath products? I set aside the note and lifted the lid.

Half a dozen books and pamphlets stared at me from the box. I picked up one with a blue cover and an image of a woman looking in the distance. The title read: *"How to Survive the Jail Sentence of a Loved One."* I scanned through the rest of the titles, the theme the same on them all. Books about coping with a loved one in jail.

I gaped at the books, my heart beating forcefully in my chest. In a quick movement, I swiped Julie's note from the table, slicing the envelope seal with my fingernail. One line: Thought these might help. Love, J.

I was so fixated on the note and the books that I didn't realize Zach was behind me.

He picked up a book. "What are these?"

I glanced at him. "I don't know. Julie, Ms. Kasler, dropped them off."

Zach read the back of the blue book. "Mrs. Kasler gave you these? Why? Does she think I'm going to jail?" He picked up a second book, then dropped it. "Is that what everyone thinks?" He sounded angry, but panicked too. It was almost as if the books made incarceration more likely.

I inhaled a breath before speaking. "Zach, stop. No one thinks that, okay. I don't know why Mrs. Kasler sent these." I put the books back in the box, set the lid on top. "I think she thinks she's being helpful."

"Whatever." Zach looked the closed box then shut his eyes. "I wish I'd never gone to that stupid Halloween party."

I said nothing. I'd thought the same. One night, one sequence of bad choices, had altered the course of our lives.

Zach continued. "I don't even remember half the night. How can I defend myself if I don't remember?"

"I know, Zach. I –" I couldn't think of anything, my motherly well of platitudes dry from exhaustion.

"I'm going to bed."

He clomped up the stairs; I let him go. Emotions were high right now. For both of us.

I sat on the edge of a kitchen chair and put my head in my

hands. Silent tears streaked down my face. I allowed them to fall without restraint until my body emptied. After, I pulled the box of books toward me, lifted them out, one by one. In the last book, one with a gray cover and a couple holding hands through a cell, a blue business card stuck out like a flag. I pulled on it: 'Not Alone, Support for the incarcerated and their families.' I held the card between my thumb and forefinger, it's sharp edges digging into my skin.

Not Alone.

I wanted to no part of a support group like this. I didn't want to sit with other parents or spouses or siblings and discuss the potential jail sentences of our loved ones. And what would be the purpose of the group for Zach? To give him the lowdown about prison? To tell him how to survive? My heart seized. A vision of Zach sitting amongst a group of unsavory looking individuals formed in my mind. I forced it away. Zach wasn't unsavory. Who was to say these men or women would be?

Still.

The concept of jail support was a stark contrast from what I thought Zach would doing his senior year. He was supposed to finalize his college choice, select dorm supplies, and attend a freshman orientation full of silly ice-breaker games. I'd even started collecting quarters for the college washing machines; I didn't want him to run out. I shook my head at the thought. The time when Zach running out of quarters for wash had been a valid concern of mine seemed a lifetime ago.

Would we still make all the college preparations? Pay the deposit, pick the classes, apply for housing? Zach would have to, I realized. The trial was in May. If – when – Zach was exonerated, he'd go to school in the Fall. If not –

I gripped the business card harder. Then, with a sudden decisiveness, I found my purse, pulled out my wallet, stuffed the card inside.

I told myself I wouldn't need it.

36

Two days after receiving the books from Julie, I sat across from Donna at The Roasted Bean, a coffee shop in town. "Julie did not send you those." Donna hit her hand on the table, her mouth a wide "O".

"She did." I blew at my mug, sat back in a heavy chair with faded, well-worn fabric. Of all places in Crasmere, The Roasted Bean was my favorite. Besides the obvious, coffee, I loved the ambience. Dark leather couches, cushy chairs, and end tables with stained-glass lamps filled the space. There was a long coffee bar across one wall, a chalkboard with daily specials in scrawled cursive behind it. Old books sat in stacks on side tables or lined up haphazardly on shelves next to board games in taped up, faded boxes.

"Did she say why?"

"Nope. The note just said 'thought these might help'," I made air quotes as I said the phrase. The recounting of Julie's gift made the shock of it less painful, the focus on Julie's behavior, not the reason behind it.

"Julie can be such a bitch." Donna bit into a thick cookie,

examined it, then took a second bite. "I think there's macadamia in here." She extended the cookie. "Try it."

I took the cookie and bit into it. "Definitely macadamia."

"Did you tell her off?"

"No. She meant well. Julie's prickly, you know. I'm sure she has no idea that sending the books might be seen as offensive." I took a long sip of coffee. Outside, a woman ran behind a giant baby jogger, two tow-headed boys inside.

I looked back to Donna. "You know, it was almost funny. I was all excited when the package was there. I thought it was a present. Then I open it and it's *that*."

Donna snorted. "Oh, my God. That would suck. Knowing you, you thought it was food."

"I thought it was bath products. You know I love a good bath."

Donna took another bite of the cookie, then broke a piece off and put it on my napkin. "Hey. I'll send you a present. A good one." She pulled out her phone and punched at it. "I'm setting a reminder." She looked up. "So, what do you want? Cookies? Vodka?"

I waved at her. "You don't have to send me a present."

"I'm sending one. Last chance for input." She waved her phone around; I shook my head. "Nothing? Vodka it is then."

"You're crazy."

"Like a fox." Donna leaned forward. "So how is the case going? Anything turn up?"

"Nothing tangible. Did I tell you about the girl in the bathroom?"

She straightened. "I don't think so."

I explained about Zach's recollection of being in the bathroom, of the girl he saw in there. "The only feature he remembers distinctly about her is that she had a four-leaf clover tattoo on her calf."

Donna popped the last bite of cookie into her mouth. "Well,

that should make her easy to find."

"You'd think, but none of the kids from the party seem to know anyone with a tattoo. Maybe the tattoo was temporary, or something new, I don't know." I exhaled and fought the panicked feeling that arose whenever I talked too long about Zach's case.

"Crasmere is a pretty small town. If there's a girl with a four-leaf clover tattoo, you'll find her. She might even be here." Donna looked around in an exaggerated gesture.

"Stop it."

"Seriously, she'll turn up."

A young barista in a green apron, Caroline, stepped to our table. "More coffee?" Caroline tipped her head as she asked, a bouncy, black ponytail swung with the movement.

I exchanged a look with Donna, then held up two fingers. "Two, please."

"Okay." Caroline said the word in a way that made it seem that retrieving two coffees would make her day. When she walked away, Donna called after her, "and a second cookie."

Caroline turned and threw us a wide smile, a dimple in her cheek. "Two coffees and a cookie coming right up, ladies."

I watched Caroline disappear behind the coffee bar. She was the type of girl that I would have once thought cute for Zach. I, in that past life, would have mentioned her to him, the happy girl with the swingy ponytail at The Roasted Bean. I might have even suggested he stop in and ask her out.

No way would I do that now. It would seem inappropriate for Zach to date in light of the pending charges. And it would be unlikely that Caroline, or any girl, would go out with him now. I felt anger rise at the thought; Donna spoke before it could take hold.

"Hey, what's up with your friend by the way?"

I looked away from the cute barista. "My friend?"

"The single, hot lawyer. The one you live with?"

"Oh. Peter." I pulled up an image of Peter on the Flynn's porch in his bare feet. I visualized his lopsided smile as he held out the tickets to the lantern festival.

"Yeah, Peter," Donna continued. "Are you setting us up or what?"

"Oh." I sat a moment, stupidly silent, before blurting out, "I'll check with him."

"Good. Let me know. He sounds like a hot piece."

"Yeah, pretty hot." I felt a surge of emotion. I hated the idea of Peter going on a date with Donna. Frankly, I hated the idea of Peter going on a date with anyone. I knew my possessiveness was wrong and unfair and, most likely, one-sided. But I felt it anyway.

"Maybe you could text him now?" She tapped on my phone.

"Right." I stared at the phone, unable and unwilling to pick it up and make the text. "Wait, he's in court today," I lied. "I don't want to interrupt." I stood, swiped the phone from the table. "I have to go to the ladies' room."

I made my way to the small unisex restroom in the corner and slipped inside. I sat on the closed toilet seat, my head in my hands. What was I doing? I had a mess on my hands with Zach and I was jealous about Peter potentially going on a date with Donna? It was ridiculous. It would be good for Peter to get out with someone fun-loving like Donna. God knows Zach and I and our situation had caused him enough stress. I vowed to send the text when I got back to the table.

I stood, put my hands on the pedestal sink, and straightened my arms. A version of myself looked back at me from a streaky oval mirror. My face was gaunt, dark circles noticeable under my eyes. Pieces of hair hung in stringy streaks, though I could have sworn I'd styled it just that morning. I looked exactly like what I was: a sleep-deprived, worried, single mom whose son had been bound over for trial on serious criminal charges.

A knock sounded at the door.

"Just a minute." I gave a last glance to the almost unrecognizable woman in the mirror then stepped back out. I walked toward my seat, around the man who'd been waiting.

Two fresh coffees sat on the table, a new cookie on a napkin in the center. I sat down across from Donna just as a cluster of teenage girls entered the shop. They set overstuffed Jansen backpacks at the door, placed fuzzy, name brand coats on top. I watched as they made their way toward the coffee bar. My heart lurched when I saw the last girl in line. Paige Dixon.

My stomach dropped; panic set in. Was I even allowed to be in the same place as my son's accuser? I inhaled a quick breath and reminded myself that I did not have a restraint against being near Paige, Zach did. I had just as much a right to be at The Roasted Bean as anyone.

I took a sip of my coffee, tried to forget Paige was there. But she stood in my line of vision, and I couldn't help but notice her. She was smaller than I remembered. Paler. She'd pulled back her hair into a severe ponytail.

The girls in line ahead of her spoke animatedly, loudly. I caught snippets of conversation about history, gym, and that weekend's football game. Paige looked uncomfortable in contrast. Nothing like the bubbly kid I'd seen out the window at Reed's uncanny hootenanny.

The thought came to me with a start. Paige looked like Natasha had. My mind pulled up an image of Natasha in our freshman year dorm, after we'd spoken to the Dean of Students about the rape. She'd seemed defeated and ashamed. In the days after, she'd been forgetful and disoriented. She'd pick up a book, then stare out the window. She'd ask to meet for lunch then fail to show up. She forgot a test, then a paper, then dropped out entirely.

Donna's hand tapped mine. "What is it? You look super pale."

I shook my head, glanced at Paige, then pushed back my chair. "Don, sorry, I have to go." I gathered my coat and purse.

She stared at me. "Um. We came together."

"Oh. Right. I'll meet you outside." I walked to the door.

Donna called after me. "Rude."

I walked a block away from The Roasted Bean and leaned on a brick wall in between a card store and a bicycle shop. The latter advertised a pre-Christmas special, a family display of bikes in a window sprayed with fake snow. I crossed my arms and looked at The Roasted Bean, willing Donna to come out. I hoped she didn't recognize Paige or that she wouldn't say anything if she did. I never knew with Donna.

I shut my eyes, took three deep breaths. When I opened them, Donna was hurrying toward me, takeout cups in her hand.

She thrust one in my direction. "What happened?"

"Paige Dixon was in there."

Donna looked back at The Roasted Bean, then at me. "So."

I didn't respond.

Donna leaned on one leg. "Don't tell me you're intimidated by a teenager?"

"I'm not intimidated, okay. I'm just in a weird headspace right now." I took a last glance at The Roasted Bean then walked. Donna fell in step next to me. After a few steps, I stopped. "She didn't look right."

Donna threw me a quizzical look.

"Paige. She looked sad, different. Like something happened."

Donna looked down for a moment, then back at me. "Maybe something did happen," she said. "It doesn't mean Zach did it."

"Yeah. I know. I just – I just feel bad for her, you know."

Donna shook her head. "You can't feel bad for her, Meredith. She – "

I stamped my foot. “What if she got attacked? What if Zach did it?” I clamped my hand over my mouth, wished I hadn’t said the words out loud.

Donna shook her head. “He didn’t.” She pointed at me. “That’s your position as his mother and that doesn’t change.” She turned her head and looked directly in my eyes. “Every mother puts their own child first. That’s just the way it is. It’s natural. All animals do that.”

“Animals?” We started walking again.

“Yeah. Crocodiles carry their babies in their mouth to protect them. Not that I’m saying you should do that.”

“Obviously.”

“I’m just saying Moms need to protect their own. Paige Dixon has her own mother, you need to protect Zach.”

We reached my car. “Alright. Fine. I won’t worry about Paige.” I handed Donna my coffee cup, dug into my purse.

Donna leaned against the car, blew out a breath.

I felt around for my keys, couldn’t find them. Honestly. My purse wasn’t that big. I felt something metal, pulled out a pen.

“Mer.” Donna tapped me on the shoulder.

“What?” I asked. I opened my purse and looked inside. The key were in the side pocket. No wonder I couldn’t find them.

“Mer, look.”

I held up the keys. “Got them.”

“Meredith.” Her tone was harsh now, almost urgent. “Look.”

I looked up, followed Donna’s line of vision to a teenage girl locking her bicycle. “And?”

“Do you see?” Donna whispered.

I started at the direction of the girl with a blank look; Donna physically moved my head downward.

The girl bent down to pick up a bag. She had on half-tights, the bottoms of her legs visible. I saw it then; my breath caught.

On the girl’s calf was a four-leaf clover tattoo.

37

Peter

One week after Meredith spotted her, Darby Brooks, aka the girl with the four-leaf clover tattoo, sat in the office conference room. Nervous energy coursed through my body; I'd never been part of a witness interview before. I tapped my pen, a nervous habit; Bo shot me a look. I set the pen down and took in Darby.

Darby Brooks was, in every sense, the polar opposite of Paige Dixon. Rather than preppy, Darby gave off an emo vibe. She wore all black except for the silver chains that hung, different lengths, down her chest. Her nose, ears, and lips featured multiple piercings. Her hair, dyed jet black, hung straight down, its ends uneven and spiky. Fuchsia socks peeked out the tops to heavy, black boots with thick laces.

Meeting at the office had been Darby's idea. She wanted to talk somewhere "official". Though there was nothing more official about the legal office than any other venue, Bo didn't argue.

After she'd established Darby was eighteen and after the introductory niceties, Bo swiped a pack of crackers from a bowl she'd set out prior to the meeting. The bag opened with a pop.

Bo pulled out an orange square, then a second. But for the crunching, it was silent. I waited. Maybe this is how interviews went? I didn't know.

Darby grabbed a bag of chocolate chip minis. The women continued to eat in silence until, finally, Bo extracted three pictures of Zach from the file: his senior portrait, one from Halloween, and a candid of him standing in front of a backyard pond with koi. Bo slid the pictures over to Darby. "Is this the boy you saw?"

Darby scarcely looked at the photos. "That's him."

Bo lifted an eyebrow. "How can you be so sure?"

"I know because I saw him." Darby reached in the snack bag and pulled out another cookie. She popped it in her mouth, chewed, then swallowed. "I knew most of the kids at that party," she continued, "but I'd never seen this kid before. It made him easy to remember, you know."

"Even though he was in costume?" Bo sat back and adjusted her shirt.

Darby tapped on Zach's graduation picture. "I remember his hair, the cowlick." She pointed to her own hair. "Plus, he told me his name."

I sat up. "He did?"

Darby nodded. "He said his name was Zach."

"Tell me about when you saw Zach," Bo continued.

Darby recounted that Zach was on the floor of the bathroom when she came in. Other than Zach saying his name, they didn't converse. She didn't mention what Zach did, that she'd shot something in her arm. My heart sank at the omission; it made Darby seem less credible.

Bo followed up with specific questions about what Darby did before and after she was in the bathroom. The people she'd seen, the conversations she'd had. She asked more specifics about Zach. Was he disheveled? Did he seem drunk? Just when I thought Bo had exhausted one line of inquiry, she'd start another, dutifully recording Darby's recollections in a black, spiral notebook. Finally, she asked, "do you remember the time you saw Zach in the bathroom?"

My breath caught. I leaned forward. The question was pivotal. According to the criminal complaint, Olivia Wade, the prosecution's main witness, had told the police the attack took place at 11:39. Zach needed to be somewhere else at that time.

Darby didn't answer. Instead, she reached down, unzipped her backpack, and pulled out a phone. I started at her. Why wasn't she answering? I gave Bo a look over Darby's bent head. She shrugged.

"Do you remember what time you saw Zach?" Bo repeated.

"Hold up," Darby said. She examined her phone, punching at it with skilled fingers.

Come on. Come on.

Finally, she looked up. "11:36."

"You saw him at 11:36?" Bo confirmed.

"Yes."

"How can you be so precise?"

Darby slid her sweater downward over her shoulder, revealing a round, white object, the size of a quarter, on her upper arm. She pointed at it. "I'm diabetic," she explained. "This is my glucose monitoring device." Darby pulled up her sweater and continued. "It tells me when my blood sugar is low. If it gets too low, it sounds an alarm."

"Did the alarm go off? On the night of the party?"

"Yeah. That's why I went to the bathroom. I didn't know anyone was in there, but I couldn't wait, you know. I needed insulin."

Bo leaned forward. "And how did you remember that time?"

Darby lifted up her phone. "I record the times I take insulin shots on an app."

"Can I see that?" Bo asked. Darby handed her the phone.

She held it out so I could see. Darby had made a clear record. She had given herself an insulin shot on October 18th, 11:36 p.m.

"Does the time sync with your phone?" I asked. "Or do you enter it manually?"

"I enter the time," Darby said. "But I look at my phone before I do it. It's supposed to be correct, you know? There'd be no point in doing it otherwise."

I nodded. "Makes sense."

Bo gave me a near imperceptible nod.

Relief flooded my body. I wasn't a trial attorney but, from what I could tell, Darby Brooks was a good witness, a valid one. She had reason to remember Zach and reason to know the precise time she saw him. And she'd recorded the time on an app. I couldn't wait to tell Meredith.

Bo asked follow-up questions then said. "I think that's it." She looked to me. "Anything I missed?"

I shook my head. "No. I think you covered it."

"Anything else you think we should know, Darby?" Bo asked.

Darby stood, picked up a heavy backpack, then stopped. "You guys know about the sex club, right?"

38

Sex club? I looked at Bo.

She was already shaking her head. "I don't know about the sex club," she acknowledged.

Darby sat back down. "It's a challenge. The kids in it get different points for different sex acts. I don't know all the details." She paused, then held her hands up. "I'm not in it."

I looked at Bo, her eyebrows arched, a mirror of my own. Under ordinary circumstances, the idea of a sex club would repel me; instead, I was thrilled. The existence of a sex club would give motive for someone else to assault Paige. It had to play into reasonable doubt.

Bo maintained a neutral expression. "And were any of these kids from the sex club at the party?"

Darby nodded. "Some were. I mean, again, I don't know that much about it."

"Could you give me names?" Bo already had a pen in her hand.

Darby rattled off five or six names. No Zach. Thank God.

Bo asked more questions. Did Darby know if there were points for assault? Did she hear anyone brag about an encounter with Paige? Had she seen any of the kids in it on the upper floor near the time of the attack?

Darby wasn't lying when she said she didn't know much. It didn't matter. Bo had enough leads to find out more.

After a few final questions, Bo thanked Darby again, asked if she could call if she had further questions. Darby agreed and picked up her backpack. A group of key-chains dangled from the zipper; they bumped against the material as she walked toward the door. When it shut behind her, I turned to Bo. She threw me a wide grin. "I think we may have just found our reasonable doubt."

As expected, Meredith and Zach were ecstatic about the Darby interview. Nate had set a post-Thanksgiving meeting to discuss the case. The beginning of the end? God, I hoped so. The old Meredith, the one without heavy dark circles under her eyes, the one whose conversations weren't peppered with pregnant, worried pauses, was back. Just the day before, she'd told me a Thanksgiving-themed joke while mucking a horse stall.

"Why did the police arrest the turkey?" She'd held the pitchfork upright and waited for my answer.

I waited a moment. "Okay. You got me. I don't know. Why did the police arrest the turkey?"

"Because they suspected fowl play!"

I bumped my head with my hand. "Please do not tell that joke at Thanksgiving tomorrow."

Meredith smiled. "Oh, I'm telling it," she said, continuing to muck. "And I have more where that came from."

I laughed. "I can only imagine."

Mom had asked Meredith and Zach to come to my Aunt Leigh's and Uncle Mason's for the annual Harrison Thanksgiving. I didn't think she'd say yes, but it was Reed's year with his girls and Lara still held all the cards on that front. Her parents were in England; she and Zach had nowhere to go.

I had mixed feelings about Meredith and Zach coming to the Harrison Thanksgiving. It wasn't that I didn't want to spend time with them. But the event was over-the-top crazy. The centerpiece of the festivities, beside food, were the annual Thanksgiving Olympics. The challenges had initially been a mastermind of the mothers, a way to keep young kids active. But, as the kids morphed into teens, then adults, the contest took on a new level of intensity. I'd tried to explain the dynamic to Meredith.

"You play competitive lawn games on Thanksgiving?"

"Yes. I know it sounds stupid, but the whole thing has gotten super cut-throat."

She'd thrown me an amused expression.

"Seriously, some of my relatives are like those crazy Little League Dads. I'm telling you, it's intense."

She reached out and touched my arm, a mock serious expression on her face. "I promise Zach and I will be prepared."

My face reddened. "I just didn't want you to be caught by surprise, like wear a dress or something."

She held up a hand. "Zach and I will dress to compete."

True to her word, Zach and Meredith dressed for competition on Thanksgiving. Both wore old jeans, running shoes, and athletic sweatshirts. Meredith snapped a rubber band on her wrist at me. "To put my hair up during challenges."

"Glad you're prepared," I said, smiling.

The dynamic, the feel, was so different with Meredith than it had been with Sadie. Sadie hated the Harrison Thanksgiving. Her Thanksgivings growing up had been formal affairs with real china, wine, and Sunday best clothes. She'd never embraced the paper plates or casual attire and, for the first few years, insisted on getting dressed up, heels sinking into the lawn as she walked. She'd only once participated in the games.

Mom spent the car ride over filling Meredith and Zach in on the people they would meet. Once at the Harrisons, we made our way up the driveway laden with Tupperware containers of our annual meal contributions: cucumber dip, fresh baked rolls, and chocolate cake.

It was a perfect day. A near cloudless blue sky and a bright sun made it seem hotter than the mid-fifties. There was a gentle breeze, enough to blow stray leaves and make it feel like fall.

We rounded the back of the property. I spied pumpkin cutouts for the ball toss, a giant tarp for the greased ham challenge. Looming from the deck stood the immense scoreboard one of my cousins had constructed a few years back. He'd divided the board in two – Team Turkey on one side, Team Stuffing on the other.

We reached the edge of the patio. Mom guided Dad toward a circle of people. I stood on the outskirts with Meredith and Zach, suddenly graceless. I'd never been great with large gatherings, never understood how some people could so seamlessly flit in and out. Meredith and Zach's presence magnified my standard discomfort.

"Let's get drinks," I said finally. We made our way to a cooler and stood in a circle. I felt a pair of hands squeeze my shoulders.

"Peter."

I turned. "Dex." I shook Dex's hand and breathed a sigh of relief. Of all the people for Meredith and Zach to meet first, Dex would be a good one. He was easy to talk to, didn't take himself too seriously. "Hey." I rapped him on the shoulder. "How've you been?"

"I'm good. I'm good. You? You look like you lost like thirty pounds." He hit my belly lightly with an open hand.

"Eh. Something like that." I pointed toward Meredith and Zach but, before I could introduce them, Dex leaned into Meredith.

"Don't tell me you got roped into dating this joker." He jerked his thumb toward me.

Meredith smiled. "I'm Meredith," she shook his hand. "This is my son, Zach."

I waited for her to correct Dex's assumption about being my girlfriend. She didn't. I opened my mouth to set the record straight, Meredith was a friend, not a girlfriend, but I didn't. I'd endured enough terrible Thanksgivings with Sadie. If Dex, or any of my other relatives, assumed I had a beautiful date, what did it matter? It wasn't like she would see them again.

The rest of the mingling period and the dinner passed less painfully than I'd remembered from years past. Dad seemed his old self, Mom was in her element, and both Zach and Meredith fit right in. I couldn't believe how fast the time passed when I didn't have to endure Sadie's crossed arms and eye rolls.

During dinner, Dex clinked his glass and stood. "Time to announce this year's Thanksgiving Olympic teams."

Meredith gave me a sideways glance and rubbed her hands together as if she'd been awaiting the moment all day.

Dex continued in the voice of a game show host. "Uncle Mason. Time to announce Team Turkey."

Uncle Mason stood with a list of team members. Aunt Leigh held up this year's t-shirt, green with the words Team Turkey on the front, a decal of a turkey running underneath. As Mason read the names, Leigh passed out the shirts. Mason announced Meredith's name, then Zach's. They half-raised their hands and Liz came by with their t-shirts. "Welcome to Team Turkey."

I didn't get called for Team Turkey; Meredith leaned into me. "Rivals," she whispered.

Once the teams assembled, we met outside for game one, the Pumpkin Toss. I spotted Meredith amongst the Team Turkey teammates, Zach in line as a participant.

The afternoon continued. Dex and I got edged out in the three-legged sack race. He pushed me forward to compete in a new game, Shake Your Tail Feathers. "I'm not doing that," he'd said.

I didn't know what the game entailed, but I spied Meredith in line for Team Turkey and took a place next to her.

"I'm going to win this," she mouthed.

"No," I said, my face deadpan. "I'm a professional."

Uncle Mason handed me a shoebox with a belt. There was an opening in the back, a massive amount of colorful feathers inside. I held it out to Meredith as if I knew exactly what it was. "Yeah. See. And this is my box of feathers."

She held up her own. "Yup. I got one too."

Uncle Mason explained. We were supposed to belt on the boxes and shake. The first person to empty all the feathers from the box won. I visualized how ridiculous I would look, felt a flash of regret. Then I glanced at Meredith. She examined the box, smiling. She looked up at me. "You're going down, Flynn."

I made a mock serious face and belted on my shoebox. "Don't be so sure," I said. "I've been practicing on the sly." I wiggled my hips. Meredith laughed.

"Okay," Mason yelled, his hand up. "Shake your tail feathers in three, two, one." He jerked his arm downward.

We jumped, feathers flying. The movement felt awkward. I stole a glance at Meredith who had perfected a kind of jump wiggle. She should have looked ridiculous; she looked adorable instead. Her ponytail flew as she jumped, her cheeks pink from the cold. I watched her a moment, transfixed, until Dex yelled out. "Come on, Flynn. Eyes off the girl."

I averted my gaze, hoped my face didn't turn red, and jumped. Meredith saw me and intensified her own efforts, feathers flying out the back.

Mason leaned forward, clapping with intensity. "Come on, Meredith, you got this!" She seemed to be in the lead, members of Team Turkey joined Mason in the cheers.

It struck me as funny then, the whole thing. I laughed as I

jumped and lost my momentum. I tried to maintain my composure but couldn't. It was just too ridiculous.

"Come on, Pete!" Dex yelled. "Get back in it!"

Dex's cheer made me laugh harder. Meredith saw me; laughed too.

"Concentrate, Meredith," Mason yelled.

Like Dex's cheer, Mason's instruction made Meredith laugh harder, feathers flew out less rapidly. Then, in an intense effort, she jumped a dozen times a row, her final feather flew out and zig-zagged to the ground. Her teammates cheered.

I picked up the final feather, tapped her on the arm. "Beginner's luck."

She smiled, pointed to the turkey on the shirt. "Team Turkey is on the rise."

"Careful what you wish for. Between Zach's pumpkin toss and your performance right there, the two of you will be locked into coming here forever."

Meredith looked around. "That's fine with me. This had been one of my favorite Thanksgivings."

I swallowed. "Me too. It's nice to have you and Zach here." I looked down, hoping the words had sounded casual.

When I looked up, she was smiling at me. "I can't tell you what a nice break this has been," she said. "It feels like things are almost back to normal, you know?" She gestured toward Zach, who was throwing a football with two members of Team Turkey. "He's more himself, too."

I looked toward Zach as he threw the ball. He had seemed more relaxed today than he had been the past few times I'd seen him. His face was no longer hollow, his demeanor more lighthearted. He still didn't talk much, but his silence seemed more borne out of politeness than stress. I looked back to Meredith. "He's a good kid."

She shut her eyes, opened them. "He is."

Before either of us could say anything further, Huey called

for the greased ham challenge. Meredith and I watched as our respective teams worked to push a greased ham across a tarp to their score line. Team Stuffing won the event, but Team Turkey won overall. Mason called his team over for a picture. Meredith handed me her phone. "Take one for me."

"Sure." I waited as the team gathered. Zach and Meredith stood in the back smiling, arms slung around their teammates as though they'd been coming to the Harrison Thanksgiving all their lives. I took the shot, stared at it on the still screen after. Would this be a one-year thing? Or was Meredith back for good?

I handed Meredith back the phone.

I really hoped it was the latter.

39

Meredith

I walked down Crasmere's Main Street, transformed since the Thanksgiving holiday a week before. White lights wound around three-pronged green lampposts, wreaths with red bows centered at the tops. Decorated greens framed most store doors, potted Christmas trees out front. Garlands with white snowflakes ran across the street on wires. The snowflakes lit up each night, illuminating the dark, winter sky.

I made my way down the street, feeling more normal than I had in weeks. Yvonne Williams, the deputy district attorney assigned to the case for Zach's trial, had set up a conference call with Nate for that afternoon. Nate thought their investigator had found out about Darby. I hoped, believed really, that the meeting would end with the prosecution agreeing to drop the charges. Now that Zach had an alibi, how could they possibly proceed? That the whole ordeal was practically over put me in an almost euphoric mood. The hard knots in my shoulder were gone, my jaw no longer clenched. The night before, I'd had my first uninterrupted sleep in weeks.

I pulled open the door to Katie's Closet, a funky store with one-of-a-kind jewelry, handmade scarves, and unique vintage clothing. I picked up a pair of hand knitted gloves with stripes the color of a rainbow. Would Donna like those? Maybe. I set the gloves down and looked at the matching hat, one with a puffy, purple pom-pom on top. She would definitely like that. I could picture her in it, bustling around in the cold weather, pom-pom bouncing in time with her steps. The hat and gloves had just the right amount of whimsy but were practical too. I bought both; the clerk wrapped them in thick red paper, adorned the package with a giant white bow.

I carried out the box with satisfaction, thinking of Donna. I hadn't seen or talked to her since before Thanksgiving. My failure to follow up had been thoughtless. She'd been worried about sharing the holiday with Max. For all Donna had supported me these past weeks, I should have checked in.

The Katie's Closet bag swung on my elbow as I made my way down the street. I spied the Crasmere Chocolatier across the way, a giant chocolate Santa in its window. On a whim, I crossed the street, entered, and ordered a box of the chocolate-covered pretzels. I'd surprise Donna with the gift and pretzels on the way home, leave a note if she wasn't there.

I drove to Donna's with the festive packages on my passenger seat and Christmas songs blaring on the radio. *All I Want for Christmas is You* sounded through the car. I recalled Reed singing the song on a car trip to see his parents the year before. His deep baritone had contrasted with Mariah Carey's melodious voice in a way that was comical. I remembered laughing, trying to sing along too.

I fingered the engagement ring, unsure how I felt about Reed anymore. We talked on the phone or met for meals once or twice a week. The encounters, whether on the phone or in person, were awkward. My thoughts were consumed with Zach, and Reed barely asked about him. We filled the gaps in conversation with recaps of sports games or non-inflammatory political discussions.

The tense times with Reed contrasted to relaxed ones with Peter — feeding the horses, eating his mother's home-cooked meals, laughing about old times. If I thought about either Reed or Peter too long, my emotions became jumbled and confused which, given the situation with Zach, was the last thing I needed. So, as much as I could I pushed thoughts of them to the recesses of my brain and focused on the only person that mattered right now: Zach.

Donna's small colonial loomed ahead with festive colored lights and a blow-up Santa she'd had since our kids were small. I felt a happy anticipation as I stepped out, packages in hand. I stamped on a tree-themed doormat and rang the bell. Owen opened the door.

"Hey Owen."

He nodded at me but didn't speak. I stepped in the foyer and pulled open the front closet for my coat. Giant rolls of Christmas-themed wrapping paper spilled out. I shook my head and tucked them back inside. Knowing Donna, the wrapping rolls had been there since last year's sales.

I caught Owen's expression when I turned around. Confused? Upset? "All okay there, O?"

He started at me, eyes wide. "Let me get my Mom."

"I can get her, hon," I stepped past him into the family room, made a mental note to ask Donna what was going on. Maybe Thanksgiving hadn't gone well. I cursed myself for not checking in sooner.

I moved to the bottom of the stairs. "Don, it's me." No answer. "I come bearing gifts." Still nothing. She was probably in the shower. Or getting dressed.

I set her gifts on the coffee table and looked around the familiar space, already decorated for Christmas. Fat colored lights adorned a white spruce in the corner, a hodgepodge of ornaments hung from thick branches. I moved toward the tree and looked more carefully at the little paper Santas and Snowmen, clearly made by Owen and Carter during the preschool years. Each of these had a square school picture glued to the center, a festive curled ribbon at the top for hanging. So little then. Tiny, happy babies.

I fingered a Christmas tree constructed from sprayed-green popsicle sticks. Above it hung the ceramic snowman I'd made during a huge winter storm. The school district had cancelled classes; Zach and I braved the weather to get to Donna's. The boys spent the morning creating an arsenal of snowballs for a fight with the neighbors. While they were out, Donna and I made salt dough for handmade Christmas ornaments; we figured it would be a fun activity for the boys. They had no interest, so she and I passed the afternoon drinking wine and decorating cookie cutter shaped decorations with paint, glitter, and ribbon. That night, Zach and Donna's boys ate hot dogs and watched Christmas specials while Max made us a meal "fit for queens." I smiled at the memory.

"What are you doing in my house?" Donna's voice boomed in a manner so different from how she normally spoke, I assumed she was kidding.

I held up the little snowman. "Stealing this valuable ornament, of course." I hung it back on the tree.

"Psst." She made a spitting noise, crossed the room, and grabbed the ornament from the tree. She thrust it in my direction. "Take it."

I stood back and studied her. Was she joking? "I have gifts." I gestured to the presents on the coffee table.

She didn't look.

"What's wrong?"

"What's wrong?" She put her hand on her hips and bugged her eyes out.

"Yes. There's clearly something wrong. What is it?"

She didn't answer.

"Look, I'm sorry I didn't call before Thanksgiving. It was thoughtless. I'm sorry." I paused. "Did it go alright?"

"It went fine, thanks. Time to go." She took a step toward the front door.

I crossed my arms, rooted my feet to the floor. "I'm not leaving until you tell me what's going on."

She tilted her head, a quizzical look in her eyes. "You seriously don't know."

"No. I don't."

She picked her phone up from a side table, pulled something up, and handed me the device. "I got this from the principal. Bo Brooker – remember her? – she's apparently poking around, she wants names of the kids involved."

I scanned the email then looked up, confused. "But this is about the sex club."

Donna said nothing; I realized the implication. "The boys?"

She pursed her lips. "Just Owen. I didn't know. But Max has the list now. I'm sure he gave it to his lawyer. They'll use it against me, you know. They'll use it in court."

"Oh, Donna –"

"Don't even." She held her hand out. "Because that's not the only thing. Bo's been asking the boys more questions. The implication seems to be that, since they were dressed like Zach, one of them did it. That you would stoop so low as to try to pin this on one of my boys. It's unforgivable."

I took a step back. I didn't know Bo was talking to the school principal or interviewing Donna's boys. "I –"

She held out her hand. "Stop." She crossed the room, pulled something from her purse, and handed it to me.

I looked at it, a photograph of Owen and Carter in the Halloween costumes from that night. They stood in front of a bonfire, arms slung around each other shoulders. She pulled the picture from my hand and flipped it over. "See that?" she said, pointed to a date and time on the back. “My boys weren’t near that girl at the time of the attack. Witnesses back them too. They were outside, Meredith.” She crossed her arms.

I held out the photo. “Donna. I –”

She waved at the picture. “Keep it. Show it to Bo. I have copies, believe me. You never know when you’re going to have to defend your own, you know?” She moved to the door and pulled it open.

I opened my mouth; no sound came out. Was this really happening? Did Donna honestly believe I was trying to get Owen or Carter in trouble?

She held her hand out toward the step. “You need to leave.”

I pulled my coat out of the closet, tubes of wrapping paper spilled out. “I –” I started and took a step outside. “I didn’t know,” I finally blurted but the door shut behind me and I didn’t know if she’d heard. “I didn’t know,” I said again, a whisper. I walked to my car in a daze, bits of the conversation whirring in my mind.

I slid into the driver’s seat and started the engine. I exhaled. Best to let her calm down. I could make it clear later that I’d never suggested that Bo investigate Carter and Owen, that I didn’t know who was in the sex club.

I pulled to a stop at a traffic light when my phone pinged with a text message. I shook my head. It was probably Donna, calling to further insult me. I glanced at my phone just as the light turned green.

The text was from Nate: Just got off the phone with Yvonne Williams. Call me.

40

My heart pounded. Nate had just gotten off the phone with Yvonne. He wanted me to call him. Good news? It had to be.

I swung the wheel of the car toward the entrance of a strip mall. I hadn't put on my directional; the man in the car behind me blared his horn. I held up a hand. Sorry. But not sorry! Don't you know, guy? I'm about to wake up from a nightmare.

A twinge of excitement fluttered in my chest as I reached for my phone. The case was almost over. I could feel it. My life would no longer be on hold. That foreboding feeling that something terrible was around the bend? Gone. I could make up with Donna, figure out my love life, help Zach plan for his freshman year in college. Everything would go back to normal.

I dialed Nate.

He answered, spoke without a greeting. "Um, Meredith."

I'd expected his first words to be 'good news' or 'guess what?' 'Um Meredith?' It wasn't a good start.

"So I talked to Yvonne."

Nate paused, the silence excruciating. A woman exited the CVS, a baby in her arms. *Come on, Nate.*

"She knows about Darby," he said finally. "They did their own investigation."

He paused. Too long. "And?" I prompted.

"They say she's unreliable and that she could have easily put any time in her app."

"But her insulin? Why would she –"

"I know. I told them." Nate sounded genuinely dejected. He continued, the rest of his words passing in blurry misery. Evidently, Darby had lied to protect a friend in a police investigation the year before. And, now, the prosecution had a second eyewitness, a boy who said he saw Zach in the hall outside the bedroom at the time of the attack. Yvonne would not consider dropping the charges, under any circumstance, she'd apparently told Nate. She did make a plea offer.

"So," Nate said, stumbling over his words, "if Zach pleads guilty to sexual assault and attempted rape, they would agree to a four-year jail sentence."

Nate paused. I didn't, couldn't, speak.

"But he'd have to register as a sex offender." Nate said this last sentence quickly, as if he hoped I'd miss it.

"Why would he agree to that?" I spat out the words.

"It's four years, maybe less. If he's convicted at trial, he could get as many as ten."

"Ten years." I repeated the words. "Ten years for one incident that he doesn't even remember. If he even did it."

I squeezed my eyes shut; the number whirled in my mind. Ten years. Zach would be nearly thirty by the time he got out. But four years? It wasn't much better. Instead of four years in college, Zach would spend four years in jail. What then? Would he enroll at age twenty-two, a convicted felon? He'd have to tell colleges when he applied. Hell. He'd have to tell everyone. With registration, he'd be a sex offender for life.

Zach in jail, marked forever.

This could not be the outcome.

"What if we can prove Darby entered the right time? Or what about bringing up the sex club. That's reasonable doubt, right?" My throat felt dry; I touched it.

"We'll try to do that of course. We'll keep trying. We'll keep investigating. This isn't over. Zach doesn't have to take the plea."

I exhaled. Right. We didn't have to take it. We didn't have to accept a four-year jail sentence.

"Meredith."

The sound of my name brought me back to the present.

"I called you first as a courtesy, but Zach's the client. I have to call him and ask if he wants to accept the offer."

"He won't accept it," I said, the mother in me rising to the surface with force. "No way."

"I have to ask him."

"Fine, but can you wait until tomorrow? I'd like to talk to him first."

"Ummm –"

"I need to be the one to tell my son, Nate. He thinks this is almost over. We both did."

Another pause. "Okay," Nate said finally. "But I'm calling him in the morning."

"He'll be in school."

Nate exhaled. "Afternoon then. But tomorrow."

I pressed the off button. Sensations of dread, thick like mud, poured back into my body. More months of worry, stress, and wondering. More months of nightmarish dreams of Zach in jail. More guilt about Paige and what she may be going through. I tipped my head back against the car seat. How would I cope until May? It was barely December.

I opened my purse and slipped my phone inside. As it slid to the bottom, I spied the edge of the bright blue business card peeking from my wallet, the one Julie had given me with the books. I pulled on it and read the words. *Not Alone.* My eyes fell to the address. It was less than an hour's drive.

As if some force outside my body was operating my limbs, I punched the address into Maps and followed the directions. My purpose, even to myself, was unclear. What would I do when I got there? I had no idea. But it wouldn't hurt to check out the space. Maybe it would be open, maybe I could find out more. The bit of a plan, even if it was just to drive to an address, calmed my nerves. With everything suddenly out of control, at least I was doing something.

I blindly followed the instructions until I pulled in front of a house on a tree-lined side street. 129. This was it. I navigated the van into a space across and looked at the structure, a narrow, two-story house with bright yellow siding and blue shutters. Near identical houses in more muted hues buttressed the home on either side. A wrought-iron gate siphoned the dwelling from a cracked sidewalk in front, a mailbox with a crooked wreath on its edge. The front of the residence featured a large stoop, and I pictured the owner sitting on it as a summer evening slid into night, lemonade in hand. Then, as if to complete the vision, a white-haired woman emerged from the doorframe, a bright red purse on the crook of her arm. She wore sturdy white sneakers.

Was this the right place? I checked the number on the card. 129. This was it. I looked again at the woman. She didn't present as a person who would know someone involved in the criminal system. Then again, I probably didn't either. What exactly would that person look like anyway?

The woman ambled down the steps, using a side banister for support. She peered at my car, made eye contact, then gave a small wave.

I sat there. I should just pull out and leave. But there was a kindness about the woman's features that kept me in place. I stepped out of the car.

The woman met my eyes. "Not Alone?" Her voice was kind.

I gave an almost imperceptible nod.

She waved a veiny hand in my direction. "Come on in, dear. Let's get a cup of tea." She waited at the bottom of the step.

"Weren't you going somewhere?" I gestured to her clothing.

"Nothing I can't do later. I'm Phyllis, by the way."

"Meredith."

"Nice to meet you, Meredith." Phyllis started back up the stairs. I followed, then stopped. It seemed unwise to follow a stranger, even an elderly one, into an unknown home.

Phyllis held open the door. "It's fine, dear," she said.

There was something about her voice, grandmotherly and warm, that compelled me forward. I followed Phyllis down a narrow hallway to a small galley kitchen with a round table at its end. Plants lined a window with a sun catcher in its center, the light from it creating small rainbows on the wall. She pulled out a kettle and filled it with water. "If you have a moment, I'll tell the story of Not Alone."

Curious, I sat at the table.

"My husband was convicted of embezzlement forty years ago," Phyllis started. "When he was arrested, our kids were eight, six, and two. I'd never worked outside the home before. No one considers that, you know. When Don went to jail, our family, me and three kids, we were without an income." She pulled two bright mugs from a cabinet. "But there was no sympathy. It wasn't like Don had been sick or died. No one seemed to care. I felt like a pariah."

She set the mugs down and fished around a second cabinet.

"One day, I was here in Trenton for a meeting with the IRS about taxes." She shook her head. "After that IRS meeting, a woman, Rae, approached me. Rae's husband was in jail too." Phyllis smiled. "Rae and I leaned on each other, gave each other the support society doesn't have for families of the incarcerated. I don't know what I would have done without her." Phyllis paused. "Long story short, we started this group to help others like us."

A lump formed in my throat. I felt a kinship with Phyllis already. Someone who understood, who knew how it felt to be embroiled in a legal proceeding over which you had no control. "My son's been arrested," I whispered.

The kettle whistled. Phyllis took it off the stove and filled waiting mugs with steaming water. "I'm sorry."

The simplicity of the statement struck me. I'd become accustomed to shocked faces and open mouths, to the inevitable question: "what for?" Though others had expressed sorrow for my plight, the sentiment had always been bound with questions and veiled judgments. Phyllis seemed only sorry.

She put the steaming tea in front of me and sat down. "How are you coping?"

"Not so well. I thought it was over. Long story, but I thought the whole nightmare was over. Then the attorney called, and it's not. It's not."

Phyllis put her hand on top of mine, said nothing.

I took a deep breath and shared the sequence of events since the Halloween party. "What should I do?" I whispered after recounting the story. "I don't know anyone who's been through this. What do people do when this happens?"

Phyllis got up, opened a small drawer, pulled out a rectangular card, and handed it to me. "If it seems likely Zach will go to jail, here are some recommended steps to prepare."

I scanned the list. Medical and dental exams. Stocking up on medication. Putting aside funds for the commissary. Arranging magazine subscriptions. Strangely, some items were identical to those on college preparation checklists.

I looked up. "What about Zach? How should he prepare? I mean, I've looked on the internet but --" I couldn't finish my sentence.

Phyllis picked up the card she'd given me and turned it over. She pointed to a notation about a support group. "Have Zach go. People in that group, they've been through it. They'll know."

I stared at the dates; the entire scenario felt surreal.

"It's strange to be in a world you know nothing about," Phyllis said, reading my mind. "I remember." She looked thoughtful for a moment. "Can I give you some advice?"

"Of course."

"Your son hasn't been convicted. He might not be. Keep the faith. Prepare the best you can but, outside of that, live your life." She took a piece of paper, jotted down her phone number, and handed it to me. "Now I can't tell you everything will be alright because I don't know that. I can tell you that you are no longer alone in this."

I thanked Phyllis and left. Her story permeated my mind on the drive home. To be without an income and responsible for three young children? For a crime she didn't commit? It would be awful. And forty years ago, there was no internet, no source of instant information. Nor would it be, I supposed, easy to get a decent paying job as a woman with no experience. Phyllis had turned her tragedy into hopeful assistance for an underserved population, families of the accused. No one thought about them, it seemed. I hadn't. Not until now.

As I edged closer to home, my thoughts switched from Phyllis to Zach. I knew the feeling of possessing information that, once disclosed, would tilt the axis of Zach's world. I'd felt the same way after Noah had died. I recalled standing outside then seven-year-old Zach's door watching him build a Lego structure in the shape of a blocky monster. His small hands placed one piece on top of another, his father still alive in his mind. I hadn't wanted to break the illusion. I felt the same way now.

I pulled up the driveway. I could make out Zach's frame at

the kitchen table, his laptop illuminated, a textbook open on one side, a can of pineapple Fanta on the other. He pushed his hair away from his forehead and leaned back, a telltale sign he was thinking. After a moment, he took a sip of soda and started to type.

Still looking at Zach, I pushed open the car door, my arms and legs heavy like weights. I stepped out and stood; a barn cat skittered in my path. I jumped and watched the cat race after a squirrel, disappearing in a thick of trees. I stared at the trees, unmoving, heard Zach's voice in the doorway.

"Mom?"

"Yeah, hon." I inhaled a breath.

"There's something I have to tell you."

41

My head shot up. Did he know? Had Nate told him?

Barkley bounded outside and circled me, sniffing.

I stepped inside, examined Zach's features. He was smiling. Smiling?

"I got in!"

I couldn't process the meaning of the words. Got in? What was he talking about?

Zach swiped a paper from the kitchen counter and extended his hand. "I got in," he repeated.

I scanned the letterhead: University of Pittsburgh Admissions Department. My hands flew to my face. Oh! He'd gotten in. Zach had gotten into PITT. "Zach. Congratulations!" I wrapped my arms around him and squeezed. "I'm so proud of you," I said into his shoulder. "I'm so, so proud of you."

"Thanks, Mom." Zach stepped back; I took him in. His face was unclouded, shoulders no longer by his ears. His smile was easy, happy. He looked like the boy I knew.

I made the instant decision that Zach should have this moment. Nate's call with Yvonne, the horrid plea offer, it would all be there tomorrow. This moment wouldn't. I beamed. "Well," I said, waving the letter, "this calls for a celebration."

Zach pulled out the drawers where we kept the takeout menus. "Pizza?"

"No. I think we should go out." I forced levity into my tone.

"Really? You hate going out." He picked up the takeout menu again.

"Nope. I want to celebrate the right way. MaGerks?" It was Zach's favorite restaurant.

Zach flashed a look of surprise. He shrugged, but with the hint of a smile. "Sure."

We grabbed coats and walked to the car. "Of course, there's a chance --" Zach started.

"You'll go," I said, not allowing him to finish the sentence, not allowing myself to think about the information I'd yet to disclose. "I'm so happy for you."

Once at MaGerks, we sat at a high table in front of a giant television, a college basketball game on the screen. We ordered and ate, half-watched the game. I pulled up images of PITT on my phone and, together, we scrolled through them: the majestic cathedral dubbed Cathy, the winding streets of Pittsburgh, the basketball arena affectionately nicknamed The Pete. Zach talked about possible majors; he planned to play club soccer. The pending accusation came up only once, during a discussion about finding a roommate. "No one will want to room with me," Zach concluded. "They'll google me and see all this stuff."

"They won't," I lied.

"Have you googled me? It's bad."

I had, of course, googled Zach. He wasn't wrong. Almost every article assumed he was a criminal. More than a few referenced his suspension. But there was no sense in Zach worrying. Not tonight. Tonight, we would just be an ordinary mother and son celebrating a big achievement. "It will all be fine Zach," I said with authority.

A server appeared with a circular tray of desserts, pointed to each with a long finger. "Key lime, double chocolate, apple cobbler." I spied a peanut butter pie; I knew Zach would pick it. Sure enough, Zach pointed at it. "Could I get one of those, please?"

I held up two fingers. "Could you make it two?"

The server affirmed and left with the tray. Zach shook his head. "Your own dessert? I don't think I've ever seen you order your own dessert."

"Well, not every day's a celebration." I jutted my hand out and put it on top of his. "I'm so proud of you Zach. Proud to be your Mom. Proud of you as a person."

Zach's face darkened.

"So proud," I repeated.

"Thanks Mom."

The server returned and set slices of pie topped with whipped cream in front of us. I fished through my purse and pulled out my phone. "Picture?" I looked to Zach. He hated pictures, especially selfies; I'd expected him to say no. Instead, he extracted the phone from my hand. "It'll be better if I do it. My arm's longer."

I leaned into him; the camera flashed. I examined the photograph after. Our heads were together, both smiling, tips of the peanut butter pies visible on the bottom. "It's a good picture." I swallowed, a lump in my throat. "I'll send it to you." I forwarded the picture and gathered myself. We finished the pie, paid the bill, and made our way out of the restaurant.

I drove home the long way. I told myself it was for old times, a throwback to the days where Zach and I would wind through neighborhood streets and look at light displays, Christmas songs blaring on the radio. But in truth, I didn't want the night to end, didn't want this brief reprieve from Zach's case to be over.

I pushed the thought aside and drove through back neighborhood streets. We passed houses with multiple blow-up characters, some with bag lights on bushes. One home featured a giant, blow-up nutcracker, taller than the house itself. The lone decoration waved in the breeze.

"That's ominous," Zach commented.

I slowed down. "Oh my gosh, it is." We stared at the nutcracker a moment before I drove ahead, toward my favorite house, one decorated with over-the-top decorations that I'd loved as a girl. Zach had seen it, but not in years. Still, he knew where I was going.

"Crazy house?"

"You know it." I turned up the volume of *Jingle Bell Rock* and tapped the steering wheel. I forced my mind to stay on the music, the decorations, PITT.

I pulled on to the street with the house, the lights bright even from a block away. I pulled up behind two other cars and looked out. Red and green lights outlined the frame of a ranch house, a plastic Santa and his reindeer on the roof. The brick walkway, flanked in lit candy canes, led to a front door centered between two small pine trees with colored lights. A small, Christmas themed carousel stood on the right lawn; a moving Ferris wheel on the left. Both featured stuffed animals as the riders, a feature I'd loved as a child. Red and green lights covered the trunks of the four trees near the sidewalk. Between these trees, wires held lit snowflakes, the effect a tiny shower of dazzling electronic snow.

"You love this house," Zach commented.

"I do. I have good memories of going to see it with my Mom and Dad and good memories of seeing it with you. It just seems so happy to me." As a kid, I'd imagined the inside: a giant tree teeming with beautifully wrapped packages, the smell of freshly baked cookies, pajama-clad children racing about.

I gave the house a last glance and pulled away, heart heavy. I couldn't put off the inevitable anymore. I punched the radio off and glanced at Zach, the PITT letter unfolded on his lap. "Hey Zach."

"Yeah."

"Nate called earlier."

Zach stiffened.

"The prosecutor's not dropping the charges." I paused. 'Not yet," I added quickly.

Zach angled his face toward me. "But why? Darby said she saw me. I have an alibi."

"The prosecution's not fully convinced. Yet. I mean, it's not over." I stumbled over my words. "It's just going to take more time." I told Zach about the plea offer.

"Four years in jail?"

I pulled to a stop at a traffic light. "I know. You shouldn't take it. It's ridiculous."

"Four years," Zach repeated.

"It doesn't have to be. Really, Zach. We'll talk to Nate and Bo --"

"What's the alternative? To the four years. What if I lose at trial?"

I paused. I wanted to sugarcoat the alternative to the plea. Up to ten years, Zach. No big deal. Just more than half your life so far.

"Mom?"

"Nate said it could be up to ten." I drove the car up the driveway, pulled to a stop and looked him.

He stared straight ahead, not speaking. After a moment, he pulled at the door handle and pushed it open. Cold air blasted the car.

"We can still beat this, Zach."

He turned. “It’s not we, Mom. It’s me.” He stepped out. “And I might just want to take the four.” He dropped the PITT letter on the passenger seat. “So much for that.” He stomped toward the house, footsteps heavy.

“Zach,” I called after him.

He didn’t turn around.

42

"I might want to take the four." Zach's words repeated themselves in my mind on a loop. He didn't mean it; he wouldn't do it.

Would he?

I didn't know what was going through his mind. If he was innocent, if he didn't attack Paige, why wouldn't he keep wanting to look for the evidence to prove it? Unless. I tried to push the next natural thought, the alternative to innocence, away.

There were countless reasons for Zach to consider the plea. Surprise. Worry. The potential of ten years.

I fell into bed and endured a fitful sleep. I woke in a sweat, my sheets tangled around me, my jaw sore from stress-induced teeth-clenching. I felt the same way I might have had I been in a fist fight, sore and defeated. I sat up, kneaded the muscles in my shoulders and thought about how different this morning would have been had the charges been dropped. I'd get donuts or scramble eggs, craft an over-the-top Facebook post about Zach's acceptance to PITT. Instead, I anticipated the day with the kind of dread I hadn't felt since Noah died.

The refrigerator opened and closed, dishes clanked.

Zach was awake.

I needed to talk to him. I pulled myself up, stumbled into the bathroom, and brushed my teeth. I found Zach in the kitchen, hunched over a bowl of Fruit Loops, long legs smushed under a table meant for a smaller boy. "Hey."

Zach nodded in response. The sound of his metal spoon on the ceramic bowl filled the room.

I forced myself to remain silent. I put water in the coffeemaker, watched the thin band stream into an orange-rimmed glass pot. The sound of its trickle coordinated with the bowl scrapes. Clink. Trickle. Clink. Trickle. Ordinary sounds of morning that, under a different circumstance, might beckon the promise of a new day. The tense atmosphere made the noise ominous instead.

Zach tipped his empty cereal bowl and drank the leftover milk. I had repeatedly chastised him for that habit; the concern seemed foolish now. Who cared if Zach drank the leftover milk from a cereal bowl? Honestly, it shamed me that my life had been so easy that bowl-drinking cereal milk had been a valid concern.

I slid into the chair next to Zach, my hand gripped around a thick mug of coffee. He shifted in his seat, then got up and put his bowl in the sink. He leaned against the counter, arms locked, head down. I stared at his back. *Talk to me, Zach. Talk to me.*

"I think it would be easier if I took the plea."

His back was still to me. Had I heard him right? "Did you just say it would be easier if you took the plea?"

He turned, his expression solemn. "Yeah. It's stressful. It's money. And I don't even know if a jury will believe me. If I take the plea, at least I know what's going to happen. I know it won't be ten years. I can prepare. So can you." He spoke with the manner of a young soldier, ready to sacrifice himself for the greater good.

I shook my head. "Zach. No. That's ridiculous. It would most definitely not be easier if you were in jail. God. No. I'd be worried sick." I picked up my mug then set it down with a jolt, brown liquid sloshed over the side. "The evidence is out there. We just have to find it."

Zach turned back to the sink. He flipped on the faucet, filled his bowl with soap. He washed it methodically with a sponge, placed it in the plastic bin for dried dishes, then turned to look at me. "What if it's ten years?"

"It won't be."

"You don't know that."

He looked like a boy in a man's body, eyes wide, face pulled downward. His nails were bitten into rough, jagged lines.

"What if I did it? What if I did it and I just don't remember?"

"You didn't," I said automatically.

He rolled his eyes. "Paige said it was me. There's a witness. It's kind of adding up that I did this, Mom." He crossed the room, sat on the couch, head in his hands. "You might have to accept that." He looked up at me, eyes wet. "I'm sorry."

"Oh, Zach." I sat next to him on the couch, squeezed his hunched form. I was about to bring up Darby, Zach's character, the fact that I just knew, viscerally, he wouldn't overpower a girl, but Zach spoke first, his voice a whisper.

"I'm scared."

Me too.

I didn't say the words. I couldn't say the words. My role, as I saw it, was to be strong and comforting. Admitting fear didn't fall into either of those categories.

"There's still time to find more evidence," I said with bravado I did not feel. "This isn't over."

He said nothing and I sat, helpless. I had no control. I didn't know what additional evidence the prosecution would find, and I didn't know what a jury would think of it. The only thing I could do was share the information I'd gotten from Phyllis the day before. I retrieved the flyer for the support group from my purse and sat next to him on the couch. I held it out. "This might help."

Zach glanced at it. "It's a support group for people that might go to jail?"

I nodded. "It's not that I think –"

"I know," Zach interrupted. He took the flyer from my hand, put in his lap in a defeated gesture. He stared at the paper. "I'll go to it," he said, finally.

We sat silent a moment; I checked the kitchen clock. "You have school."

"Can I skip?"

A piece of me, the rule-following, controlling piece, wanted to say no. Deviation from the routine felt like giving in. Still. Everything was different now. Adhering to the normal protocol seemed unimportant, akin to insisting someone go to a scheduled appointment in the middle of a hurricane.

I tipped my head. "Up to you."

Zach went back to bed. I finished my coffee in silence, stared vacantly at the barn. Peter was likely inside for morning care. I pictured him. Talking to the horses as he refilled their hay, petting errant barn cats as they passed. I wondered if he knew about Nate's conversation with Yvonne. If he knew about the plea.

As if to answer my internal question, Peter's form emerged from the barn. I found Barkley, then stepped outside. Barkley ran after Peter, circled him. "There you go, Bark," Peter said, petting his moving body. "There you go."

Barkley fell to his back and wiggled. Abruptly, he twisted to his feet, chased a barn cat. Peter looked at me. "How's Zach?" He caught up to Barkley and grabbed his leash.

"Terrible." I opened my mouth to say something more, to soften the sentiment, then decided against it. No reason to candy-coat things.

"I'm sorry. Nate texted me yesterday. I stopped down last night, but you weren't home."

"Zach got into PITT. We went out to celebrate."

Peter paused, seeming to process the sudden change in subject. Then he smiled. "Oh. Good. That's really good. Tell him I said congratulations."

I followed Peter toward the edge of the property. "Wait. Where are you going?"

"The trail." He looked at me. "You didn't know about the trail?"

"No."

Peter stepped on to a tree-lined path. "It's pretty short. Just a loop in the woods my granddad made when he lived here. But I used to love it as a kid. There's a cool view, I'll show you." He gestured forward, then strode ahead, Barkley at his side. I followed him, the path lined with wood chips and scattered dead leaves. The rising sun felt good on my face, the air crisp and clean. On any other day, it would have seemed a great beginning.

I followed Peter around a bend, leaves crunching with our steps. We came to a part in the path obstructed by a fallen log. He stepped on it, held out his hand. The log wasn't particularly high, I took the small assist anyway. Peter jumped down after me.

"It's just up there." He pointed to a small incline. I stepped up to a landing and looked down. Acres of trees filled a landscape of majestic homes linked by a small, windy road. A few cars chugged along the roadway. Smoke blew out of one chimney, its black swirls dissipating into the morning air. At another house, a toddler rode a tricycle in circles, thrilled parents behind. The house closest to us featured a tall evergreen covered with thick Christmas bulbs.

"This is stunning."

"Yeah," Peter acknowledged. "I forget it's here sometimes. I should have told you about it. Sorry." He gestured to a small bench set back from the edge. "I made this bench with my Dad." He tapped on it, smiled.

I sat on the bench, jostled my body with mock force. I patted the wood with an open palm. "Sturdy. I'm impressed."

Peter sat beside me, Barkley's leash slack in his hands. "See? I have skills you didn't know about, even after all these years."

"Bench making," I said, nodding. "I see how that one could come in handy. You never know when you might have to whip up a bench."

"You mock me." Peter punched me lightly on the shoulder. "Even as you sit on my handiwork, you mock me."

"No. Never. Bench making is serious." A giggle escaped; I covered my mouth. The bit of levity felt wrong.

Peter seemed to sense the change in my demeanor. He stopped joking, put his elbows on his knees and looked down. A breeze blew the leaves. Barkley pulled on his leash at the sighting of a squirrel; Peter reigned him in. "Nate and Bo think we need to look harder at Zach's friends," he said. "The ones dressed like him at the party."

"Owen and Carter." I shook my head. "Not them." I filled Peter in on the altercation with Donna. "She gave me a time-stamped picture. Her boys were outside when it happened. They have witnesses too. Kids who were with them."

"Nate doesn't have to pin it on them. He just needs to show it's possible, that it could be one of Donna's boys instead of Zach."

I exhaled. An Explorer chugged along the road and turned into a driveway buttressed by lion statues. "Donna's going through a custody battle. I don't think suggesting her sons might have been involved in a sex crime would go over too well." My mind flew to the look of hatred on Donna's face during our last conversation. "She's already incensed that Bo is looking into the sex club. Owen was in it, apparently."

Peter caught a falling leaf. "Really?"

"She says she wasn't aware, but who knows? Anyway, Donna's fiercely protective. She wouldn't want her boys involved."

He dropped the leaf, it fell haphazardly to the ground. "Mothers."

"Mothers," I repeated. "We are a sad, crazy lot." I stood. "Speaking of mothers, I should probably check on Zach."

Peter got up; we walked back in companionable silence. When we reached the edge of the path, he handed me Barkley's leash. I took it, my hand grazing his. I held his eyes a moment, inhaled the scent of his soap.

What would I do without him?

"Thanks." The word felt inadequate. "I mean, I –" I stood still, unable to verbalize my feelings.

"You mean I'm the greatest?" he teased.

"Yes," I said, my tension pierced by his levity. "That's exactly what I mean, Peter Flynn. You are the greatest."

"As long as we have that straight, things should be good." He squeezed my shoulder. "Hey, call if you need anything. I'm always here for you."

I looked into his eyes. "I know," I whispered.

43

Peter

Zach didn't take the plea. I didn't want him to take the offer. Still, the burden of the continued uncertainty was wearing. Whenever I spent time with Meredith and Zach, there was an undercurrent of worry, like a sports score tape running at the bottom of a regularly scheduled game. And, despite what I knew had to be debilitating anxiety, Meredith continually made a valiant effort to make things seem normal which was, in equal parts, sweet and heartbreaking.

I was glad at least that, tonight, she and Zach would go to the Chinese Lantern Festival. My client had given me parking passes the day before. I set out to deliver them to Meredith; she and Zach were outside. Zach stood on a ladder, Meredith below with a string of Christmas bulbs. Her cheeks were ruddy. She waved in my direction. "We decorated a bit. Hope that's okay."

"Of course, it's okay." I looked to Zach. "Need a hand?"

"Nah. I got it."

"Zach's helped with me the Christmas lights for years." She patted his foot on the ladder. "We used to do a lot more but, you know." Meredith held up the string of lights. "This will do for now."

I looked at the single string of bulbs in her hand, recalled Meredith's love of Christmas décor. "But you love Christmas decorations."

She waved at me as if she really didn't like Christmas all that much. "This is fine. My decorations are at Reed's anyway."

I said nothing, my eyes on the sad, single string of lights. She must have read my expression because she squeezed my shoulder. "Really, it's good. We even got a tree." She gestured toward a small tree, hardly bigger than the one on the old Charlie Brown Christmas special.

"All right," I said, eyeing the tree. "If you're sure."

"I'm sure." I gave her the parking passes. "Send me pictures."

I left them alone, didn't want to intrude on what had clearly been an annual tradition. Still, the idea of Meredith with a single string of lights and a sad little tree stayed with me. It had been a rough couple months, and things wouldn't get easier as the trial date approached. This year of all years, Meredith and Zach could use some Christmas cheer.

The idea came to me with a start. What if I got her decorations from Reed? The more I thought about the idea, the more it took hold. I could add her own decorations while she was at the festival with Zach. It would be a fun surprise, something light amid of all the awfulness.

Meredith left to pick up sandwiches for lunch. I pulled Zach aside and asked what he thought. He liked the idea, arranged for the pick-up of the decorations through Jamie.

After they left for the festival, I drove to Reed's. It occurred to me on the way that Reed might not be too psyched about another man surprising his fiancée. But that was his problem, not mine. He could have, should have, dropped off the decorations on his own. He had to know how much Meredith loved Christmas.

As the house came into view, I pushed my feelings about Reed aside. I'd get the decorations and leave. No big deal. I pulled into the driveway. The garage opened, Reed inside, a stack of boxes at his feet.

I cut the engine, exited the car, and examined his features. He looked bewildered instead of angry, as if couldn't quite figure out how his relationship had gotten to this point. I held up a hand. "Reed."

"Peter." He gestured to the boxes labeled 'Christmas' in Meredith's familiar scrawl. "I would have brought these over."

I shook my head. "No trouble. I've got it." I picked up a box. Reed piled two on top of each other, set them in my truck cavity. We repeated the sequence once more, the entirety of the effort taking less than a minute.

I scanned the remaining boxes, neatly lined up in rows on the outskirts of the garage. A vision of Meredith packing them materialized in my mind, lip curled, hair hanging down around her face in straight sheens. She'd have packed with care: covered glass with bubble wrap, folded clothes to emerge wrinkle-free. She'd probably have paired her socks in little balls; she'd shown me how to do that once. I gestured to the boxes. "Should I take any of these? Clear out some space?"

Reed looked back in the direction I'd pointed, seemed not to comprehend the question.

"I've got room." I pointed to the near-empty truck cavity.

Reed shook his head. "No. They can stay." He stood, hands dangling uselessly by his sides.

I took a step toward my truck.

"How is she?" he called out.

I turned back at the question.

"I mean, I've called, I've talked to her. But I can't really get a read on how she is for real."

The absurdity of the question floored me. Reed was her fiancé. He ought to know how Meredith was doing. And if he didn't, he should be able to fathom a guess. She'd been asked to leave her home, was ostracized by most of her friends, and her son faced serious criminal charges. How did he think she would be?

I didn't answer and he met my gaze, a look of guilt on his features. "Things get more complicated when kids are involved. My ex-wife, Lara, well, she's –"

The anger in my gut bubbled over. "Lara's your ex," I said. "Maybe you ought to focus on your fiancée." I opened my truck door, slid in the driver's seat, and shut it.

Reed stared at me from the driveway. I fought the urge to roll down the window and tell him off and, instead, pulled out of the driveway and on to the road in a single fluid move of the wheel. I glanced at the review mirror; Reed still in the driveway, a hapless look on his face. What a tool.

I pulled on to the main road, tried to put Reed out of my mind. I glanced back, saw Meredith's Christmas boxes. There wasn't as much there as I'd hoped. Not for the kind of surprise I had in mind.

I passed a Home Depot, made a last-minute decision to pull in. I'd supplement Meredith's decorations with a few things, make at least this one night festive and memorable. I scanned the aisles for decorations she might like. A light-up penguin in an igloo? Moving reindeer framed with white lights? An inflatable snowman? It struck me that all the decorations I thought Meredith would like, Sadie would have hated. Sadie was a candle-in-the-window kind of girl. Meredith was all color.

I grabbed a few strings of colored bulbs like the ones Meredith had already hung. I passed through each aisle, ideas forming in my mind as scanned the shelves. I filled the entire shopping cart, then took my place in a long line at checkout.

"Well if it isn't Peter Flynn."

I turned and saw Lucy in a red Christmas sweater, a light-up tree in its center. Though she was still the landlord for my office building, she hadn't come by much since the Black Cat Ball. I felt a surge of guilt for the way I'd treated her; I'd never made good on my promise for make-up dinner. She pointed to my cart. "Nice haul there. Decorating an entire storefront, are you?"

I looked down at the cart, realizing then that the sheer quantity of the items was ridiculous. Even Lucy seemed to think the décor absurd. And she was wearing a sweater with lights embedded inside.

"Just trying to liven things up."

"For the office?" She raised an eyebrow. "Because you'd have to run that by your landlord, you know."

I smiled, relieved she'd made a joke. "Nope. Not for the office." I held up a hand. "I promise." Lucy met my eyes. It seemed a good time to set things right. "I think I still owe you a dinner."

She waved her hand in my direction. "We don't have to go to dinner. It's fine."

"Really, I –"

"Peter," she said, "her voice now serious. It's alright. You like her, your friend Meredith. I could tell."

"Oh no," I said shaking my head, "we're just friends."

Lucy snorted. "Okay."

"No, really," I protested.

"It's fine if you like her, Pete." She gave me a tap on the shoulder. "Have a good holiday." She disappeared down an aisle of light fixtures.

I watched her go; my face flushed. Were my feelings for Meredith that transparent? I looked at the items in the cart. Clearly, yes. First, I'd given her tickets to a festival I'd actually wanted to attend. Then I'd spent the entire afternoon planning to decorate her house. I shook my head. God. I was a chump.

I started at the items, willing myself to put them back. No

big deal. Meredith didn't know about the plan. She wouldn't be disappointed. I'd put up her own decorations; it would still be a surprise. The line snaked forward, I pushed the cart, the light up penguin jostledwith the movement.

Screw it.

Meredith would love these decorations. Whatever my feelings for her, I could stay in the friend zone. Hell. I'd been in the friend zone for decades, and I'd managed just fine. My *friend* needed something to smile about, and the hodgepodge of over-the-top Christmas-themed items in my cart would get it done.

I purchased the decorations, loaded them into my truck, and started home. I unpacked them at the house, carried Meredith's boxes inside. Barkley greeted me with tail thumps. After unloading the boxes, I pulled an eight-foot spruce from the back property into the home. I set the tree on a stand and opened Meredith's boxes with care. I hung her lights and ornaments on the tree.

Once finished with the indoor decorations, I checked my phone. Meredith had texted a picture of herself and Zach, a selfie, in front of a dragon made to look as if it were swimming in the Schuylkill river.

So fun. Thanks, Peter.

I looked at their faces, both smiling. I was glad I'd given Meredith the tickets, particularly now that we knew the prosecution was proceeding. They'd needed this diversion.

I took a last look at the photo, then switched the phone to off. I spread the boxes around where I thought they should go, then put lights along the pathway. I unspooled one string; it took forever to hang. Longer than I'd remembered from years past. I strung a second as dusk fell, dim lights from the bulbs evident in the darkened sky.

I unspooled the third set when I heard the door to the main house slam. Dad made his way toward me with strong physical steps that belied his dementia. "What's going on here?" He leaned closer. "Your mother wants to know."

I explained. Dad nodded, then took the light string from my hand. "Alright. How about I give you a hand?"

"That would be great." I watched Dad with the light string, a lump in my throat. My mind flew to past projects we'd done together - repairing the deck at the old house, washing and waxing our cars, making a vegetable garden for Mom. I didn't know how many more opportunities I would have like this. I touched his shoulder. "Really. Thanks, Dad."

We worked in tandem, Dad seeming to enjoy the physical activity. After hanging the lights, I set up a group of happy penguins near a light up igloo. Once finished, I followed Dad back to the main house. Mom poured us mugs of coffee and nodded toward the newly decorated carriage house. "That's a nice thing you did."

I shrugged. "It's nothing."

My phone buzzed. Zach. *Ten minutes out.*

"They're almost here." I took a sip of coffee, rapped Dad on the back. "Thanks for the help." I made my way back to the carriage house and adjusted a few of the lights before I heard Meredith's car in the driveway, saw the flash of her headlights.

Her arrival imminent, I felt suddenly foolish for the grand gesture. What if she didn't like it? Maybe she'd wanted an understated Christmas. Worse, what if she'd picked up on my feelings for her? Saw my efforts not as a gesture of friendship, but a romantic overture?

Too late. The car stopped. I glanced at her in the driver's seat but could only see her profile. I couldn't see her expression. She stepped out of the car. This was it.

44

Meredith stood in the glow of the Christmas lights on the carriage house for a moment, her hand over her mouth. "Wow. This is crazy."

Zach emerged from the car, spotted me on the outskirts. "Mr. Flynn," he called. "It looks fantastic."

Meredith's head whirled toward me. "This was you?"

"Me and Zach. But only if you like it."

"Like it?" She moved toward me and pushed at my shoulder. "I love it. It's like a mini crazy house."

She stepped back. I stood by her side and looked in the direction of her gaze. Red and green lights outlined the house, candy canes flanked the walk. No carousel, but there was a fully lit igloo, two glittery penguins inside. Lights covered the trees out front; a giant wreath centered the door. A plastic Santa and reindeer sat square on the small roof.

"This is amazing." She reached out and fingered a candy cane. "I always wanted a walk lined with these." She looked to me. "Oh my gosh, and thanks for tonight. The festival was unbelievable. Now this. It's crazy."

"There's more inside."

"More?"

I gestured toward the house. Meredith pushed open the door and stepped into its frame. She said nothing, her figure unmoving in the door. Was it too much? Had I overstepped? I took a step back, as if doing so might distance me from my efforts.

She turned and looked at me, eyes damp.

I let out a relieved breath.

"They're my decorations. How did you get my decorations?"

I inclined my head toward Zach, now standing next to me. "Zach arranged the pickup. I just drove the car."

"You guys are too much." She swung open the door and gestured for us to come inside. "What a fantastic surprise. And the festival. It was awesome." She took off her coat and looked up and down the tree again. "Thank you. Thank you so much."

I shrugged. "It was nothing."

"It's definitely something. I was trying not to make a big deal, but I really missed my Christmas stuff." She sat and patted the couch cushion beside her. "Hey. Come check out our pictures from tonight. It was unreal."

I took off my coat and sat next to Meredith on the couch, Zach on a reclining chair nearby. She pulled up the camera roll on her phone. "This one," she said, pointing, "was our favorite."

The photo featured a giant pagoda lit up with yellow, red, and white lights. I tapped on it. "How tall was that?"

She exchanged a look with Zach. "Twenty-five feet, maybe?" Zach nodded. "Go ahead," Meredith nodded toward me. "Scroll through."

She left me with her phone, stood, and looked down at her clothes. "Let me go change. I'm such a baby with wearing regular clothes anymore." She disappeared down the hall and emerged in fuzzy sweatpants and an oversized sweatshirt. She opened the fridge and returned to the couch holding two beers and a Pineapple Fanta. She handed a beer to me, the Fanta to Zach.

"You still like Sam Adams, right?"

I held up the bottle. "Still my favorite."

She sat on the end of the couch, pulled her feet up, and crossed them. Her toenails were red, polish chipped at the tips. She picked up the remote and switched on the television, ESPN on the screen. We watched sports highlights in silence, NBA scores scrolled across the bottom on a ticker tape. "Sixers won," Meredith commented.

Zach looked up from his phone. "Embiid had 28."

"Still like Simmons better." I winked at him and took a sip of beer.

"Really?" He rolled his eyes.

I sipped my beer again, felt at home in a way I hadn't previously. I glanced at Meredith. Did she feel the same? "Hey," I said suddenly. "Do you think it's too late for a fire?" I nodded toward the doorway. "There're logs right outside."

Meredith smiled. "I'd love a fire. Good with you, Zach?"

"Fine."

"Okay then." I stepped into the cold, picked up logs from a nearby stack.

Headlights illuminated the space behind me. I turned. A truck rattled up the drive. I squinted at it, unable to appropriately see over its bright lights. It pulled to a stop. Reed stepped out and stared at the carriage house before looking in my direction. "Oh. Hey."

Still holding the logs, I nodded. "Hey." He held a small package in his hand, a red bow centered on top.

"I thought about what you said today. I'm here to check on Meredith." He reached out and tapped my shoulder like we were old chums.

The door swung open. Meredith stepped out in oversized

snow boots, her sweatshirt pulled over her hands. She squinted. “Reed?”

I couldn’t read the tenor of her voice. Excited? Surprised?

He moved toward her, his back now to me. “Meredith. Hi.” He gave her an awkward peck on the cheek. “I texted you. You didn’t respond, so I just swung by. Hope that’s alright.”

Meredith straightened. “Zach and I were at the Chinese Lantern Festival in Philadelphia.”

“Oh.” Reed appeared to process the fact that Meredith had done something without him. “Was it fun?”

“Amazing.”

I willed myself to leave, but my feet remained planted in place, my arms still around the log pile. I starred at the two of them, frozen.

“That’s quite a display.” He pointed to the house with the hand holding the gift. “Oh,” he said, looking at the present. “This is for you.” He held the package in her direction.

“Peter did the lights,” Meredith said. She looked down at Reed’s present then back up at him. I couldn’t make out her expression in the dim light.

“I’m sorry.” He stepped closer to her. “I’ve been a total jackass. I realized it after Peter stopped by today. I should have stood up to Lara instead of --” He let the sentence trail off.

Meredith took the gift from his extended hand.

I stood still with the logs, my eyes trained on Meredith. I wanted her to give the gift back at Reed, tell him off. But instead, she slipped a finger under the wrapping. I couldn’t watch anymore. I set down the logs and started toward the main house.

“You don’t have to go, Peter,” Meredith called.

I turned. She looked happy in the glow of the lights, Reed’s eyes fixed on her. He loved her. I could see it on his face.

“I really should check on my Dad.” I picked up my hand in a half wave. “Have a good night.”

Meredith jogged after me, Reed's half opened package in her hand. "Thanks so much for tonight, Peter. For the lights, the tickets. Everything."

"Sure, of course." I looked at her, still in her sweatshirt. She must be freezing. "You should get inside." I hurried toward the door to the main house before Meredith could call after me again.

Gratefully, there was no sound from the kitchen or family room, my parents likely asleep. I trudged up the stairs, found sweatpants in the closet. I stepped to the window to close the blinds, saw Reed's truck in the driveway. He and Meredith were no longer outside.

I stood at the window, visualized myself with Zach and Meredith in the light of the Christmas tree. The ease of sitting with them, hanging out in comfortable clothes, watching sports in the background. It could have been the three of us at the light festival, the three of us decorating the house.

I snapped the blinds shut.

Things with Meredith were not meant to be. She saw me as a friend. She always had. I'd made my big move with the kiss after Noah died; the answer had been a clear and resounding no. And now, she sat with another man in the light of the decorations I'd spent the day putting up. They'd probably made the fire.

Humiliation snaked through me. She had made her feelings clear yet I'd spent the day grand-gesturing in the name of friendship.

I crawled into bed, pulled the covers to my neck, and fell into a fitful asleep. Hours later, morning sunlight filtered in the room. I stared at the ceiling, at the outline of the glow-in-the-dark stars my grandparents had put there when I was small. The fact that I was still in this room? It was pathetic. I knew my parents needed me, but the situation suddenly felt impossibly frustrating. How could I meet anyone, let alone a girl like

Meredith, when I still lived with my parents? When I slept in a room with glow-in-the-dark stars on the ceiling and a lamp shaped like a planet?

I swung my legs over the bed and sat up. I needed to get out and think. I pulled on jeans and heavy sweatshirt, finger-combed my hair. I descended the stairs quietly, grabbed my coat from the rack near the back door and snuck out, feeling more like a teenager than a grown man.

The first thing I noticed: it was snowing. Light powdery flakes had already coated the ground, heavier clumps fell in a steady rhythm.

The second thing I noticed: Reed's truck was gone.

I exhaled. It wasn't my business what Meredith did, but I was glad Reed didn't spend the night or, at least, that he wasn't still here. I'd felt embarrassed enough by the sequence of events; I'd didn't need another reminder of where I stood in Meredith's eyes.

I navigated toward the path I'd shown her earlier in the week, shoved my hands in my pockets. My breath smoked as I walked. The stillness of the woods calmed me. It would all be fine. I'd assist with Zach's trial, find a caregiver to help Dad, and move on with my life. I'd stop this infatuation with Meredith, ease her and Zach out of my life in the least painful way possible. I might even move to another state. I'd always liked Colorado.

The plan in mind, I felt better. I maneuvered over the giant log that blocked the trail and made my way toward the incline. I stepped toward the bench I'd made with my grandfather.

I wasn't alone.

45

Meredith sat still on the bench, Barkley by her side. I took a step back, not wanting to disturb her. Or talk to her. But Barkley saw me and jumped up, circled my body in happy leaps. “Hey there, boy. Hey there.” I pet Barkley on the head.

Meredith turned and smiled. She had on a hat with a giant pom-pom that made her look cute and ridiculous all at once. “Hey.”

“Hey.”

Barkley finished circling and returned to Meredith’s side, breathless. She tapped the bench. “Do you want to sit?”

I didn’t. It felt imperative that I create a boundary between myself and Meredith. Hanging out with her on a tall hill overlooking a majestic winter scene as snow gently fell around us? That would be the opposite of a boundary.

She seemed to sense my hesitation.

“Please.”

I didn’t want to sit, but I didn’t want her to think I was angry about Reed, didn’t want to seem petty. But, really? She had to have guessed that last night might have been humiliating. Not knowing how to verbalize any of this, I stood still with my mouth shut, my hand on the edge of the bench.

She oriented her face to look into mine, held my gaze. "I gave Reed his engagement ring back last night," she said finally. "Even though we weren't living together, things weren't officially off. Now they are."

I stepped back, processing. She'd broken it off. Reed was out of the picture. My heart leapt; I tamped it down. Just because Meredith broke up with Reed didn't mean she had feelings for me. I still needed to keep my distance.

"I'm sorry," I said. I brushed a clump of snow from my hair and glanced at her ring finger, now bare.

She shrugged. "I'm sad of course, but, and this sounds awful –" She paused. "Part of me is relieved. I thought Reed and I would have that family I always wanted. You know, the kind of house where they have barbeques for the kids and their friends on Saturday nights." She looked at me. "Kind of like your house growing up." Barkley rested his head on her thigh, she pet him. "And we had days like that. It felt perfect sometimes but, just as often, I missed when it was just me and Zach. I missed our tiny condo with the square patio and our stupid little stove that didn't work half the time. And I missed my beanbag."

"Your beanbag?"

She smiled. "Yes, my beanbag. I had this purple beanbag chair my Gram gave me for Christmas when I was eight or something. It had my name embroidered on it in big block letters."

"I remember it." I'd only been in Meredith's bedroom a few times growing up, but I remembered that beanbag. Bright purple. "In the corner, right?"

She nodded.

"That purple beanbag has been in every bedroom I've ever had, even with Noah."

That I didn't know. "Well, what happened to it?"

"Right before I moved in with Reed, I gave it to the Salvation Army. His house was just too perfect."

"Did Reed ask you to give it away?" I felt a flash of anger.

"No. Of course not." She looked out, her gaze unfocused. "I didn't want to clutter up my perfect new life, even for the beanbag. Then Zach got arrested and, boom, the illusion was over." She swept snow off the bench with a gloved hand; it scattered on Barkley. She brushed it from his torso.

I reflected on her words. I understood. I'd tried hard to create an ideal life with Sadie. She'd tried too, if I was honest. "I think perfection is fragile."

Meredith stayed silent, her expression thoughtful. "You know, I think you're right," she said after a moment. "If you're trying for perfection, only one thing has to go wrong to ruin it. Trying to attain perfection is like trying to be happy all the time. It's an unattainable goal."

I looked at her. Pink cheeks from the cold, blue eyes framed with tiny laugh lines. A broad inviting smile; wisps of hair that blew in the breeze. Life with Meredith, casual nights like the one we'd had before Reed showed up, might just be perfect enough for me. But I couldn't tell her that.

"Do you want to start back?" The question was abrupt; I needed to keep my new boundary in place.

"Sure." Meredith stood next to me, paused a moment, her eyes on the scene below. "It's beautiful in the snow."

I followed her gaze. Acres of now partially snow-covered woods blanketed the ground. The sun had moved to the center of a solid blue sky, its rays bringing bits of warmth.

Meredith looked at me. "Maybe the best you can do," she said seriously, "is find that person you can be completely yourself with. Happy, not happy. Perfect, not perfect. Like an old blanket." She paused, still looking at scene below. "I think the key to love is finding that person who gives you comfort no matter what."

I stared at her upturned face.

"Is that stupid?" she asked, her face inches from mine. "To compare love to an old blanket?"

My heart beat harder; I stepped away. I wanted to think she was talking about me, that I was the person who gave her comfort. But was she? I didn't know.

"I don't think it's stupid," I said after a beat. "Everyone loves an old blanket." I spoke in a purposely casual tone, hoped to diffuse the tension I felt in my body.

Meredith blinked. "Yeah, right. Everyone loves old blankets." She shrugged and stepped toward the path, down the small incline.

The moment, if there had been one at all, was over. We walked down the path and I pushed any imagined intimacy out of my mind, affirming the vow I'd made just that morning. I'd help her and Zach through the trial, then gently extricate myself from her life. Anything else was too emotionally difficult. I knew that now. My feelings for Meredith were too strong to stay in the friend zone.

Barkley charged ahead, pulled at her arm before stopping suddenly and sniffing the ground with vigorous attention. We both stared at the dog. My body felt rigid; I wondered if Meredith sensed the tension. The last thing I needed was her to ask me about it. I had to lighten the mood.

I gestured toward Barkley. "Do you ever wonder what they smell?" I asked. "Like what is it about that spot?"

She fingered the pom pom on her hat. "Maybe another animal peed there?"

"Well, that's a pretty boring answer."

She turned to me, a hand on her hip. "What do you think then?"

"I think it's gold," I said decisively. "All these years, dogs have been trying to tell their owners something. Dig here. Dig here. And we just ignore them. But there's gold under there." I pointed to the spot Barkley had sniffed.

She laughed. "You think so."

"I know so."

"Well, I'll be sure to return with a shovel then."

"Not if I get there first."

"You're crazy." She looked at me, her expression different than it had been in the past. Searching? Or was I reading into things once again? I looked away.

"Peter?" She gently moved my head to look at her, her face impossibly close.

"Yeah, Mer."

"I think you're my old blanket."

46

I stared at Meredith, snow falling gently around us.

I think you're my old blanket.

Did she mean it the way I thought? I looked at her, her eyes steady on mine, head tilted up, lips inches away. I felt exactly as I had almost a decade before, positive Meredith wanted to kiss me.

And I sure remembered how that turned out.

Plus, she had just been through a lot. The failed hoped that the prosecution would dismiss the charges, breaking up with Reed. Meredith was vulnerable. This wasn't the time.

I looked into her eyes, intending to step back and diffuse the moment with a wacky joke or silly gesture. But she pulled me toward her instead, kissed me softly on the lips. When I stepped back, she shook her head. "Sorry, I –"

I pulled her to me. "Don't be sorry. You have no idea how badly I have wanted to do that." I pressed my body to hers, skimmed my hands downward, and kissed her, longer this time, searching. I would have lost myself in the moment, but Barkley jumped up, front paws on my waist. The movement was enough to break apart the kiss.

"Way to ruin the moment, Bark," Meredith chastised, teasing.

I looked down, raked my hand through my hair. "Wow. That is not what I expected this morning."

"But good?"

"Good? I don't think the word good really gives justice to that kiss. That was -" I couldn't find words. I'd visualized kissing Meredith. Of course, I had. But the real thing? It was one hundred times better than I'd imagined.

She looked at me; her face flushed. "Why didn't you tell me you could kiss like that?"

"Why didn't you tell me you could?" I brushed a bit of snow off her hair, elated. I'd expected Meredith to give me a smile, kiss me again. Instead, her face darkened.

No.

She opened her mouth. I sensed what she was about to say wouldn't be good. I wanted to pull her to me and kiss her again, forestall whatever her next words would be, ones I was fairly certain would puncture my heart.

She pushed at the accumulating snow with a booted foot. "I really like you."

I inhaled, waited for the inevitable 'but'.

"But –"

There it was.

She blinked. "The last forty-eight hours have been insane. That horrible plea agreement, breaking up with Reed, your unbelievable grand gesture." She jerked her thumb in the direction of the carriage house. "My head's spinning."

I dropped my gaze. I knew it. It was too soon, Meredith's temporary passion was borne out of stress rather than genuine feelings for me.

"The truth is," she looked down and back up at me, "the only good thing to come out of this awful experience was finding you again. And this time –" She twisted her hands around the strings to my coat hood and pulled me forward, "this time, you're not a married man." She pressed her lips on mine. We kissed again, stayed in a long embrace after, snow falling gently around us. When we finally parted, she poked my chest with her index finger. "We just may have a little chemistry, Peter Flynn."

I smiled, shook my head. "I think we just might."

I took her hand, and we walked back to the edge, the carriage and main house in sight. Barkley ran ahead, leash trailing behind. I stopped and looked at her.

"I'm going to need to take this slow," she said and took both of my hands in hers. "It's not you or that." She inclined her head in the direction where we'd just kissed. "*That* was amazing. It's more everything else that's going on." She looked up at me. Snow dotted her dark eyelashes, flakes fell on her cheeks. "Is that okay? Will you wait for me?"

I wiped the snowflakes off her face with my thumb. "Will I wait for you?" I smiled, shook my head. "Don't you know I've been waiting for you most of my life?" She closed her eyes; I kissed the lids. "I'll wait as long as you need."

~

AS IT TURNED OUT, we didn't take it slow.

Three days after the kiss, Zach was in school. Meredith had the day off. She suggested I work remotely from the carriage house. I looked at my calendar, attended a ten a.m. consult at work, then headed back, laptop and files in tow.

We sat on the couch near the Christmas tree, colored lights dim in the daylight. Meredith had lit a fire before I got there, and the smell of burning wood underscored the already homey atmosphere. A plate of powdered cookies (courtesy of Mom) sat on the coffee table next to warm coffee in snowman-shaped mugs.

Meredith wore leggings and what I now knew to be her favorite oversized sweatshirt. Her hair was damp from a shower and hung in freshly combed pieces around her almost makeup free face. She had on fuzzy socks featuring little penguins on skis. She looked adorable and sexy, and I almost regretted coming. Maintaining the physical distance she'd asked for would be difficult, especially since we were alone.

I balanced my laptop on my knees and spread the papers I needed on the cushion next to me. I started a will. A cool tip I learned from this: boring estate work calms the libido. I focused on the document. Next to me, Meredith crossed her legs under her thighs and swiped a cookie from the plate. She bit into it, tapped at her phone. "Sixers Celtics this weekend."

I gave her a sideways glance. "Should be a good one."

"As long as Embiid stays healthy." She took another bite of the cookie, bits of powder clung to her lips.

I nodded toward her. "You've got some sugar on your lips."

"Oh." She tipped her head, widened her eyes.

The gesture seemed suggestive. Or maybe I just *wanted* it to look suggestive. I'd made a promise to take things slow, and I wasn't going to fail that pledge on day three. I averted my gaze from her soft, and now sugary, lips and looked back down at my computer. I couldn't remember where I had been.

Out of the corner of my eye, I saw her take another bite. More powder clung to her lips. "Better?"

I looked at her. She had the same sensuous expression as before, the same seductive look in her eyes. "No. It's still there." I looked back to the laptop.

"This sugar on my lips is such an issue," she said. "Do you know how I might get it off?"

Okay. I was dense, but not dumb. This was clearly a come-on. I'd agreed to take thing slow if she wanted to. But if she didn't? I set my computer down on the coffee table. "Do you need some help?"

She raised her eyebrows. “Are you offering?”

“Well, it seems the courteous thing to do.” I moved my papers from the couch cushion, inched closer, and pressed my lips to hers.

47

Three months passed since that first time I made love to Meredith. We'd had sex a dozen or more times since, mostly gentle but, on occasion rough, both of us grabbing and clawing and physically acting out the stress we'd felt as the trial date inched closer.

Our lovemaking was interspersed with casual times – walking the dog, feeding the horses, movies over beers and nachos. If I thought I'd loved Meredith before, my feelings were so intense now, it was almost painful. And, as elated as I was about our relationship, Zach's trial hung between us, an invisible but ever-present force. I feared the trial, terrified of a potential conviction. Meredith was scared too and, at times, she'd drift into a deep melancholy, only pulling out of it long enough to make things seem as normal as possible for Zach.

Worry about Meredith and the case found itself into my consciousness more and more until it was a constant, steady stream. I'd hope each day for a big charges-dropped type of break in the case with the same fervor (and the same likelihood) as a little kid wishing for a pony. Instead, evidence trickled in, all of it bad. Two boys overheard Zach tell Carter about sleeping with Paige; they'd both made statements. The three boys at the party who'd been in the sex club all had alibis that placed them somewhere else. None looked like Zach; one of them had been Darby Brooks' ex-boyfriend. Apparently, they'd broken up a few days before she'd seen Zach in the bathroom.

Not good.

Bo had found one witness, a kid who'd said he'd seen Zach near the hall bathroom. She'd set up a date to interview him and another boy. It was something. Barely.

I ate with Meredith and Zach a few times a week and, today, I stood in the carriage house kitchen, Meredith breaking up ground beef in a sizzling skillet. Zach was out with the dog.

"Was it bad?" I asked.

Since the start of the new year, Meredith and Zach had attended bi-monthly support meetings for those touched by the criminal law system. The concept of the group was good; the result less so. She always came back upset.

"It's always bad." She picked up the skillet, drained it over the sink.

"I'm sorry."

She set the pan back down, opened a can of Manwich sauce, poured it in, and faced me. "Tonight, they talked about poop."

"Poop?" I was sure I misheard her.

"Yeah. Poop. Apparently, at some prisons, you need to flush at the same time you go so there's no time for it to smell." She looked at me. "I didn't ask what happened if someone forgot." She stabbed at the beef with her spatula, bits of the sauce sprayed the counter.

I grabbed a paper towel, wiped the sauce. I didn't know how to respond to the information. What did you say to something like that? I'm sorry? That sucks? "How's Zach?" I asked finally.

"Stoic. But he's scared. He's scared and there's nothing I can do about it. It's not like I can go check the jail out ahead of time." She didn't cry, didn't move. It was as though Meredith was numb, her emotions stuck in a body shut down from months of anxiety.

"I'm sorry." The words were inadequate; I didn't know what else to say.

She turned the heat off the stove and removed the skillet. "Any news from Nate?"

Her tone carried a sliver of hope that broke my heart. Nate hadn't been in the office today and, if there was something new, he'd have called. Still, I pretended a sudden break might be a possibility and pulled out my phone. I expected to see a blank home screen. Instead, there was a text from Nate.

We need to talk. It's urgent. Tomorrow? 8?

I stared at the words. Urgent? That didn't sound good. In fact, "urgent" gave off a serious and pressing vibe, not a woo-hoo-good-news one. I looked up, saw Meredith's eyes on mine. She tipped her head. "Anything?"

No use worrying her. "Nah. Nate just wants to meet in the morning."

"About the case?"

That hopeful tone again. It killed me. "Possibly. He didn't say." I pulled up the message again and typed back. *Sure thing. What's up?*

Dots, signaling Nate was writing back, appeared, then disappeared. I waited, staring at my phone. *Come on, Nate.*

He didn't respond; Zach returned with Barkley. Meredith set out plates with sloppy joes, coleslaw, and apple slices. It seemed unnecessary to call or text Nate back right then. I was meeting with him first thing in the morning.

~

When I arrived at the office fifteen minutes early, I saw Nate through the window. He had on a red tie that hung down over his desk, pooling at the bottom. His suit jacket covered the back of his chair.

I reached his window, knocked. He jerked and looked up. I'd expected a laugh, but all he gave was a sad smile.

Shit. Something was wrong. *Please don't let it be about Zach's case.* I hurried to the door, pulled it open, and found Nate in his office.

"Hey, Pete." His face was serious, his countenance muted.

"You wanted to meet?"

He did not look up, did not make eye contact. "This isn't easy." He picked at a hangnail.

I started at him. I'd never seen Nate at a loss for words. Something bad had happened. Really bad. Fuck. "What's going on?"

"Okay. First off, Lizzie's pregnant. Twins." Nate sat up straighter, as if the acknowledgement had given him courage.

I felt my shoulders drop. "Congratulations, man." I extended my hand. Maybe Nate just wanted more money? Or to be a partner? I'd been meaning to talk to him about that anyway. I let out a sigh of relief. This, I could handle.

"And second --" Nate let go of my hand. "Second, I've taken a new job."

A new job? "What? Why?"

"I got an unbelievable offer. Almost double my salary here and with the twins..." He let the statement trail off for a moment then added, "Lizzie wants to stop working."

No. Panic rose in my chest. Zach's trial was only two months away.

"When do you start?"

"Two weeks."

"Shit." I leaned against the desk, my arms straight. "Can you stay? Can you stay just until the Morgan trial?"

Nate shifted. "I would, man, but I can't. If I defer, they're offering the job to someone else."

I looked up, met Nate's eyes. "Will you help with it, though? I don't have criminal experience, I –"

"I can't." Nate shook his head. "The firm is Dixon, Baker, and Nash."

My head shot up. "Dixon. As in Scott Dixon? Are you kidding me?"

I felt that same way I might have had Nate sucker-punched me on the way in. I had not seen this coming. Of all the scenarios I might have dreamed up as to what was 'urgent', Nate leaving the firm to work for Scott Dixon would never have crossed my mind. I felt betrayed. Or set up. Dixon, Baker, and Nash, a firm with hundreds of lawyers across three states, suddenly needed Nate? "Is that even allowed?"

Nate's regretful look transformed to a firm one. "The firm doesn't represent Paige. The Commonwealth does. There's no conflict."

"Yes, there is. You might tell Scott Dixon, your new boss, our strategies. You can't do this. You can't do this, Nate."

Nate lifted his eyebrows. "You know I wouldn't tell Scott anything. Plus, they know our strategy. Darby Brooks. Zach's statements. That's all we have."

Recognition of our lack of a defense fueled my desperation. Nate had to stay. He had to see this through. "What if I could match the salary? Or what if you were a partner? I'd been meaning to talk to you about that."

Nate eyes softened. "It's not just the money," he said. "It's the opportunity. The exposure. I'm sorry." He paused. "I can stay for two weeks."

Anger snaked up my body. The thought that Nate would leave me in the lurch like this, knowing how important this case was, how much was at stake. And to work for Scott Dixon no less. I met his gaze. "No. You can leave." I began to walk out of the room, then stopped in the doorway. "Congratulations on the twins, by the way." I left before he answered.

48

Meredith

Two days after Nate quit, Peter filed a motion with the Court of Common Pleas asking for a continuance of the trial date so I could find new counsel.

I didn't want to move the trial date. A continuance meant more months of uncertainty, and Zach would likely miss the start of the semester at PITT if (when) he was exonerated.

But not moving the trial caused a bigger problem; mainly, that Peter would need to try the case. He'd been clear from the start that he didn't have criminal law experience; I couldn't put the pressure of a trial on him. Zach needed someone else.

This morning, I saw Peter leave the house for court in his black suit and dress shoes, Zach's file tucked under a muscular arm. His hair was slicked back, not rumpled the way it was in morning or on weekends. He looked confident, slick even. Like a lawyer.

I left for work not long after Peter left for court, initially grateful for the distraction. But as the clock inched minute by minute past the start time of the argument, I wished I had been able to go. At least then I would know what was going on.

I refocused my attention on my client, a five-year-old little girl named Jewel. Jewel was working on her fine motor skills by putting pieces into a Mr. Potato-head, tongue out in concentration. We each had a head and a pile of pieces. I liked the kids to think of my planned activities as collaborative fun, and we were racing to see who could finish their potato-head first. When I accidentally placed the eyes where the nose should have been, Jewel pointed at the mistake, then gave a full-bellied, hearty laugh which belied her small frame. I took in her crinkly eyes, grinning mouth, and bouncing ponytail. Her guffaws were contagious; I started laughing along, then put a pair of shoes in the slot for Mr. Potato-head's hair. This started a new round of hysterics for both of us, mine a welcome release for of stress I'd felt all morning.

Then my phone buzzed.

Peter.

Call me.

The text immediately doused my laughter; Jewel looked in my direction. She stopped laughing too, put a tiny pink-nailed hand on my upper arm. "Are you okay, Miss Mer?"

Her bit of kindness moved me, and I wiped an emerging tear with the back of my hand. "I'm good, sweetie."

She tipped her head. "Does something hurt?" Her eyes were wide, caring.

"Just on the inside."

She kneeled on her chair and gave me a quick peck on the top of my head. "That's for the inside."

I stared at her round face, her kind eyes. A vision flashed in my mind: one of Jewel years from now, a beautiful woman, vulnerable to attack. How could women still be oppressed, attacked, assaulted, in a modern society like ours? But it had happened to Natasha. And, more and more, it looked like it had happened to Paige. I squeezed my eyes shut.

Jewel's small voice interrupted me. "Miss M. Can we make the sticker zoos now?"

"Yes. Absolutely." I had promised the activity, her favorite, at the beginning of the session. "Let me get the sheets." I found sheets of animal stickers and colored paper in the supply room. Jewel spent the remaining five minutes of our session peeling off bears and tigers and giraffes and placing them in hand-drawn cages on the paper.

After the session ended, I stepped outside to call Peter. I pulled out my phone, the bright sun obscuring my vision. I moved to side of the building, leaned against its brick wall. Peter answered on the first ring.

"I lost. No continuance."

I took in the words.

"I'm sorry," he continued. "I'm really sorry. We can still try to find someone else, another lawyer."

"Right." But I knew the chances of finding another attorney were slim. Peter had already told me experienced criminal lawyers were booked months in advance. Finding someone to take over at this stage would be almost impossible. At least at rates I could afford.

"Look," Peter said, his voice hurried. "I'm getting together a list of possibilities. Talk later?"

He disconnected before I could answer. I slid down the building, sat on the cracked sidewalk adorned with rainbows made from chalk. I pulled my legs toward me, put my head on my knees. This case. This fucking case. It had robbed me of sleep and peace, my mind in a constant state of worry about Zach.

Zach in prison.

Zach with a record.

Zach's name in a database for sex offenders.

And, even if the court dismissed the charges, the internet footprint of the case would always be there. For job interviews, for graduate schools, for future love interests. No matter what happened, Zach's life would never be free of this allegation.

The only positive thing about the past few months was Peter. I looked forward to being with Peter more than anything else in my day. He'd been worried about Zach, about the trial. Nate's involvement had, at least, served as a boundary. Without it, he'd be pulled under by the weight of the stress. I'd lose my lifeline but, more than that, I'd cause Peter the kind of intense distress I'd been feeling for months. I wouldn't wish that on anyone, let alone the man I loved.

My phone chimed, signaling I had a message. I looked at it and saw Julie had made a Facebook post. I pulled up my account and saw her son had committed to Penn State. I knew I should be happy for him, for them, but I was jealous of their normal lives, of a clear college pathway that didn't involve trials and jail sentences and allegations of assault. My finger hovered over the like button; I finally pressed it. Good karma, I told myself, and stared at the phone.

For reasons I couldn't explain, I typed Kelly Dixon, Paige's mother, into the search bar of Facebook and pulled up her account. I hadn't checked her feed in weeks, hadn't wanted to see evidence of Paige's potentially bad mental state or posts about Zach. But, when I scrolled through, neither of those types of posts were there. Instead, pictures from the Dixons' recent trip to St. Martin crammed her feed. Photo after photo of white beaches, turquoise waters, and her three smiling children. In one post, Paige stood grinning in a red bikini in the center of a cove, hair around her shoulders in curly waves, bits blown back by the breeze. She looked healthy and happy, nothing like the girl I'd seen at The Roasted Bean before Christmas.

Maybe she was okay?

And, if Paige was okay, maybe Kelly would take mercy. Maybe she'd believe there was a chance Zach didn't do it, that it was some other drunk boy. And if Zach was the one, maybe Kelly would realize that Zach, just like Paige, had been drunk. That neither of them were acting in a way they would have normally. She could encourage Paige to talk to the District Attorney, to see if the Commonwealth would drop the charges. Paige and Zach could go on and live normal, productive lives and put this awful chapter behind them.

The more I thought about it, the more the idea took hold. I didn't need to find a new lawyer. I didn't need to pull Peter further into mine and Zach's mess. What I needed was to talk to Kelly.

Mother to mother.

49

Two days after deciding to talk to Kelly, I sat in my car in the upper parking lot of Crasmere Park, her white BMW in view. I knew from Facebook that Kelly walked in Crasmere Park with two girlfriends on Tuesday mornings. I stared at her empty car, felt like a stalker. Part of me, a big part, thought I should turn around. This was crazy. I wasn't even sure I was allowed to speak to her.

I glanced down, saw the picture I'd brought of Zach on the console, one of his senior class portraits. The photographer had allowed the kids to take goofy pictures along with the formal ones. One of Zach's friends bought a soccer ball, another a ukulele. Zach had brought Barkley. His face was next to the dog's in the photo; Zach smiling, Barkley looking dead center at the camera. The photo had been my favorite from the group. A larger, framed version sat on the credenza of the carriage house.

Maybe if Kelly saw the picture of Zach, she'd see what I did:

A nice kid.

A boy who wasn't a danger.

A high schooler unequipped to handle himself in jail.

I assumed Kelly would sympathize, but I didn't really know. The only time I'd ever spoken to her was outside the port-o-potties at the soccer game. She'd been angry, but that was before. Maybe the passage of time had softened her. Maybe Paige was okay.

The photo shook in my hand; I set it down. I mentally rehearsed the speech I'd devised the day before. Once. Twice. It was important I tell Kelly that I empathized with Paige; I knew from Natasha how hard it was to come forward. But Zach might be innocent. Or he might have made an alcohol-induced mistake. Either way, he'd learned his lesson. I was certain he'd never find himself in a situation like this again.

I practiced the speech a final time, then exited the vehicle, Zach's picture in hand. I checked my phone, assumed Kelly's walk would be over any minute.

I waited, then walked to the top of an asphalt trail buttressed with barren trees dotted with bits of leftover snow. A small manmade waterfall, one Zach loved as a small child, trickled; the familiar sound comforted me.

I waited a moment, the sun hot on my face, then peered around the bend. Kelly sat alone on a bench overlooking the water, a fuchsia Hydro Flask bottle beside her. Her face was down, thumbs flying over the keys of an oversized phone. She was probably posting a picture of her workout. I could almost see the post, a selfie of Kelly in her workout gear, the waterfall in the background.

I approached her from behind, my footsteps silent on the layer of soggy snow. I stopped. The inappropriateness of my being there, stalking the mother of my son's accuser, crashed over me like a wave.

I should leave.

My body would not move.

I couldn't leave.

What if this was it? What if this conversation, the one I was about to have, was the difference maker? I opened my mouth. A group of noisy joggers ran by. Kelly turned around; I stood a few feet away. She jumped, reached in her pocket, and pulled out a canister of mace.

"No. No. No." I held up my hands.

Kelly lowered the mace. "You scared me." She smiled. "I thought you were an attacker."

"Sorry." I waited for Kelly to recognize me. She seemed not to and, instead, gave a half wave. "See you later." She started toward the parking lot.

"Wait."

Kelly turned. Words escaped me. I stood mute on the path with Zach's picture.

Kelly's eyes fell to the photo; her demeanor changed. "Oh." She took a step backward, a guarded expression in her face. She reached in her pocket.

I held my hands up. "I'm sorry I startled you. I just want to talk." I tried to make my voice calm. "Mother to mother."

Kelly shook her head, took another step back. "You don't need to talk to me. There are a lot of mothers out there."

"None connected the way we are."

Kelly's face morphed from uncertainty to anger. "We are not connected. Your son attacked my daughter."

I stood still. This was it. Time for my speech. I tried and failed to recall the words, instead blurting out, "what if he's innocent?"

Kelly leaned on one foot, put a hand on her hip. "And what if he's not? That's why there's a trial process. To find out." She turned and strode toward the parking lot, her water bottle swinging as she walked. She pulled out keys and pressed a button. The BMW clicked with recognition.

I jogged after her, my limbs carried forward by a frantic, invisible force. "I know he seems guilty," I said, still moving. "But he might not be. And he's a good kid. I know my son."

Kelly reached her car; I stopped a few feet in front of her.

"Zach can't go to jail," I panted. "Please. He's my only child." I felt desperate. I searched Kelly's face for signs of empathy. Seeing none, I babbled on. "And Paige. She's seems alright. Would she really want to send Zach to jail? They were both drinking and---"

"Excuse me?"

I stopped my monologue and took in Kelly's demeanor: furious eyes, flared nostrils, an athletic stance.

"I mean –" I started.

Kelly held her hand out. "Did you just say Paige seems alright?"

"I –" Had I said that? I'd been so caught up in my own emotions. "I saw a picture on –" I stopped. I couldn't tell Kelly I had been stalking her Facebook posts. I'd look crazy. Maybe I was.

Kelly pointed in my direction. "You know, I don't give a hoot what you saw or think you saw. Paige isn't okay. She's embarrassed, upset, withdrawn, depressed. She's in therapy if you must know." Kelly looked away. A man jogged by; a woman pulled into the lot, emerged from her car with two giant dogs. Kelly looked back at me, lowered her voice. "The kids talk about her, you know. A bunch of them, older kids, call her 'The Tattler'." She made quotes with manicured fingers. "Other kids want to help. They want to be part of the cause. But Paige doesn't want to be a social icon against sex crimes. She's just wants to be a regular kid. She wants this behind her."

"So does Zach," I blurted. "He's not a danger. He's not a violent kid. If Paige can talk to the DA, if they drop the case, both of them can go back normal. They can be regular kids." I exhaled, the solution obvious in my mind.

She looked at me, eyes wide.

"It makes sense," I added.

"It makes sense to tell my daughter to just forget Zach

violated her because he doesn't want to deal with the consequences?"

Stated the way Kelly put it, the idea sounded terrible. "I didn't mean it that way."

"How did you mean it then?" She cocked her head, clearly waiting for the response I didn't have.

I looked at the ground. "He was drunk. They both were. Maybe neither of them really remembers."

Kelly opened her car door, threw her keys and water bottle on the seat. She stood a moment, her back to me, then turned around. "Would you feel differently if Zach had killed her?"

I startled at the question. "What? Of course."

She turned around. "Yeah. I thought so. Drunken killings are rare. They happen. Hardly ever. Do you know why?"

Still shocked by the initial question, I took a step back. Kelly was the one who seemed unhinged now.

She adjusted her ponytail. "It's because people instinctively know killing is wrong. Society teaches that from birth. No one would get away with saying 'oh so I drank too much, and I killed someone. Can we just forget it?' Not true with sex crimes." Kelly slid into her car. "Society must change the way it views these encounters. If kids like your son are let off the hook, if girls like my daughter are told to stand down, nothing will ever change. It will remain okay to violate women. Not a big deal. Not a real crime. I can't let that happen." Kelly gritted her teeth then glanced at the picture of Zach. Her face softened; she met my eyes. "I am sorry for you and your son." She shut the door, started her car, and drove out.

Her car made a left and disappeared on a tree-lined road. I stood, Zach's picture dormant in my hand.

I'd just made things worse.

50

After the failed encounter with Kelly, I drove toward the carriage house, my body on autopilot. What had made me think Kelly would understand? And why had I assumed Paige was okay? Zach appeared fine in photos too. Pictures never told the real story.

I pulled into the driveway, wiped stray tears with the back of my hand. I gulped down a breath, then saw Donna's car at the top of the drive. I hadn't talked to her since the blow up before Christmas. When we'd seen each other at work, she had made a show of not talking to me -- moving her break room chair in an exaggerated manner, or turning in the opposite direction if she saw me in the hall. She no longer included me in any social invitations with the other soccer moms, the group, save Julie, seeming to pick Donna in the friendship divorce.

And now she was here.

I couldn't handle another combative encounter. Not today.

I stepped out and looked in her car. Empty. I scanned the area, spotted her by the fence in front of the horse field. Thirty feet away. Looking straight at me.

"I can't do this today." I turned on my heel, head down, key out. Her footsteps clomped behind me. "Really," I said, not turning around. "You need to go."

"I'm sorry."

I paused, my key in the door. She was sorry?

Donna was never sorry.

Interest piqued, I turned. She stood with a hunched posture, her eyes dull. She wore no make-up, curly hair pulled back into a haphazard ponytail. Her coat was open over a sweatshirt with a coffee stain. A cellophane-wrapped basket hung limp in her hand.

"I'm sorry," she repeated. "I know you didn't peg my boys, you were just trying to do what was best for Zach. I get it. I shouldn't have reacted the way I did." She kicked at a bit of gravel-encrusted snow. "And I heard about you and Reed. I'm sorry."

I waved my hand in her direction. "The break-up was months ago. Why are you really here?"

She paused. "I'm just sorry, okay. I was a bad friend. I just --" She looked down, then back up at me. "I just wanted to tell you that."

Barkley jumped at the window, tail wagging. I glanced at him then back at Donna. "Apology accepted." My tone was brusque. I'd meant it to signal the end of the conversation.

"I brought you these." She held up the basket.

I glanced at the contents. Bath products.

I wanted to shut her out. Like Reed, she'd hadn't been there at the time I needed her most.

Then again, I was already isolated. Should I really to turn away one of the few people who still wanted to be my friend? I pushed open the door. "Come in." Donna stepped forward; I sniffed the basket of products. "Smells like peppermint."

She shrugged. "After Christmas clearance."

I shook her head and took the basket. "Cheapskate." I said

the word with affection, felt the familiar rhythm of our friendship.

She tossed her coat on a chair near the door. "Hey. Who says peppermint is just for December?"

I laughed and turned on the coffee pot. She sat at the kitchen table and gestured to the framed picture of Zach and Barkley, the larger version of the one I'd waved around during my encounter with Kelly.

"That's a good shot." Donna stared at the photo with a melancholic expression. "How are you?" she asked softly.

I pulled out two mugs. "Do you want the truth or the version I tell myself when I don't want to break down and cry?"

"The truth."

"It's awful." I explained about the support group meetings, and how Zach had become increasingly withdrawn. I told her about Nate leaving and the potential of a ten-year jail sentence.

She took in my words, eyes wide, but said nothing. "What's the good version?" she asked finally.

I exhaled. "In the good version, there's a break in the case. Or the jury believes our main witness, Darby –" I stopped, recalling that Donna was with me when they found her. "You remember."

"Right." Donna straightened. "And why wouldn't they believe her? She saw Zach in the bathroom, right?"

"Right." I poured us each a coffee, put cream into Donna's. I explained about the manual nature of Darby's insulin app and the fact her former boyfriend had been in the sex club. "The prosecution doesn't think Darby's a lock solid witness." I slid a mug to her and took a seat across.

"Well, they're crazy. She saw him, she recorded the time. That's that." She patted her hands against each other as if wiping away the issue.

"Yeah, well, maybe you could be on the jury."

She blew at her coffee, then took a sip. "Anything else?"

"Not really." I shared the few small leads Bo was pursuing.

I kept the meeting with Kelly Dixon to myself. Too raw. I visualized myself in the park, waving Zach's picture, running after Kelly, begging her to talk to Paige. I must have looked crazy. And I had stalked her. I'd literally staked out her location. Knowing the Dixons, they'd probably file harassment charges.

Donna reached over and squeezed my hand. "So awful. I'm sorry."

I shrugged. "Not your fault." I took a sip of coffee and realized then I'd asked nothing about her, about the divorce. "How about you? What's happening with Max?"

Her face clouded; she looked away. "Hearing got put off until June. Until then, we're sharing. One week on, one week off." She rolled her eyes. "I don't think I'll be able to afford the house when this goes through."

"I'm sorry." My mind pulled up a vision of Donna's house, a home that had welcomed me and Zach for decades. "We had a lot of good times in that house."

"Yeah. That's why it's so hard to give it up."

We both fell into silence, my mind a barrage of memories of an earlier, better time. Peter's figure, heading to the barn, jolted me to the present. He wore jeans and hiking boots, a thick, gray sweatshirt pulled tight across broad shoulders.

Donna sat up, seeming suddenly energized. "Hey. Is that the hot –"

"Off the market."

She cocked her head; I felt my cheeks get hot.

She slammed the table. "No."

I smiled. "Yes."

She leaned back. "Well, he's better than Reed, that's for sure."

I rolled my eyes. "You never liked Reed."

"Just saying. You know, when I saw him, he didn't even

admit you two had broken up. He acted like everything was fine."

"He's probably afraid of you."

She shook her head. "He's such a pussy."

"Donna."

"Sorry. True."

Peter corralled Fritter back to the barn, his manner gentle but firm.

She nodded toward him. "Now that's hot."

Before I could agree, the door swung open. Zach entered, slung his backpack on the floor.

Donna stood. "Hey Zach." Her intonation was different. Pitying.

Zach nodded toward her. "Hey, Mrs. Sullivan." He made his way to the kitchen, opened the fridge door and grabbed a slice of cold pizza. He ripped off a piece of crust with his teeth.

Donna took a step away from the table. "How are you? Carter says you've missed some school."

Zach shrugged. "A few days here and there." He took another bite of pizza, dropped a piece of the crust for Barkley.

She looked like she wanted to say something, stood staring at him instead.

I'd become immune to these types of encounters, ones where people instantly became mute when Zach came into view, like his circumstance was contagious. And, though those occurrences hurt, the people involved didn't really know him. Not like Donna. She'd known Zach since he was eight-years-old. She was practically a second mother. That she couldn't carry on a normal conversation with him? It stung.

She picked up her coat. "I should go."

I wanted to stop her, shake her, make her talk and joke with my son the way she used to. But Zach had already disappeared up the loft. Forcing him to come down so I could make the point seemed unnecessary. But I could say something to Donna.

I opened my mouth to point out her faux pas but shut it when I saw her face. She looked ashen, her eyes glazed. "Are you alright?"

She pulled open the door, stepped outside, and fanned herself. "I'm alright. Just needed some air. Sorry." She moved toward her car, then turned, catapulted toward me, and engulfed me in a hug. I felt her tears on my shoulder; I rubbed her back.

"I'm sorry," she said, pulling back. "You're the one going through all this and I'm the one crying." She wiped her face with her coat sleeve.

I hadn't known Donna to be a crier; her reaction surprised me. But it touched me too. It felt good that she cared so deeply about me and Zach.

I reached out and squeezed her hand. "Thank you for caring," I said, tears starting in my own eyes.

She pulled me back toward her, gave my body another tight squeeze. "Zach will win," she whispered.

51

Peter

"Is it bad?" Meredith leaned against a tree outside the carriage house. She'd just finished recounting her conversation with Kelly Dixon that morning.

"I don't think so," I said. "Neither of you is a party to the case. It's not like you're legally banned from talking to Paige or her relatives." The statement made sense; I hoped it was true.

She exhaled. "Alright. Thanks. I thought I blew it."

"You're fine." I kissed her gently on the head and looked at my watch. "I've got to get ready for a meeting."

I dressed in more formal clothes and left to meet attorney Drew Kirkland, an experienced criminal attorney recommended by Nate.

Nate, apparently having heard that I lost the motion for a continuance, emailed Kim a list of attorneys who might come in late. When Kim first gave me the list, I'd made a ridiculous show of ripping it in half. Kim reached down, grabbed the pieces and taped them together. "Don't be a jackass," she'd said, handing me the paper.

Methodically, I'd called the lawyers in the order Nate had

listed, paying close attention to the words he'd written next to each name: Arrogant. Pricy. Hates Yvonne.

The first lawyer on the list, Lydia Tweedy, was too busy. Same for Maddox Moran. And Mark Grygotis. Mara Rankin was interested. Her retainer, she said matter-of-factly, was $150,000. Just to start. Jan Stanek said she'd think about it, later called and said no. Jed Looney and Sam Harrrison didn't even return my voice messages.

One by one, I eliminated lawyers from the list until I had reached the final name, Drew Kirkland, the word 'wild' next to it in boldface type. Wild? I conjured up the image of a caveman; I couldn't find a photo of Drew online.

I sat in Drew's waiting room now, a stack of old magazines on the table beside me. The woman who'd taken my name smacked gum behind her desk. She pecked at a keyboard with her index fingers, then blew a giant, pink bubble. It popped on her face; she wiped it with the back of her hand. Behind her, a framed black and white sketch of former President Millard Filmore hung off center on the wall. It looked like something that might have been purchased at a garage sale.

I exhaled. It was not the best first impression.

"Peter Flynn?"

I stood. A tall man with chiseled features in a perfect suit stood in the door frame. He looked normal, not wild. Nate was insane.

I extended my hand. "Drew. Great to meet you."

The man shook his head. "Oh, no. I'm not Drew." He adjusted his lapel. "I'm Hunter, his assistant. Come on back." I followed Hunter past a room containing an old-fashioned coffee maker and Styrofoam cups. A copy machine in the hall operated on its own, legal documents spitting from its mouth. He gestured to a water cooler, triangular cups affixed to the side.

"Water?"

"No thanks."

Hunter knocked on a closed door at the end of the hall, simultaneously opening it. "Peter Flynn's here." Hunter pushed the door wider. I stepped through.

Drew sat behind an enormous desk covered with piles of papers. His hair was jet black, a few cowlicks protruding from the back like spikes. He pushed smeared glassed up his nose and half stood. "Peter. Nice to meet you." He extended his hand across the desk. I shook it.

"Sit, sit." He gestured to two chairs with stacked with papers filled with cross-outs and illegible scrawl.

"Move anything," he said, his manner jovial. "Make yourself at home."

I moved a stack to the floor and sat down. I looked at Drew. He had on a blue oxford shirt; the buttons pulled across the beginnings of a potbelly. It was hard to gauge his age. Thirty-five? Forty, maybe?

"Do you golf?" he asked.

"Some." Normally, I was fine with small talk but, today, it seemed an irritation. Who could talk about golf with Zach's trial so close?

"I just got a Maverick driver. Callaway." He swiveled his chair toward a bag of golf clubs set against the wall. In a fluid movement, he stood, removed a club, then pulled off a cover that looked like a gorilla head. He pushed the club head in my direction. "Check her out."

I nodded at it. "Nice."

He put the club back, sat back down. I eyed an oversized box of munchkins on the edge of his desk.

Drew followed my gaze. "Want one? They're all chocolate."

I held up my hand. "No, thanks."

He held one up. "This is gourmet right here." He popped it in his mouth. "So," he said, still chewing. "Rumor has it, you're looking for co-counsel." He plucked his glasses off his face, rubbed the lenses on his shirt. When he put them back on, there were still smears on the glass.

"I'm interviewing a few candidates."

Drew grabbed a pen shaped like a golf tee, tapped it on the desk. "Any luck? It's kind of last minute."

I kept my expression neutral. "I'm narrowing down the options."

"Really?" He put down the pen and leaned back. "Because I heard no one wants to touch this case. It's fine to lose cases no one knows about. But the Morgan case is prime time. Bad for the reputation to lose one of those."

My heart banged in my chest. "What makes you think we'll lose?"

He shrugged. "There are eye-witnesses, right? And Yvonne Williams, man. She's tough. She will not want to lose this one." He paused. "But you must have something. What's your case? What do you got?"

I opened my mouth, then shut it. We had nothing, not compared to the evidence the prosecution had amassed.

My heart hammered, my head spun with images of Meredith and Zach. Zach on the couch, a Fanta in his hand, Barkley in a brown curl beside him. Meredith holding up a hand of cards in the sunroom opposite Dad. Her face when she saw the carriage house lit up for Christmas. Image after image clicked in my mind like a slideshow. I held the last one, one of Meredith in the light of the fire after the first time we'd made love, hair spilling down her back.

"I need some air."

I stood up abruptly and made my way out on to the sidewalk in front of the bland office complex. Cars sped on the highway in front. I exhaled, put my hands on my knees. Fuck. I couldn't handle Zach's case. I couldn't even talk about it. Shit. Shit. Shit. I kicked the building wall. Shit. I kicked the wall again, too hard. Pain seared in my foot; I hopped backward.

"Ouch."

I looked up. It was Drew. He took a pack of cigarettes and a lighter from his pocket. He lit one and inhaled. "You alright?"

"Yeah –" I forced myself to stop hopping and set my foot on the ground. "I'm alright."

I glanced at Drew. He was tall, over six feet, and now wore a long tweed coat. He'd taken off his glasses; his hair less wild. He looked normal.

What the hell? It wasn't like I would ever see him again. "Actually no, Drew, I am not alright."

He held the pack of cigarettes in my direction. I'd smoked only a handful of times and hated it. I took one anyway.

He threw me the lighter. "I didn't use to smoke, you know. I started after I lost my first case. Never stopped." He blew out smoke in a ring.

I lit my cigarette. Inhale. Exhale. Inhale. Exhale. The rhythm relaxed me. My shoulders dropped.

"I've known Zach Morgan's mom since seventh grade. We were biology lab partners." I visualized Meredith dissecting the frog in lab, her head bent over with the knife, ponytail swung to one side. "I can't lose this case."

"You might."

"I can't."

"I'll help you."

I took a drag from the cigarette, let it dangle in my fingers after. Red embers fell to the ground. I made eye contact with Drew. "Why would you do that?"

"Good question." He took another drag before continuing. "My first real client, the first case I handled on my own, was a kid Zach's age. Jesse Cook. Same kind of scenario. He said, she said." His eyes were distant as he spoke, almost as if he was conjuring an image of Jesse in his mind. "He was a nice kid. I thought he was innocent. Maybe he wasn't. I still don't know for sure. He got four years; the plea offer was one. Not the worst sentence. But for a kid that age?" He threw down his cigarette and stepped on it. "Four years is everything."

I nodded, the concern the same one I'd had for Zach. Two years, four years, ten years. Doing time of any length would never be easy. But a kid being plucked from their prime, before they got grounded in adulthood? A four-year sentence in that time period would be especially heart-wrenching.

Drew continued. "That sentence changed the trajectory of Jesse's life, I'm sure of it. I've always blamed myself. So helping Zach, it's –" Drew let his thought trail off.

"Redemption?"

"Yeah. Redemption. Absolution. Mercy. All of it."

I watched the cars whizz by. Tractor trailers, SUVs, minivans shuttling down the highway.

"When's the trial?" Drew asked.

"Four weeks."

Drew threw his cigarette on the ground and twisted his foot over its end. "Tell you what. Let me review the case. I'll give you my thoughts, get you prepared. I'll come to as many trial days as I can."

I looked at him. A few minutes ago, I never would have considered teaming up with Drew. The idea didn't seem so terrible anymore. "What would you charge?"

He met my gaze. "What are you charging?"

"Nothing."

"I'll charge the same."

I reached my hand out and shook Drew's.

"Welcome to the case."

52

Drew dove in right away. Within two weeks, he'd become a regular at the office; remnants of his presence left after each visit -- a stray Rubik's cube on the conference table, a pair of dice next to the copier. Next to Kim's desk, he'd left a pair of old ice skates.

Kim held them up. "Really?"

I glanced at the skates. "He's eccentric."

"Crazy's more like it." She set them down, a hint of a smile on her face.

I leaned forward. "You like him."

"I don't. He's nuts." She turned back to her computer monitor.

"Nuts in a nice way, though, right?"

Kim's cheeks reddened. "Okay. Maybe it's a little nice having Drew around."

As if on cue, the office door swung open. Drew stepped inside, a six pack in each hand. "Happy hour?" He placed the beers on Kim's desk. "I brewed these myself. I call it Drew's Dynamite." He moved his hands as if underscoring the words.

Kim smirked.

"So," Drew said, picking up a beer. "You in?"

I looked at the beers then back to the pile of documents, both for Zach's case and all those I needed to keep the firm going.

I had a ton to do.

I needed a break.

"Why the hell not?" I set the files on Kim's desk and held up my phone. "I'll even order pizza."

I placed an order for pizza and joined Kim and Drew in the conference room. Drew slid a longneck bottle across the table.

I caught the beer, twisted the top off, part of me hesitant to drink something that Drew had brewed God-knows-where. I sniffed at the beer, citrus filled my senses.

"Lemon." Drew said. He jutted his chin in my direction. "Come on, try it."

I put the bottle to my lips and took a long drink. It was good, robust and full-bodied. "Nice."

Drew clinked my bottle with his own. "Second career, baby."

"I'm with you, man. I'm with you." I took another swig.

Drew told stories about growing up on an alpaca farm; Kim, about her former job as a nanny. I found myself laughing, real laughs from my gut. How long it had been since I'd laughed that hard? I couldn't remember. Thanksgiving?

The pizza arrived. I grabbed a second beer and went to get it just as Bo shuffled in, phone in hand. She held it up. "Someone texted about a party?"

Drew held his hands up. "Guilty." He handed her a beer.

I paid the pizza guy and thought of Meredith. Should I call her? Would she like this?

No. The answer came automatically.

I loved Meredith, but her being here would alter the mood. She'd said it herself after returning from what was supposed to be a fun night out with alleged friends: "If you want to ruin a party, just invite the mother of the accused." I'd rubbed her shoulders with a deep circular motion, assured her she'd imagined the tension and awkwardness. But she hadn't. We both knew that.

I oriented myself to the present, tried to catch on to a story Bo was telling.

"And then I realized he was in his pajamas!"

It was the punchline. Drew and Kim laughed. I joined in, the sound hollow in my throat, my thoughts unable to leave Meredith. She would be home with Zach, exhausting herself with valiant attempts to make things seem normal. She could use a laugh. She could use camaraderie. Hell, she could use a beer.

I held up my phone. "Let me call Meredith and invite her down."

Immediate silence.

I looked up, finger poised over the call button. "What?" I put the phone down. "What?" I asked again.

Bo and Drew exchanged a look. The atmosphere, jovial a moment ago, was now thick with tension.

"I should get going." Kim stood up, cleared her plate and stepped out.

The door shut behind Kim, and I faced Drew and Bo. "Is one of you going to tell me what's going on?" My stomach filled with the now familiar sensation of anxiety and fear.

"We were going to talk to you about this Monday," Drew started. "I finished my review of the case."

"And."

"Unless you get a perfect jury, Zach's not going to win."

I dropped my head. I knew it. Deep down I knew it. Shit.

Drew bent down and pulled a thick file from his briefcase. "We'll show you."

Over the next hour, Bo and Drew meticulously laid out the pros of the case for each side. In an awful visual, Drew listed them on a wipe board, Zach's name on the left, Commonwealth on the right. Ten pros to two. I leaned back, thinking the list was compete, when Drew picked up a marker and wrote Yvonne Williams under the Commonwealth side.

I pulled my fingers through my hair, felt the itch of hives. There had to be something. "Any way we can turn it around?"

"That's just it, Peter." Bo said in a voice so uncharacteristically soft, it felt more alarming than it would have had she spoke in her normal, blunt tone. "We've exhausted every avenue legally and investigation-wise. There are no more witnesses to interview, no more legal motions to file. The case is as good as it's going to get."

I put my head in my hands. No. I looked up, glanced at the wipe board. "Well, I can't just take my ball and go home."

"You need to talk to Yvonne," Drew interjected. "Get a plea offer."

"I won't get one without jail time."

Drew's voice was firm. "Don't let Zach be your Jesse." He paused. "Four years, maybe less, is significantly different from a decade behind bars."

"What's the harm in asking?" Bo tipped her head. "The plea might be good. Yvonne might want to get this off the docket."

"I'll be on the call with you," Drew volunteered. "I'm free all afternoon tomorrow."

I blew out a breath. "Alright," I said simply. "I'll set it up."

I left shortly after. My phone pinged with a text as I drove. I stop at a traffic light, glanced at it. One word from Meredith. *Beers?*

My heart lifted at the thought of having beers with Meredith. I would love a quiet night with her, watching television or sports or lounging around reading magazines or thrillers. I wanted to feel her body next to mine under a shared afghan, our elevated bare feet on the coffee table. I wanted to talk to Zach about the latest Sixers game, take Barkley for a walk in the woods. I wanted to hold Meredith in bed at night, have breakfast with her in the morning.

I wanted a normal life with Meredith so badly, my body ached. But it wouldn't happen if – when? – a jury convicted Zach. She'd never forgive me and, even if she did, I'd never forgive myself. I'd picture Zach in jail every day. The same curse Drew had had with Jesse, only worse.

Drew hadn't been in love with Jesse's mother.

The text pinged again. *Beers?*

I pulled over and texted a lie about a stomachache, then drove home and went to bed. My phone pinged again as I laid there. Meredith. *Feel better. Love you.* Heart. Heart. Heart.

"Love you too," I whispered.

I didn't answer the text.

~

I SAT at my desk the next morning, a list of the arguments for a plea on a legal pad. I dialed the District Attorney's office to set up a time for Drew and I to talk to Yvonne.

The phone rang once, a woman's voice filled the line. "District Attorney's office. Yvonne Williams speaking."

I sat up. Yvonne had answered the main phone? Why? I looked at my own phone as if the answer to the unexpected occurrence would materialize on the screen.

"Hello? Can I help you?"

"Yes. Um. Yvonne. It's Peter Flynn. I'm calling on the Morgan case. I wanted to set up a time to talk later, a conference call."

"Well, I'm on the phone now." She remained silent, clearly waiting for me to speak. I could hardly tell her I needed Drew on the line. I was an adult. And an attorney. I exhaled. I knew what the arguments were. I could do this.

"I wanted to talk about a plea," I started. I went through my argument without interruption, gaining confidence as I ticked off each of the items on my list. "So," I concluded, "we're looking for a plea without jail time. Or dismissal of the case."

Silence. I opened my mouth to say more, shut it. Maybe she was thinking about the offer?

Time stretched on. I stared at my list.

Yvonne's voice, when she finally spoke, was crisp. "Thank you for that succinct overview of your case, Mr. Flynn. The Commonwealth will not be offering another plea in this matter."

The phone clicked off. She'd hung up. No offer, not even a bad one.

I cradled my head in my arms. I'd been concerned a plea offer from Yvonne would be bad but, at least, it would be something to work with. Maybe I could have gotten it down to something palatable. But no plea offer? I wasn't prepared for that.

Shit.

I picked up a metal pen holder and threw it to the ground. The pens rolled out haphazardly. I kicked one; it skittered against the wall. Fuck. Fuck. Fuck.

No plea offer.

No evidence.

No out.

I took a deep breath, recalled my conversation with Bo and Drew.

There was one chance for Zach to get acquitted.

I'd have to pick a perfect jury.

53

Jury selection was a Friday, the same day, it turned out, as Zach's senior prom. He hadn't planned to go, but the juxtaposition of what was actually happening versus what could have been was nonetheless jarring. On a day when he should have been picking up a corsage for his date and readying himself for one-of-a-kind night with friends, Zach was, instead, dressing for court.

In lieu of a suit, we'd decided on khakis and an army green button down shirt. The hope was that Zach wouldn't look like a court defendant but, instead, clean-cut and ordinary, the kind of kid who might bag up groceries at the Stop and Shop or mow neighborhood lawns for money. It wasn't a stretch. Zach *was* that kid. But potential jurors didn't know that.

Meredith stood back, examined Zach, then stepped forward and moved a stray cowlick, adjusted his collar. She pressed both of her hands on his shoulders and moved back a second time to take in his entire body. The whole scenario reminded me of Suzanne Collins' book, *The Hunger Games*, Zach a tribute about to appear before the judges, and Meredith the stoic mother trying to make her son look as impressive as possible.

"You missed a loop," she said, pointing, "for your belt."

Zach looked down.

"He'll be sitting," I said. "I think it's okay." But her worried gaze remained fixed on the stray belt loop. I wasn't sure what adverse conclusion she thought potential jurors would come to over it, or how they would even see it, but her concern over the missed loop was clear. I looked to Zach. "Maybe just fix it."

Zach undid his belt buckle, and I put my arm on Meredith's shoulder. "It will be alright." I said the words as though I had things under control which was a complete lie. I couldn't even think clearly. I'd barely slept in weeks; stress coursed through my veins like its life source. The only thing that kept me going was the knowledge that my assurances, fake or not, seemed to be what kept Meredith together.

She looked at me, eyes trusting. "Okay."

I wanted to vomit, to leave, to do anything but endure the next hours and the next week. Instead, I kissed Meredith on the cheek and drove her only son to the courthouse where I would hand-select people to decide his fate.

Meredith had wanted to come to the selection; I'd discouraged it. She'd made the point that, if Zach was sick in the hospital, she'd be in the waiting room. In her mind, this situation was no different. But it was. At a hospital, everyone had the same goal: get the patient better. It was the opposite in court. One whole side, the larger one fueled by tax dollars and a government agency, was set to prove Zach wrong.

Ultimately, she'd agreed to stay home, a decision for which I was grateful. I wasn't sure I could handle Meredith's anxiety on top of my own, though I knew I'd have to do that for the trial next week.

Once in court, I sat at counsel table, Drew on one side, Zach on the other. As my firm was the trial counsel attached to the case, I'd do the *voir dire,* but Drew had promised constant support. He'd set a yellow legal pad between us for notes.

The potential jurors sat in the courtroom along with us, waiting for the judge, and Yvonne Williams, to arrive. In a general sense, the jurors gave the impression of an annoyed audience awaiting the start of a terrible show. Only two jurors looked remotely pleased to be there – a man in a MAGA t-shirt and an older woman with shock white hair.

Yvonne swung into the courtroom. She pulled a jet black briefcase on wheels, the initials YKW on its front. She nodded at me and Drew, lips parting in a half-smile. A young attorney, twentyish, followed behind her, head high, her expression one of nervous awe. The women sat. Yvonne pulled out a file, spread paperclipped documents across the table, then folded her hands and waited. The young girl mimicked her movements. They reminded me of teachers waiting for class to settle down. The room did become noticeably quieter.

"All rise." Judge Richardson's court clerk stepped through the door, the judge behind him. "Please be seated."

I'd seen Judge Richardson, the judge assigned the case, during the hearing for my failed application for a continuance. She was older with gray, sprayed hair, a round face, and rosy cheeks that made her seem like a modern Mrs. Claus. Her voice, sweet and grandmotherly, made her seem kind. She wasn't, at least not as a judge. She ran her courtroom with a tough authority that, had I not been on the receiving end of it, I would have found impressive.

Judge Richardson gave instructions to the jurors, and it started then, the *voir dire*. I stumbled with my questions at first, then fell into a rhythm. The court dismissed the man with the MAGA t-shirt for cause after he acknowledged a bias against women accusers.

I used my first peremptory challenge on a young girl with pink hair after Drew had furiously scribbled "no way" on the pad. When I'd hesitated, he'd underlined the phrase.

A middle-aged bank teller named Charlotte became the

first member of the jury. Mother of two, one of them a boy, age twelve. Charlotte felt like a win. We were trying to fill the box with mothers of boys, mirrors of Meredith.

The second juror was an older man, the third a woman with a red scarf tied in an elaborate knot around her neck. Scarf woman fiddled with an armful of bangle bracelets then greeted the next juror, a short order cook named Milt, in a manner which suggested they were both part of an exclusive club. Both Milt and scarf woman were parents of boys.

By 1:30, we'd selected all the jurors. They sat in two rows, seven men, five women. I stared at the group. It felt strange they would stand in judgment of Zach, a boy I'd gotten to know so well. Zach was a good kid. But how would the jury know that? The only version of him they would get was the teen boy who drank too much and attacked girls. Then again, Zach's goodness, or lack thereof, didn't matter under the law.

Judge Richardson gave final instructions. We'd reconvene for the trial on Monday. The weekend, I knew, would be horrific. How could I look at Zach without thinking: this might be the last weekend you get to pet your dog, grab a soda, use the bathroom without concern? How could I continue to placate Meredith with false hope, pretend as though it was just as likely as not that, at the end of the trial, she'd drive home with her son in the passenger seat, his giant feet on the dash?

As the courtroom cleared out, I saw Meredith in the back row, her lips a grim line. She held her hand up in a half wave, and I wondered when it was that she'd slipped in. I walked to where she now stood, Zach behind me. "Do you think it's a good jury?" Her eyes were wide.

"Yes. Lots of boy mothers." The thought was that mothers of boys would have an underlying bias in favor of Zach but who knew? That Yvonne had let the Moms pass on to the jury concerned me. Was the strategy faulty? What did Yvonne know that we didn't?

Meredith nodded, her expression distant before she shook her head and oriented herself to the present. "Can I take Zach home?"

I looked back at Drew, who remained at counsel table, pieces of the file spread out before him. "I don't see why not," I said, turning back to her.

Meredith and Zach left. I tried not to think of how they would spend the afternoon. Meredith had doubled up on her efforts to make things seem normal, the effect of which was way worse than it would have been had she just acknowledged the awfulness. She'd probably force Zach into an awkward mother-son lunch or some other activity he was too kind to decline. But I couldn't worry about Meredith and Zach; I had to focus on Monday's trial. I stepped up to counsel table, tapped on it. "Ready to go?"

Drew looked up. "I am." He stuffed a few juror files into the overfilled cross-shoulder bag he used as a briefcase. He stood, then inclined his head toward Yvonne Williams, still sitting at counsel table.

As if she could sense the gesture, Yvonne whipped her head in our direction, her expression unreadable.

I started at her, this woman fighting for justice who I'd vilified in my mind. Our eyes locked, neither of us averting our gaze in what felt like an unspoken battle of wills. "Peter," she said finally, breaking the contest.

I startled. She'd never addressed me by my first name.

She stood, all six feet of her, and looked down at me.

"I'm going to do something unusual."

54

I met Yvonne's gaze and, despite my heart moving into my throat, I tried to maintain a neutral expression.

She tipped her head. "I'm going back on my statement that the Commonwealth will not offer a plea." She smoothed out her suit skirt. "I don't usually do that once a jury is empaneled."

I adjusted my lapel. Why was she doing this? Did she not like the jury? Did she think Zach had a chance?

Yvonne produced a paper and placed it on the table before me and Drew. "Two years in jail, eligible for probation in one. Your client can plead no contest."

No contest, I knew, was a means by which Zach could agree to the punishment without admitting he committed the offense.

Yvonne tapped on the terms. "Offer's good until the trial starts Monday." She grabbed the handle of her wheeled briefcase and started toward the door.

I looked at the paper. Why had she changed her position? She'd been adamant that the Commonwealth would not offer a plea. To make an offer now? It seemed a red flag. I called out to her. "Why the change of heart?"

She stopped and, though I couldn't see her expression, I could visualize it, perturbed and annoyed. Lowly Peter Flynn was questioning her clear good will? She stood still in the aisle. I half expected her to turn and recant, a penalty for my recalcitrance. My heart beat harder. I fought the urge to take back the question.

What felt like a full minute elapsed before Yvonne turned. She narrowed her eyes in a way that, but for the circumstances, might have seemed comical. "Do you not want to bring my offer to your client?"

I shifted my weight from one leg to the other. "I just want to know why you changed your mind."

Yvonne paused before answering. "You may not realize this, Mr. Flynn, but very public trials can be hard on the accused. Paige Dixon would like this to be over. She asked me to make this offer."

She turned and left, the heavy door of the courtroom shut behind her. I looked at Drew. "Well?"

Drew leaned back with the offer, set it down on the table. "It's a gift."

"Do you think we can counter?" I asked, my mind whirring. "Meredith won't like the jail time."

"It's a gift." Drew repeated. "Two minutes ago, Zach was looking at the possibility of ten years."

"Mer –" I started.

"Meredith's not the client, Peter. Zach is." Drew's voice was uncharacteristically harsh. He put his head in his hands before looking at me again. "Look, Peter. It's obvious how you feel about Meredith, but you can't let your emotions get in the way. It's not fair to Zach." He blew out a breath, then continued. "If you get Meredith involved, if she talks Zach out of this plea because she can't stand the thought of her little boy in jail for a single second, how does that play out if he gets convicted, if he goes to jail for the maximum? She'll never forgive herself."

The court clerk appeared from the door behind us. "Got to get set up for a hearing." He stepped toward the tables with a stack of fresh cups.

"I know it will be hard to do," Drew said, grabbing the file and plea offer, "but you've got to give Zach this offer without Meredith's input. The choice has to be his." Drew put his hand on my shoulder, nodded toward the door. "We got to go."

I followed Drew out, thinking of his counsel. It was an impossible situation. If I allowed Zach to take the plea without telling Meredith, she'd never forgive me. But, if Zach didn't take the plea because she talked him out of it, she'd never forgive herself if he lost.

We reached the glass courthouse door; Drew pushed it open. Raindrops pelted the surrounding ground. Drew met my gaze. "Talk to Zach alone, Peter. It's the right thing to do." He rapped me on the shoulder then raced down the stairs, hand over his head like a makeshift umbrella.

I pulled a real umbrella from my briefcase, stood on the steps. I recalled Meredith's expression after she'd gotten the call from Zach at the Black Cat ball. It seemed a lifetime ago, the possibility that the entire event was a terrible mix-up still real. And now? If Zach took the plea, he would go to jail on Monday. I exhaled.

How would I be able to keep this from Meredith?

55

That night, I did not want to have pizza at the carriage house in what had become the standard Friday tradition. The idea of sitting with Meredith and pretending the plea offer didn't exist felt wrong. I thought about feigning an excuse but didn't. Meredith needed me there to maintain the routine, even if the night would be excruciating. And I needed to get Zach alone. So, I sat in the carriage house with the two of them, a barely eaten pizza in the center of the table between us.

Meredith pushed the box toward me. "Have another."

The last thing I wanted was more food, but I dutifully pulled a slice toward my plate.

"I got extra cheese," she commented. She picked up a plastic knife and cut the strings which stretched from the box to my plate.

"Good call."

It was awful, the atmosphere so tense that we may as well have been sitting inside of a black cloud. None of us wanted to talk about the jury selection or the upcoming trial but, really, what else was there to talk about? The beautiful night that would have been Zach's senior prom? The Phillies winning streak? PITT? Any subject, except the case, seemed frivolous or emotionally charged or both. We sat in silence, every sound amplified. Chewing, the rattle of ice cubes. Even Barkley's breathing seemed loud.

Zach's second slice remained untouched on his plate. Meredith swallowed, nodded toward it. "You need to eat, honey."

He pushed his plate away. "I'm good." He tore off a piece of crust and threw it to Barkley. The dog jumped and caught it in his mouth. Zach threw a second then stood. "I'm going to take Bark for a walk." He grabbed the leash and clipped it to the dog's collar.

"I'll go." I jumped up, too quick.

Meredith gestured to the uneaten slice of pizza I'd just put on my plate. "You don't want this?"

I shrugged. "Maybe when I get back. I could really use some fresh air."

She nodded, the look on her face defeated. It was as if she'd realized that there'd be no sense in insisting people eat, on pretending that things were even somewhat normal.

"I'll be right back," I said, though this was likely untrue.

I found Zach and Barkley in the driveway, waiting. I followed them in silence to the road, stalling the conversation I didn't want to have. Barkley's tail wagged in time with our steps. I took a deep breath, wished I had no ulterior motive, that Zach and I were truly out for a dog walk on an ordinary evening. "So I had a conversation with Yvonne Williams at the courthouse today."

Zach didn't respond verbally, but his steps quickened.

"She offered a plea." I explained the terms of the deal, the consequences of it. Zach remained silent. I didn't blame him. It was a lot to take in. "You don't have to decide right now."

Barkley stopped to sniff a patch of grass; Zach in front of

him, his face away from mine. "Did you tell my Mom?" he asked finally.

"No."

"She won't like it."

"I know."

We walked, our footsteps heavy on the sidewalk. I visualized Meredith back at the house, clearing the plates, putting the leftover pizza in the fridge. She wasn't in a good place, not with the trial Monday, but she had no idea Zach's fate might be decided in the next few minutes. My stomach seized again at the thought of keeping her in the dark.

A BMW zoomed past us, music blaring. Zach pulled on Barkley's leash. "I think I should take the offer."

He spoke without looking at me. I didn't respond, my voice in my throat. It was the conclusion I wanted him to come to, but hearing Zach say it made the inevitable closer. No chance of an acquittal. His jail sentence would start Monday.

"Do you agree?" His voice was small.

I exhaled, not wanting to give the advice but knowing I had to. "Yes."

We stopped at the driveway. Zach bent down and pet Barkley; the dog to licked his face with a sloppy pink tongue. "Hey, boy. Hey, boy." He looked up. "My Mom won't want me to take it, you know."

I looked down, mustering the energy for the words that felt like a betrayal. I looked up into Zach's eyes, painfully like his mother's.

"That's why I don't think you should tell her."

56

Meredith

My heart beat so hard I thought its outline could be seen in my chest.

Zach sat next to Peter at the defense counsel table. Zach in the navy-blue suit we'd gotten two weeks ago. A stray tag stuck out the back. I wanted to tuck it in. A tiny, motherly gesture. One I would not have thought twice about months ago. But, now, Zach was on a trial for sexual assault and there was a literal barrier between me and my son. A security officer too.

Our conversation that morning, the final one, had not been the best. I'd tried to assure Zach, and myself, that the jury may believe his side of the story, that he might get acquitted. He'd shaken his head. "I know what I'm up against, Mom."

He'd looked at me strangely, then pet Barkley, the dog's giant tail thumping on the hard floor. Zach had stared straight ahead on the car ride over, swallowing then clearing his throat in a nervous rhythm. His hand trembled.

"You've got to believe in your own case," I'd admonished, desperate to instill a sense of confidence.

He'd given me a sideways look, then reached out and squeezed my shoulder in a gesture of comfort.

It was worse than if he had argued.

Now, in the courtroom, I had to force myself to look away from him. I averted my eyes from his back, looked around. Judge Patricia Richardson's courtroom was stately, more so than the little district court we'd been in for the preliminary proceedings. A massive desk, the judge's bench, sat in the front, a space for a court reporter on one side, a law clerk on the other. Behind the desk, American and Pennsylvania flags buttressed a gold-embossed State seal affixed to the wall. Brown panels lined the walls which, combined with the absence of windows, made me feel trapped. Anxiety intensified my sense of smell, and I fought off nausea from the competing odors of perfume and sweat inside the crowded space.

A woman filled water pitchers at the counsel table. She approached the court reporter after, their heads together. The court reporter laughed.

A regular day in their life.

The worst day of mine.

A man with a giant sketchpad made his way down the aisle, dragging an easel behind him. He set up in the front, near where the jury would sit. I could see his pad from my front-row vantage point, a white canvas to be filled with hand-drawn scenes of the trial. I stared at the empty juror seats which would soon be filled by the twelve strangers who would decide the course of Zach's life.

And my own.

I glanced around, saw a few familiar faces. Julie was the only representative of the soccer moms. Donna would have been there, she'd said, but there had a been a last-minute change in the work schedule. I spied Reed in the back, his plain brown shirt blending into the wall panels. He put his hand up in a half-wave. I touched the empty space where my engagement ring had been. Had my life not been completely derailed, Reed and I would have been on our honeymoon right now.

Most of the crowd, I realized, sat on the prosecution side behind the Dixons. Kelly and Scott, Paige's parents, sat in the front row as I did, a macabre version of the sides in a wedding ceremony.

"All rise."

The courtroom silenced immediately.

Vomit formed in my throat; I steadied myself on the banister.

Judge Richardson followed her law clerk, a thick file under her arm. She had a round, wrinkled face and rosy cheeks. She'd pulled her grayish hair away from her face in a way that accentuated clear, blue eyes. She looked like a sweet grandma. Normally, her appearance would have given me comfort but I knew from Peter that her looks were a ruse. Judge Richardson was tough and rigid and seemed to lack even a trace of empathy. She was no doting grandma.

"Please be seated." The judge sat down, adjusted her robe, pulled the court microphone closer to her mouth. "We are here on the matter of Commonwealth vs. Zachary Noah Morgan, docket number CP-25-CR-4288091-2020."

I wanted to stop her, slow down time. *Stop. Stop. I'm not ready. I can't handle what comes next.*

The judge spoke over my internal concerns. "Counsel? Your appearances for the record."

Yvonne Williams and Peter both stood. Yvonne, in two-inch black pumps, had three inches on Peter. She reminded me of a gazelle, elegant and graceful. Her red-nailed fingertips pressed against counsel table. "Yvonne Williams for the Commonwealth of Pennsylvania."

"Thank you, Ms. Williams." Judge Richardson looked to Peter.

"Peter Flynn, Your Honor." He transferred his weight from one foot to the other.

Judge Richardson raised an eyebrow. "Can you state for the record who it is you represent, Mr. Flynn?"

Modest laughter filled the courtroom; Peter corrected the error. "Of course, Your Honor. I represent the Defendant. Zach, Zachary Morgan."

I hung my head. The botched appearance would rattle Peter. He was clearly nervous. His foot jiggled under counsel table. Twice, I'd seen him wipe his palms on his suit pants. I'd barely spoken to him since Friday night, our paths crossing only twice. Both times, Peter seemed almost unable to look at me, our conversations rushed and shallow. I would have asked him what was wrong, but I knew already. The pressure of this day – representing the son of your childhood best friend – had taken its toll.

Judge Richardson directed her attention to Yvonne. "I understand the Commonwealth has a preliminary matter."

"Yes. Your Honor." Yvonne stood. "I know this is unusual on the day of trial, but the Commonwealth and the defense have reached –"

Bang.

I twisted in the direction of the noise. The back door had been swung open. Bo Brooker stepped through. My eyes widened. Bo hurried down the aisle without explanation or apology, her blonde ponytail streaking behind. She stopped at Peter, slid him a note.

He scanned it, looked at Bo.

She nodded.

Peter stood. "I request a recess, Your Honor."

57

Judge Richardson pushed her glasses down, peered at Peter over the rims. "The trial started less than a minute ago, Mr. Flynn."

"There's additional evidence, Your Honor. There's –"

"Objection." Yvonne's voice burst from the prosecution table.

Judge Richardson tapped gnarled fingers on the desk then stood, black robes swimming around her. She waved a hand. "Counsel. Chambers."

Peter followed Yvonne and Judge Richardson through the door behind the bench, Bo's note clutched in his hand. When the door shut, the courtroom buzzed, the atmosphere akin to a classroom without a teacher. The sketch artist flipped the page on her easel.

What in the world? New evidence? Now? I tapped Zach on the back; he turned.

"Do you know what's happening?" I mouthed. He shook his head.

I stared at the door, willing Judge Richardson to come out,

bang her gavel, and dismiss the case. My gaze was so intense that, when Judge Richardson did emerge ten minutes later, it felt almost as if I'd made it happen by the pure force of my will. The judge stepped to the bench, picked up her gavel.

I put my hand to my mouth, squeezed my eyes shut. *Please. Please. Please.*

Bang. "Court is in recess for twenty minutes." I opened my eyes, let out a breath.

Peter touched Zach's arm. The two stood and started down the aisle toward the rear of the courtroom. Neither looked at me. I watched them, helplessly, hopefully. Should I follow? How could I not?

I stood, my legs unsteady. I grabbed the front railing for support, stepped over the one woman who'd seen fit to sit in the front row, accidentally kicking her oversized purse as I navigated the narrow space. I stepped into the aisle. Julie threw me a tentative smile; I worked to make my face reciprocate. I reached the door and pushed it open, saw Zach and Peter down the corridor, walking away from me.

"Wait." My voice was small. "Wait," I said, louder. They turned; Peter waved for me to catch up.

I followed them toward a room much like the one I'd sat in months before, after the preliminary hearing. Peter pushed open the door. Bo was inside.

So was Carter Sullivan. Donna's son.

He sat alone in a chair in old jeans and a red Temple t-shirt, a paper on the pocked table before him. Bo stood behind Carter, her hand on his shoulder. She gave off a motherly presence, one I had not seen before.

I stepped forward. "Carter. What is it? What did you find?" I focused on his face, stopped short. His features were drawn, his eyes almost hollow. Had he found out something bad? Something against Zach?

Carter lifted his eyes and looked in mine. I saw the little boy

I had known. The one who loved Oreos and fed Barkley leftovers under the table. The one who told me at a sleepover that there were monsters under his bed. I put my hand over his. "Carter. What is it?"

"I'm sorry, Mrs. Morgan." He looked to Zach, a pained expression on his face. "I'm sorry." He pushed the paper in Zach's direction. "Here."

I looked at Zach as he scanned the paper, his eyes wide. What was it? It was all I could do not to grab it from his hands.

Zach held the paper a long moment. Finally, he set it down. "It was you?"

Carter dropped his head. He didn't answer Zach.

I took a step from the table; I felt Peter's hand on my back.

"Carter called me this morning," Bo explained. "Zach told him last night he was going to take a plea. He couldn't let him go through with it. He's signed a confession." Bo gestured to the document, again put her hand on Carter's shoulder.

I leaned against the paneled wall, my mind spinning. Carter had signed a confession? Zach was going to take a plea? I stared at the paper, unable to process the change of events. Carter? He'd done this?

I looked toward Zach, his expression a mirror of my own: confusion, betrayal, surprise. But, also, relief. If Carter confessed, they couldn't try Zach.

I felt my heart lift, then fall. Donna. Oh, Donna. She would go through what I'd been through. Worse than what I'd gone through. There would be no hope of acquittal for Carter.

Zach's voice interrupted my thoughts. "What about the pictures? The ones of you and Owen from the party? You were outside when it happened."

"We doctored them," Carter mumbled. "At the pharmacy. Owen stamped a different date and time. He works there."

I processed the statement, stunned. The time and date on

the photo Donna had shown me had been perfectly clear. It had never occurred to me it was fake. How could it? I'd never have imagined Carter attacking Paige. I'd never imagined he'd frame Zach. Anger rose in my gut.

"And the witnesses? Your alibis?" Zach questioned. "At least six people swore they were with you."

Carter put his head in his arms on the table.

Zach eyes bored into the back of his head. "You were going to let me go to jail." He whispered the words.

Carter lifted his head, shook it vigorously. "No. You had a witness. My Mom said you would get off. She was sure of it. Zach, if I thought that ---" He let the words trail off.

My mind spun. Carter's mother. Donna.

Donna knew?

I shook my head as if to eradicate the idea. It couldn't be right. Donna couldn't have known. I looked at Carter. "Did your mother know about this?"

He said nothing, guilt etched in his face. I took another step forward, put my hand on the back on his. "Does she know you're here? Does she know you signed a confession?"

He looked at me, skin blotchy and tear-stained. "She thinks I'm at school."

"Oh." I stood back. My mind flew back to the last conversation I'd had with her. She'd been so concerned about Zach. About me. And she'd known Zach was innocent. I sat, the weight of the betrayal heavy on my shoulders. She knew. Donna knew.

Carter lifted his head. "She said Zach would get off," he choked.

I opened my mouth just as a door opened, a court officer behind it. "Court recess is up. You're due back in court."

Zach walked out without another word. I stayed a moment, stared at Carter's sad form. He was the reason we were in this situation but, also, the reason we were out of it. Despite his own mother telling him not to, he'd done the right thing in the end. I rubbed his back. "Thank you, Carter."

I stepped out and shut the door behind me, leaving Bo and Carter inside. I strode ahead, caught up to Peter and Zach. "Is this it? Will Yvonne drop the charges?"

"She should," Peter said. "Zach didn't do it."

"Was Zach going to take a plea?"

Peter didn't respond; his silence my answer. It struck me then. We had been moments away from a certain jail sentence. And I didn't even know. Another betrayal.

Carter.

Donna.

Now, Zach and Peter.

Later, I'd expect that I would scream at the injustice of it, admonish Zach and Peter for their secret. But right now, all I could do was focus on the present, on the real possibility the Commonwealth would drop the charges against Zach. I walked toward the courtroom, heels clicking on the floor. The charges *should* be dropped, Peter had said. But it wasn't a definite. Not yet.

Once inside the courtroom, Peter asked for a sidebar; he and Yvonne approached. He disappeared with the judge and Yvonne into chambers, the confession in his hand.

I sat back and exhaled. My mind fell on the Dixons in the front row, Kelly's head in her hands, thick locks hanging around her face. Did she know about Carter yet? I imagined for a moment how it would be for Kelly to tell Paige that the case would go on. There would likely be press coverage and attention, neither of which she would want. My ordeal and Zach's might be over; Paige's would continue.

Judge Richardson swung open the door, Yvonne and Peter behind her. The judge took her place behind the bench, the lawyers at their respective counsel tables. Judge Richardson called the case; Yvonne stood.

"The Commonwealth hereby dismisses all charges against Zachary N. Morgan."

58

The courtroom erupted around me. Peter's Mom engulfed me in a hug. Julie patted my back. Reed stared from the back row, held up his hand in a partial wave.

It was over.

Relief flooded through my body, tempered by what I had learned over the past hour.

Donna knew Zach was on trial for a crime he didn't commit.

Zach was going to take a plea.

And Peter?

I'd trusted him completely. The fact that he'd hidden Zach's plan from me? That he might, even, have encouraged it? It felt like the ultimate betrayal.

Zach turned in my direction. He wiped his face with the back of his hand. I hugged him over the half-wall, saw Kelly and Scott over his shoulder, deep in conversation with Yvonne. I took in the celebrations on my side of the aisle, forced my face to be neutral. The ordeal wasn't over for everyone.

"Can we go home?" Zach spoke over the din of the courtroom, the shuffling of bodies and bags. Only the sketch artist remained in place, the new sketch one of Yvonne and the Dixon's, Kelly's mane outlined in thick, black pencil strokes.

"I don't know. I think so." I looked to Peter. He stood at counsel table shifting documents, head down. "Can we leave?" I worked to keep my voice steady.

He looked in my direction, not meeting my eyes. "The court is preparing the dismissal order. Wait for that." He lowered his head, then lifted it. "Actually, you and Zach can just go. I'll wait for the order."

I stared at him. A feeling of anger overwhelmed my already fraught emotions. But for Carter Sullivan, Zach would be in transit to prison right now. And I hadn't known. Peter was going to let me be sucker-punched.

I stepped toward him. "Carter coming forward doesn't change things. I trusted you." I spat out the words. "I'll never forgive you for this."

Peter looked at me straight on. "I'm sorry." He held my gaze a moment, regret in his eyes. Love too. Didn't matter. What he had done was indefensible.

I grabbed my bag, slung it over my shoulder. Peter's Mom touched my arm. "I'll make a cake," she said, clearly oblivious to the exchange I'd just had with her son. "You and Zach should come for dinner."

I smiled, unable to verbally decline the invitation. I'd bow out later by text.

"Chocolate chip," Evelyn added. "Zach's favorite."

I lifted a hand in acknowledgment, stepped into the aisle. Zach and I made our way to the courtroom door, the space around us less crowded now. As we neared, a pot-bellied sheriff's officer moved into the aisle and blocked the door.

I held my breath. What now? I half expected him to stop Zach, to say there'd been a mistake or that he had to be processed at the station. Instead he smiled, a gap between his teeth. He pulled open the door and held it. I stepped through, unable to process the gesture. Zach said thank you behind me.

We made our way down the hall, toward the front door. Light streaked through old windows with paint peeled frames. A half dozen people waited in line, bags and briefcases churned through x-ray machines. A sheriff's officer waved a wand over a woman in a sundress.

I opened the door and stepped out on the steps, the sun warm on my face. I inhaled. Free. I felt free. I grabbed Zach and hugged him tight. My boy, my son. It was over.

I opened my eyes and released Zach. A woman hurried up the steps. My breath caught.

No.

I squinted.

It was Donna.

59

Donna strode up the courthouse steps in jeans and a t-shirt, hair pulled back in a makeshift bun. She spied me and Zach and waved.

"Meredith!" She bounded up the stairs, two at a time, her face in a broad smile. It was almost as if she'd been searching for us. She puffed out a breath when she reached us. "What's going on? I got a text from Carter to come down here." She shook her head with exasperated affection. "That kid played hooky to be here for Zach. And it's over now? The charges are dismissed?"

She smiled again, the signature lipstick smear on her front tooth.

I tilted my head. "Do you not know?"

"Know what? I just got here." She held up her phone. "Carter said to come down. I figured it was good news." She looked from me to Zach. "Isn't it?"

Donna's ignorance set me off-balance. In the few moments I'd had to think about her since Carter confessed, I'd envisioned unleashing on her in a tirade of anger. But now, I felt almost sorry. Donna's life was about to explode. These were her last minutes of normalcy.

"Well?" Donna said, after a moment. "Is one of you going to fill me in?"

"Carter confessed." Zach said the words, his tone matter-of-fact.

Donna's features transformed; her bright smile contorted to a panicked one. "Confessed what?" She gripped the strap of her purse. "What do you mean?"

"We know it was Carter. He signed a statement. The police probably have him in custody." I gestured to the courthouse.

She looked from the courthouse to me. "Carter didn't assault anyone. Why are you saying this?" Her eyes were wild.

"I'm saying it because it's true." I took a step back. The momentary empathy I'd felt vanished. Donna was still lying, even after Carter's confession. "He told us you knew he did it, that you told him not to tell." Emotion overtook my voice; I could barely speak. "How could you do that to us?" I whispered.

Donna shook her head. "No. No. No. I didn't, I --" She stared at the courthouse steps, then met my eyes. Like Peter's, I saw regret there. And love. "I didn't know until a few weeks ago," she whispered. "I wanted to tell you, I came to your house to tell you but, then, it all sounded so awful. And then you said there was a witness and it seemed, it seemed –" She stopped and took a breath. "It seemed like Zach would get off and it would all be okay."

Anger exploded like fireworks in my body. "But it was a gamble you took with my son, Donna. With my son." I thought about Kelly and my conversation with Paige. "And what about the girl? What about Paige? She's suffering real pain as a result of what Carter did." I stepped closer to her. I felt unmoored, like a piece of me had broken off and become someone else.

A hand on my shoulder. Zach. "Come on, Mom."

His words made me step back.

"I'm sorry," Donna whispered. She pushed past us, her bun loosening as she ascended the stairs, pulled open the heavy courtroom door and disappeared. Confusion lay ahead. Police interrogations. Arraignment. Plenary hearing. Or maybe none of those. I didn't know the process, how it differed if there was a confession. And I'd always had Peter to ask.

Peter.

The thought of him made me angry. Donna's betrayal was initially shocking, but not surprising in retrospect. She'd always been fiercely protective when it came to her kids. But Peter? I'd have trusted him with my life. I did, in fact, trust him with my life.

I'd trusted him with Zach.

60

On the way home from the courthouse, I got Zach a large chocolate milkshake. The mundane act of waiting in the drive-thru calmed me. Zach sucked up the drink, placed the empty plastic cup on the holder between us. I knew the cup would sit there, bits of chocolate congealing on its sides. Zach was predictably forgetful when it came to taking his trash from the car. Another former pet peeve now endearing.

Barkley circled us when we entered the house, the dog blissfully unaware of what had transpired over the last hours. He thumped his tail; Zach scratched his chin.

The lack of a sense of foreboding for the upcoming trial felt strange, the sensation strikingly similar to those of the first days of summer vacation. What to do with the time? The freedom?

The endless possibilities overwhelming, Zach fell asleep in his bed next to Barkley. I texted Evelyn to decline her dinner invitation, then fell asleep on the couch, a lopsided afghan pulled up to my chin.

When I woke, it was dusk. I fumbled for a light, made a disoriented path to the kitchen. I reached for my phone, then set it down. I didn't want to know what the news outlets said, didn't want to hear about what was happening with Carter Sullivan or the Dixon family. Not yet. I wanted to stay in the bubble where I'd lived before this all happened.

My stomach rumbled, I took out cereal and milk. I opened the cabinet to find a bowl and saw a note leaned up against the stack, the word "Mom" in Zach's messy scrawl. I grabbed it, held it. My heart beat so hard I had to remind herself that Zach was upstairs, safe in his bed, Barkley curled around him.

I perched on a kitchen chair, unfolded the note.

Mom,

By the time you read this, I will have taken the plea and begun my jail sentence. Please do not worry about me. I am prepared. I do not remember assaulting Paige but would rather take a certain sentence of two years than face the possibility of ten. I am sorry I did not tell you about the plea. I knew you would want me to fight and, if I lost, I did not want you to feel any blame. Mr. Flynn felt the same way.

Please remember, it is only two years. You can visit every week. Please let Barkley sleep next to you while I'm gone. I think he'll miss me.

I love you.

Zach

I STARED at the words a long moment, pictured Zach, hunched over the table, writing them last night. I recalled his actions from the morning with new eyes: the way he had hugged Barkley, the final stare at the house from the doorway, his comforting squeeze of my arm on the ride over.

I folded the note back up, felt the weight of its contents in my chest. Zach must have been terrified. He must have felt so alone.

I thought of Zach's explanation in the note, that Peter didn't want me to talk him out of the plea.

Would I have? Probably.

Did that make the secret right? I didn't know.

What I did know was, but for Carter Sullivan, Zach would be in jail.

On Peter's recommendation.

My stomach churned; emotions coursed through me. I stared at Zach's note, ripped it in half, then in half again. And again. I threw the pieces in the trash bin as if doing so would eradicate all memories of the allegation, the trial, the plea.

I stared at the ripped pieces, bits of Zach's familiar handwriting on jagged paper strips. Feelings of relief and happiness competed with ones of exhaustion and betrayal. I leaned against the kitchen counter, arms locked.

I didn't know what to feel anymore.

Donna was easy. Her actions were abhorrent, atrocious, loathsome. But, also, "on brand" as they say.

But Peter? Peter had been there for me since the moment I got that awful call from Zach at the Black Cat ball. He listened to my worries, held me when I cried. He'd tried to distract me, tried to make me laugh. He stayed on as my lawyer despite mounting emotional pressure.

Was I being too harsh? Too unforgiving? Was Peter, as Zach said in his note, just trying to protect me from my own instincts? The motherly ones, borne from love, but lacking in sound judgment.

A sound from the loft interrupted my thoughts. Zach was up. Barkley too. I'd need to get dinner. Gratitude surged through me at the thought. Dinner for two, not dinner alone.

Barkley bounded down the stairs.

"Hey boy," I pet his square head.

He stood by the door, expectant, tail wagging. I opened it to let him out. Barkley shot straight into Peter who stood on the doorstep in a gray t-shirt and jeans, hair askew. I pulled at my dress, the one I'd worn to the trial, wrinkled now.

"I'm sorry." Peter raked his fingers through his hair, cast his eyes downward. "I should have encouraged Zach to talk it through with you. You're his Mom. You —"

My psyche shifted at the sight of him, at the sound of his voice. Peter didn't want to cause me or Zach pain. He had been trying to do what he thought was right. I'd put him in an impossible situation.

"I should have —"

I shook my head. "No."

He looked up at me, met my eyes.

"You were trying to save me from my instincts. I probably would have encouraged Zach to fight and he might have gotten ten years. I don't know." I paused. "I know you did what you thought was right."

Peter kept his eyes steady on mine. "I felt awful."

"I know."

"I never would have —" he continued.

I stepped closer to him. "I know."

He looked down at me. "Are we okay?"

I put my hand over my heart. "I am. Are you? You're not sick of me? Of all the issues I've caused?"

He pulled me closed, kissed my lips a moment before pulling back. "I could never be sick of you, Mer." He smiled down at at me. "You're my old blanket."

61

FIVE YEARS LATER

My car winds through the streets of Oakland, a suburb of Pittsburgh, Zach's new home.

The day is spectacular. Sky the blue of a child's drawing, puffy clouds set around a yellow ball of a sun. The air is breezy but warm, the temperature so perfect it doesn't register as hot or cold. A boy, eight maybe, whizzes past on a bike. A mother holds the hand of a toddler with a yellow toy truck.

Peter, driving, squeezes my hand. My engagement ring and wedding band dig into his palm. We married a few months after the trial.

"You alright?" he asks.

I glance at him just as the sun dips behind a single cloud, dimming his face.

He's not asking about meeting Zach's girlfriend's family –

our main purpose for the trip. Peter knows I like the girl, Tanisha.

Actually, I love Tanisha. They met Zach's junior year at PITT and, unlike other people, she didn't make assumptions about the digital footprint of the allegations that follow him, notwithstanding acquittal. Instead, according to Zach, she'd held out an article about the trial on her phone and said: "What's up with this? This isn't you."

It's clear, Tanisha loves my son and treats him well. Just last week, she texted me to ask me for my mac and cheese recipe, Zach's favorite. She planned to make the dish as a surprise.

Peter's question isn't about Zach; it's about the date. May 15th. The day of the trial. Most of the time, I'm pretty good at forgetting that horrid one year period in my life. Peter and I moved to New Jersey after the wedding. It was close enough to Crasmere to keep our jobs, to help with Peter's parents when Karl's new caregiver was unavailable. But our new home was far enough away that the landmarks of Zach's case – district court, jail, even the high school – are no longer plainly in view.

Still, without fail, each time May 15th rolls around, I'm transported to that courtroom. I can smell the competing odors, see Judge Richardson's falsely cherubic face behind the bench. Zach's there too, in his new suit next to Peter, his hand visibly shaking. Bile forms in my throat at the clear image; fear lodges in my stomach.

I exhale and turn to Peter.

"I'm okay."

I am, actually, most of the time. Zach is too. Going to PITT the fall after the trial was best thing for him. New people, new surroundings.

I don't know much about Paige or Kelly. I ran into Kelly in downtown Crasmere a month after Zach's trial and, unlike our other meetings, she remembered me. We sidestepped each other as if we were strangers but, as I paced down the block, the encounter felt wrong. "I'm sorry about what happened," I called. Kelly turned toward me. I recognized her pain, that of a mother. She nodded, held up a hand. "I'm sorry too," she said. I heard Paige is in college now. A good sign, I think. I hope so.

Carter has been out of jail two years. I know this from Donna. Zach's been adamant in his unforgiveness. I don't blame him. I might not have forgiven Donna except that, in the months after the trial, she'd been such a tragic figure. She lost her house, custody of both boys, and served six-month jail sentence for withholding information about a crime. She'd relentlessly tried to contact me – text, phone, social media, flowers. I'd finally broken down with the apology strip-o-gram she'd sent to me at work. It had been too Donna.

Our relationship will never be the same, but I did understand the panic she'd felt at the thought of Carter in jail. Of course, I did. I'd felt it too. I'd like to think I'd have made a different choice than Donna, but I can't entirely be sure.

We reach Zach's apartment, on a side street in Oakland, near PITT's main campus. I spy he and Tanisha through the window. They work to set a small table for dinner. She squeezes his forearm; he kisses her head. Both seem natural interactions; happiness floods my body. Zach is fine, safe, and content with a partner he loves. I look to Peter.

And so am I.

ACKNOWLEDGMENTS

I am very excited to have published my second book! I would not have been able to do so without help.

Thanks to my developmental editor, Sheila Athens, who helped me tell a more compelling story and gave me the confidence to believe in it.

Thanks to Leslie Pike and Megan Stumpf, both experienced criminal attorneys, for sharing your expertise so I could make the legal aspects of the story stronger.

Thanks to Katie Treese for reading the first, second, and other countless drafts of this book. And for catching all my missing commas!

Thanks to Brittany Glassman, Leslie Hyman, Megan Stumpf, and Cassidy Treese for reading the final manuscript and giving your feedback.

Thanks to Kevin Treese for helping with my plot issues during our many COVID dog walks.

Thanks to Jena R. Collins for your amazing cover design.

As always, last but not least, thanks to Jason Treese for your love and support. If I only have one fan, I'm glad it's you!

A NOTE FROM THE AUTHOR

There are millions of books out there and I don't take it lightly that you took the time to read mine. Thank you! If you enjoyed *Mother of the Accused*, I would be deeply grateful if you would leave a review on Amazon or your retailer of choice. Reviews help other readers find my book.

I would also love to hear from you. I post monthly book vlogs about what I am reading on Instagram (@leannetreese) and on Facebook (@authorleanne50). I also post updates about my releases and, perhaps more important, pictures of my dogs! In addition, I have a monthly newsletter with exclusive offers. Sign up on my website at www.leannetreese.com. I look forward to connecting with you!

ABOUT THE AUTHOR

Leanne lives in New Jersey with her husband of twenty-five years and their three wonderful children. When Leanne is not cheering her kids on in their activities, she can be found running, reading, and spoiling her two beloved dogs. Favorite locations include the Jersey shore, Martha's Vineyard, and any place that sells books or coffee, preferably both. A passionate student, Leanne's dream life would include going back to college and majoring in everything.

Leanne is a graduate of Lafayette College and The Dickinson School of Law. She is a former attorney who is now lucky enough to write full-time. She is the author of *Their Last Chance*, *Love Locked*, and *Mother of the Accused*. She is busy at work on a Christmas romance, *The Santa Games*.

ALSO BY LEANNE TREESE:

"This nuanced and empathetic novel balances the difficult and the heartwarming." Kirkus Reviews

"This is an excellent drama. It reads like you are watching an episode of *This is Us*." @readinggirlreviews

"It's root is a beautiful love story." @bookapotomus

"Captivating and immersive." @nursebookie

Hannah and Will Abbott define the American dream: two kids, a home in the suburbs, and a seemingly perfect marriage. But discontent lurks beneath the surface of their outwardly happy lives.

Will and Hannah each suspect the other of infidelity. When they independently consult divorce attorneys, the conflict escalates and Hannah flees with the children against a court order. Hannah's snap decision starts a social media firestorm and, suddenly, the Abbott divorce is big news.

With family stress and legal fees rising, Will and Hannah accept an invitation to appear on a reality television show for divorcing couples. During filming on the beautiful island of St. John, the Abbotts must decide once and for all: can their love survive their past?

WINNER: 2021 BOOK EXCELLENCE AWARD

Made in the USA
Middletown, DE
11 July 2021